"Great. We've got dragons."

"If Catherine allowed herself to be eaten by a dragon, I have no sympathy for her at all. Unless you're a virgin sacrifice, which she most certainly is not, they're easy enough to avoid."

"They know where the store is, Auntie Jane," Allie said.

"Of course they do, they can sense the power. If you follow them, you'll probably find them acknowledging every power signature in Edmonton."

"Calgary."

"What?"

"I'm in Calgary."

"Are you asking me to join you there?"

"No!"

"Then don't start complaining to me about geography. Dragons are not this family's business."

"Unless one ate Gran."

After a long pause, Auntie Jane sighed. "Yes, unless one ate your grandmother."

"How do I . . . ?"

"Oh, for pity's sake, Alysha, just consider it for a moment. You'll need to examine the scat for the nasty indigestible bits."

She was almost afraid Auntie Jane hadn't been kidding.

TANYA HUFF

The Enchantment Emporium

DAW BOOKS, INC.

DONALD A. WOLLHEIM, FOUNDER

375 Hudson Street, New York, NY 10014

ELIZABETH R. WOLLHEIM

SHEILA E. GILBERT

PUBLISHERS

www.dawbooks.com

First Paperback Printing, June 2010
1 2 3 4 5 6 7 8 9

For Sue and Tom.
For True Love.
For Happily Ever After.

ONE

Shoot the moon was considered to be one of the more dangerous yoyo tricks. Not particularly complicated—nothing like the crossovers of a *Texas Star*—but a moment's inattention and the odds were good that 35.7 grams of hardwood would be impacting painfully off the front curve of the human skull. There were rumors that, back in '37, Canadian and World Champion, Joe Young had once bounced a *Shoot the Moon* and continued to ace the competition with no one the wiser until the next day when the bruise began to develop. She didn't know about that, and she didn't put much trust in rumors, but she did know that when Joe Young died during the war, the sport lost a master.

She executed the trick perfectly.

Pulled a glow-in-the-dark yoyo from the box, turned off the lights in the store, and did it again.

Perfectly.

Pity there was no one around to see.

In a valiant but ultimately futile effort to keep herself amused, she had a yoyo on each hand and was walking alternate dogs when the shadow finally blocked out the light from the street spilling through the grimy glass of the door. It took her a moment to pull the string off the second finger of her left hand and, in that moment, the metal doorjamb began to groan.

Another moment and it would buckle.

Lips pressed into a thin, irritated line, she shoved both toys more-or-less away and strode over to the door. It wasn't locked, but that was clearly a detail these sorts of late-night visitors never bothered to check.

Yanking it open, she squinted up at the misshapen silhouette and snapped, "What took you so long?"

This was clearly not the expected response.

"Were you planning on getting up any time soon?"

Allie pulled the pillow over her head, hoping her mother would consider that answer enough. She was twenty-four years old, unemployed, friendless, and back home with no prospects. As far as she was concerned, she was entitled to stay in bed all day if she felt like it.

The silence, weighted heavily with unspoken advice, ended with a nearly audible eye roll, and the sound of her bedroom door closing.

Good. The last thing she needed right now was the kind of practical, levelheaded analysis of the situation her mother excelled at.

Pillow still over her head, she stretched out her left arm and patted the empty spot in the bed. Charlie was gone. Given how cool the sheets were, she'd probably been gone for a while. Stretching out her right arm, she patted the other side of the bed. Dmitri was gone, too. Face pressed into the bottom sheet that smelled faintly of fabric softener and sex, Allie frowned and tried to remember what day it was.

Her job as a research assistant at the Royal Ontario

Museum had ended on Tuesday, the grant money that had paid her having finally run out with no hope of renewal. With almost a month's warning, she'd been trying to get the last of the Cypriot artifacts into the new cataloging program. The Classical/Hellenistic period—the bulk of the collection—had made it in, but it seemed as though the Cypro-Geometric period never would. She hated leaving things unfinished.

She hated leaving.

Or more specifically—she hated having to leave. Hated the feeling that her life was out of her control.

It wasn't as though she'd loved the job—although in all fairness, she'd enjoyed rummaging about the back rooms at the museum attempting to bring order out of chaos—it was just that she wasn't finding the old joke about fine arts degrees and "would you like fries with that" particularly funny these days.

Her Uncle Richard and three cousins had arrived on Wednesday to help pack up her tiny apartment and haul home the stuff she hadn't sold or handed off to other cousins in the city. The family didn't exactly own things communally, but there were cooking pots still being passed around that predated frozen food. Charlie had stayed with her, they'd spent Wednesday night on an air mattress; she'd handed the keys in Thursday before they'd crammed the last bits and pieces of her life into the back of a borrowed car and left the city—Charlie complaining all the way home about the mode of transport—so today had to be Friday.

Friday, April 30th.

Which answered that question at least—Dmitri was at school.

Charlie could be anywhere.

Once again, she'd been left alone.

Her fingers plucked at the quilt the aunties had made

for her, not needing to remove the pillow to find the square centered with a piece of one of Michael's old shirts.

Left alone just like stupid Michael with his stupid perfect boyfriend and his stupid perfect job out in Vancouver had left her alone.

"Alysha Catherine Gale!" Age had not stopped Auntie Jane's voice from carrying clearly up to the second floor. As if age would dare. "If you aren't out of that bed and downstairs in this kitchen in fifteen minutes, I will make you sorry you were ever born!"

No chance Auntie Jane would leave her alone.

And an even smaller chance that every word she'd said wasn't to be taken literally.

Sometime in the night, Dmitri had sketched a charm on her right calf. He'd probably thought she wouldn't notice it down there, but then he was young and still incredibly indulged. Eyes rolling, she erased it, smiled fondly at the old charm Charlie had retraced on her shoulder, and stepped out of the shower to find Samson, one of the family's four border collies, drinking out of the toilet.

"Don't tell me you've learned to go around the door," she muttered, grabbing him by the scruff of the neck and hauling him back. She hadn't bothered to stuff the old rusty hook into the equally rusty eye, but the bathroom door was still closed.

Tail slapping into her knees, Samson ignored her.

Allie made it downstairs with twelve and a half seconds to spare, wrapping an elastic band around the end of her hair and tossing the wet braid back over her shoulder. As expected, her mother and Auntie Jane were in the big farmhouse kitchen baking pies, the two of them both working at one end of the old rectangular table. Allie paused on the bottom step.

Gale girls had sisters, that was a given.

There were inevitably four or five girls in the family to every boy.

Her gran, her mother's mother, Auntie Jane's youngest sister, had three girls. No boy. That was strange but not unheard of.

Allie had a brother, David. He was four years older and hadn't that set the aunties to talking. Boys were never born first.

She had no sisters.

"He got the Gale that should have been spread out over half a dozen girls," Auntie Jane had been heard to sniff, her dark eyes watching David. *"What's he going to do with it, that's the question."*

This close to ritual, the kitchen should have been full of Gale girls, laughing, talking, making sure the right things went into the pies.

"Your Aunt Ruth will be over later with Katie and Maria," her mother said, without looking up from the block of shortening she was cutting into the flour. "And your Auntie Ruby has just gone down to the cellar for more apples."

"Senile old bat'll probably forget what she's down there for," Auntie Jane snorted, expertly flipping the rolled pastry onto a pie plate, a move she'd probably made a million times. The family was big on pie and Auntie Jane admitted to being over eighty—although she got nasty when people tried to be more specific. A minimum of eighty years and say a minimum of a hundred pies a year ... "And if you'd hauled your lazy carcass out of bed before noon," she continued, interrupting Allie's attempt at math, "there'd have been four of us all along. So, stop seeing the empty places at the table and get over here. The family's coming home, and pies don't make themselves."

Unable to argue with the familiar and clearly inarguable observation, Allie grabbed an apron off the hook by the door but circled the table until she reached the coffeepot over by the big six-burner stove. "You *want* me caffeinated," she said before either woman could comment on the delay. "In the interest of only having apples go into the pies."

"Ruth is bringing rhubarb from her cold frame," Auntie Jane sniffed, dark eyes disapproving—of her attitude not the rhubarb, Allie assumed. "If you're sufficiently *caffeinated* before she arrives, you can start preparing the pastry."

"Apples, rhubarb . . ." Allie pulled her favorite mug from the cupboard and filled it. ". . . either's better than a helping of 'I don't give a flying fuck.' "

"Alysha!"

Oh, crap. Had she said that out loud? Had she missed one of Dmitri's charms? He was still young enough to find putting her on the spot funny. Unfortunately, it turned out she had nothing to blame but her own big mouth.

"Sorry, Mom." Ears burning she took a long swallow and stared at her reflection in the dark liquid. "It's just that . . ."

"You lost your job, and Michael's in Vancouver with Brian. We know, honey." The sympathy in her mother's voice drew Allie's gaze up off the coffee. "But tomorrow's May Day, most of the family will be home, so, if you could, get over yourself."

Were her mother's eyes a darker gray than they'd been when she'd been home last? Mary Gale was fifty. That was all. Fifty. Allie'd taken a week off work for the big family party back in the fall. Fifty was too young.

"Change happens, Alysha." Auntie Jane seemed grimly amused by the inevitable. "Although the girl has a point, Mary. Remember what happened when Ruth let her mind wander that time during peach season? We were months sorting out the mess."

"I was sixteen, Auntie Jane. Let it go." The screen door slammed and Allie's Aunt Ruth pushed past her to dump an enormous armload of rhubarb in the sink. Her eyes were still Gale gray, but then Aunt Ruth was three years younger than her sister and . . .

"Allie!"

She managed to slide her mug to safety on the counter in time to return her cousin Katie's hug. "Shouldn't you be out flogging swamp land to unsuspecting city folk?"

Katie grinned. "I took a personal day. Pies won't bake themselves."

Impossible not to grin back. "So I keep hearing."

"And I thought you were friendless," Auntie Jane snorted as the two girls giggled together over the inevitability of family.

"Is Michael still out west?" Katie asked sympathetically, snagging Allie's mug and draining it.

Keeping one arm linked with her cousin, Allie grabbed another apron and dropped it over Katie's head. "Apparently he loves his job, and he and Brian are disgustingly happy."

"That sucks."

"Tell me about it."

"I'll send him a pie."

They turned together to stare at Auntie Jane.

"What?" Upending the big earthenware bowl, she dumped the mass of pastry out onto the table. "Michael's as much as family, and he loves my blueberry pie."

"We don't have any blueberries."

Dark eyes narrowed. "We do if I'm making blueberry pie."

That was also inarguable.

"You gave him a charm?" Allie asked as Aunt Ruth, clearly assuming they'd never get to it on their own, deposited Katie at the sink and shoved her toward the huge scarred cutting board beside it.

Auntie Jane sniffed as she separated the dough into fist-sized balls. "Why not?"

"Because he moved away." Allie chopped the flared end off a piece of freshly washed rhubarb with more force than was strictly necessary.

"No reason to give him a charm if he'd stayed in Darsden." A round of dough slapped down onto the table hard enough that it continued to quiver for moments after. "You let him leave when you refused to change his mind."

Sure, she could have changed his mind, made him believe what she wanted him to believe, but that would have changed Michael. Made him not!Michael. And what would have been the point in that?

He wouldn't be in Vancouver with Brian right now.

Shut up.

"I stood by him." And occasionally in front of him, shoulder to shoulder with her cousins. Gale girls protected their own. Not that Michael, smart, handsome, and on every sports team Darsden East High School offered had needed a lot of protection. "I let him be who he was."

"He was fifteen. He wouldn't have even noticed."

"He's not family, Auntie Jane."

Things were done for the sake of family that weren't done to an outsider no matter how close to family he was.

"He could have been, Alysha Catherine!"

Everyone had adored Michael still adored Michael—and the aunties, all expecting a chance to integrate Michael's line, blamed Allie for his absence.

Allie scooped the *could haves* away into the bowl with the cut rhubarb—the could haves of her and Michael and a life she could see so clearly she sometimes forgot which life she was waking into—and gave thanks, not for the first time, that she hadn't inherited her gran's ability. In a family that drew an arbitrarily adjustable line between maintaining the status quo and interfering with the outside world, foresight was a curse. She totally understood why Gran had gone wild, leaving home and the nagging of the aunties. The *other* aunties.

Because, of course, Gran was also an auntie.

Although not hers.

Sometimes family life got complicated.

The screen door slammed again and Katie's younger sister, Maria, backed into the kitchen, the top of a stack of aluminum pie plates tucked in under the prominent curve of her breasts. She wasn't as tall as either Katie or Allie but was definitely curvier. A distinction the scoop-necked T-shirt had been clearly chosen to emphasize. "Delilah's in the apple tree again, Aunt Mary."

Muttering about the damned dog, Allie's mother wiped her hands on her apron and headed out into the yard.

Maria dropped the pie plates on the table. "Still don't see why it matters."

"Best to stop it before it matters; border collies can cause a lot of blossom damage." Auntie Jane glared a spinning plate to a stop just at the table's edge. "And she'll knock the young apples off later in the season. Are these all Christie had?"

"They're all Auntie Christie *said* she had," Maria told

her. Then she turned to face the counter, full upper lip curled. "Allie."

Allie blinked. That had sounded like a challenge.

"Ignore her." Katie dropped the last of the cleaned rhubarb onto the cutting board and dried her hands on her apron. "She's just being a bitch because Dmitri slept here last night."

Aunt Ruth glanced up from setting wrapped dough balls in the fridge to rest. "Don't call your sister a bitch, Katie."

"Sorry. She's being a cow because Dmitri slept here last night. She has plans for him."

With barely more than a year between them, Dmitri and Maria wouldn't be a bad match, but Dmitri was only just finishing high school and it would likely be years before he chose. Still, with so few Gale boys available, attempting to stake an early claim wasn't an entirely bad idea. By the time Dmitri was ready to settle down, Maria might have discouraged some of her competition.

"Don't worry about me." Setting the bowl of cut fruit on the table, ceramic ringing against the wood, Allie reached past it for the sugar. "He was only here because he's working his way through his list and I haven't been around much."

The arch plucked into Maria's brows rose higher still. "You can't be on his list."

"Alysha and Dmitri are as far apart as you and Dmitri," Auntie Jane pointed out.

"But she's old!"

"Thank you so much." Allie didn't bother watching her tone. It was rhubarb. It was going to be tart anyway. "He's been eighteen for a month; I may be elderly, but I'm well inside the seven-year break."

"Well, fine . . ." Maria poked her finger into a block of

shortening. ". . . you're on his list; that's why he wanted to sleep with you. Why did you sleep with him?"

The sudden silence in the kitchen was complete. The only sound, the distant command that Delilah was to get down out of the tree. Immediately.

Allie stared at her cousin. Knew Katie had turned from the sink and was staring as well. Aunt Ruth snorted. Auntie Jane answered for them all. "Turn down a Gale boy?"

Maria's blush dipped down to tint her cleavage. "Never mind."

She looked so miserable, Allie took pity on her. "Charlie was here, too."

Charlie, at nearly twenty-six, was definitely not on Dmitri's list. Her presence made it clear Allie wasn't remotely serious about making an actual connection with her young cousin. Charlie, like Gran, was one of those oddities the family threw up every now and then and was, because of what she could do, nearly as indulged as one of the boys. Half the aunties wanted to see if they could breed her ability back into the lines, stabilizing it, while the other half insisted its very instability argued against tying up one of the Gale boys on the attempt. Charlie ignored both halves, and no one doubted, given her talents, that one day she'd go wild.

Allie adored her, embraced the uniqueness the rest of the family used but didn't exactly approve of, and harbored half-formed thoughts about taming the wildness. Next to Michael, she loved Charlie best.

"Where is Charlie?" Aunt Ruth asked as Maria grabbed herself an apron and a rolling pin.

Charlie was the exception to the rule that all Gale girls cooked. Younger members of the family scared still younger members with whispered stories of chocolate cupcakes gone horribly wrong. And when a cupcake went horribly wrong in the Gale family, the word "horribly" was not an exaggeration.

Allie shrugged, hoping it looked like she didn't care. "I don't know. She wasn't there when I got up."

"Because you wasted all that time wallowing in self-pity. Charlotte has gone to bring Roland home from Cincinnati," Auntie Jane added before Allie could protest that she hadn't been wallowing. Exactly. "That fool Kirby sent him out to get a deposition."

"Sent him to Cincinnati? Right before May Day?" Aunt Ruth rolled her eyes, the expression strengthening her resemblance to her sister although her eyes were clearly a lighter gray.

"Charlotte will have him home in time."

It was possible Charlie could have him home before he left, but that wasn't the point. When a Gale said he needed time off, he got it. Given the obsidian gleam in Auntie Jane's eyes during the discussion, Allie actually felt a little sorry for Roland's boss. Drawing the ire of the aunties was never smart. Alan Kirby had lived in Darsden East his whole life. He should have known that.

"It's only Cincinnati," Maria snorted. "They have an airport, you know. Okay, it's across the river in Kentucky, which is kind of stupid, but why doesn't he just fly home for the weekend then fly back?"

"No reason why he should." Auntie Jane's tone nearly frosted the windows.

"Dad says no one's seen Granddad for weeks," Katie said hurriedly, changing the subject before the mood affected the pies.

For a moment it looked like Auntie Jane would refuse to allow the subject changed, then she snorted. "He'll be here tomorrow."

Aunt Ruth frowned, slowly unwrapping another

pound of shortening, fingertips dimpling the soft brick. "He's getting wilder."

"He'll be here tomorrow," Auntie Jane snapped. "We can't replace him. David's not ready."

"For what?"

Allie suddenly found measuring dry ingredients fascinating as her mother returned to the kitchen trailed by a clearly unrepentant Delilah. Auntie Jane was convinced that David was destined to be the next head of the family. Her mother was convinced that Auntie Jane was tottering on the edge of senility. David was too powerful, too independent to be tied so definitively to place.

Too like Granddad had been once? Allie wondered.

"David's not ready for what?" her mother repeated.

As the inevitable argument began, Katie sidled closer and murmured, "You okay?"

Given the concern in Katie's low voice, Allie figured that sudden flash of fear had shown on her face.

"Don't worry," her cousin continued. "Even if David does take over from Granddad, he's young. Really young. It'll be years, decades, before . . ."

"Don't." The flour slipped through her fingers like silk. Impossible to hold.

"He gets tied down, it'll keep him from going all darkside," Maria said quietly, pulling a stalk of rhubarb from her mouth, the plump curve of her lower lip stained pink.

"He's not going darkside!"

"He's powerful." Maria flipped up a finger as she counted off the points Allie had just made to herself. "He's a loner . . ."

"So what? So's Gran. So's Charlie more often than not."

"He's a male."

And there was yet another inarguable point. There were times Allie wished she could argue with her family a little more. Of course, right at the moment, they wouldn't be able to hear her over her mother and Auntie Jane.

"My son is not hoarding power!"

"Oh, and that's an unbiased opinion, is it?"

"Don't be ridiculous! How could it be unbiased, I'm his mother!"

"Don't talk to me about mothers! Not when your own mother is careening about the world like a tetherball!"

"What does my mother have to do with my son?"

"Nothing at all." Bits of dough flew off her fingers, spattering the kitchen like a soft hail as Auntie Jane spread her arms. Those not involved in the argument ducked. "For pity's sake, Mary, keep up. We've moved on."

A sudden shadow flickering past the window over the sink cut off a response Allie suspected would be memorable.

Muttering how no one should be worried about what the *girls* were going to add to the pies, Aunt Ruth leaned forward to check it out.

"It's Auntie Ruby," she sighed, head twisted to one side so she could see past the upper edge of the window. "She's found a broom."

"I told you she was senile!" More dough spattered as Auntie Jane punched the air in triumph. Allie brushed a bit off Katie's cheek.

Aunt Ruth sighed again. "And she's cackling."

Charlie moved through the Wood along the path of Roland's song. Most days she'd have been there by now—in the Wood, the actual distance between Aunt Mary's porch and Cincinnati was irrelevant. But today . . .

The path kept skirting the edges of the dark places beneath the oldest trees. Places Charlie'd just as soon not have to cross. Places she shouldn't have had to go near. Not for Roland.

Reaching back, she tugged her guitar around and strummed a questing chord.

The path shifted onto higher ground.

She picked up her pace and, when her shoulders brushed between the smooth trunks of young aspens, turned to look back the way she'd come.

Shadows had already claimed the path although, in all honesty, she couldn't say if it was a multitude of smaller shadows or one large one.

Either way, it wasn't good.

The clerk at the front desk tracked her disapprovingly as she crossed the lobby and Charlie only just barely managed to keep from flipping her the bird. The shadows had dogged her footsteps for the rest of the trip, and all the cliché lurking had pissed her right off.

She walked on to the elevator and, as the door closed behind her, swung her guitar back around to the front and began to pick a discordant pattern, trying to give the shadows form now she was out of the Wood. There'd been something almost familiar about them—or it—but she just couldn't . . .

"So, uh, what floor did you need?"

Startled, she glanced over at the man standing beside the controls, had a vague memory of him being there when she'd entered, and said, "Ten."

He gave her a smile that said, *Well here we are, stuck together in a small space,* and nodded down at the place where her hand remained curled protectively over the strings. "Do you play?"

"No," she told him as the *almost familiar* slipped away, "I just like to carry a guitar around with me."

"Right. Stupid question." Smile faltering slightly, his gesture drew her attention to her reflection in the stainless steel walls. "You know, you look more like the electric than acoustic type."

She tossed a strand of her blue, chin-length hair back off her face and growled, "Do you have any idea what a battery pack for an amp weighs?"

"Uh . . . No."

"Well, there you go then."

He shuffled back a step and raised his eyes to the numbers flicking by as though seven, eight, nine had suddenly become the most interesting things in his world. Out the door on nine, he turned, opened his mouth, and closed it again as the elevator door slid shut between them.

The fluorescent lights banished all shadows from the elevator.

Charlie kept an eye on the corners anyway.

Roland was in 1015, one of the small corner suites. Charlie knew damned well Alan Kirby hadn't booked a suite. Roland's boss was, in the words of Auntie Grace, tighter than bark on a tree. But Roland was a Gale; if there were upgrades to be had, he'd have them.

His door was slightly ajar—obviously he'd been expecting her.

"Charlie, hey!" Roland closed his laptop when he spotted her walking the short hall and began shoving paperwork into his backpack. "Thanks for this. I could have gotten a flight home, but getting back here on Sunday would have been a nightmare."

"Yeah, whatever."

He paused. Frowned. "I know you hate playing taxi, but . . ."

"I hate people assuming I'll play taxi, not the same thing." As a general rule, she didn't mind making life easier for the family, but that did not include being on call for those too stupid to read a calendar and needing a quick trip home.

"Then if you don't mind my asking, what crawled up your ass and died?"

"What? Oh, sorry." She crossed the room to the desk, boots making next to no noise on the carpet. "Nothing to do with you. Just some guy trying to be all friendly in the elevator."

Roland winced. "How badly did you damage him?"

"Not *that* friendly. Just friendly."

He ducked away from the punch she aimed at his shoulder. "The horror."

"It wasn't him." A bit of laminate was loose on the edge of the desk. She absently charmed it back down. "There's something funky happening in the Wood."

"Define funky."

"Can't. If I could, I wouldn't be so . . ."

"Cranky?"

"Bite me. Three year olds get cranky." But she couldn't stop herself from smiling back at him. Damned Gale boys anyway. "You ready?"

"Well, since your arrival establishes precedent that funky, however *funky*, is safe—almost." Laptop secured, he stretched, back cracking. "You know, I could have flown down here Monday. The deposition won't be ready until first thing Tuesday morning—but Alan was adamant I be here for the final court dates."

"The aunties are pissed."

"I think that was his intention."

"To get the aunties pissed?" Charlie asked, wandering into the bathroom to pocket the tiny bottles of shampoo and conditioner. "The man has a death wish?"

Roland shrugged as she came back into the sitting room. "They haven't done anything obvious in a while."

"So he's poking at them with a you-shaped stick? Moron. What the hell is that?"

With the ease of a man who'd grown up with five sisters, he deftly avoided her grab and tucked the glittering pink unicorn into the larger of the pack's outside pockets. "It's a present for Lyla. I always bring her something when I get back from a trip."

"Technically, you won't be back from this trip until next Wednesday."

"I'll bring her something else then." He looked so sweetly besotted talking about his three-year-old daughter that Charlie gave half a thought to jumping him. Sweater vests or not, he was David's age, only twenty-eight, and while law might have left him a little physically soft around the edges, none of the Gales had been short-shrifted in the looks department. Rayne and Lucy, Lyla's mothers, certainly wouldn't care.

"So, how's your band doing?"

"Which one?" Charlie wondered, opening what turned out to be a fake chest of drawers and finding the television.

"The New Age techno head banging thing I saw you do at that . . ." When the pause extended, she turned to see him standing, half into his jacket, and frowning. ". . . club."

"We broke up."

"I'm sorry."

"Really?"

"No."

And so much for doing Roland. Sweet guy, for a lawyer, but his idea of music stopped and started around John Williams and usually involved light sabers. She tossed the TV remote on the sofa and spent a moment making sure her strings were in tune. Her B had a tendency to flatten in the Wood. "If we leave now, we'll be back before Lyla gets home from school."

"I'd like that. Thanks." He slipped his backpack over one shoulder. "Where do we leave from?"

"Across the street from the hotel. There's a shrubbery in that little park."

Holding the suite's door open for her, Roland frowned. "You can get in from a shrubbery?"

"I can." She patted his cheek as she passed. "Because I'm just that good."

The shadows dogged their heels all the way home.

"Traveling the Wood is never the same twice," Auntie Jane scoffed. "And all sorts of things lurk by the path."

"This was something new," Charlie insisted.

"What part of *never the same twice* are you having trouble understanding, Charlotte?"

"But . . ."

"It's coming up on May Day," Auntie Ellen pointed out—unnecessarily as far as Allie was concerned, given that the house already overflowed with family and Uncle Richard had just parked his RV in the yard. "Things are stirring."

Charlie took a deep breath, visibly holding her temper, and tried again. "I've never seen anything like this."

"You've never seen anything like it?" Auntie Jane sniffed.

"It's new to your vast experience?" Auntie Ellen sneered.

Auntie Muriel snorted but kept her attention on her knitting. Rumor said Auntie Muriel had been quite the traveler in her youth although, as she had most definitely not gone wild, the traveling in question probably had more to do with planes, trains, and automobiles rather than metaphysical pathways with no actual form.

As Charlie tensed up to respond, Allie wrapped one hand around her arm, anchoring her in place, and pointed out the big front windows with the other. "Look!" she said, loudly. "David's home!" She had the uncomfortable feeling that Auntie Jane's eyes literally lit up. Auntie Muriel, her knitting tossed aside to spill in a multicolored tangle off the big leather ottoman, led the charge out of the house. "They'll never admit you know something they don't." She pulled Charlie up against her as they watched the aunties part the sea of younger cousins crowded around David's car. Gale girls, regardless of age, were attracted to power. "Sooner or later, they'll send someone to check it out."

"And then claim omnipotence in family matters."

"Do you care?"

"Yes. No." Charlie sighed and pushed a fold into the worn rug with the scuffed toe of her boot. "Probably not. They just get up my ass sometimes, you know?"

"They do it on purpose."

"Well, duh. You going out to see David?"

Watching her brother lift five-year-old Callie up onto one shoulder, Allie grinned and shook her head. "Not

this close to May Day; he's already showing horn." Even
for her, the pull was nearly irresistible. "You go ahead,
though."

"Tomorrow's soon enough for that." Charlie bent to
pick up her guitar case, paused, and frowned at the spill
of yarn. "What the hell is Auntie Muriel knitting?"

"I have no idea." Allie shuffled a little farther away
from the ottoman. "I was afraid to ask in case she offered it to me."

Every now and then, one of the dimmer bulbs from
Darsden East or the surrounding county tried to discover just what exactly went on in the Grove. These
days, the family was large enough that David—too
powerful for any circle but the first—and those who,
for one reason or another, preferred to opt out of the
ritual entirely, made up a fourth circle of protection for
the other three.

In the old days, the aunties dealt with it.

Auntie Ruby swore her dahlias hadn't been the same
since they stopped.

Stepping into the Grove, Allie nudged Charlie with
her hip and nodded across at Dmitri, already dealing
with both Marie and either Carrie or Ashley. Without
clothing it was almost impossible to tell Charlie's twin
sisters apart.

"Boy needs to pace himself," Charlie snickered. "It's
going to be a long day."

Dusk had painted shadows where shadows weren't, trying to fool the eye, but experience and training helped

him separate the real from the imagined. In his job, the difference, when there actually was one, could be crucial.

Although he knew the glyphs he wore offered more protection from discovery than camouflage and the dubious shelter of a bush ever could, he pushed himself a little more firmly against the ground when he heard the distinctive sound of his targets arriving. Camouflage and a bush provided a physical comfort the glyphs did not and death would be the best he could hope for if his targets spotted him.

Elbows making a tripod with his body, he peered through the scope, the sigils carved into the metal allowing him to see true forms. He had to admit, the horns were impressive.

His employer had been adamant that this was a recon mission, nothing more, but he couldn't stop himself from lining up a perfect shot.

Finger curled loosely around the trigger, he whispered, "Bang."

One moment Allie was sound asleep, the next she was staring through the curtain of her hair at a water stain on the ceiling and wondering who'd called her. Charlie remained asleep beside her, one arm thrown up over her head, blue hair fanned out against the pale skin. Next to Charlie, Katie frowned, eyes twitching behind her lids as she dreamed.

Easing out of bed so as not to wake them, Allie headed for the window, picking a careful path around the half dozen girl cousins, Samson, and a strange cat who'd crashed out on mattresses on her floor after the ritual had ended. The sun was up, but only just. Given that he'd no doubt spent most of yesterday being chased around by members of the family too young to go to the Grove, Mozart, the rooster, was probably still asleep in the henhouse, allowing the sun to rise without him. One of the barn cats walked purposefully along the rail fence by the lane. Across the south pasture, at the edge of the woods, a stag lifted his head to test the breeze.

That explained it.

On her way to the door, Allie grabbed a pair of jeans she thought were hers and a McGill sweatshirt that had to belong to Holly. Samson watched her go, one ear up, but didn't follow.

She couldn't find a matching pair of rubber boots that fit in the jumbled pile on the back porch, so she pulled on a green boot to go with the black one she already wore. Saturday's unseasonably adjusted warm temperature had already begun to cool but hadn't fallen far enough for Allie to take yet more time to find a jacket. Skirting the edge of the pasture where the new green was just beginning to show, she reached the point where she'd seen the stag and pushed her way in under the trees.

"Granddad?"

"Over here, Allie." He was sitting on a fallen log, in an old, stained pair of work pants and a quilted plaid jacket. There were caches of clothing all around the county, the girls taking turns to maintain the protective charms. Above his head, the air shimmered; antlers still very much evident.

Allie frowned and tried to remember the last time she'd seen him without them. Or for that matter, the last time she'd seen him up at the house.

"Is that face for me, little one?"

"Sorry." He smelled wonderful, like the woods and the wind, and, when he hugged her, his grip was strong, his arms sure. If he'd taken any damage the day before, he wasn't letting it show. No one really wanted to replace him, but when their blood was up, Gale boys—from Uncle Richard to Zachary, who'd only just joined the circles—tended to act first and think later.

"Worrying too much, Allie. Just be."

Dropping down beside him on the log, she rested her cheek on his shoulder. "It's hard to just be when you're out in the world, Granddad."

"Good thing you're here, then." He kissed the top of her head. "I can't protect the ones who wander. Off to school. Off to jobs."

She wondered if he ever wished he could leave, if ever he wanted to roam farther than the land the family claimed. If that was even something he *could* want after being the family's tie to place for so long.

"We always come home, Granddad." It was all she could offer him. For herself, well, it wasn't coming home she objected to. Home and family defined her as much as it defined any Gale. It was the failing at having a life thing she found less than stellar.

"Not everyone comes home." His snort had little humanity in it. Allie wrapped one of his callused hands in both of hers, skin to skin, to hold him in this shape a little longer. "There are always those who make other choices," he said at last and, from his tone, she realized he wasn't talking about her.

She'd expected Gran back for May Day, expected her to appear and demand to know just what, exactly, everyone thought they were doing. She hadn't been the only one.

"Be just like Catherine to show up at the last minute," Auntie Jane had muttered entering the Grove. *"Make us shift the whole first circle to accommodate her."*

But she hadn't come, and Auntie Muriel had anchored the day with Granddad. It would have been wilder with Gran there. Allie was old enough now to know that wasn't always a good thing. This part of the world had storms enough and no one appreciated a rain of frogs.

Especially not the frogs.

They sat quietly together as dawn shifted to morning, and then Granddad drew his hand from hers.

"Your brother is on his way. We have to talk, he and I."

"David's not . . ."

"Just talk," he told her as he stood. But the shimmer had grown more pronounced, and she could see the point where the antlers grew up out of bone. "We aren't controlled by what the old women think is likely to happen." When Allie couldn't control her expression in time, he grinned. "Although it's easier to maintain that belief out here in the woods—and you didn't hear me say it." He bent, carefully, to kiss her cheek. "Come and find me again to say good-bye before you go."

"Where am I going?"

"*That* choice, little one, is yours."

Somehow she managed to keep her reaction to that bit of Yoda philosophy from showing on her face.

David met her halfway across the meadow and they adjusted their paths to leave a little more room between them, knowing the steps of the dance without having to consciously consider them. By tomorrow or the next day they'd be fine, but this morning, with David still showing an impressive rack of horn, better to be safe than sorry.

"Your boots don't match."

"It's a new style." She pointed at the red curve cut into his cheek, centered within a purpling arc of bruises. "Tell me that wasn't Dmitri."

"It wasn't." When she continued to stare pointedly at him, he rolled his eyes. "Uncle Evan."

"How's he?"

David shrugged one broad shoulder, as though the information wasn't worth the effort of moving them both. "He'll live."

"Good. Granddad's just inside . . ."

"I know."

Allie rolled her eyes and kept walking. Never exactly chatty at the best of times, David was clearly having one of his more taciturn mornings. She wondered how his moods went over at work—surely the police forces that called in Dr. David Gale, brilliant young criminologist, expected a little more verbal bang for their consultant buck. Or maybe, as long as he got it right when he took the stand, they didn't care. She'd ask him later, he was always in a better mood when he'd stopped manifesting.

Crossing the yard, she caught sight of a familiar figure heading into the henhouse. It was still early enough that her father, as one of the rare Gales by marriage, was likely to be the only male of ritual age awake—well, except for David who preferred to be the exception to most rules. Her dad and Michael used to do things together while the rest of the family moved through the circles and she wondered if he missed having Michael around. She took a step toward the henhouse, chasing the long line of her shadow.

Paused.

No. Missing Michael was not on the morning's agenda.

Surrounded by family, she had plenty of things to do.

Much like pies, pancakes, and sausages didn't make themselves and there'd be people looking for breakfast soon enough.

Around nine thirty, Uncle Richard and Aunt Marion began herding their branch of the family back into the RV, Uncle Richard favoring his left side. At nine forty, they discovered they were one short. At nine fifty, Allie found their four-year-old granddaughter, Merry, sound asleep in the tree house, a sausage clutched in one chubby fist.

"She wanted to spend the night up there," Brianna sighed, handing her daughter up to her exhausted looking husband. "I told her she was too young." Then she grinned, gray eyes sparkling. "David and I spent the night up there after senior prom. I was so sure he'd choose me."

"But you and Kevin . . ."

"Are completely happy, Allie, never fear. He loves the farm as much as I do. David would have gone insane."

All three of them winced as a long blast from the RV horn set the dogs barking.

"I think Dad wants to get going."

Allie kissed one cousin good-bye, waved at the other, and blew kisses at Merry who laughed and blew kisses out the back window all the way down the lane.

Just past eleven, the last group emerged from the haymow.

"For pity's sake, boy," Auntie Jane snorted as Dmitri shuffled carefully into the kitchen, "there's salve for that. Use it before those trousers rub you raw. Downstairs bathroom. And you lot," she snapped at the girls who gathered around the table as he left the room, "stop giggling. He didn't get in that condition all on his lonesome."

Allie pulled a platter of pancakes out of the oven where they'd been keeping warm. "He needs to learn to pace himself."

"He's young. He'll recover."

By two that afternoon, only Aunt Ruth and her family remained, helping to put the house to rights.

By supper, there was only Charlie.

"This is nice." Auntie Ruby poked at her vegetables with her fork. "Although in my day, we actually cooked the carrots. I guess no one cares what old people think anymore."

Allie looked around the table and moved her leg just far enough to touch Charlie's knee with hers. Her parents, David, Auntie Ruby—who'd lived with them all of Allie's life—Auntie Jane—who'd moved into the old farmhouse after her husband had died—and Charlie, who'd had lunch with her immediate family and returned by midafternoon announcing that if she spent another moment with the twins, she'd strangle them both. Auntie Ruby was right; it *was* nice. Okay, so she didn't have a job and she didn't have Michael and she'd moved back in with her parents at—God forbid—the ripe old age of twenty-four, but she still had family.

For a Gale, family was everything.

David left after supper, needing to be back in Ottawa for work first thing Monday morning. His current job involved very hush-hush consulting with the Mounties, although he refused to give specifics.

"We don't keep secrets in this family, David Edward Gale."

David bent and kissed the top of Auntie Jane's head. "If I told you what I was doing, I'd have to shoot you."

"I'd like to see you try." She hooked a finger through his belt loops to hold him in place. Allie held her breath until it became obvious he wasn't about to try and break free. "In my day, David Edward, Gale boys chose by twenty."

"But in your day, Auntie Jane, you were one of the choices."

"I'm not saying that wasn't incentive . . ."

Was Auntie Jane actually blushing? David *was* scary powerful.

". . . but you are perilously close to having choices made for you. The time will come, and sooner than you think, when your duty to your family can no longer be set aside."

"But that time is not now." His tone made it entirely clear he wasn't asking for her agreement.

"No, not now." And Auntie Jane's tone added, *but soon*. It also added: *We have every intention of bringing all that power you're flashing around back into the lines one way or another, young man, and this delay is not helping your case as far as our suspicions about you are concerned. We'd prefer you to come willingly, but we're perfectly willing to bind you if you don't, and our patience is running short. Also, you need to call your mother more often. She worries.*

The aunties hadn't invented subtext—at least these particular aunties hadn't, Allie didn't want to make assumptions about the originals—but they squeezed every possible nuance out of it.

Charlie left the next morning after breakfast.

"I've got a friend in Halifax going into the studio today," she explained, tossing David's old hockey bag over one shoulder and picking up her guitar. "I told him I'd sit in." Head cocked, a strand of blue hair fell down over her eyes as she studied Allie's face. "I'll stay if you need me to."

"To hold my hand because I'm friendless and unemployed?"

"Something like that."

Allie kissed her quickly and gave her a shove off the porch. "I'm fine."

"You sure?"

"Just go."

"All right, then."

"You can't keep Charlie in one place, Allie-kitten."

Allie leaned back against her father's arm and watched the shimmer between the apple trees dissipate. "I know."

"She'll come back to you. She always does."

"I know."

"She reminds me a lot of your grandmother."

"Didn't need to hear that."

He gave her one final squeeze, and grabbed his backpack. "Gotta go, kid. High school history doesn't teach itself." He paused, halfway to his truck. "You could always think about teaching, Kitten. Add a master's of education to that fine arts degree. As I recall, you used to have mad skills with macaroni and glue."

"I'll think about it, Dad."

"You want something to do with your life besides standing around and feeling sorry for yourself?" Auntie Jane yanked open the door and thrust a basket into her hands. "Go get the eggs."

The hens had no advice to offer. Mozart tried to eat her shoelaces.

By the time the mail came that afternoon, she'd made three batches of cookies and a lemon loaf.

"There's something for you, Allie." Her mother tossed a pile of sales flyers onto the table and held out a manila envelope. "No return address. Maybe it's a job offer."

"I haven't applied for any jobs, Mom."

"That might be why you're not working, then."

"I just lost the last one," Allie muttered, opening the

envelope. "And Dr. Yan was positive we were going to get that funding renewed so why would I have been looking?"

"Are you asking me?"

"No." She pulled two sheets of paper from the envelope, unfolded them, read them, and frowned. "This isn't . . . I mean, it's not . . ."

"Isn't not what?" Auntie Jane demanded, plugging the kettle in.

"It's from Gran. It says if I'm reading this, she's dead."

TWO

"I, Catherine Amanda Gale, being of sound mind . . ."

"That's always been debatable," Auntie Jane snorted.

". . . and body do hereby leave all my worldly possessions to my granddaughter, Alysha Catherine Gale. These possessions include the building at 1223 9th Avenue S.E., Calgary, Alberta and all its contents." Allie set the handwritten sheet of paper down and took a deep breath. Then a second. "That's all there is. She signed it on the 28th and had it witnessed by a Joe O'Hallon. I think it's O'Hallon. I mean his penmanship sucks, but I just spent eighteen months reading some pretty hinky documentation, and field archaeologists have remarkably crappy penmanship and . . ."

"Allie."

She snapped her mouth shut and turned to her mother, reaching out to touch her shoulder. The soft nap of her sweater was still cool from walking down the lane to get the mail. Was it possible that so much had changed in such a little time? "Oh, Mom, I'm sorry. Here I'm all thrown by losing my grandmother, and you've lost your mother."

"She isn't dead."

"But . . ." Frowning, Allie tapped the letter. "She says she's dead."

If you're reading this, Alysha Catherine, I'm dead. Don't make a fuss—it's a state we all come to in the end. Except possibly for Jane who may be too mean to die. Now that it's happened, I need you to do me a favor. I have a small business in Calgary that's become crucial to the local community, and I want you to take it over. There's an apartment upstairs. I've left the keys with Kenny in the coffee shop next door. He'll hand them over when you settle my tab. Don't dawdle.

"She lies." Auntie Jane unplugged the kettle and filled the old brown teapot with boiling water. "She's always lied when it suited her."

When warm fingers closed around hers and squeezed gently, Allie turned her attention back to her mother—whose expression seemed caught halfway between comforting and exasperated. "If she was dead, sweetie, the aunties would know."

"But she didn't make it home this weekend." If she could have come home, she would have. Allie knew that. They all knew that. Rituals brought the wild ones home, even if they never stayed.

"We're not saying she isn't up to something," Auntie Jane pointed out, setting the teapot on the table. "We're just saying she isn't dead."

"Who isn't dead?" Auntie Ruby asked, shuffling into the kitchen and lowering herself carefully into one of the chairs.

"Catherine."

"Has she been buried?"

"Of course not, you old fool."

"Then what difference does it make? Pour my tea now, Jane dear. Off the top. You know I can't drink it when it turns to tar."

"Hey, Allie-cat! What's new?" Michael sounded just like he always did—happy to hear from her.

She clutched the phone a little tighter and concentrated on breathing. Her reaction was always more intense when she hadn't spoken to him for a few days.

"It's like the little mermaid," she'd told Charlie once, lying curled on her bed and emphatically not listening to Michael and his date through the suddenly too thin walls of their student apartment. *"Only instead of walking on razor blades, it's like they're filling my chest."*

"She gave up her tail for feet." On the other end of the phone, Charlie sounded merely curious. *"What did you give up?"*

"Michael."

"You didn't so much give him up as you never had him and, if you'll recall, no one forced you to share an apartment with him."

"He's my best friend. I love living with him."

"Have I told you lately that you're an idiot?"

"Allie?"

"Sorry. Got distracted." She never let it show in her voice; that wouldn't be fair to him. And his stupid perfect relationship. "It seems Gran's left me a business in Calgary."

"Left you? What do you mean, left you? She died?" He knew the family well enough to delay his reaction, but Allie could hear shock and grief waiting to emerge. Michael adored Gran, and she felt the same way about him. Of course, everyone felt the same way about him.

"The aunties don't think so."

His relief was palpable. "The aunties are usually right."

She felt almost sorry for those few seconds he'd believed the worst. Almost. She'd had to live through them, too. "Suck up."

"Hey, sucking up gets me pie. Auntie Jane has mad skills with blueberries." Memory provided a perfect shot of dimples flashing as he leaned back and stretched out long legs. "So, what are you going to do?"

"I don't know. They want me to go out there and figure out what she's up to."

"Calgary's a lot closer to Vancouver. Makes it easier for us to see each other."

She'd thought of that. "So I should go all the way out to Calgary just on the chance I'd see you more often?"

"Pretty much, yeah. Oh, crap. Allie, I've got to go. I've got an outside elevation I have to finish before the client arrives, and he just walked in."

"You're still at work?"

"You can rearrange the world for your convenience, and you can't remember a three-hour time difference?"

"I can't rearrange the *whole* world."

"So you say. Let me know what you decide. Love you."

"Love you, too." But she was talking to a dial tone.

"What did Michael say?"

"How do you know I called Michael first?"

On the other end of the phone, Charlie made a rude noise. "You always call Michael first, Allie."

Michael had received a family phone the same day Allie'd got hers—the day they left for university. Although the phones began as the cheapest pay-as-you-go handset available, by the time the aunties got through with them, they provided free, reliable cell service. There was a strong suspicion among the younger members of the family that the aunties were using the technology to eavesdrop, but—given *free, reliable cell service*—no one tried too hard to prove it.

Michael'd accidentally flushed his down the toilet during the first party they'd thrown in their shared apartment. Four days later, it had arrived in the mail; plain manila envelope, no return address, still working if a bit funky smelling.

"He said if I moved to Calgary, it'd be easier for us to get together."

"For what? Cappuccinos?" Charlie snorted, sounding frighteningly like Auntie Jane.

"For . . ." Sitting cross-legged in the tree house, Allie waved a hand, knowing Charlie'd get the intent even if she couldn't see the motion. "Why do you think she left her business to me?"

"Because you're unemployed with no emotional commitments that have any connection to reality."

"You think she saw that?"

"I think your mother called her when your grant ran out and, as your grandmother, she's understandably concerned about your creepy obsession with your gay best friend and thinks you should get a life. And I'm on the phone, dipshit!" Charlie's volume rose. "Keep your pants on, I'll be right there."

"I'm interrupting something."

"Not really. Just a prima donna who's sucking all the life out of this track by insisting it be *perfect*!"

Allie didn't quite catch the prima donna's answer, but it seemed to involve inserting instruments where they clearly wouldn't fit.

"This," Charlie added with a weary sigh, "is why I

hate session work. So what are you going to do? You've never been that far away from home."

"I know." Allie picked at a piece of splintered wood; swore as it drove in under her nail. "I think I'm going," she mumbled around the taste of blood as she sucked at her fingertip.

"You think?"

"I am." Staring across the moonlit pasture at the dark line of the woods, she wondered if Granddad was still hanging around. "You're right, I don't have anything better to do, and I'd like to know what Gran's up to as much as the aunties."

"Doubt that."

"I actually believed she was dead, Charlie." Her reaction lingered; like the phantom pain of a missing limb.

Charlie was quiet for a long moment, then she sighed. "All right, then."

"Besides, I can always come home when I need to." Like Charlie did. Well, not quite like Charlie did, but there were plenty of aunts and cousins out in the world. As each generation got larger, more of the Gale girls spread out, came home for ritual, spread out again. "You know they have these things called airplanes now."

"They smell like ass and they make you check your guitar."

"I don't have a guitar."

"It's not all about you, sweetie. Hey, you want me to come with you? You could be Nancy Drew and I can be the snappy sidekick with the gender inappropriate name. I always figured they were getting it on."

Allie grinned and leaned back against the tree house wall, the faded catalog pages that covered it crinkling under her weight. "You also figured Daphne and Velma were getting it on. If I haven't solved the mystery of the missing grandmother by the time you've finished the demo, come out then, okay?"

"Okay. And now we've got your life sorted, I'm needed elsewhere. Someone found two brain cells to rub together, and we might actually make some music tonight."

"Have fun." But she was talking to dead air. Again.

Flat on her back, feet out over the edge, she stared up through the latticework of branches and wondered why, at twenty-four, she still felt as though she were waiting for her real life to begin.

Off in the darkness, a small animal screamed and died.

She decided not to consider it an omen.

Allie left Wednesday morning. Aunt Andrea, Charlie's mother, who ran Darsden East's single travel agency, got her a last-minute ticket at a deep discount and her father took a personal day to drive her to the airport.

"They've all got reading to catch up on, Kitten," he told her, getting into the truck. "It won't kill them to sit quietly and make the attempt. Besides, I had a word with Dmitri. He'll keep our lot under control, and you know what they say . . ."

"It's better to follow a Gale than get in their way." Allie fastened her seat belt, twisted to wave at her mother and the aunties on the porch, then settled back in the seat with a sigh as they started down the lane. "Dmitri's in charge at the school?"

"Fought Cameron for it back in the fall." They drove in silence for a few kilometers, gravel pinging up against the undercarriage. Then, as they turned onto the paved county road, he added, "I think Dmitri's after your granddad's job."

"Dad, he's eighteen."

"Granted, but that'll change. He's looking ahead. Building alliances."

Allie rolled her eyes. Gale boy or not, Dmitri thought a little too highly of himself. "It doesn't work like that, and the aunties would never choose him, not if he wants it that much."

"You're sure?"

"Pretty sure, yeah." She shifted inside the confines of the seat belt, really not wanting to talk about why she was sure with her father even though he had to have known that Dmitri'd spent Thursday night. He'd given him a ride to school Friday morning, so the odds were good. "Dmitri's not powerful enough, and he's too ... tame." Not quite the best description, but anything more exact crossed over the TMI line. Way over. Gale women were attracted to power, and it took a lot to keep them from wandering off. Dmitri just didn't have what it took to hold the rituals in place.

"David ..."

Allie waited for more, but the name just hung there.

"David's not tame," she said at last, rubbing at a smudge on the window with her sleeve. And then, because it was clearly where the conversation was heading, added, "Auntie Jane wants him."

"So I've heard." The aunties shared the habit of talking amongst themselves like they were the only ones in the room and, with two of them in the old farmhouse, her father had likely heard any number of conversations he'd have been happier remaining ignorant of. "Your Auntie Jane is worried David's going to turn. Says it's been very a long time since a Gale boy went bad, and it's not going to happen on her watch."

"Really?" Allie felt her lip curl. She couldn't seem to stop it. "And who put Auntie Jane in charge?"

"I suspect Auntie Jane did."

Hard to argue with that, actually. Even among the aunties, who insisted on a lack of hierarchy, force of personality won out. Even Gran had deferred to her, although she'd done it mockingly. Allie drew in a deep breath and let it out slowly. "David's not going to turn."

"They're worried about how much time he spends away from the family."

"He's there if he's needed. And come on, Dad, he works with the police. He helps put bad guys in jail. He's . . . David. Sure he gets all dark and brooding sometimes, but hello, great power, great responsibility . . . she knows that. They all know that. Or don't they listen to the lectures they give us?"

"You're his baby sister, Kitten. You're not exactly unbiased."

"You're his father!"

"Well, fathers. Sons. It's complicated."

She glanced over at her father's smooth profile. Allie had asked her mother once if she'd been afraid the aunties would turn him down when she'd presented him. He was smart and funny and infinitely patient, but he brought nothing out of the ordinary to the family.

Fortunately, her mother had understood. *"Don't worry, Allie, when the time comes, they'll approve Michael. Everyone likes him and that's a very useful trait for the family to acquire. Or control if it comes to it. As for your father, well, your gran came home and made such a nuisance of herself that I think they agreed to accept him at least partially just to shut her up. And, who knows, maybe they saw what I saw in him."*

Of course, the aunties had never been given a chance to approve Michael and Allie'd come to see that infinite patience when dealing as an outsider with the Gale family was a wonderful thing to have. David had inherited some of that patience Allie hadn't. And none of that changed the fact that her father had no scars. He'd never gone head-to-head in a blind rut, unable to stop the need to dominate. He thought he understood his son, but really, bottom line, he couldn't.

"David won't turn," she told him. "And he'll choose when he's ready to choose. If Auntie Jane wants to tie him to ritual and the land, wants to tame him with chains of family obligation, she'll have to go through me!"

One dark brow rose. Unless he'd been practicing, it was likely they'd both gone up, but Allie could only see the one. "Tame him with chains of family obligation?"

"A little melodramatic?"

"Just a bit." But he was smiling and the tense line of his shoulders—tension she thought had come from her leaving—had eased. Which was flattering and not terribly realistic since even Auntie Gwen, whose eyes had only just darkened, could go through her opposition like a knife through meringue. "I take it you don't want me to repeat that to Auntie Jane?"

Allie literally felt her heart skip a beat. "Oh, God, no!"

"It'd help if he'd choose."

David's list was long enough that Allie suspected the aunties had bent a few lines trying to get him safely tied to one of his cousins.

"Or he could go Roland's route. I know there's cousins willing and that'd take the pressure off."

"Dad, shouldn't you be talking about this with David?"

"He gets enough of it from the aunties." He turned just far enough to flash her a self-conscious smile. "I'm not going to add to the chorus. But I still worry."

They talked about other things then; about new babies, and future plans, and what they thought Gran was really up to.

"You need to recognize that there's a chance she's actually dead, Kitten. If anyone could figure out a way to hide it from the aunties, it'd be your gran."

"But why?"

"Just to prove she could."

Yeah. That sounded like Gran. "Then I'll find out how and why it happened."

"All on your own."

"Dad, I'm twenty-four."

"And you're a Gale."

An undeniable statement of fact that could have a myriad of meanings. Allie decided she'd be happier not knowing which particular meaning her father felt applied.

They argued about music.

"I swear to you, Dad, if you say Rush one more time, I'm going to walk the rest of the way to Toronto."

And they talked about Michael although Allie put it off as long as she could.

"I'm not saying you should stop loving him, Allie. I'm just saying you should stop pining for him."

"I'm not pining." Pining meant she thought they might happen someday and she knew they wouldn't. She'd learned to work around the Michael-shaped hole in her life. "Michael was the one for me, and just because I'm not the one for him, that doesn't change things."

"It should."

"It doesn't. What if Mom hadn't wanted you? Or if the aunties hadn't approved you?"

He did her the credit of actually thinking about it for a few minutes. "I'd have moved on. Eventually."

"Well, maybe my eventually just hasn't happened yet." But she only said it because it was what he wanted to hear. "Dad! Last Tim Horton's before the airport!"

As he decelerated up the off ramp, Allie gave a quiet thanks for coffee and doughnuts. She'd eat enough fried dough with sprinkles to need larger jeans if it got her out of that particular conversation.

Gales didn't have problems with airport security and, after a short wait, Allie accepted it as her due that the plane had been overbooked and they were bumping her to first class. Or business class. Or whatever they were now calling those seats an adult could actually fit into.

Family influence did not, unfortunately, extend to providing anything worth watching while in the air. Allie read, napped a bit, and pulled her father's final warning out of memory to examine it for content she may have missed.

"Be careful, Kitten. The aunties have been wondering for some time what your grandmother's been up to and her getting you out there is no doubt a part of a much larger . . . thing. Whatever it is. Also, if you ask me, I think they're afraid."

"The aunties?"

"If your grandmother is dead, then clearly whatever killed her was something outside the norm, or we'd have heard from the proper authorities. And if something was capable of killing your grandmother, then that something is a danger to the entire family."

"Are you saying you don't want me to go?"

"Would you not go if that was what I wanted?" After a long moment, while she searched for the right words, he pulled her into a hug. *"It's all right. Just don't take anything for granted and call David if you run into something you can't handle. He's your big brother, it's his job to look after you."*

Sometimes Allie wondered if her father paid that little attention to how the family actually worked. *"Don't worry, Dad. I'll be fine."*

She'd be fine but a long way from home. She could feel family ties stretching. It wasn't a pleasant feeling.

A red light held her cab at the corner of 4th Avenue S.W. and 6th Street S.W. and Allie found her attention drawn to the north along 6th—the streets went north/south, the avenues east/west, but the ease of movement that suggested got canceled out by the compass locations. It wasn't enough to find 6th Street, it was crucial to know *which* 6th Street.

This 6th Street ended three short blocks to the north, and it looked like the entire west side of that last block was one long, two-story building.

"Excuse me." Allie twisted in the seat, trying to get a better angle. "Do you know what that building is?"

"The nice-looking one with the railing on the roof and the kind of pale stone trim? Big windows? Got all those trees out front behind the fence?"

Allie couldn't see that kind of detail but why not. "Yes, that one."

"No idea. Probably offices." He hit the gas as the light finally changed and sped along 4th Avenue mentioning points of interest as the buildings blurred by. He'd been completely silent all the way in from the airport—Allie didn't count the on-again, off-again duet he'd been performing with Country 105—but her question seemed to have tapped his inner tour guide. "The Old Spaghetti Factory's on 3rd Street, and then there . . ." A brisk nod as they raced a yellow light through the intersection. ". . . there's a good Korean barbecue and something Spanish or something and a pizza place. And this is pretty much Chinatown," he added turning south onto Center Street.

Allie would have asked what he meant by "pretty much Chinatown" but thought it might be safer if he concentrated on his driving for a while given that traffic had gone from insane to certifiable. The workday was ending and the sidewalks were fairly crowded, but not one head wore a cowboy hat. What point was there in going west if people dressed like they did in Toronto?

"Calgary Tower," he grunted, turning east on 9th.

As freestanding phallic symbols went, it was smaller than the one Allie was used to, but maybe Calgary felt it had less to prove.

The signs said they were in the southeast part of the city now. Allie had no idea where or when they'd crossed the line.

Pulling out to pass a transport, the cabbie jerked his head to the north with enough emphasis the cab swerved over the center line. "Fort Calgary. Bow River. Oh, and there's a zoo." Across a bridge, and they were suddenly on Atlantic Avenue. "I never been, but it's there."

"Where?"

"There." He jerked his head again, and Allie clutched at the edge of her seat.

"Okay."

Atlantic Avenue S.E. was also 9th Avenue S.E. And 1223 was only three long blocks in from the bridge.

Gran's business, the business that had become crucial to the local community, took up a double storefront and from the road looked to be . . .

"A junk shop?"

Her driver paused, one suitcase on the sidewalk the other hauled half out of the trunk, and peered up at the sign. "Says *The Enchantment Emporium*. Fair number of secondhand shops in this area. On the weekends, you'll get *antiquers*."

"By any other name," Allie muttered, eyes rolling at the emphasis. Gran had charms in the bottom right corner of all eight narrow windows obscuring the view—the lace curtains covering the top half meter of each gleaming glass pane were probably there to give the place an air of shabby gentility—but, from what she could see of the store's content, *junk* seemed more than accurate.

As the cabbie slowly counted out her change, Allie considered drawing a quick charm. She couldn't stop him from taking other fares to their destinations by the scenic route, but she could arrange it so passengers stayed out of his backseat. In the end she let it go, lifting her finger off the dusty metal and wiping the grime off onto her jeans. Her family didn't get screwed over, so something they'd passed on the way in from the airport had to have been important.

Or would be important.

Eventually.

At least she knew where to find a good Korean barbecue. She factored that information into his tip.

Kenny in the coffeehouse next door was an elderly Asian man who pulled Gran's keys out from under the counter, cupped his hand over the pile, and demanded twelve fifty. "You know where she's gone?"

"No." It seemed the safest answer and had the added benefit of being the truth.

"Yeah, well, she's an original, your grandmother. The things she could do with a yoyo . . ." As the pause lengthened, Allie cleared her throat and he reluctantly returned from wherever the memories had taken him, pushing the keys toward her. "If you hear from her, you let me know."

"She didn't say anything when she left the keys?"

"Just that you'd be coming for them." Kenny pulled a dark red paper cup off the stack by the cash register and turned to the row of urns behind the counter to fill it. "Alysha Catherine Gale, five foot eight, long blond hair, usually worn in a single braid, gray eyes, mole under the outside corner of her right eye, sprinkle of freckles, still bites her nails . . ."

Allie curled her fingers in.

". . . drinks her coffee black." He slid it along the same path as the key. "First one's free."

Of course it was. "Thank you, Mister . . . ?"

"Shoji. But call me Kenny, everyone does." Grinning broadly, he waved at the signed photos up on the wall. Allie recognized a few actors, a couple of politicians, one very well known hockey player, and . . .

"Is that Bob Dylan?"

"It is." Kenny leaned closer although he didn't lower his voice. "I met him at Woodstock."

"Okay." Wondering how much of his own coffee he'd sampled, she picked up her cup and backed away from the counter. "I need to go and . . ." A wave of the keys filled in the blank.

Kenny beamed, his face pleating into a hundred wrinkles, suddenly looking like one of the apple dolls Auntie Kay entered in the county fair every year. Auntie Kay's were specific to people in and around Darsden East—*"Don't be ridiculous, Allie dear, of course it's inert. Now."*—but, otherwise, the resemblance was astounding.

Her two suitcases and her carry-on bag were exactly where she'd left them, resting on a charm scuffed into the sidewalk by the junk shop's door. She paused, turned to face the street, and frowned. Something felt wrong. Off.

A teenage boy slouched past; baseball cap on backward, dark glasses covering his eyes, jeans nearly falling off nonexistent hips, the tinny sound of Rita McNeil being the wind beneath someone's wings coming from his earbuds.

An SUV, two pickup trucks, and a car that looked a lot like her Uncle Stephen's ancient Pacer drove by.

Two pigeons stared down at her from the power lines while one stared up at the sky.

Not exactly signs of an approaching apocalypse.

She was probably just reacting to the entirely new and not entirely pleasant feeling of being so far from home.

Key in the lock, she paused again and traced four lines scored lightly into the glass, the spread a little wider than her fingers. There could be a hundred explanations. Her brain kept fixating on the one involving claws, but that didn't make the other ninety-nine any less valid.

The lock turned with a definitive snick. The door opened silently, swinging in on well-maintained hinges. The bank of four light switches was just to the left of the door where light switches always were. Allie reached out with the hand holding the coffee cup and nudged the first one up with the rim.

As the lights immediately overhead came on, hot coffee spilled over her hand.

Swearing, she took four quick steps to a glass display case where she could put the cup down beside a half empty box of glow-in-the-dark yoyos and suck at the scalded skin at the base of her thumb.

It took her a moment to realize what she was staring at through the glass top of the case.

Resting on a folded paper towel, tucked in between a set of cowboy boot salt and pepper shakers and a set of four highball glasses commemorating the Winter Olympics, was a monkey's paw. The fur around the wrist had matted into triangular clumps. Only two of the darker gray, leathery fingers were folded down. It still had a wish left.

"Are you sure it's real?"

Even with the glass between them, it was making her skin crawl. "Pretty sure, yeah." There was only one way to be positive, and Allie didn't want to know that badly.

"How much is she charging for it?"

"Mom! I hardly think that's the point. This is a dangerous artifact just lying out in the open."

"You said it was in a glass case."

Reaching around, Allie slid open the nearer half of the badly fitting wooden panel and then closed it again. Quickly. "The case isn't locked. Anyone could reach in and take it."

"Sweetie, anyone stealing from your grandmother would get exactly what they deserved."

"No one deserves one of those things!" Was it moving? Was that a twitch? She tapped a finger against the glass but didn't see a reaction.

"If you can't handle it, Auntie Jane says she'd be willing to join you."

"I'm surprised none of the aunties insisted on coming with me," Allie muttered, *placing a stack of folded T-shirts into her suitcase.*

"They want to, but Mother has always made it quite clear they aren't welcome, and now they won't go without an invitation."

"Won't or can't?"

Allie's mother smiled. "At this point, it's impossible to tell. Things get tangled."

"No, it's all right." Auntie Jane or a monkey's paw; wasn't that a choice between the lesser of two evils. "I can handle things here. I was just startled a bit by . . ." Allie's eyes widened. "Mom, there's a signed photograph of a minotaur on the wall behind the counter."

"Probably Boris."

"He dotted his i with a little heart."

"Definitely Boris. Your grandmother seemed very fond of him."

Given the way Boris was built, Allie didn't doubt that in the least.

"You are in cattle country, remember." There was the faint sound of a distant horn, and her mother sighed. "Oh, wonderful; your father stopped at Ikea on the way home from the airport. That explains why it took him so long. And it looks like more bookcases. I'm glad you got there safely, don't forget to put the charm in the fridge. Tom, where are we supposed to put . . ."

Once again, Allie was listening to a dial tone. "I could start getting a complex about this," she muttered, closing the phone.

Finding the monkey's paw—for certain very small values of the word *finding* since the horrid thing would have taken work to avoid—convinced her she didn't want to deal with the store until she'd had a shower, a meal, and a good night's sleep. If Gran was keeping that powerful an artifact out in the open, there was no telling what she might have tucked in amongst the junk as a trap for the unwary. Or a not particularly funny joke. The differences could be subtle.

Flicking off the lights, Allie picked up her carry-on bag and headed for the door opposite the store entrance, eyes locked on the *employees only* sign. *If I*

don't see it, I don't have to deal with it until tomorrow.
The door led into a narrow hallway—yet another door
opposite led out into a small courtyard of scruffy grass
boxed in by buildings on all four sides, three scruffy
shrubs in a circular bed defining exact center of the
space. To her immediate left, a somewhat grubby two-
piece bath, and about ten feet to the right, the bottom
step of a long, narrow staircase.

A huge rectangular mirror covered almost half the
wall between the door into the shop and the stairs. The
glass alone had to be nearly six by four and the addition
of the triple-molded pediment and carved frame easily
added another foot each way. While her degree was actually in art history, working on the museum inventory
had given her enough exposure to antique furniture that
Allie was certain she was looking at an actual 1870's
Renaissance Victorian piece in walnut, still wearing its
original finish. Even with the few flaws she could see, it
was worth around five thousand dollars.

And then she noticed her reflection—black dress,
black stockings, black shoes, little black purse, and black
pillbox hat with a tiny net veil.

"Oh, wonderful." A number of the oldest aunties kept
magic mirrors but not on this scale and, as a rule, they
didn't leave them running. Stepping back, she folded
her arms over her white cotton sweater. Her reflection
pulled a tissue from her purse and blew her nose.

Finding meaning in any mirror most closely resem-
bled playing a surreal game of charades.

"If it helps, the aunties say Gran's not dead."

Her reflection wavered and was suddenly in sweater,
jeans, and sneakers standing in what looked like a
casino.

"Not likely. Not after the last time." Auntie Jane had
traveled to Vegas to bail her out, and she had not been

happy about it even though a dollar slot machine at the airport had paid for the trip.

Allie's reflection wavered again, and she was naked. She could see Charlie's charm glowing on her shoulder, but her breasts were a bit big.

"Cute," she muttered and started up the stairs.

With any luck, Gran had left documentation lying around somewhere. Without an instruction manual and a way to turn it off, she was stuck sharing space with a large reflective surface exhibiting a juvenile sense of humor.

No surprise; she found charms surrounding the apartment door. Most of them were the standard Gale protections, keeping out those who entered with intent to harm, but a couple were strangely specific. One of them seemed to be denying entrance to crows, and three of them, strategically located, didn't just cover the door but were part of a pattern that warded the entire apartment.

Gran had enemies?

Feeling stupid, Allie connected the dots. Of course Gran had enemies. If Gran wasn't dead, there was a good chance she was on the run from something. If she *was* dead, that something had killed her.

Allie took a deep breath. A large part of her insisted that opening the door was a bad idea. The rest of her found the right key and slid it into the lock.

All of her paused.

If Gran was dead, there was a chance that Gran's rotting, mutilated corpse could be on the other side of the door because if Gran was dead, there had to be a body. Okay, there didn't *have* to be a body. Given what it would take to kill Gran, a body after the fact had to be considered optional. And it wasn't as if she hadn't dealt with bodies before; the family maintained a hands-on approach to death.

But, if Gran *was* dead, the thing that killed her could be waiting on the other side of the door.

Reminding herself that dealing with either a week-old corpse or a something mean enough to get through Gran's charms would be preferable to dealing with Auntie Jane should she call for help before she'd even unpacked, Allie pushed the door open and stepped into an enormous room that was living room and dining room and kitchen combined. From where she was standing, she could see neither corpse nor *thing*, so she stepped further in and pulled the door closed behind her.

The last of the daylight poured into the room through tall, multipaned windows on both the street and the courtyard sides. The walls were a deep yellow and the floor a dark natural wood, the wide boards probably original to the building. The furniture was large, over-stuffed, and predominantly upholstered in dark brown velvet. A quick glance under the cushions proved both of the sofas folded out into queen-size beds. The scuffed rectangular table could easily seat eight. Ten with very little crowding. Twelve if manners weren't a factor. Gran may have left the family behind, but old habits died hard. Fairy lights had been wound around both of the thick steel poles supporting the massive beam that indicated where the interior load-bearing wall had been removed.

Not actual fairy lights, Allie was relieved to see, although she wouldn't have been surprised had Gran been dealing with the UnderRealm.

There were three doors on the far wall.

A double set of French doors, curtained in ivory lace, led into a large bedroom where the wood floor had been painted black and the walls were the same dark red as the heavy velvet drapes over the windows.

Allie glanced in at the king-sized bed and tried not to think of minotaurs. There was a duvet on the bed, the red-and-gold damask cover safely purchased and charm free. Allie'd slept under family quilts her entire life, each piece of fabric placed by the aunties to fulfill multiple purposes—Gran had left that combination of protection and influence behind. Now, so had she.

The middle door led to a narrow bathroom with a shower centered in a claw-footed tub, shower curtain hanging in a circle from the ceiling. The rug, like the duvet cover, had been bought, not made.

The third door led to another bedroom piled high with boxes and larger pieces of junk in place of a bed. Peering into a box of bright green baseball caps, Allie realized no one in the family had known exactly where Gran had settled until the letter and the will arrived. She'd come home for holidays and rituals and stayed in touch by phone, but no one had ever visited her here.

That was sad. Even the wild Gales needed family around them once in a while.

There could be a clue to her disappearance hidden somewhere amongst the junk in the spare room.

Or in the junk downstairs.

Or in the medicine cabinet.

Or under the sofa.

"Where the hell do I start?"

Her stomach growled.

"Good answer."

Pulling the door closed, Allie realized she'd have to sleep in Gran's bed.

The sheets had gone into the dryer by the time the take-out Thai arrived. Allie'd picked the restaurant at random from the half dozen stained flyers stuck to the front of the fridge. The fridge itself held only the kinds of food that could last a week or even two; whatever had happened, Gran'd had warning. Or she'd lived on soy sauce, margarine, mustard, and extra old cheese— which couldn't be ruled out. Auntie Ester had lived on gingerbread for the last two years of her very long life. Fortunately, as Allie hadn't the faintest idea of where the closest grocery store was, the freezer and the pantry were better stocked.

On her way back to the stairs, mouth watering at the scent of the Pad Thai Talay, the mirror showed her the delivery boy naked.

"You go, Gran," Allie sighed, taking the stairs two at a time. After she ate, she'd start in on the spare room and leave the store for the morning. Right now, skirting the edges of her grandmother's life was all she could cope with, and that was only because she'd found ice cream in the freezer.

"Honestly, Michael, who needs that much variation?"

"Apparently, your grandmother." He couldn't stop snickering. "Anything look interesting?"

"I don't care if one them looks like yours, I'm not even considering the word *interesting* as a reaction to a drawer full of my grandmother's sex toys. What am I supposed to do with them? Shut up," she snapped as the snickering turned into a shout of laughter. "I mean, I can't just throw them out. What if the bag breaks open and everyone knows where they came from?"

"The family doesn't have a charm for that?"

"Oh, yeah, of course we have a charm to keep garbage bags from breaking open and half a dozen dildos belonging to our grandmothers from spilling out onto the pavement."

"Problem solved, then."

"Ass."

"You love my ass."

"Oh, please . . ." Allie reached up and turned off the bedside light. ". . . everyone loves your ass."

She could see him smiling, see him stretched out on one of their stupid perfect black leather sofas wearing a pair of worn gray sweatpants and an equally worn T-shirt, the tap tap of Brian working on his laptop, the perfect quiet background noise. Stupid, perfect, quiet, background noise.

"Lonely, Allie-cat?"

She rubbed the ache in the center of her chest that told her how far she was from home. "A little."

"Where's Charlie?"

"Halifax. Working on a friend's demo." The heavy drapes blocked most of the city sounds. Allie pressed her other ear into the pillow and blocked the rest.

"Want me to stay on the phone until you fall asleep?"

The sheets smelled like fabric softener and the mattress was exactly the right combination of hard and soft. "I'm not six."

"I know. And I know you hate sleeping alone."

"Yeah, my life sucks. Gran's up to something and all I get is a business, an apartment . . ."

"An assortment of sex toys."

"I'm going to regret telling you about them, aren't I?"

"Probably."

"Good night, Michael."

She hung up before she could tell him she missed him and eventually fell asleep with the phone cradled in her hand.

"There's a Gale staying in the apartment?" Heavy black brows met in a vee over his nose. "You're certain of that?"

He shrugged. "Alysha Gale ordered take-out this evening. I just got word from one of my sources. She had it delivered to the store."

"I knew it was too good to be true when the old woman disappeared. Damn. Damn. Fucking damn!" One scarred fist pounded the words into the desktop, hard enough the silver letter opener slid off the pile of paper.

He caught it before it hit the floor.

"We're too close to the day," his boss continued, ignoring both the letter opener's fall and its subsequent retrieval. "We have no choice but to stay and see it through. No choice for me but to stay and face the danger inherent in yet another fucking Gale!"

"All right." He kept his voice low, calming. Things happened when his boss lost his temper. Things that could attract attention, and—right now—attention was the last thing they wanted to attract. He knew that for a fact because not attracting attention had been a part of every conversation they'd had since Catherine Gale had first appeared on the scene and, for the last month, not attracting attention had moved to the top of the agenda. "I'm still not exactly clear on just what you think she'll do."

"There's no way of knowing what she'll do. That's the fucking problem! You say black, and they're likely to say white just to be contrary. Controlling harpies, the whole lot of them!" Nostrils flaring, he took a deep breath, then another, and finally growled, "We need to know if she's here because of me. If Catherine Gale got suspicious before she disappeared and passed those suspicions on."

"This Alysha Gale could be here merely to take over the store. Or because of *them*. You told me that the Gale women were not known for their subtle reactions. That if Catherine Gale knew you were here, we'd know."

"I know what I told you!"

He held up a hand in apology as the vein in the older man's forehead throbbed.

"I need to know what Alysha Gale knows."

"About you?"

"About everything! The last thing I need is to have them stumble on the situation and destroy me all unknowing with their incessant need to meddle. Wouldn't those controlling harpies love that. Find out what she knows!" A beefy finger jabbed the command toward him.

"And what happens then?" He rested his hand on his weapons case.

"That depends on *what* you find out. I'll reevaluate when I have more information."

THREE

It took her a moment to realize the sound dragging her up out of sleep was her phone and a moment after that to find it in the bed.

"Alysha Catherine."

Only the aunties ever used both names. Half asleep, it was impossible to narrow it down any further. "Auntie . . . ?"

"Bea, Alysha Catherine. It's Auntie Bea."

Auntie Bea was one of the *David is too powerful to be trusted* group. Allie felt her lip curl.

"Don't curl your lip at me, young lady. Why are you still in bed?"

She took the phone away from her ear and peered at the time. "It's twenty after five."

"It's twenty after seven."

"Calgary," she sighed. "Time difference."

"That's no reason to be lying about."

Allie considered it a very good reason to be *lying* about and thought about mentioning that had she still been working in Toronto, her alarm wouldn't have gone off for another ten minutes and so she'd still be in bed and Auntie Bea could just fuck off and die, but two time zones weren't distance enough for something that stupid. She sighed. "What's the problem, Auntie Bea?"

"Have you figured out what your grandmother is up to?"

"No."

"Why not?"

"I just got here yesterday evening."

"And you're still in bed?"

"Twenty after five," Allie repeated, yawning. "Goodbye, Auntie Bea."

There may have been a protest, but Allie barely heard it as she closed the phone. No one should have to deal with an auntie at five twenty in the morning.

Or at five twenty-three.

Or five thirty.

Her body, still on Ontario time, insisted it was time to get up . . .

Five forty-five.

. . . and refused to be convinced otherwise no matter that the room was dark and the bed, although empty, was comfortable.

"Fine."

Auntie Vera called as she got into the shower. Auntie Meredith called during her not entirely successful attempt to make coffee with the space age coffeemaker she found in one of the kitchen cupboards. Allie wasn't willing to agree with her father that the aunties were frightened, but this level of annoying meant they were definitely worried.

Dmitri's youngest sister, Ashley—one of the pre-ritual mass of cousins—called just as she pulled her jeans out from under the bed and discovered that a lemon meringue pie didn't exactly fit in the watch pocket.

"It's just Kristen's being all like totally annoying, and

I could come out as soon as school's over so that you won't be alone."

"If I'm still here," Allie pointed out, using the legs of her jeans to wipe up the mess.

"Why wouldn't you be? I heard Auntie Catherine left you a junk store."

"How do you know about the store?"

"I heard my mom and Auntie Carol talking. Your mom told Aunt Ruth and Aunt Ruth told Auntie Vera and Auntie Vera told Auntie Carol and Auntie Carol . . ."

"I know how it works." She dumped the pie still clinging to her jeans in the toilet and caught the charmed penny as it fell. As long as the penny was not currently holding a pie, anyone in first or second circle could provide baked goods. Dead or alive, Gran wouldn't appreciate her plumbing clogged with pastry. "If I'm still here, Charlie'll be here."

"Charlie never stays."

Ouch. But true enough. Allie rinsed the penny off in the kitchen sink and carried it to the fridge. Charmed change kept most Gales alive through college and university. "We'll see."

But they both knew it meant yes.

"You're my *absolutely favorite* cousin ever! Gotta go. First bell. Bye!"

And it was all of six thirty-two.

She looked at the penny lying in solitary state on the second shelf, set the phone down beside it, and closed the refrigerator door. Charlie liked to send hers on taxi rides, but Allie preferred to keep hers closer to hand, just in case.

She toasted and ate a bagel—Gran had left a bag in the freezer—drank a bad cup of coffee, stared out the window at the traffic passing below, and reminded herself that she'd made the decision to come west so she could just cope with how weird it felt and get to . . .

Coffee slopped over the side of the mug as she jerked back from the glass.

Shadow.

Big shadow.

Big fast-moving shadow.

Too big. Too fast.

Heart pounding, Allie leaned forward. The street ran essentially east/west and the long shadows thrown by the early morning sun ran parallel, so it could have been nothing more than a small plane flying north/ south. A traffic plane. Up there to report on the traffic. Unfortunately, a traffic plane didn't explain the pigeons she could see crammed under a newspaper box across the street.

Or the way the trailing end of the shadow seemed to be lashing.

Her fingers were not trembling as she retrieved her phone. The spilled coffee had been hot, that was all. There were six missed calls and a text message from Katie.

Spnt nght cxng A Ruby off H2O twr. Come home.

Tempting.

Allie took a deep breath as she snapped the phone closed.

But no.

She didn't know if it was smart or stupid or just bloody-minded to step outside the store, to cross the sidewalk to the curb, and to look up. At some point between the time she'd left the window and arrived at the curb, the pigeons had come out from under the newspaper box and flown to perch along the low stone parapet of her building like nine small, feathered gargoyles. Eight of them were staring at whatever it was pigeons stared at. One of them watched the sky.

Allie tipped her head back, following its line of sight. As far as she could see, the sky held nothing but a bit of cloud the heat would burn off before too long and the distant, familiar silhouette of a bird of prey. She'd seen more kestrels in Toronto than out at the farm; they nested in most major cities in Canada, adapting to cliffs of concrete and steel, feeding well off the fat-and-oblivious birds who'd dulled their survival instincts with French fries and cigarette butts.

Squinting, one hand raised to block the sun, Allie tried to get a better look at the hawk, only certain it *was* a hawk by the way it moved. Predators were unmistakable in the air. Unfortunately, it was just too damned high for her to pick out details.

"Hey, Blondie! Nice ass!"

She turned just in time to see a muscular young man leering out the window of a passing pickup before he was swept away on the tide of morning traffic. Too far away and moving too fast to toss a charm after him. And besides, it *was* a nice ass and a little moderately skeevy appreciation never hurt.

It took her a moment's search to find the kestrel again, a tapered black cross rising still higher against the blue.

How high would that passing shadow have had to have climbed in order to look like a small hawk from below?

Wondering where that thought had come from, and really wishing it had stayed there, Allie moved closer to the building until she found herself standing with one hand on the door. According to the sign taped to the bottom of the nearest window, the store was open 10 AM to 6 PM Wednesday, Thursday, Saturday, and Sunday. 10 AM to midnight Friday. Closed Monday and Tuesday.

It was Thursday at seven forty.

Two hours and twenty minutes to search for clues . . .

"Oh, dear God, I *am* turning into Nancy Drew."

. . . before she was expected to open and become a crucial part of the local community.

The store didn't look significantly better than it had yesterday although, in all fairness, it didn't look any worse. It was a bright, sunny morning, but the light spilling through the windows seemed unwilling to move very far away from the glass.

"All right, then." She took a deep breath and flicked on the overhead fluorescents, banishing some but not all of the more interesting shadows. Piled high on tables, spilling off of shelves, in boxes opened for rummaging—the amount of crap gathered together in this one place was overwhelming. What were the odds of finding a clue to her grandmother's disappearance in that amount of crap?

"I am so screwed."

If she'd dragged half a dozen cousins to Calgary with her, they might have a chance to bring something resembling order out of chaos.

Actually . . .

She flipped open her phone.

And closed it, frowning, half an hour later wondering what the odds were that every single cousin she'd called was busy and expected to remain busy for the immediate future. Betsy, after a winter of almost no teaching gigs, had been called in to finish out the school year in Odessa. Uncle Don had fallen out of the mow and broken his leg, leaving Carol and Theresa to deal with the fieldwork. Sandi, ready to give up acting and become an accountant like her mother, had actually gotten a part as Chava's understudy in a revival of *Fiddler on the Roof*. Bonny was giving serious thought to bringing a member of the county road crew home to meet the aunties.

"If they approve him, they'll get plowed out first all winter."

"They already get plowed out first," Allie reminded her.

"But this way, they won't have to put any effort into it."

Allie had her doubts that the aunties put any effort into it, relying instead on reputation, but she wished Bonny luck and snapped the phone closed.Until the younger kids finished school, it looked like she *was* the only member of the family unemployed and/or emotionally uncommitted.

"Well, don't I feel special."

On her own, the store would take her months to catalog and, unless she stumbled over her grandmother's diary, months longer to start piecing together any relevant information even if she used the cataloging software she'd acquired at her last job.

And that was ignoring the time she'd have to put into running a business to pay the bills.

Not to mention ignoring whatever had flown over the store at dawn.

Actually, ignoring whatever had flown over the store at dawn seemed like a great idea. Any weirdness going on in the airspace over the city of Calgary was not her concern.

"Here's a thought," she said to the obligatory velvet Elvis fronting a box of bad art. "Why don't I assume Gran knows what she's doing and, if she's not dead, she'll fill us in when she's good and ready?"

Velvet Elvis offered no opinion.

All things considered, Allie was actually pretty happy about that.

Instead of a cash register, Gran had a heavily charmed cashbox containing four hundred and seventeen dollars and twenty-seven cents on a shelf under the counter. Next to it, three ledgers that looked liked they'd been picked up at a yard sale given by a Victorian mortgage broker. In mint condition, they'd be worth serious money to a collector although *Store, Extras,* and *Yoyos* scrawled in black marker on the oxblood leather had likely devalued them a bit.

On the wall behind the counter was a seven-by-three grid of cubbyholes numbered from one to twenty-one. Some of them held . . .

"Mail?" Allie stared down at the envelope she'd pulled from cubby number one. The name looked vaguely Eastern European and the address was definitely the store's. Gran seemed to have been allowing the homeless to use the store as a mail drop. Surprisingly community minded, Allie allowed, putting the envelope back in the cubby where she'd found it.

Next to the cubbyholes, a locked cabinet.

Turning to pick up the keys from the counter, she screamed.

The translucent young man, face and hands plastered to the glass as he peered into the store, jumped back, mouth open, eyes wide.

Heart pounding, Allie took a deep breath and then another, and reminded herself that most of the lingering dead were harmless. Granted, some of them had issues they took out on the living, but this redheaded twenty-something she could see traffic through seemed more the former sort. He'd been at least as startled by her as she was by him.

She could almost hear the aunties telling her to ignore him.

Although, if peering into the store was part of his regular morning routine, then it made more sense to pump him for information. He might have seen something, or heard something, or—depending on how long he'd been dead—actually been part of something to do with Gran's disappearance.

When she got to the door, he was still standing where he'd landed, leaning forward slightly, gaze tracking her movements. That was good. The revenants with a little lingering self-determination were easier to talk to.

When she opened the door, the young man solidified.

Allie stared at him. Frowned. And closed the door.

Definitely translucent.

Open, opaque.

Closed, translucent.

Open . . .

"What the hell are you doing?" He looked ready to bolt.

She touched his shoulder and felt substance, although it gave a little under her finger. "You're not dead."

"I'm not what?" he demanded, jerking away from her touch.

"Dead."

"Why would you be thinking I'm dead?"

"Give me a minute." Closing the door again, she searched it for charms and found a clear-sight drawn on the painted steel frame that held the glass. So what she saw through the glass was the young man's true appearance. But he wasn't dead. Interesting.

This time when she opened the door, he rattled out, "Are you Alysha Catherine Gale?" before she could speak. "Your grandmother said I could trust you."

"And you are?"

"Joe O'Hallan."

The other signature on the will. That could mean she was supposed to trust him in return. It could mean nothing more than Gran had found him conveniently available at the time. It was hard to say.

"I've come for my drink." Indicating his own body with a grubby hand nearly hidden in a gray sweater at least two sizes too big, he added, "I'm a bit beyond due, but you weren't here yesterday."

Allie ducked her head back and took another look at him through the glass door. Red hair, gray sweater, brown cords with cord worn off in places, work boots with the steel cap showing through the torn leather on one toe. Bit of ginger stubble along a narrow jaw. Purple/ gray half circles under worried eyes. Still translucent. "You'd better come inside." Whatever Gran was up to, explanations out on the sidewalk were a bad idea.

Joe appeared solid inside the store and, once over the threshold, a lot less skittish. Given the possible claw marks gouged into the outside of the door, maybe that wasn't so surprising. "Your grandmother said you'd be taking over her stuff."

Allie spent a moment not thinking about the toys in the bedside table. "That's right."

Thin shoulders rose and fell. "I need my drink, then."

That was the second time he'd mentioned a drink. It wasn't completely out of the question that Gran had been running some kind of weird after-hours club. Where *weird* meant translucent clientele. And *after-hours* meant eight in the morning.

"Let's pretend that Gran left me no information about her stuff. Which should be easy because it's true." Reaching past him, she relocked the door. "You're going to have to tell me everything."

Ginger brows drew in. "Everything?"

"Everything. Let's start with who you are, what this drink is, and, when it comes to it, where I can find it."

"It's in . . ."

She raised a hand and cut him off like he was one of her younger cousins. "It hasn't come to it. First, tell me who you are."

"You know my name."

Allie sighed. As names went, Joe O'Hallan wasn't very descriptive. "You want to expand on that a bit?"

Joe stared at her for a long moment and then he sighed. "Look, you don't . . ."

"Yes, I do."

"Fine." His chin rose. "I'm a leprechaun."

"A leprechaun?" She hadn't expected that; given how many Newfoundlanders were working the Alberta oilfields, she'd assumed his accent was east coast. "Aren't you a little tall for a leprechaun?" He wasn't that much shorter than she was. Five-six. Five-five maybe. And scowling.

"Am I? Faith and begorrah, sure, and no one's ever pointed that out before!"

Allie blinked at him. "Bitter much?"

"You started it with the cultural stereotypes." His hands disappeared inside his ragged cuffs as he folded his arms over his chest. "I'm a changeling, okay? I was raised as human, but the babe I got changed for has died."

"Of what?"

"What difference does it make?" Joe rolled his eyes—inhumanly green now she knew what to look for—at her expression. "Fine. Whatever. Probably old age. Point is, without it there, I've no counterbalance to keep me here, so I fade as I'm Called back under the hill."

Under the hill was the mythic reference to the Under-Realm. It was strange to hear one of the Fey use the Human term.

"Your grandmother made a drink that unfades me," he added.

He seemed to be waiting for a response. "She did?"

"Why the hell would I lie about something like that, then?"

Good point.

"Don't you want to go home?" She could feel the ache of her own home pulling at her.

He snorted. "Not even. The food's crap and the music sucks. Oh, and let's not forget . . ." He scowled. ". . . my loving family traded me off for a human when I was a babe. And it's not like they even want me, do they? The Court just hates the thought of a pureblood not under their control. They can Call until Finnbhennach comes home."

"Who?"

"White bull of Connacht. Far as I'm concerned, I *am* home. Your grandmother keeps the drinks in the locked cabinet behind the counter."

He seemed pretty sure she was going to give it to him.

"I can pay for it," he growled as she hesitated. "It's not charity." One grubby hand indicated the shelves of junk. "It's part of the business."

"Of course it is," Allie muttered, searching the ring for the right key. Trust Gran not to mention which community her business had become crucial to.

There were three shelves inside the cabinet crammed with bottles and jars that looked like they'd originally held condiments. All of the aunties had similar cabinets although, back home, they were never locked. The aunties liked to weed out those members of the family they considered too stupid to breed.

Probably why they never labeled anything either.

"Do you know . . . ?"

He frowned and leaned over the counter. "I think it's . . . uh . . . no. That one."

"This one."

His pointing finger didn't move. "No, *that* one."

"This one?" When he nodded, she lifted what looked like a ketchup bottle carefully from the shelf. "You sure?"

"Mostly. It's the right color."

It was the only liquid that virulent a shade of orange. When she passed it over, Joe cradled it for a moment between both hands before unscrewing the lid and draining the bottle. He didn't look any solider but he felt more . . . there. Slipping a thin hand in past the worn edges of his pants pocket, he pulled out a lump of . . .

"Fairy gold."

"Yeah, what of it?"

"Well, it's fairy gold," Allie repeated, wondering if he was trying this out on her because she was new. He could move about under his own power, so he hadn't tried it on Gran. "When the sun touches it, it'll turn to earth. Or leaves. Or dog shit."

"You think I'm after cheating you?"

Allie gestured at the fairy gold on his palm, letting it speak for itself.

"You think I'm after cheating Catherine Gale's granddaughter? Obviously, you think I'm a complete idiot." He slapped the pale yellow lump down on the counter and glared at her. "I like my balls right where they are, thank you very much. Just put the gold in the cashbox like always."

"And?"

He blinked. "And? And after twenty-four hours it's coin of the realm. Well, paper money of the realm anyway." Another blink wiped the remaining anger away as realization began to dawn. "She really didn't tell you anything?"

"She really didn't." Allie pulled the cashbox out from under the counter, stared into it, and rolled the fairy gold between her fingers. "So, about my grand-mother . . ." When she looked up, he'd started to fidget. "Do you know where she's gone?"

"Hard to say." His smile wouldn't have fooled a three year old. "Heaven wouldn't want her and Hell couldn't hold her."

True enough as far as it went.

"So you believe she's dead?"

Except for his eyes, he went completely still. His gaze flicked first left then right as though he was afraid there might be eavesdroppers in the shadows. "I believe what she wants me to believe."

The words came out in a rush and so quietly that Allie had to strain to hear them. The subtext was obvi-ous; she'd better believe the same.

Allie sighed. "Am I going to get a visit from a large man in an expensive suit looking for a lot of money?"

"No," Joe told her indignantly. Paused. "Probably not."

"Great. Did she tell you why she wants me here?"

"She had to leave her stuff to someone, right?"

"But why me?"

He snorted. "Why not you? All I know is . . ." He was watching the shadows again. ". . . she had me sign that paper and she let me have your name. And then she wasn't here for a few days. And then you were here."

"How many days?"

"Store's been closed since last Friday."

"I got the letter on Monday. She must've mailed it . . ."

"Before." He scratched at the back of one hand. "Before she was gone. Yeah. Said she couldn't trust the post to get it there after."

"The letter said, if you're reading this I'm dead, so she either knew she was going to die or she knew she was going to disappear."

"Well, yeah." Joe stared at her like she was slightly simple. "She knew things, didn't she?"

"Good point." She'd probably *seen* Allie accept and her reason for leaving things the way she had didn't need to be any more complicated than that. Allie couldn't decide if that took the pressure off or added some kind of unwanted destiny factor.

I'm your grandmother, Luke.

She dropped the fairy gold in the box, reached out to close it, and saw Joe swallow, prominent Adam's apple bobbing up and down in his throat.

"I'd go get coffee for your grandmother sometimes," he said hurriedly when she paused. "You know, when she didn't want to lock up the store."

Allie glanced over at the closed sign still facing the street.

"But yeah, I guess I'm early today so, you know, I'll just leave you to it." Hands shoved into his pockets he turned away from the counter. And then back again. "Oh, and don't be forgetting to mark that I got my bottle down in the special ledger. The accountant comes in every Friday afternoon to do the bookkeeping, and he gets right shitty if he's got to ask about stuff. He's old school."

"Right. The special ledger." Joe had gotten as far as the door and was shifting his weight from foot to foot as he waited for her to let him out and lock it behind him.

More than Joe seemed to be waiting.

"You know what?" Allie said slowly, feeling her way

but growing more confident with every word that she was moving in the right direction. "A coffee sounds like a good idea." She pulled a twenty from the cashbox. "And a muffin if Kenny's got anything edible. And the same for you. I know it's an imposition," she added hurriedly before he could speak, "but I'm floundering here. If you don't mind staying for a while . . . ?"

"To help?"

"Yeah."

"Here?"

"Yeah. You seem to know what's going on. More than I do anyway."

It was entirely possible that Joe was older than her grandmother, but just for a moment, the moment between uncertainty and his smile, he looked painfully young.

"How'd you take your coffee, then?" he asked, pulling the twenty from her grip.

"Black."

"The Saskatoon berry muffins are killer."

"Great." Then she rethought it. "That is great, right? You weren't warning me?"

"No, it's great. Coffee and muffins, then. You don't need to lock the door behind me, I'll only be a tick."

He looked solid through the door. Solid, and completely alone. Allie checked off a box in her mental actually-figured-out-what-Gran-wanted column. Feeding one of her strays wasn't much, but it was a start.

"Wait a minute, you can't be Irish."

Joe picked the last of his muffin crumbs off the counter with one finger. "Leprechaun."

"Okay, ethnically Irish, but you said you were raised by human parents."

"In Ireland."

"Oh. Right. Then what are you doing in Calgary?" Allie asked hurriedly, feeling a little stupid for having missed the obvious answer.

"Why not Calgary? Things are happening here. It's a good place to start a new life."

She didn't point out that his new life seemed to suck a bit.

At ten, Allie turned the sign, opened the store, and went reluctantly back behind the counter. All three account books were up on the glass—one for the yoyos, one for the potions and the mailbox accounts, one for the store. "Okay. Let's try an easy question. Did Gran ever explain *why* she kept the yoyo sales in a separate book?"

Joe shrugged. "Not big on explaining herself, your grandmother, but I'm guessing it's because she's got so many of them."

There was the box of plastic, glow-in-the-dark yoyos on the counter, a box of old-fashioned wooden yoyos enameled in primary colors on one of the shelves next to three stacks of saucers that seemed to have lost their cups, and there was a box of miniature yoyos, each about as big around as a twoonie, on the floor next to a box of old musical scores.

Allie opened her mouth, about to protest that three boxes weren't that many, then reconsidered. "There's more than I can see from here, isn't there?"

"In the storeroom."

She drained the last drop of cold coffee and, as fortified as she was going to get, said, "Show me."

He nodded toward the door. "What if someone comes in while we're gone?"

"That's a risk they'll just have to take."

"Don't you mean a risk you'll have to take?"

Allie thought about the monkey's paw and tips of icebergs. "Nope."

The basement had a packed dirt floor, stone walls patched in a couple of places with concrete blocks, and bare bulbs, dusty and dim, hanging from the underside of the floor joists. Piles of boxes filled nearly the entire space with only narrow passageways between them for access.

"This isn't a storeroom," Allie muttered, ducking under a spiderweb, "this is a horror movie cliché waiting to happen."

The stained boxes nearest the stairs were packed with smaller, unopened boxes of yoyos.

"She only brought new ones up when the old boxes were completely emptied," Joe offered, crouched by the trapdoor.

"And the rest of the stuff?"

"Stuff."

"Specifically?"

"People bring your grandmother boxes of stuff, and she buys them. Bought them." Allie could hear the frown in his voice as he changed verbs. "Used to buy them. You know, stuff like the last bit of crap you can't get rid of at a yard sale or the odds and sods an estate auction won't touch."

That explained the smell. The storeroom reeked of other people's lives, a melancholy mix of the stale perfumes left behind by withered dreams, lost hopes, and forgotten promises—with a faint hint of cat pee. And mold, Allie acknowledged, as she made her way carefully back up the steep stairs and headed into the tiny store bathroom to blow her nose on a handful of toilet paper.

"Your grandmother told me once that nine out of ten people throw away the answer all unawares like." Joe closed the trapdoor and straightened, arching his back. "She also said nine out of ten people don't know what the fuck the question is." He turned, cupped both hands over his corduroy-covered crotch, and scowled at his reflection in the mirror, his ears suddenly redder than his hair. "I hate it when it does that!"

Allie glanced over. "That's why it does it. For the reaction."

"It doesn't bother you, then?"

She shrugged. "I have a lot of cousins; if you freak at a live frog in your lunch bag, next time it's pepper in your pompoms."

"What in your what?"

"Pepper in your pompoms." Allie pointed at the mirror now showing her reflection in full cheerleader rig. "Red and gold," she corrected, and the colors changed. "Most of the Gale girls are cheerleaders in high school. Even Gran."

"Scary thought," Joe muttered following her back into the store.

"We're less scary when we're young."

"Differently scary."

"Fair enough. Auntie Jane says Gran was deadly with a field hockey stick."

"Actually deadly?"

"It's always safer not to make assumptions." She slipped back behind the counter. "No customers while we were gone. No surprise." Although the traffic along 9th Avenue was steady, the sidewalks were empty.

"I should go." Joe headed for the door. "Your grandmother didn't like me hanging around all day."

"Gran's not here." When Joe turned to check the shadows, Allie managed to keep her eyes locked on him rather than join in the search. Just managed. "Listen, if you could stay just a little longer, I could get started checking this place for . . ." She examined and discarded a couple of descriptive phrases that would have gotten her mouth washed out with soap at a much younger age. ". . . less than normal merchandise."

"Like the monkey's paw?"

"Hopefully not."

"There's that velvet Elvis." He nodded toward the box.

"I saw."

"It's like its eyes follow you."

"Optical illusion."

"If you say so. The thing creeps me the fuck out."

"Okay, that's . . ." Her phone rang before she could finish.

"Your mother says Catherine's crucial business is a junk shop," Auntie Jane announced without preamble.

"That's right, but . . ."

"Ha!" she said, and hung up.

"Auntie Jane." Allie slipped her phone back into her pocket. "Long-distance mocking." His shrug suggested he didn't care. "So, are you staying? I'll throw in lunch."

"Lunch?"

"The meal in the middle of the day. I'm a good cook. I was thinking grilled cheese sandwiches, a bowl of homemade tomato soup . . ." Gran may have gone wild, but she was still a Gale. The pantry was full of canning. ". . . and pie."

He rolled his eyes. "Grilled cheese sandwiches aren't exactly hard to cook."

"You don't have to stay." She tried to sound like she didn't care either way and suspected she'd failed dismally. Joe wasn't just a connection to her missing grandmother, he was the only person she knew in Calgary.

"What kind of pie?"

"I don't know yet." She pulled another bill out of the cashbox. "We can start with more coffee."

"I'm not staying all day, mind. I've got things to do."

"Okay."

Joe tugged the bill from her hand. "You want another muffin with that?"

The charms the old woman had put on the windows were still in effect. He could see the reflection of the street—traffic passing, the storefront directly opposite, himself in ballcap and dark glasses struggling to get a paper from the box—but nothing past the glass. His employer hadn't liked that Joe O'Hallan had been hanging around the old woman, his concern only slightly tempered by the evidence that Catherine Gale had barely tolerated the changeling. He really wouldn't appreciate him striking up a friendship with this new Gale and, unless Joe had snuck out the back way, he'd been in there for hours.

He'd trailed Joe for three days back after he'd first shown up, his employer suspicious of anything that might interfere with him building a power base in the city. There was a danger inherent in tracking purebloods—some of them literally had eyes in the backs of their heads, and they very much disliked interference in their business. Where disliked meant if caught, expect to be ripped limb from limb. Leprechauns like the changeling were not only nasty little sons of bitches, but they'd taken to Human weapons like cops took to Timmy's. They might throw a curse of seven years of bad luck but were just as likely to pull a submachine gun from a convenient pocket universe and use the spray of bullets like a scythe, cutting anyone they'd caught trailing them off at the ankles, leaving them to flop around in shock, and eventually bleed to death. He figured all that attitude had something to do with them being the shortest out of the box.

The trick was not to get caught.

He was very good at what he did.

This changeling, though, except for pulling the old fairy gold scam, he appeared to be living Human. And living rough. Not only had trading lumps of what looked to be raw gold for cash gotten more complicated since the old days, but the cash it brought didn't go far. If the glyphs on his scope hadn't allowed him to see what his target truly was, he'd have dismissed him as a mutt dumped to fend for himself. His report on Joe's pathetic existence had been enough to tag him no threat.

In retrospect, that might have been a mistake.

The Courts had to know what was going down by now. No way movement of that magnitude hadn't been flagged. Generally, they didn't give a crap about what happened in the MidRealm, but Joe was still of the blood, no matter how long he'd been gone, and damned near living on top of the epicenter. It was possible, however unlikely, they'd warned him.

It was possible Joe had taken that information straight to the new owner of the shop.

It would certainly explain why he'd been in there for so long.

He rattled the door of the newspaper box one last time—as an excuse to linger the damned things were near foolproof—gathered up his *Herald,* checked the sky, and headed west. His orders had been to find out what Alysha Gale knew, but he couldn't do that as long as the changeling was with her. Joe was as suspicious as all hell just generally. In case the Courts hadn't been in contact, the last thing he wanted to do was give him a reason to call home.

If it turned out Joe had told the Gale woman nothing of note, he wondered how they were going to keep it that way. The Courts were possessive of their own; taking out a pureblood would attract more unwanted attention from yet another source.

His right index finger squeezed the memory of a trigger. It was always harder when they looked Human.

The pie was rhubarb—not terribly surprising given the season. Joe devoured a second piece in spite of the two sandwiches and the large bowl of soup that came before it. They ate in the store, sitting on a pair of stools behind the counter, Allie flipping through her gran's recipe book, wiping grease off her fingers to mark the entries that referred to the bottles in the cabinet.

All the Gale girls dabbled—there'd never been a school dance where one of them hadn't spiked the punch—but this was on another scale entirely. Allie had a feeling it might be smartest to trade Gran's recipes to one of the aunties for services rendered rather than risk the kind of disaster that had made her junior prom an object lesson in winging it.

"Joe, when do you start fading again?"

"Four weeks last Monday. Who wants to know?"

She tapped the page in front of her. "The person who'll keep it from happening."

"You?"

"What? You thought Gran was coming back from the grave to mix drinks? Metaphorically speaking, since there isn't a grave or a body to put in one."

He sighed and slid off the stool onto his feet. "Look, I

did some stuff for her, but she didn't even like me much, okay? So if you're being nice to me because you think she was my friend, I should just go."

"You should just sit."

Looking a little surprised, he sat. The food as much as the potion had firmed up his edges. Remembering how he'd looked through the door, Allie came to a decision.

"Do you want a job?"

"What?"

"I need to find out what my grandmother is up to. That's why I came here. If there's a clue in the store, I'm going to have to weed through everything to try and find it. I can't do that and deal with customers."

"Customers?"

"We must have them," Allie told him dryly. "Someone has to be buying all the yoyos."

"Why don't you just close the store while you search?"

"Because Gran left it to me to run."

"But if it's yours . . ."

"Is it?"

His gaze skittered past the shadows again.

Allie nodded. "Exactly. Minimum wage, flexible hours, one full meal a day provided. And I'll pay you cash at the end of every shift."

"You don't even know me," he sighed, and she could almost see him refusing to hope. "I could be a danger to you."

"I trust you."

"Because your grandmother said you could."

"Not likely; I don't trust her." She nodded at his empty plate. "But you had a second piece of pie, and Aunt Ruth isn't too happy about my being so far from home. She's worried about me, and she's worried I'll give some of her girls ideas." Allie'd been able to taste the charm with every bite. She wondered what she'd flushed with her mother's pie.

He shifted as far from the sticky residue on the plate as the circumference of the stool would allow. "What if I *had* been a danger to you?"

"We wouldn't be having this conversation."

"Okay, then." He looked like he was ready to bolt. "What if I don't want to work for you?"

"Then don't."

"As simple as that, then?"

"Yes."

"Can I think about it?"

"No." When his eyes widened far enough to show whites all around, she sighed. "That was a joke."

Returning to the store after taking the dishes upstairs, she paused by the back door and peered out into the courtyard, frowning slightly at the path beaten into the scruffy grass. "Joe, what's on the other side of the courtyard?"

"Garage."

"Gran had a car?"

"How would I know?"

Given that Gran had a garage, Allie figured it only made sense to see what she had in it. Or if *she'd* been left in it, tucked under a bench of half-empty paint cans and covered in an oily tarp.

All alone in Calgary, Gran hadn't used the open earth for even basic ritual. Yet, given that the only windows overlooking the courtyard were from her own apartment, Allie didn't see why she couldn't. Except that she was also alone in Calgary. She poked at a trio of scraggly bushes as she passed, wondering if Gran had used them to access the Wood. Even if she hadn't, Charlie could and would probably appreciate having an entrance right outside their back door.

"You sound like you're thinking of staying," she muttered, searching the ring for the key to the padlock on the garage door. "Get a grip."

Up on the roof, a trio of pigeons made noises that sounded like agreement.

Gran's body had not been left under the bench of half-empty paint cans.

And she very definitely had a car.

A 1976, lime-green, convertible Super Beetle, restored to mint condition. It was a car that blended into traffic with all the subtlety Allie had come to expect of her grandmother. The registration and insurance were in the glove box and the name on the ownership remained Catherine Amanda Gale.

"Translation," Allie told the silence as she carefully closed the door and went around to the front of the car. "It's not mine. There's a key so I can drive it, but I'm not to be surprised if she shows up to reclaim it."

Even given the half dozen charms she could see without actually searching, it didn't seem like a particularly practical car for a Calgary winter—or occasionally a Calgary July, Allie amended, if the stories she'd heard were true.

That put a check in the *Gran's just buggered off* column.

Unless she'd been ripped to pieces and stuffed into the trunk when she came out to change the ownership.

Allie paused, fingers around the high, chromed trunk handle, thumb on the release.

Unlikely. But possible.

The chrome warmed under her grip. It was the

potential for *pieces* that stopped her cold, exposing a previously unsuspected squeamishness.

"On three." Deep breath. "One, two . . . three."

The trunk contained a leather glove, a collapsible shovel, and a bag of kitty litter.

Against one end wall of the garage, a flight of stairs rose up to a small landing and an unlocked door that led into a second-floor loft. Bales of insulation, some two by fours, and a stack of drywall had been left in the middle of the floor and, at the far end, plumbing had been roughed in for a small bathroom and a kitchen sink. Someone had clearly started to turn the space into a studio apartment. Given the housing crunch in the province, that wasn't a bad idea. Gran as a landlord, however, slid significantly past bad idea into *moving to Vancouver so as not to freeze to death while sleeping under a bridge is a much better idea* territory.

Heading back to the store, Allie paused in front of the mirror to make sure she'd got all the cobwebs out of her hair and found herself actually looking at her reflection.

Fully clothed.

Standing in the back hall.

Weird.

Joe was putting one of the ledgers away when she reached the counter. He glanced up at her and grinned, obviously pleased with himself. "I sold a yoyo while you were gone. One of the glow-in-the-dark ones."

The sidewalk outside the store was empty although traffic had begun to pick up as evening rush hour approached.

Joe turned to see what she was looking at and shrugged. "They're gone now."

"They?"

"Yeah, couple of kids." He grinned. "Customers."

"I knew we had to have them."

Pale cheeks flushed at being included. "I thought about what you said. About a job."

"And?" He needed it. She needed him. But he wasn't family, and besides, she didn't think she could force the issue on one of the Fey no matter how Human he wanted to be.

"And okay, I'll work here. Flexible hours, though." He might have thought he sounded tough, but the fine veneer of bravado barely covered an emotion too complex to be merely called relief. "I'll come in first thing tomorrow, but I have to go now. I have to get . . ." He couldn't say home. It was the next word, Allie could almost hear it, but he couldn't say it. "You should maybe think about closing early," he added as she pulled three twenties out of the cashbox and handed them over. "There's a storm coming."

Allie took another look out the window. What little she could see of the sky was clear.

"This is Calgary," Joe snorted. "If you don't like the weather, wait ten minutes." He paused at the door. "You know you're . . . *we're* open until midnight tomorrow, right?"

"I know."

"It's just that after dark . . ."

"I *know*."

Ginger brows drew in. "Because you're her granddaughter?"

Allie rolled her eyes. "Because you're a leprechaun. Also there's a signed picture of a minotaur over the counter, plus another seven potions in the cabinet, and I suspect the name on the first mailbox isn't in a Human language. Not that hard to connect the dots, Joe. The only thing that's confusing me —about this specifically," she amended, "is why *Calgary*?"

He shrugged, much like he had the last time she'd brought it up, and said, "Things are happening here. I'll see you tomorrow, Alysha Catherine Gale."

Put like that, it was a binding promise.

"I'll see you tomorrow, Joe O'Hallan."

He'd barely moved out of sight, heading west at a slow run after a quick look up at the sky, when her phone rang.

"Well?" Auntie Jane demanded.

Until Allie found out what her grandmother was up to, there would be only one question. "I've hired someone who can watch the store while I look into things."

"For pity's sake, Alysha, ignore the store."

Allie picked a yoyo out of the box and turned it between her fingers. "No," she said, and hung up.

The crack of thunder that sounded as she closed her phone was probably a coincidence given the three-thousand-odd kilometers and all.

It hadn't taken quite the ten minutes Joe said the weather required before dark clouds filled the sky. The first scud of rain, barely enough to dampen the sidewalk, seemed to be a test run. Then thunder cracked, lightning flashed, and Allie could suddenly no longer see the road through the sheets of falling water.

Closing early might not be a bad idea. It was nearly five, and there wouldn't be any . . .

The umbrella entered the door first, followed by a dark trench coat and a lot of water. A tanned, long-fingered hand wrestled the umbrella closed, and Allie got her first look at a pair of extraordinarily blue eyes. Not the more common bluish gray but a bright, cerulean blue. A Maxfield Parrish sky-blue.

"Sorry about dripping all over the floor."

"That's very blue."

"Pardon?" His voice was rough. A whiskey voice, Auntie Ruby would call it. Actually, Auntie Ruby was losing it, so she could easily call it a carpet voice, but that was beside the point. It stroked against Allie's skin like a cat's tongue, lifting all the hair on the back of her neck.

"All right. I meant, that's all right. About dripping on the floor." The remarkably blue eyes were in a pleasant enough face with a straight nose—a bit on the short side—over a longish upper lip and distinctly long chin. Not Brian Mulroney or Jay Leno long, but long. The eyes were tucked under nicely shaped brows on a high forehead tucked in turn under medium brown hair that could use a trim although, to be fair, the storm had destroyed whatever style he might have started the day with. He wasn't very tall, had maybe two inches on her tops, but then he smiled and his eyes crinkled at the corners, and Allie forgot all about his height.

She was suddenly entirely aware of the bit of pie filling smudged on the front of her sweater. If she'd known he was coming, she'd have changed. Hell, if she'd known he was coming, she'd have baked a cake.

"I'm looking for Alysha Gale."

"I'm Alysha Gale."

"You're Alysha Gale?"

"Yes."

"You're not . . ." He frowned, clearly trying to marshal his thoughts and having a hard time doing it. ". . . old."

That was just strange enough, Allie wrestled cognitive thought back on-line. "Excuse me?"

"God, that had to have sounded inane. I promise you, I don't usually sound inane." He reached in past the lapels of his dripping trench coat into the inner pocket of a distinctly cheap suit. Although the tie was nice. The narrow stripe across the gray was the same color as his eyes.

"Ms. Gale?"

Cognitive thought hadn't lasted long. She stared down at the white rectangle of paper. Oh. A business card. "Graham Buchanan?"

"That's right."

"And *The Western Star*?"

"It's a newspaper. I'm a reporter. For the newspaper. Hang on." He reached into the inner pocket on his trench coat and pulled out a folded newspaper and passed it over. "It's last week's, we're a weekly and okay, it's a tabloid, but . . ." His eyes crinkled again. "It's a job. That's uh, me." One finger tapped the page. He kept his nails very short. "My byline. There."

"Hauntings on the LRT?"

"Some people saw things in the glass."

"Actual things?"

"Probably not."

She liked that he said probably. That he was open to the possibility. That could come in handy later.

"Anyway, I was talking to Catherine Gale last week, about her business, this business, about how it's mostly made up of odds and ends of people's lives, trying to convince her there's a terrific human interest story here . . ."

Graham Buchanan was a very good liar. If Allie hadn't been watching his eyes so closely, she'd never have realized it. If he thought there was a story here — and he did—it wasn't a story about *other* people's lives. She had no idea what her grandmother had done to make him suspicious, but—in less than a minute—his willingness to see beyond the expected had gone from being a good thing to a potential problem.

And he worked for a tabloid.

Those idiots would print anything.

This sort of thing never came up at home, and the wild ones, while they sometimes made headlines, they just laughed and moved on, but here and now Allie had neither the safety of home nor the luxury to leave.

". . . but no matter how hard I tried, I didn't seem to be getting anywhere. Then she told me she'd be leaving, but one of her relatives would be taking it over and I should talk to her. All she gave me was your name. I don't know why I thought you'd be old." He shrugged, the movement surprisingly graceful under all his damp layers. "I mean, it was just a name. You're . . ."

"Her granddaughter."

"Of course."

Thunder.

Lightning.

The lights went out.

When the lights came back on a moment later, he'd moved closer. Not a lot, but the puddle he'd been in the middle of was mostly behind him and Allie doubted the puddle had shifted. If he'd hoped to throw her off by his sudden proximity, then she could definitely count on at least one thing he didn't know about the Gale girls.

This close, he smelled amazing.

When she smiled, he blinked and shuffled back a step. "I, uh, I dropped in to set up a time we could talk. If you were willing to talk to me, that is. Just because Ms. Gale, your grandmother, thought you would be, doesn't mean you'd be. Willing. To talk." He seemed confused by his reaction. This was not a man, Allie concluded, in the habit of losing control.

This close, she could see the faint shadow of stubble along his upper lip and jaw. "We could talk now. I doubt

anyone's going to brave the storm for a mismatched set
of silver spoons and a yoyo."

"A yoyo?"

A nod toward the box on the counter. "They're our
best sellers."

"Of course." Cerulean eyes crinkled at the corners,
and even though his smile had become a little masklike,
it was still a very, very nice smile.

She was going to enjoy finding out what he thought
he knew.

As soon as her friends had yelled one final good-bye
out the car window and driven safely out of sight, Charlie pulled her guitar from the gig bag, stuffed the gig bag
into the duffel bag, and settled the latter on her back.
Given that Halifax Stanfield International Airport was
thirty-five kilometers from downtown Halifax, and they
knew how broke she was, she couldn't really refuse the
ride. Fortunately, airport improvements meant airport
construction meant a near total lack of parking so
they'd merely dropped her off and kept going. It was
why she'd chosen to "fly." They'd have hung around the
train station or bus station, keeping her company until
she boarded.

Three quick steps up and over the curb and she was
sinking into loose dirt as she slipped between skinny
trees newly planted and into the Wood.

Allie's song was one Charlie'd been following most
of her life. She'd followed it out her first time in when
she'd very nearly become just another cautionary tale
the aunties told about the family oddities.

"Oh, traveling sounds like fun," they'd say. *"But it's a*

lot less fun if you're lost in the Wood and can't find your way home."

No argument from her. Lost was definitely a whole fuck of a lot less fun and had involved near panic resolved by projectile vomiting when she'd finally stumbled into Aunt Mary's kitchen. Allie, home alone finishing a history essay, had cleaned her up, tucked her into bed, and kept the gathering aunties out of the room until Charlie's parents could come to claim her.

Charlie'd asked later how she'd done it, and Allie, just turned thirteen and all knees and elbows, had spit the end of her braid out of her mouth and shrugged, saying, *"I stood in front of the door,"* like it was no big deal to hold off a whole flock of the circling buzzards.

Even for Gale girls, the two years between fifteen and thirteen were a bit of a gap, but that had bridged it.

So following Allie's song should not require the kind of attention she was having to give it to stay on course.

And then a few notes went missing.

Shadows began to gather . . .

The path began to shift.

"Excuse me?" Charlie touched the old woman gently on the shoulder, hoping her breath didn't smell liked she'd just puked up her last three meals against the rough bark of what looked like a coconut palm. "Can you tell me where I am?"

The old woman frowned, mahogany skin pleating. *"Oh, merveilleux. Un autre Américain touriste perdu."*

Not exactly a hard translation, even with Canadian high school French. *"Je ne suis pas Américain. Je suis Canadien. Mais vous avez raison, je suis peu un perdu. Quelle ville est-ce que je suis dedans?"*

The frown didn't change significantly. So much for Canadians being universally loved abroad. *"Port-au-Prince."*

"Haiti?"

"Oui. Haiti." The old woman rolled her eyes, and walked away along the cracked sidewalk, muttering under her breath.

What the hell was she doing in Haiti? The last thing Charlie remembered before the puking was Allie's song spiraling out of her control and the shadows gathering under the trees. Or maybe shadow, singular. She was pretty sure she'd felt focused intent, and that was new. And terrifying. The aunties could kiss her ass if they didn't believe her this time.

Carefully setting her guitar down, ignoring the way her fingers trembled, she pulled the duffel bag around and unzipped the small end pocket. Empty.

Not in the duffel bag. Not in the gig bag.

Where the hell was her phone?

FOUR

"I mean, you've got to wonder, who'd ever buy one of these in the first place, right?" Graham was smiling as he slid open the back of the case. His fingers were actually over the monkey's paw when Allie grabbed his wrist and pulled his hand back.

"It's old," she said quickly, as his smile slipped. "I'm afraid it'll fall apart if it's handled."

"Sorry."

"It's okay. You couldn't have known." But it was interesting that he'd gone straight for the artifact. Was he testing to see if she knew what it was? She wondered what he'd have done if she hadn't stopped him. How would he have reacted when the severed paw squirmed in his grip? Not that it mattered because she'd have stopped him regardless. Allie had no idea who'd made those first two wishes, had no idea what they'd wished for, but she knew it had ended in horror and regret. It always ended in horror and regret. "If I had a choice, I'd lock it away out of sight."

"Don't you have a choice?" That was the reporter asking. Just a little too emphatic for a polite inquiry.

"I don't think my grandmother would like that much."

"Ah." When he nodded, Allie wasted a moment thinking about brushing his hair back off his face. Would it feel as silky sliding through her fingers as it looked? "She's coming back, then. Is she all right?"

The aunties' opinion aside, it seemed safest to stick to the party line. "She's dead."

His face blanked for a moment before sympathy took over, but she couldn't tell for certain if his reaction was to the news or the way she'd delivered it. "I didn't know." Not exactly the truth but his lies were better hidden than they had been. "It must've been sudden."

He said he'd been talking to her last week. "It was."

"Forgive me for saying this . . ." Head dipped slightly, he studied her through the shield of his lashes. ". . . but you don't seem too upset."

"I don't think I've really accepted it yet." And that, at least, had the benefit of being the absolute truth.

Outside the store, thunder rolled, gentled by distance, and while the rain continued to fall, it was now possible to actually see the other side of the street. The storm had moved east, heading for the prairies.

"Uh, Ms. Gale."

"Allie."

"Okay." He didn't step away from her smile this time. Good for him. "You're still holding my wrist."

Oh.

They were standing close enough that fabric touched—his open suit jacket brushing against her sweater. Close enough shared body heat had warmed the air between them.

His pulse beat strong and fast under her fingertips. A little faster than it should given it was the pulse of an apparently healthy young man just standing and dripping rainwater onto a hardwood floor. Allie suddenly realized she'd actually traced most of a charm onto the smooth skin of his inner wrist without thinking and swiped it clear as she released him, her fingers lingering just a moment longer than necessary. Gale girls took what they wanted ...

Down at the other end of the counter, her phone rang. Long distance, but not one of the family rings.

"Are you going to get that?"

He expected her to say no. Which, to be fair, was her intention. She opened her mouth to say, *let it ring*. What she actually heard herself say was, "I'll just be a moment."

Telemarketers did not call Gale phones and she could count the number of non-family members who had the number on the fingers of one hand. When an anonymous voice asked if she'd accept a collect call from Charlie Gale, muscles she didn't remember tensing relaxed.

"Charlie?" Allie mouthed *my cousin* at Graham. "Did you lose your phone again?"

"I think I left it in Halifax."

"Left it? Where are you?"

"Brazil."

"What are you doing in Brazil?"

"I got pushed out of the Wood. Four times now."

"Shit." She turned, her back to the reporter, her body curled protectively around the phone as though she could send that protection through to Charlie. With her free hand, she traced a charm against the countertop, and her voice slid sideways, out of eavesdropping range. "By what?"

"I couldn't tell. Shadows." Charlie sighed, bone-deep weariness apparent in the sound. "Well, shadow, singular, probably ... I think it was the same fucking thing every time."

"Are you all right?"

"I'm tired and I'm angry and I've puked up everything I've eaten for the last six years, but yeah, I'm all right. I'm just in Brazil. Rio. I think it's trying to keep me from you."

"What?"

"For fucksake, Allie, pay attention. I said, I think . . ."

"I heard you." Fear, not for herself but for Charlie, sharpened her tone. "That was an exclamation of surprise, not a request for you to repeat yourself. If you can't get to me, go home!"

"Oh, stupid me, not to think of that!"

She gentled her tone, pulled Charlie back from the edge. "You tried?"

"I tried. Every time I go in, fucking shadow bounces me out. Doesn't matter where I'm pointed."

"Then why do you think it has to do with me?"

"I just . . . I can hear your song in the way the Wood changes, okay? And yeah, I know that doesn't make sense to you, but it does to me, so be careful. Don't trust anyone outside the family. I'm on my way."

"How . . . ?"

"They have these things called planes."

"Yeah, but they smell like ass and they make you check your guitar." Allie could hear Charlie smiling in the silence. "Have you got the cash to . . . ?"

"Credit card. I'm on a flight that's boarding in about forty-five minutes. It's going to take a while, though." She could hear paper rustling and maybe, now she knew what to listen for, a distant security announcement. "It's Rio to San Paulo to O'Hare to Denver to Calgary. Thirty-six hours and fifty minutes. I'll get in about six thirty in the morning on Saturday if there's no delays . . . except that I'm going through O'Hare, so delays are fucking inevitable."

The layout of the runways at O'Hare meant that two or three times a day, planes heading east sketched a dark charm on the airport. Had the family needed to fly into Chicago with any regularity, they'd have done something about it. As it was, it was easier to just to avoid the city.

"Wait a minute, O'Hare to Denver to Calgary?" Allie mapped it out against the counter. "That's going back south before you go north."

"Beggars and choosers, babe. At least I'll get caught up on some sleep."

Charlie didn't have her phone; she'd have thirty-two hours and twenty minutes of peace and quiet. "You haven't called the aunties yet, have you?"

"Figured you should get a heads up first."

"You're too good to me."

"I know it."

"Charlie . . ."

Charlie's interruption was more of a snort than a snicker. "I'll be careful if you keep from doing anything stupid."

"Define stupid?"

"Bite me."

"Love you, too."

She pressed a kiss to the phone before she closed it and turned back to Graham. His brows rose, and questions about why he suddenly couldn't understand a word she'd said swam just under the surface of his expression. "Problem?"

"Unexpected travel screwup." She still needed to know what he knew, but she really didn't need the distraction of his eyes and his scent and his smile and his hands and all the lovely that cheap suit was covering while dealing with the inevitable calls from the aunties.

"Family member?"

Interesting phrasing.

"Cousin."

"In Brazil?"

"Yes." But that much he'd overheard. "She's a musician."

"I should go." He didn't want to, and he wasn't bothering to hide it. Easy enough to see that his desire to stay mostly had to do with wanting confirmation of whatever he thought was going on. With the store. With her grandmother. With a cousin in Brazil. She could almost see him drawing lines, connecting dots he thought he had. But that wasn't the part he let her see; she took a look at that all on her own. The part he let her see had more to do with her, personally, and she really wished she had the time to appreciate the sentiment.

"Yeah, you should go." Her fingers tightened around the phone. "It's going to get very . . . *family* around here soon."

Graham smiled at that, like he understood what she meant. He really didn't. He really couldn't, but she appreciated the thought and caught herself wondering about his family as he said, "I'd like to see you again. To talk about the store. For my article."

Nice save. She wondered why he felt he had to make it. He wasn't wearing a ring, but that didn't mean there wasn't a significant other attached. "How about coffee tomorrow?"

"Coffee's good."

"I'll see you around eleven, then."

"Great."

Graham hadn't expected to have quite so visceral a reaction to Alysha Gale. He stepped wide off the curb avoiding a puddle, ignored the shouted, *Watch where the fuck you're going!* from a passing truck, tried to stop thinking of her as everything he'd ever looked for in a woman—news to him he'd been looking—and tried to start *thinking*.

He could do this. He could do his job and keep it from getting personal.

If his watch was right, and the cheap piece of shit hadn't been ruined in the rain, it was only a little better than seventeen hours until he could talk to her again.

Lying flat on the roof, holding a directional microphone instead of his rifle, he watched Alysha Gale walk down 9th to the twenty-four hour convenience store at 11th Street. She'd headed out to shop almost immediately after she'd closed the store and received two phone calls on the way down the street—two liters of milk, a pound of butter, a dozen eggs, and three lemons—three calls on the way back. This particular microphone could pick up fly farts at three kilometers, but he had no doubt she could block it if she cared to.

Strangely, she didn't care to.

"I'm fine. Everything's fine. You know as much as I do. No, no sign of her. I'd rather you didn't, I can manage."

And around again. And again. Her end of the conversation barely changed there and back.

Maybe her lack of concern for eavesdroppers wasn't that strange after all.

The sound cut off when she reentered the store; before she'd disappeared, the old woman had put security in place even his boss couldn't crack. The boss had upped his own security the moment Catherine Gale showed up on the radar. Given the security he'd already put in place, that was saying something.

"She obviously doesn't know I'm here, and I'm fucking well going to keep it that way."

Given what he'd been told about the Gales, the youth of this newest family member to show up in the city had come as a bit of a surprise. Gale females of any age had the potential to be dangerous adversaries, but in the older women, all that potential had been realized and they were apparently borderline bugfuck besides. Was the girl a trap? Was her function to lull them into a false sense of security? Distract them while the others gathered?

He could wait here and hope she left the building again, or he could be more productive and have a few *words* with the changeling.

Six aunties, her mother, Charlie's mother, and two of Charlie's sisters later, Allie got the one call she wasn't expecting.

"Do I need to come out there?"

"David?"

"I'll be finished with the job I'm doing currently in seventy-two hours, but I can be there in forty-eight if you need me."

Phone trapped between ear and shoulder, Allie broke the third and final egg onto the third and final cup of flour. "To do what?"

"Mom says you're in trouble."

"Me? Charlie's the one who got bounced."

"Four times. Trying to get to you."

"It didn't matter where she was going."

"But she said it had to do with you."

"Nothing's happening here." As the ancient, upright mixer struggled to fold air into the thick batter, she glanced over at the window, opened her mouth to tell David about the shadow, and closed it again. She didn't need to bring big brother all the way to Calgary to chase shadows. "There's no sign of Gran, and I hired a leprechaun to work in the store."

"A leprechaun?"

"Yeah."

"Full-blood?"

"Changeling."

"The family doesn't mess with the Fey, Allie."

"I'm not messing with him." Hadn't even occurred to her actually, and that was a bit weird; he was cute in a scruffy sort of way. "He needed a job and, if I'm going to figure out what's going on, I needed part-time help."

"So you hired a *leprechaun*?"

"Let it go, David."

"What's a leprechaun doing in Calgary anyway?"

"He tells me that things are happening here." She hadn't been able to find a tube pan, but a bundt pan would do.

"I'll be there in forty-eight hours."

"Not *those* kind of things."

"You sure?"

And she convinced him that she was. For all his power, David was still a Gale boy, and they took Gale girls at face value. It was safer that way.

The traditional way to catch leprechauns was to sneak up behind them while they worked on their shoes. Count on them being particularly obsessed if they're whistling. People in his line of work who relied on folklore rather than more mundane skills tended to die young. Or wish they had.

He stared at Joe through the night vision goggles—the changeling had one foot up on the park bench, tunelessly whistling "Mime Abduction" as he struggled with a knot in one bootlace—thought about irony, and hit him with the Taser. The current theory among those in the know was that, as well as overwhelming the nervous system and causing temporary paralysis, a Taser could be used to disrupt the more exotic abilities of the Fey. He hadn't actually seen Joe use any of those exotic abilities, but the redundantly careful lived longer.

Cable ties were in place around grimy wrists before the paralysis wore off, even given the Fey's accelerated recovery time. Under the baggy clothes, the boy—*Not a boy,* he reminded himself—was surprisingly thin. Maybe he'd swapped bulk for height. Didn't matter. Facedown on the asphalt path, hands secured in the small of his back, a knee between his shoulder blades and the end of the silencer tucked under one pointed ear, Joe O'Hallan wasn't going anywhere.

"Blessed rounds," he growled as Joe tried to twist his head far enough to see his attacker. "Stay still."

The changeling froze, his muscles spasming as they finished throwing off the effect of the Taser. From this point on, it was the threat of a true death and the belief that his captor would pull the trigger that held him. A full-blood just up from the UnderRealm wouldn't believe the threat—it would take a certain kind of scary crazy to go up against the Courts—but Joe had been living Human long enough he probably had no idea he was protected.

"We talk, then you can go." Using his free hand to pull the back of the sweater down, he pressed the pendant against the damp, pale skin just under the hairline and watched goose bumps rise at the touch of the cool metal. "What do you know about what's happening in the city?"

As the silence extended, he thought maybe he'd been a bit too obscure. He hadn't wanted to give away any answers, but perhaps *what's happening* hadn't been specific enough. Then the changeling shivered as though he'd worked his way through to the actual question, snorted, and said, "I know what's come through, don't I? I'm not blind, and they don't give a fuck who sees them."

"Have you told anyone?"

"No! I'm not fucking stupid either! Best way to deal with them is to keep your head down."

The pendant forced the truth. Anger added the flourishes—the Fey hated being bested by Humans. Anger *usually* added the flourishes. In this case, it sounded a lot more like fear.

"Have you had word from the UnderRealm?" If he had, he'd know why as well as what.

"No. They don't give a fuck about me, and I wouldn't listen to the fuckers if they did!"

It seemed the changeling hadn't learned not to let sentiment stand in the way of survival. Good. And Alysha Gale hadn't been given even the minimal information he had about their visitors. Better.

Still that did raise the question of what he'd been doing in the store for so long.

"I'm after working there, aren't I."

"Working?" There were any number of jobs a leprechaun's strength and speed could be useful for. "What are you doing?"

"Selling shit."

"Selling shit?"

"And going for coffees."

"You're working retail?" That was ... unexpected. "Why?" He repeated the question with a little more physical emphasis when the silence extended.

"I think ..." Pureblood or not, the changeling's voice had nothing of the UnderRealm in it, sounding more young and terrified than immortal and devious. "I think she felt sorry for me."

Pity made sense. He was starting to feel a bit uncomfortably like a bully and had to remind himself Joe O'Hallan was not Human.

He wanted to ask specifically about Alysha Gale, to see if the details of her story changed with her audience, but rumor had it that the family had an uncanny way of knowing when they were the topic of conversation, and he didn't want to risk tipping her off.

Pressing the gun just a little harder against Joe's head, he slid his knife blade through the ties, and freed Joe's hands. "If I wanted you dead, you'd be dead." Muscles tensed under his weight, a clear indication he'd been believed. "Talk about this, and I'll want you dead."

"I'm not going to be saying anything! I swear!"

The pendant felt warm as he dropped it into his pocket. "Count to fifty before you get up."

Allie told herself that the time difference had hauled her ass out of bed at dawn, but standing at the window, hands cupped around a mug of coffee, she knew that was a lie. Mostly a lie. After the cake came out of the oven, she'd stayed up until midnight cataloging the contents of the spare room and finding nothing, so the two-hour time shift had certainly helped her haul her ass out of bed.

If the shadow returned, then yesterday's pass over the store hadn't been random.

And?

And then yesterday's pass over the store hadn't been random.

There really wasn't a lot more information a shadow passing at that speed could impart.

Well, except for the obvious.

When the pigeons crowded back under the newspaper box, she braced herself.

There.

And gone.

And not alone.

"Great." Allie finished her coffee in one long swallow. "We've got dragons."

"If Catherine allowed herself to be eaten by a dragon, I have no sympathy for her at all. Unless you're a virgin sacrifice, which she most certainly is not, they're easy enough to avoid."

"They know where the store is, Auntie Jane."

"Of course they do, they can sense the power. If you follow them, you'll probably find them acknowledging every power signature in Edmonton."

"Calgary."

"What?"

"I'm in Calgary."

"Are you asking me to join you there?"

"No!"

"Then don't start complaining to me about geography. Dragons are not this family's business."

"Unless one ate Gran."

After a long pause, Auntie Jane sighed. "Yes, unless one ate your grandmother."

"How do I . . . ?"

"Oh, for pity's sake, Alysha, just consider it for a moment. You'll need to examine the scat for the nasty indigestible bits."

She was almost afraid Auntie Jane hadn't been kidding.

When she paused in front of the mirror and murmured, "Dragons?" her reflection lifted a familiar tabloid. The headline read *"Not all THUNDER LIZARDS Come out of the Ground at Drumheller."* And under it, in slightly less strident type, *"Thousand-Year-Old Lizard Baby."* She was worried for a moment that the tabloid had already been reporting on the dragons when she saw that the date on the paper was closer to the end of the month.

"Trust me, I wasn't going to tell Graham about this." Giving the frame a quick pat, she moved on into the store figuring she could use the ninety minutes until opening to begin cataloging.

Joe sat tucked up into the small offset of the door, head against the glass, arms wrapped around his knees.

Allie dropped her laptop on the counter and hurried across the store. When she turned the lock, his head jerked back and he stared up at her with wide, terrified eyes. Then he blinked and only looked tired as he pulled himself to his feet, one palm against the door.

"Joe? What are you doing here?"

"You want me here. You do want me here?"

"Of course I do. I only meant that it's early."

"I don't . . ."

. . . have anywhere else to go.

The subtext was so loud, he might as well have said it.

She stepped aside and watched how his shoulders relaxed when he crossed the threshold. Whatever had happened to him, he believed it couldn't follow him into the store. She hated to disillusion him, but down here in the store, Gran hadn't set things up to keep anyone out. She'd just wanted to know what was coming.

When the lock snapped into place, he raised a hand and brushed his hair back out of his eyes. He probably figured that Allie'd ignore the way his fingers were trembling.

Not likely.

"Have you eaten?"

"What?"

"Breakfast? Have you eaten? No, of course you haven't. Come on, then, upstairs. I'll make pancakes."

He stared at her in disbelief. "You'll what?"

"Make pancakes. Unless they call them flapjacks out here in the west, then I'll make flapjacks."

"Upstairs?"

"It's where the kitchen is." Hand in the small of his back, not terribly happy about the way she could feel the knobs of his spine through his sweater, she moved him across the store toward the other door.

"I can't . . ." His need for sanctuary rolled off him like smoke. He wasn't fighting her, he hadn't even stopped walking, but he needed reassurance.

"Why can't you?"

"Your grandmother . . ."

"Isn't here. I am. Don't look in the mirror, just keep walking."

If he'd been Human, he wouldn't have made it up the stairs. She could feel him trembling, forcing each leg to rise and pull himself up the next step. She didn't help, but she made it clear she'd be there if he fell.

When he was standing, staring stupidly around the

apartment's big open room, she gave him a gentle shove toward the bathroom. "Go shower and toss your clothes out, I was going to run a load of laundry, and I can easily throw them in. If you don't mind that it says *Niko,* I've got sweats you can wear until they're dry."

"Niko?"

"Misprints. There's a couple of boxes of them in the spare room. Go on," she added when it looked like he might be gathering enough energy to argue. "Pancakes will be ready when you are."

He blinked at her, shook his head like he couldn't quite believe he was doing it, and shuffled off to the bathroom.

Allie snorted as she pulled the big mixing bowl down off the shelf. Twenty-four years of handling Gale boys made handling the Fey a piece of cake. She'd been getting David to the table since she was five.

When Joe sat down, his hair tucked wet behind his ears, points exposed, she slid a plate of six steaming pancakes—nearly as big around as the plate they were on and half an inch thick—in front of him. "I'm afraid we've only got maple syrup," she told him, sliding the bottle across. "There's a bottle of blueberry syrup in the pantry, but since it probably came from Auntie Jane, it'd be safer if we didn't open it."

"She charmed it, then?"

"If she made it for Gran, she likely poisoned it."

"Poisoned?" His voice rose a little on the second syllable. Not quite far enough to be called a squeak.

"Apples are more traditional, but Auntie Jane has a thing for blueberries."

"You're kidding?"

Allie smiled. "Eat up, you don't want your pancakes to get cold."

The first forkful dripping with butter and syrup slid

tentatively between pale lips. The second forkful rose a lot more enthusiastically. "These are good!"

"Of course they are." Allie had two smaller pancakes on her plate, mostly just to keep him company while he ate. When he finished, she smiled and said, "So what happened last night?"

While it was true that the way to a man's heart was through his stomach, Gale girls tended to believe food should be more inclusive.

Joe pushed the last bit of syrup around his plate with his fingertip. "I got jumped by a guy with a gun."

"*You* got jumped?" Her turn to stare in disbelief. Calgary had some hard-assed petty criminals if the Fey were getting mugged.

"He knew what I was, didn't he? Tasered me first. Tied my hands."

"Tied?" She took one hand in hers and gently pushed the sweatshirt cuff up. Not even the faintest residue of a binding.

"Well, it wasn't just the ties, was it? I could have broke them, sure, but he had a gun, here." Two stiffened fingers tapped his head just below his right ear. "Told me he had Blessed rounds, then he asked me what I knew. Asked if the UnderRealm had been in contact with me."

"So what *do* you know, Joe?"

"I know about the dragons."

"I've seen them." Still holding his hand, she glanced toward the window. "Well, seen them pass, which is almost the same thing."

"No, it's not. They're . . ."

Bigger. Scalier. Toothier. Definitely scarier in person. "It's okay. I know. *Has* the UnderRealm been in contact with you?"

"No, and like I told him, I wouldn't fucking listen if

they had. Then he wanted to know what I was doing in the store. I told him I was working here." His eyes widened as he suddenly realized what he'd been saying, and he yanked his hand free. "You enchanted me!"

"Yes."

"He told me he'd kill me if I told anyone!"

Allie kept her tone matter-of-fact. "How will he know you told me?"

"He has a truth thing! A silver thing. You can't lie when it's on you! He'll know I told you and he'll kill me! He had Blessed rounds! True death!"

"Joe! Stop it!" When he froze, she took his hands, thumbs stroking the backs. "If he threatens you again, he's in for a surprise."

"What have you . . ." He stared at the backs of his hands, eyes wide, the charms clearly visible to him. "You can't."

Allie shrugged. "I just did."

"You don't speak for your whole family!"

"Actually, we all speak for the whole family." She knew better than to look deep into his eyes so she stared sincerely at a freckle in the middle of his forehead. "That's what family is, Joe, we stand by each other, no matter what."

"You just told me your Auntie Jane was trying to poison your grandmother!"

"Doesn't count. If I call, they'll come. If he touches you, he'll know that."

"And if he shoots me from a distance?"

"Then it won't matter if you told me or not since he clearly has his own agenda."

Joe frowned, shifting the freckle. "That's not particularly comforting!"

"Sorry. He didn't happen to mention what that agenda was, did he? I mean, the level of threat does not match the level of his interrogation. We've got a big, big threat." She spread their joined hands apart, then moved them closer together. "Little bitty questions."

"He wasn't after explaining himself, if that's what you're asking."

"Pity."

"You think he had something to do with your grandmother's disappearance, then?"

"I think my grandmother disappeared, and now there's an armed man threatening someone who just started working at her store. My store. There's got to be a connection. There's the wash done." She let go of his hands. "I'll just toss everything in the dryer."

He rubbed his right hand over the back of his left and had no effect on the charm. "What does it actually say?"

"It's complicated, but basically . . ." Allie thought of him translucent one day and panicked the next, curled up on her doorstep terrified, and gentled her voice. ". . . it says, hands off."

He seemed almost content about that, so she didn't regret lying to him.

A more accurate translation would be *mine*.

"Someone's watching the store."

"Who?"

Allie rolled her eyes and glanced toward the bathroom door. Joe wouldn't be in there much longer. "I don't know who, Auntie Jane. But he carries a gun with Blessed rounds and has access to an artifact charmed to force the truth."

"It's entirely possible he bought the artifact from your grandmother," Auntie Jane snorted. "I assume

Catherine has charms in place keeping the family business from being broadcast to all and sundry?"

"Yes, but . . ."

"Then let him watch. If he actually wants to see
something, he'll have to come through the door."

"And then?"

"Oh, for pity's sake, Alysha Catherine, use your
imagination."

"A reporter?"

"For *The Western Star*." Allie restacked the latest
pile of saucers and added the number to the catalog. So
far, she'd counted fifty-seven saucers with no cups and
two cups with no saucers.

"That piece of shite." Joe swept the dirt into the
dustpan and straightened. "And he was talking to your
grandmother?"

"Apparently."

"You don't believe him, then?"

"I believe he has his own agenda and the bluest eyes
I've ever seen."

"So you're having coffee with him because of his
eyes?"

Allie shrugged, pulled out a basket of oddly shaped
candles, and put it back onto the shelf, not up to dealing with the mix of scents. "I need to know what his
agenda is. How much he thinks he knows about the
family."

"He won't know anything about the family, will he?
Worst he'll know is bits about your grandmother."

"That's bits about the family."

"You lot are right clannish."

"That's what I keep trying to tell you."

"I doubt she told him the truth about anything."

"Unless she decided to do a bit of shit disturbing."

Joe's expression suggested that from what he knew about Catherine Gale, that was entirely possible. "So you're doing damage control?"

"If it needs doing."

"And if he knows too much?" Brows up, Joe drew a questioning line across his throat.

"Please, we can be much subtler than that." They weren't always, but they could be.

She was sorting through a box of mismatched sterling silver cutlery—*Fill in your set. Priced by weight.*—when Graham came through the door. She'd wanted a good look at him through the clear-sight charm but not enough to be lingering by the counter so it looked as though she'd been waiting for him. She had no intention of crossing the fine line between not playing stupid games and looking way too eager.

His eyes were just as blue in the morning.

Which was quite possibly the stupidest observation she'd ever made about anyone.

He stopped by the end of the counter, once again a little too close to that damned monkey's paw. Shoving the box of silver to one side, Allie hurried over to him, afraid he might make another grab for the paw. It might be an old, ugly, hacked-off primate hand, yet the power it held made it remarkably seductive. But then, power was always seductive.

"Eleven o'clock, you're right on time."

His smile was as enthralling as she remembered. "I pride myself on being punctual. Can you leave?" He turned a not particularly approving glance toward Joe. Since Joe still looked a bit rough, that was hardly surprising.

"I think I can handle the crowds," Joe muttered,

squaring up the box of yoyos with the edge of the counter.

"We'll just be next door if anything happens," Allie told him and waved Graham back toward the front of the store.

"What would be likely to happen?" Graham wondered as they emerged out onto the sidewalk.

"Could get a run of little old ladies who desperately need cat saucers." Allie glanced up, saw that the pigeons were missing from the edge of the building, and quickly checked the space under the newspaper box. Empty.

"Looking for something?"

She glanced over to find him watching her and liked the way his gaze lingered. "I thought I saw a kestrel the other day."

Which was true. She'd been wrong, but it had been what she'd thought at the time.

"It's possible," he allowed as they walked to the coffee shop. "They seem to be taking to city life, and Calgary is a city where things are happening. We were named the best Canadian city to live in by the Canadian conference board," he added, holding the door open for her. "And the third best in North America."

"You know people keep telling me things are happening here . . ." She brushed up against him as she passed, almost accidentally, and spent a moment appreciating the feel of muscle under the same cheap suit he'd had on the night before. ". . . but so far all I've seen is the airport, the route in from the airport, the store, and this coffee shop. Oh, and the convenience store down the road."

"We'll have to do something about that," he murmured, close behind her and the low, whiskey rasp of his voice lifted the hair off the back of her neck.

It took her a moment to realize that Kenny was staring

at her expectantly from behind the counter. "Uh, two coffees please, for here, and . . ." She half turned and laid a hand on his forearm, just because he was up and in her personal space like an invitation. ". . . the Saskatoon berry muffins are great."

He blinked, but since the new angle gave him a deliberate glimpse of lace and the swell of breasts inside the vee of her shirt, that was only to be expected. If he thought he could fluster a Gale girl by standing too close and smelling terrific, he didn't know as much about the family as she feared he did. And he'd clearly never tried this on her grandmother.

She smiled at the thought. Graham looked startled for a moment, then smiled back.

"So are you having the muffins?"

When she turned back to the counter, a pair of big red mugs filled with coffee waited by two empty plates although she hadn't heard Kenny move—not to take the mugs from the rack, not to fill them at the urns. He held a pair of tongs over the muffin baskets.

"Yes," Graham answered for them both. "We are. Thank you."

While he paid, Allie carried both mugs and plates over to the most isolated of the small tables by the front windows. "I waitressed in a bar while I was in university," she explained as he joined her, brows up at the display of plate shuffling. "Right kind of place and I still get the urge to clear tables and refill coffees. Charlie says I do it deliberately to embarrass her."

"That your cousin, the musician, in Brazil."

"That's her." She could see him filing away the whole *Charlie's a her* thing.

But all he said was, "You don't seem the bar waitress type."

"Well, Michael got the job first. He was bartending

and when one of the girls quit . . ." She'd quit because Allie had wanted to be with Michael and had been more than willing to arrange things to get it. She was a little embarrassed about that now. Right now. Which was strange because she never had been before.

"Michael's an old boyfriend?"

"Michael's . . . it's complicated."

"Yeah, I have a couple of those, too. So . . ." Graham took a long swallow of coffee—two cream, two sugars—and pulled out a small black notebook. "Let's talk about why your grandmother decided to open a store in Calgary so far from the rest of her family."

Allie shrugged. "Things are happening here."

"Seriously."

"She told you that, that she was far from her family?"

"She did." He wore a "trust me" face. Allie might have trusted him more if he hadn't been so obviously wearing it over his actual expression. He was good, though; she couldn't see beneath it. "It must have come as a huge shock to you when she died."

"It did."

"What happened to the body?"

Allie froze, a piece of muffin halfway to her mouth. "The what?"

"Your grandmother's body. When there's a death, there's a body. I wondered what happened to it. Was she buried here or back home?"

Or eaten by dragons. Allie had to bite back an inappropriate desire to giggle. "We have a family burial plot back home."

"That doesn't exactly answer my question."

"Which wasn't *exactly* about the store."

"Background information."

"About someone who no longer has anything to do with the store."

Graham acknowledged the point with a nod and drank a little more coffee. Allie watched muscles move in the tanned column of his throat and met his gaze with nothing more than a lifted brow when he caught her at it. He brushed his hair back off his face, although it didn't really need brushing, and checked his notes. "So your grandmother left you the store; does she own the building?"

"She said she did."

"But you haven't seen the paperwork?"

Allie shrugged so he could watch the motion. Fair was fair. "I don't even know where the paperwork is," she admitted. "That's remarkably blonde, isn't it?"

"A little," he admitted in turn. "And I don't think ignoring the legalities is something even you can get away with."

"Even me?" she purred, leaning forward.

A flash of something that might have been annoyance at the slip, but it was gone too fast for her to be certain. "A beautiful blonde." He reached across the table and lifted the end of her braid out of her coffee.

He waited for her to laugh before he did. She liked that. A lot. And she was a little afraid of how much she liked his laugh, so she fumbled her phone out to hide her reaction. Some of her reaction.

"Do you mind? This'll only take a minute, but you're right and I should get it dealt with." When he nodded, she called Roland and repeated Graham's point, or possibly points, about the paperwork.

"You're talking to a reporter?"

"Get past that."

"Okay . . ." She could hear definite speculation in the pause and thanked any gods who might be listening that he wasn't likely to repeat that speculation to the aunties. "He's right."

"I already told him that."

"I take it you'd like me to deal with it?"

"If you can."

"No problem. In fact, you couldn't have called at a better time since I can be out there in a couple of days. My boss is retiring, leaving me temporarily unemployed."

"Retiring?" Alan Kirby had always struck her as more the "die in the saddle" type, Matlocking his way through increasingly lame court cases until one of his clerks finally noticed he'd started to decay.

"The aunties suggested it."

That made more sense. The aunties had probably also suggested an alternative.

"I'll pass on the details," Roland continued, "when I've booked the flight."

"You don't mind leaving home?" She'd expected to send the information to him.

"Right now, I think being away from home would do me good." His voice had picked up a definite edge. It wasn't always easy being among the cosseted few.

"If they give you any trouble . . ."

"I'll have them call you."

"Thanks, Rol. Cousin," she explained, closing the phone. "He's a lawyer. He's flying in to deal with it."

"You have a lot of cousins."

"How do you figure? I've only mentioned two."

"It's the way you say *cousin* like it should be obvious."

Okay, she'd give him that one. "You're right. I have a lot of cousins."

"Brothers and sisters?"

So stupid to miss sisters she'd never had. "Just an older brother. You?"

"I had six and two sisters." Graham dropped his

crumpled napkin on his empty plate and frowned, like he was trying to remember. Not an obvious movement, but Allie caught it. "They uh, they died with my parents when I was thirteen. Fire. I wasn't home; everyone else was."

"I'm so sorry."

"Yeah. Thanks. I, uh, I have a fair number of cousins myself, though." He shook the sadder memories off with what looked like the ease of long practice, as though so terrible a thing had happened to someone else, and Allie thought that was almost worse than the memory itself. "Lots of aunts and uncles. My father's family was huge; eight of them survived to have kids of their own, and I expect by now those kids have kids."

"You expect?"

"We're not close."

"How often do you see them?"

Graham frowned again. "I don't."

"You don't see them often?"

"I don't see them at all. Not since I left for university." He seemed to be reaching for a memory, didn't quite get there, and shook off the attempt with a wry twist of his mouth. "But then most of them are still in Blanc-Sablon. The town in Quebec where I was born."

"Quebec? You don't sound French."

He smiled then. "I can, but it's a cheap imitation accent. In spite of what the rest of Canada thinks about rural Quebec, most of the people where I'm from are English speakers."

"And they never call? You never call them?"

"Like I said, we're not close."

In twenty-four years, Allie had never gone an entire day without talking to at least one member of her family. There'd been days when she hadn't gone twenty-four minutes. "Ever think of starting a family of your own?" she asked absently, tracking the breadth of his shoulders.

Graham's expression seemed to be asking where *that* had come from. Allie was wondering the same thing. In spite of the shoulders. "I haven't, no."

"So you don't want kids?"

"Actually . . ." From the outside, it seemed as though he'd found something unexpected tucked into a forgotten corner of his head. "Actually, yeah, I do. Not eight, but I always figured I'd have a few. What about you?"

"Not eight," she agreed, smiling. "So, your family . . ." His eyes shuttered again and although she didn't want him to close off, she couldn't let it go. Family was everything to a Gale. "Your family is farther away than mine." The pull of distance remained a steady ache. "Why move so far from home?"

"My boss at the paper is an old mentor of mine. He was the reason I managed to get to university, to get out of Blanc-Sablon—which is a beautiful place, don't get me wrong . . ." A raised hand cut off questions she hadn't intended to ask. ". . . but I was on my own and wanted to see the rest of the world. When he offered me a job, I took it."

There was an obvious truth to what he'd just told her, like he didn't think he needed to lie. In contrast to when he spoke about his family, when he spoke about his mentor/boss, it almost sounded rehearsed; spilling out freely as if she'd charmed him. She hadn't, although she'd certainly thought about it during those moments she'd been alone with his muffin. And wow, that sounded dirty.

She was half tempted to toss out, *"Did you know we have dragons?"* just to see what he'd say. She didn't. She wasn't that lost in his eyes.

Then he frowned and reached into his pocket to pull

out his own phone, still vibrating. "It's my boss. I have to take this."

Eavesdroppers might never hear good of themselves, but Allie, sketching patterns against the white Formica tabletop in a bit of the coffee she'd wrung from her braid couldn't hear anything at all beyond the low murmur of a male voice. Graham had turned to put his body between her and the phone, much as she had the night before. Nothing more than an obvious move to gain a little privacy in close quarters but, given the distance, it seemed to be enough to block her.

"I'm sorry," he told her as he hung up, "but I have to go. Something broke on a big story we're following, and I need to take advantage of it."

Again, no lie in his voice. Of course she hadn't lied to him either. "Hey, I understand about doing the job." She stood when he did, wiping out the pattern with the napkin. "I used to be gainfully employed."

"And now?"

She surprised herself by her answer. "I honestly don't know."

He paused, half turned toward the door. Apparently, she'd surprised him, too. "I'd like to continue this. Dinner?"

About to say yes, she remembered. "I can't tonight. We're open until midnight."

"I can't tonight anyway. Story."

"Right."

"Tomorrow?"

"That would be great." Then he actually held the door open for her. She'd have gone through it also except Kenny called her to the counter.

"Watch this one," he said quietly. "He prefers to drink his coffee black, but he put milk and sugar in."

"Okay . . ."

"He is not honest with you."

Yes and no, actually. "You'd be surprised."

"Probably not at my age," he snorted and pushed a take-out cup across the counter. "For Joe, triple triple. Waste of decent coffee. I never played hockey, but you still owe me $2.79."

Graham walked her back to the store but didn't go in. "I have to go."

"So you said."

"Yeah."

"I should get inside. Joe's coffee ..."

"Yeah."

The door opened, and Joe leaned out. "Is that for me?" he asked pointedly.

When Allie handed it to him, he stayed where he was.

Graham glared for a moment, but since Joe was staring fixedly at the sidewalk, it wasn't very effective. "I'll see you tomorrow," he said at last. "Six thirty?"

"Terrific."

"Casual." When she raised a brow, he grinned. "I've heard women like to know. It's a shoe thing." He was walking away before she remembered the charm on the door. Which didn't work if she was on the same side of it he was. By the time she got inside, it was too late.

"I sold a couple of yoyos when you were gone," Joe told her. "One of the glow-in-the-dark ones and one of the little ones. Oh, and some old lady bought some saucers for her sprites."

"She's drinking soda pop out of a saucer?"

"No, *sprites*. You know, about yea big ..." His thumb and forefinger were around five centimeters apart. "... double wings, not really good for sweet fuck all but looking cute, and they'll eat you out of house and home if you let them." He sucked back a mouthful of coffee like he needed it. "She's got seven. I think she expected me to care. So you're going to dinner with him tomorrow?"

Still thinking about the sprites, Allie just barely managed to make the lateral move to her personal life. "I am."

"Just dinner?"

"None of your business, Mom."

He flushed and ducked his head. "Just, you've got no family here and . . ."

"It's okay." How cute was an overprotective leprechaun? "And there's family coming. My cousin Charlie'll be here early tomorrow and my cousin Roland's coming in next week."

"Oh." Pale skin went paler, the freckles standing out. "Then I guess, I . . . uh . . ."

When he started to move toward the door, she understood, reached out, and gently took hold of his arm—all skin and bones and oversized sweater. "Joe, Charlie's a musician and Roland's a lawyer. They're not here to help in the store. I'll still need you."

"I don't . . ."

So many fears unfinished.

"I know. Hey, I made almond cake last night, want some?"

His eyes narrowed. "What'll it make me do?"

She grinned. "Gain weight."

They spent the next few hours in companionable silence as Joe sorted through a few boxes filled with the jumbled debris of a stranger's life and Allie continued to build her catalog, inventing categories as she went.

About an hour after lunch, she was sitting cross-legged on the floor staring at a small painting of a seascape and wondering if she could really see the waves move or if the dust and mold had started to cause hallucinations. She glanced up when the door opened and saw a small man of indeterminate age dressed in a dark green suit step into the store and head for the counter. The word dapper popped into her head uninvited as she stood. No question of where it had come from; it fit the little man perfectly.

So did supercilious and disapproving.

She could only see his profile, but from the way a muscle jumped in his jaw, she'd bet his teeth were clenched and his lips pressed into a thin, pale line. Wondering what had climbed up his ass and died, she'd taken a single step toward him when he snapped out a word definitely not in English—nor covered by high school French—and Joe growled, "Fuck you."

Allie knew bravado when she heard it. "Joe?"

The little man turned toward her and she saw the weight of centuries in his eyes. Unlike Joe, who looked Human with only a faint overlay of *not,* this guy was not!Human all the way through. His slow inspection—head to toe and back again—was clearly intended to intimidate. "So you'll be the new Gale, then?"

His accent was Joe's distilled and filtered through a peat bog by way of a box of Lucky Charms.

"And you are?"

"Sure and I *was* Catherine Gale's accountant, and if you're the new Gale in her place, then I'll be seeing to your numbers as well—but I'll not work around the likes of him. Blood traitor!" Color began to rise in his face as he turned his attention back to Joe, spitting out a long line of invective, tone providing sufficient translation.

Joe gripped the edge of the counter, fingertips white, lower lip caught between his teeth, breath beginning to quicken.

As the little man began to surge forward, Allie slid between him and the counter.

He stared up at her in astonishment. "You don't understand, Gale. He has been Called and he does not answer! Roaming about free in the MidRealm indeed! I have every right to force him home."

"No, you don't understand Gales. Get out."

The silence that fell was so complete she was pretty sure both members of her audience had momentarily stopped breathing.

The little man recovered first. "You can't . . ."

"Yes . . ." She used the edge on her voice to cut him off. ". . . I can."

"Allie, it's okay. I can go."

She gentled her voice for him. "There's no need, Joe."

"Do you dare, Gale-child? Do you know who you are dealing with?"

Allie knew the power of age; immortality didn't intimidate her. Very much. "My grandmother's accountant."

He bristled and jabbed a pale finger past her toward Joe. "I see your marks on him. You would dare to take control from the Courts? You would truly choose that, then?"

"Have chosen. And it's him, not that. And he has a name. And a place. You, on the other hand, are not wanted here." She called up Auntie Jane's best *don't make me come over there* expression. "I'd prefer to say good-bye and nothing more, but we both know there's more I could say."

All his attention shifted suddenly to her, lifting the hair off the back of her neck. "You would dare?" he demanded incredulously.

In spite of the way her heart had lodged up somewhere in her throat, she managed a fairly nonchalant shrug. "Your choice."

"No, your choice, Gale-child." His upper lip curled

exposing stained teeth. "Your grandmother would not approve."

"My grandmother isn't here." Auntie Jane's expression slid off, leaving no buffer between them. "I am."

He stared at her for a long moment, then he snorted. "So you are. My debt to your family is cleared by my leaving." He nodded once, turned, and walked to the door. Outside, he paused to give her a long look at his true shape before he strutted off into the west.

"Give me a break," Allie muttered, sagging back against the counter. "You're a leprechaun; that's not exactly visually terrifying."

Joe charged around the counter and stuffed a stool under her as she continued to sag. "Allie? You okay?"

"I'm fine. Adrenaline crash, that's all." As David had so helpfully reminded her, the family didn't mess with the Fey. Other side of the coin, though, the Fey didn't mess with the family. She'd just never been the one pointing that out before. The weight of Joe's regard finally spun her far enough on the stool for her to face his concern. "What?"

"You've made an enemy."

"No, I cashed in my grandmother's debt. Him and me, we're even now. If he comes back, I'll make an enemy."

"Don't even be joking about that!"

"I'm not."

Joe swallowed once, eyes suspiciously bright, then proved he was Human enough by heading straight past the chick flick moment and saying, "I wonder how he got in debt to your grandmother in the first place?"

"I can think of a few ways."

"Yeah. Me, too."

They shuddered together.

Maybe word had gotten around. Maybe early May

was a slow time in the antiques/junk biz. Whatever the reason, the store remained empty until Allie went upstairs to pull something out of the freezer for supper.

"Another yoyo," Joe told her.

She set the plates of porcini mushroom tortellini on the counter with a sharp crack, the pasta sliding precariously close to the edge. "You're kidding me."

"Uh-uh. And this lady was asking if you'd keep an eye out for some old teapot." He pushed a piece of paper toward her. "I wrote it down."

Royal Albert bone china, Lady Hamilton pattern. "Did Gran do that?"

"Dunno." Half a careful shrug. "But she's not here."

For the first time since Allie'd met him, he didn't check the shadows when talking about her gran.

Neither of them spoke about how late he intended to stay.

Charlie called as they finished eating. The delay at O'Hare had screwed with her connection in Denver. "So I'll be coming in around nine twenty."

"Do you want me to pick you up?"

"You have something to pick me up in?"

"Gran's car."

"Then, yes. Please. Bring food."

Just after dusk, Allie found a Hand of Glory in with the candles then, having accidentally touched it, spent twenty minutes washing her own hands while wondering what the hell Gran had been thinking.

At ten twenty, the current owner of mailbox number four came in. Allie had been searching through a box of costume jewelry, amusing herself by running a mood ring through its paces, so once again she missed a chance to use the clear-sight on the door. Tall and thin and of indeterminate age—at least from the back—the woman had long, almost blond hair and wore a shapeless gray cardigan over an equally shapeless gray skirt. She had on worn sneakers and gray ankle socks and carried a grubby canvas shopping bag from a national grocery chain. It looked like she relaxed slightly when she saw Joe behind the counter, the stiff lines of back and shoulders curving into something more fluid.

Those curves snapped rigid again as Allie came forward and she thought for a terrible moment the woman, who'd spun around to face her, was going to cry.

"Hi. I'm the new ... proprietor." Until she knew what she was dealing with, it seemed safest not to hold out her hand or smile too broadly.

"I just came for my mail." Long fingers clutched at the bundle of papers Joe had set on the counter.

"Okay."

"I'm not doing anything wrong."

"I didn't think you ..."

"I have the money for this month!" She reached into the canvas bag and thrust a moist envelope at Allie. "I didn't mean to be late."

"Don't worry about ..."

"I won't be late again! I'm so sorry!" Before Allie could reassure her, she spun on one heel and hurried toward the door, leaving damp footprints behind her. She didn't look a lot different through the glass although strands of long gray hair swirled about her like she was moving underwater.

"Loireag," Joe said, wiping a few drops of water off the counter with his sleeve. "Lives in the river by the weir."

"She seemed afraid." The bills in the envelope were limp but appeared to be actual legal tender.

"Yeah, we got lucky. She doesn't deal with new things

very well. Once she gets to know you, she'll talk your ear off about how depressed she is and how much her life sucks and other shit like that."

"You think she knows about the guy with the gun?"

"Knows?"

"Just wondering how many of the Fey he's threatened."

Joe rolled his eyes, but Allie noticed that he was rubbing the charm on the back of his hand. "Don't need a guy with a gun to threaten her. She'd get threatened by an old lady waving a bran muffin."

"Don't underestimate old ladies or muffins," Allie told him, dropping the envelope into the cashbox. "That said, I *was* expecting something more dangerous to come out after dark."

"Not her, not out of the water," Joe snorted. "Drown you soon as look at you if you're swimming too close to her hidey-hole, though."

"I'll try and remember that."

"Yeah, well, city's got this Bow River weir project, right? And part of it's to deal with the . . ." Fingers sketched air quotes. ". . . extreme drowning hazard." He shook his head, and shoved the resulting fall of hair back off his face. "Most people got no idea, do they?" Then he frowned. "You're not going to be doing something about that, are you? I mean about her?"

"My family's smart enough not to swim near a loireag. Or in a river that goes through a major metropolitan area. I mean, eww."

"It's not so bad."

"Except for the extreme drowning hazard."

"Well, yeah."

Just before midnight, Joe glanced out to the empty street and sighed. "I guess I'd best be going then."

"You can sleep on my couch if you like."

He froze, hand on the door. "Upstairs?"

"It's where the couch is."

"Why? You think you can keep me safe up there."

Allie thought about lying but not for very long. "Yes, actually."

In spite of the fear that showed in his eyes, he shook his head. "I can't bring that on you."

"It'll be fine. It's not a big thing."

"You can stop bullets?"

"Well . . ." She considered lying about that as well but didn't. ". . . no."

"I'll see you tomorrow, then." The fingers not wrapped around the door handle were trembling. He probably thought she couldn't see them. "Can't be spending my life hiding behind your skirts, can I?"

A glance down at her jeans. "I'm not wearing a skirt."

"Don't be so damned difficult, Allie. I need to . . ."

"Be a guy?" Sighing, she shelved the idea of asking just where exactly he was going.

"Maybe that. Besides . . ." Mouth twisted into a close approximation of a smile, Joe held up a marked hand as he stepped over the threshold. ". . . isn't this supposed to keep me safe?"

"Not from bullets," Allie said as the door closed behind him. If anything happened to him, she'd bury the city in aunties, but as sweet as revenge might be, it wouldn't bring him back. "Stay safe," she told his back and gave some serious thought to adding new charms that would keep him from wandering.

All things considered, chief among them the condition she'd found him in that morning, Allie wasn't surprised when at a quarter past one, a pounding on the store door interrupted her brushing her teeth before bed. Joe couldn't be too badly hurt, not if he still had

the energy to pound, but that didn't mean there wasn't
something on his heels. She all but flew down the stairs
and through the store and rocked to a sudden stop
when she saw who was standing on the sidewalk.

"Michael?"

FIVE

Allie didn't have to ask what was wrong, Michael told her as soon as she opened the door.

"I caught Brian fucking one of the guys at the construction site."

He didn't sound angry; he sounded weary, and that was a thousand times worse.

"Oh, sweetie." She grabbed the strap of the duffel bag hanging from his shoulder, dragged him over the threshold, and wrapped as much of him as possible in a hug. "I'll call Auntie Jane."

She was mostly kidding. Calling in the aunties for a cheating boyfriend was like calling in a nuclear strike on the asshat who'd parked diagonally across two spots at the mall. This didn't mean she wouldn't call them if Michael wanted her to.

He laughed a little, like she'd hoped he would, and if it sounded like he was laughing to keep from crying, well, that was okay, too. They'd take that next step when they weren't standing in an open doorway. Anger had probably got him packed and to the airport and onto the plane where he'd had nothing to do for a couple of hours but think about how his life had fallen apart.

"Let's leave the aunties out of this; you know how they overreact."

"They salt the earth because they care. Come on." Unwrapping herself only as far as necessary, she tugged him a little farther into the store and locked the door behind him. "Upstairs. I made cake."

"Magic cake?" He sounded about twelve—or as much like a twelve-year-old as a man who'd topped out at six foot five and then put on the muscle bulk to match could sound.

"Is there any other kind?"

Arm around his waist, she steered him through the store and past the mirror . . .

"Is that . . . ?"

"Don't even look, Michael, trust me."

. . . and up the stairs and into the apartment where she stepped back and took a good long look at him. He wore a shirt and blazer over jeans and work boots, the uniform for an architect visiting the site, and he'd obviously been in them since early Friday morning. His hazel eyes were shadowed, there were flecks of dried blood in the corner of his lower lip where he'd chewed off a bit of dried skin, and dark stubble buried curves where his dimples were hidden. Michael had always shown his heart on his face.

"Fuck the aunties. I'm going to kill him myself."

"Allie . . . it's just . . ." The duffel bag slid to the floor and he dropped into one of the kitchen chairs like his strings had been cut. "Just don't. You know what Brian's like. Hell, I know what Brian's like."

"I thought he'd changed."

"Yeah. Me, too."

It had been Brian's idea that Michael take the job with his father's firm, allowing them to finish their internship together. Brian's idea that they live together in Vancouver. Although he hadn't stopped fucking around the first year after he and Michael had hooked up, Allie knew for a fact that the last year the three of them had been at Carleton, Brian had actually managed monogamy. Not without temptation and not without a few alcohol-fueled rants about having been neutered, but he'd kept it in his pants.

She should never have let that charm fade.

She should have given him a different one as a going away present. One that came with consequences.

"I thought you said there'd be cake?"

"Yeah, I did." Allie bent to kiss the top his head, although given his height she didn't bend far, then pulled the cake out of the fridge and sliced off a hefty wedge. Filling the largest glass in the cabinet with milk, she set them on the table in front of him and slid into the next chair, tucking a bare foot up under her.

"You're not eating?" He frowned at her red boxers and over them the worn and armless remnant of one of David's old high school football jerseys. "You were in bed."

"One, not yet." Tugging at the frayed hem of the jersey, she was just glad it wasn't his; under the circumstances, just a bit creepy. "Two, it wouldn't have mattered. And three, if I'm going to eat cake at two in the morning I might as well apply it directly to my ass. Eat."

The left dimple made half an appearance. "You sound like your mother."

"Could be worse." Frowning, she watched him stuff a huge forkful of cake into his mouth. "Did you eat supper?"

"It's worse."

Reaching out, she smacked him lightly on the shoulder. "Just answer the question."

"I had something at the airport. And I bought a sandwich on the plane. Two actually."

"Good." If he could still eat, he wasn't completely broken. So far there'd been nothing in Michael's life so terrible it had killed his appetite. Except, if anything, this should . . .

"Because I was expecting it."

Allie blinked. Not at Michael knowing what she was thinking before she got there herself, they'd been able to do that to each other since they were kids, but at the actual words. After a moment, she managed a quiet, "Why?" her reaction waiting on his answer.

"It was too perfect, wasn't it?"

With his stupid perfect life and his stupid perfect boyfriend.

At least she'd got the stupid boyfriend right.

"No. It wasn't *too* perfect. It was exactly as perfect as you deserve."

His mouth twisted. "Apparently."

"Oh, sweetie, that's not what I meant!" It was easier to hold him with him sitting down. Arms wrapped around him, head tucked into the curve of her throat, she rested her cheek on the top of his head and murmured, "Brian's an ass, he doesn't deserve you. And you deserve better."

"But I still want him."

"Yeah. I know."

After a long moment, he sighed. "I need a shower."

"I didn't want to mention it."

Both sofas opened into queen-sized beds. Allie didn't bother setting up either of them. Michael was one of the most tactile people she knew and when he was hurting, he needed touch.

Emerging from the bathroom clean and shaved, chestnut hair damp and curling slightly over his ears, he glanced over at the sofas and then at Allie standing in the bedroom door.

"It's a big bed," she said softly.

A little of the tension went out of his shoulders and he almost smiled. "Promise to keep your hands to yourself?"

"Nope."

They'd shared a bed, or certain variations of the word bed, off and on since they were five. There'd been a few rocky months in their teens before Allie had been convinced he really wasn't interested . . .

"Can't you just close your eyes and pretend I'm a guy?"

"Can you close your eyes and pretend I'm a girl?"

"Why would I want to do that?"

"Why would I?"

. . . but in the end she settled for having as much of him as she could. Charlie thought she was a little too fond of self-flagellation, but the comfort they took from each other outweighed the unrequited bits. Usually. And maybe Charlie wasn't entirely wrong.

She wondered if it hurt more that he'd caught Brian with another guy. If maybe a girl would have hurt less. Michael might not be interested, but Brian was as firmly in the enthusiastically nondiscriminating camp as any Gale. One very cold February night after Brian had essentially moved into their student apartment, the heat had gone off and the three of them had shared a bed. Allie and Brian had held a silent and speculative conversation, then placed Michael definitively between them.

Head on Michael's shoulder, his arm a warm, familiar weight against her back, she inhaled the scent of clean skin and fabric softener from his worn T-shirt and murmured, "What did Brian say?"

"When? Oh . . ." A disdainful snort in the darkness. "He didn't see me. I saw him, went back to the apartment, packed some shit, and left."

"So you didn't give him a chance to explain?"

"Explain what? That he was just standing there between the trailer and the crane minding his own business when some guy in a hard hat threw himself on his dick a few dozen times?"

"It's just . . ." Strange? Weird? Unlikely? None of the above, given that he'd been caught in the act. "What did you do with your phone?"

"Left it at the condo."

"I wonder why he hasn't called *me*."

"He's afraid of your reaction."

"Smarter than he looks."

"Obviously."

She spread her fingers out over his heart, feeling it beat through muscle and bone. Feeling the ragged edges of the break rubbing against each other.

"Allie?" Something in his voice suggested she wasn't going to be happy about the question.

"Yeah?"

"What drawer are Gran's sex toys in?"

She couldn't see him grinning in the dark, but she knew the dimples had reappeared. "Shut up!"

"Two more?"

He shrugged as he stripped out of his camouflage, using the movement to work the knots out of his shoulders.

"That's all of them, then. This would be the one thing

in millennia they've agreed on." Heavy brows drew in. "Perhaps I *should* have had you deal with them as they emerged."

He'd spent thirteen years dealing with the horrors drawn to his boss' power—creatures that crawled and walked and flew out of nightmare, creatures that didn't belong in this world however Human they looked—and this was the first time he'd ever heard him sound unsure. Whatever was coming had him rattled. Off his game. "If I knew what we were all waiting for. . . ."

"You know what you need to. You know what you always have. And you know I depend on you. If this creature gets loose in the world, I will be in mortal danger." The dark eyes narrowed. "You need to kill it. They're watching for me now, they'll be watching for me when it arrives, but they don't know about you. That's why you couldn't deal with them as they emerged. If they find out about you . . ." He spread blunt-fingered hands, rings glittering under the fluorescent light. "Capture. Torture. Eventually, you'll tell them where I am. Best to keep a low profile."

"Best for both of us from the sounds of it."

"Of course."

"What about after it's dead? What will they do then?"

"After?" The older man snorted. "After, they'll very likely try to kill you, but with no reason to hide, you can pick them out of the sky as they come in for the attack."

"Provided they attack one at a time."

"Which they will. As I said, they don't agree on much and, furthermore, with only a single shot to base their assessment on, there's no way they'll anticipate how dangerous *you* are. *After*, they'll be furious and you can take advantage of that lack of finesse."

True. Checking that his M24 rested secure against the padded lining of the case, he frowned. It sounded reasonable—for those definitions of reasonable that referred to the more important part of how he made a living—but there seemed to be more variables every time they talked. For the first time in a long time, he wondered if he did know what he needed to.

Brian called at 8:10 just as Allie eased the ancient Beetle onto Deerfoot Trail heading for the airport. *Eased* because one of Gran's charms appeared to be a NASCAR derivative and maintaining a speed less than 20K over the 100 KPH limit proved to be taxing. Fortunately, Saturday morning traffic was sparse compared to the usual commuter tangles so, after glancing down to see the call display, Allie picked up the phone.

"Is he there?" Brian sounded wrecked.

She'd left Michael communing with the coffeemaker, eyes squinted nearly shut, hair sticking up in at least three different directions. He'd slept through the dragons' flyby—probably for the best—but had hopefully regained enough consciousness to understand her instructions for opening the store.

"Allie, *please*. Is Michael with you?"

He deserved to know that much.

"Yes," she told him. And hung up.

"Hi, you must be Joe. I'm Michael, a friend of Allie's. She's gone to pick Charlie up at the airport, but she should be back by eleven unless Charlie convinces her to stop by a grocery store, which would not be a bad idea since there's a significant lack of crap in that apartment. But not a big surprise since Gale girls don't trust anything they haven't baked themselves. Which reminds me, I ate the last of the rhubarb pie for breakfast, so you're in the clear with Aunt Ruth's charm, and in case no one's warned you, pancakes are sneaky because they can pour the batter in pretty much any pattern they want. Generally, they're pretty harmless, but stick to toast and eggs if you pissed one of them off. And butter the toast yourself. Oh, and Allie says you're in charge."

He had a place here. The prickle of panic evoked by the stranger at the door stopped running up and down his back. Joe looked down at the enormous hand engulfing his and then up, way up into a friendly smile and shadowed fox eyes. "How the fuck tall *are* you?" he demanded, wondering if this Michael had a touch of the blood.

"Uh . . . six five. Ish."

"Ish?" Who actually said ish? "And could you maybe let go of my hand, then?"

"Sorry."

"It's all right; seems I can still use it." He flexed the fingers just to be sure. "So, when did you arrive?" Charlie and Roland he remembered, but Allie hadn't said anything about Michael.

"Late last night."

Front door unlocked, Joe turned the sign, and decided to be amused by how much the big man had to shorten his stride to walk beside him to the counter.

"So, uh . . . you're a leprechaun?"

"Oh, she told you that, did she?" She might as well have hung a sign around the big guy's neck saying *I trust him, so you can.* Conscious of Michael's continuing stare, Joe sighed. "Go ahead and say it."

"I don't . . ."

"Yeah. You do. Let's get it over with and move on. I'm a little *tall* for a leprechaun."

Broad shoulders rose and fell; the grin was damned near blinding. "Not from where I'm standing."

Joe spent a moment thinking of punching the guy in the nuts, considered the consequences, and pulled a ten from the cashbox. "If I'm in charge, you're going for coffee."

"I don't . . ."

"Next door."

"Okay, then."

He sold a yoyo to a kid on a skateboard while Michael was gone and was entering it in the ledger when he got back.

"The old guy next door? Kenny Shoji? He can tell exactly what kind of coffee you like. Pretty cool, eh?" The big red mugs looked small in his hands although they regained their size when he set them on the counter. "He said it makes more sense to use these than to keep wasting paper, that we should bring them back when we're done, and that if I'm staying for any length of time, he's going to get some crap coffee in so that we can abuse it without causing him pain."

Seemed that Michael was also a triple/triple man. And it seemed that coffee shop Kenny trusted him on sight. Joe, however, still had trouble trusting anyone so tall. At least a dozen members of the NBA and four MLB pitchers were half bloods, so it wasn't like the Courts didn't have a presence in the MidRealm. He slid the ledger back under the counter. "How long are you staying, then?"

Just like that, the shadows in Michael's eyes won; darkening the hazel, banishing the grin. "I don't know."

In spite of his suspicion, Joe felt like he'd kicked a

puppy. A big, half-grown, annoying puppy that he'd
best stay on the right side of, not only because of the
size of his teeth but because Allie was clearly holding
the end of his leash. Sighing, he scraped at a smudge
on the counter with a ragged fingernail. "So why'd *you*
need sanctuary, then? And don't even try to lie to me
about it."

"Because you're a leprechaun?"

"No, because any idiot can see you'd be crap at it."

Seemed for a moment like Michael wasn't going to
answer, then he shrugged. "I caught my partner fucking
around on me. You?"

So he'd caught that it went both ways. The big guy
wasn't stupid for all the air was probably right thin up
near his head. "I got my life threatened by an attitude
case with a gun and loaded Blessed rounds."

Looking thoughtful, Michael took a long swallow of
coffee. Set the mug back on the counter and said, "True
death, eh? Well, that puts infidelity in perspective. Your
life sucks worse than mine."

Joe saluted that insight with his own mug, then
kicked the second stool over. "You know you're fucking
covered in charms, right? And they're not all hers."

"You can see them?" Michael asked, sitting down.
"Sorry, stupid question. Of course you can, given who
you are." Glancing down at a tanned forearm that
screamed *don't even fucking think about* it to anyone
with the sight, he twisted it so the muscle rolled beneath
the skin. "Some of them are Charlie's, a couple are
Aunt Mary's—that's Allie's mother—at least one is her
cousin Katie's, and there's one of David's. Her brother,"
he added when Joe raised a brow.

"No aunties?"

"They try, but Allie always catches them. Her gran
actually managed to keep one in place for almost a

week once, but that was only because she drew it just before my dad dragged me off to Ottawa with him. Allie hit the roof when I got home and she found it."

"Little possessive is she, then?" Joe murmured watching the charms on the backs of his own hands catch the light.

"A little." His smile flashed bright and unconcerned about being possessed. "But she's not controlling, and the aunties are. Can be," he amended. Frowned. "Are."

"But you've family of your own?"

"Sort of." Michael took a long swallow of coffee. "Well, yeah. But my parents are politicians—back room, not elected—and they never have much time for anything that doesn't impact at the federal level. First day of kindergarten when the au pair was late, Allie took me home with her and I pretty much stayed. She's got no sisters and that's kind of an anomaly in her family." He shot Joe a knowing look. "I think that's why she collects strays."

"I'm no stray!"

"If you say so, but you're a long way from home."

As much as he wanted to, Joe couldn't argue with that.

Charlie's reflection was wearing a cowboy hat as she passed the mirror on her way into the store, but that, Allie noted, seemed to be the only embellishment. *Her* reflection stood tied to a stake surrounded by bones split for their marrow.

"Yeah. Dragons. I know," she sighed as she followed her cousin.

"You must be Joe."

Eyes wide, Joe managed to sweep his gaze from the blue hair to the lilac Docs and settle somewhere in between by the time Charlie stopped across the counter from him.

"I'm Charlie. Don't let her . . ." A toss of her head, toward Allie. ". . . boss you around."

Ginger brows drew in. "But she's my boss."

"Well, you're screwed, then." She turned and charged between the first set of shelves. "Michael!"

"Charles!"

Allie rounded the shelves in time to see Michael heave Charlie off her feet, secure her with one arm, and reach out to stop an ancient wire spinner stuffed with old *Maclean's* magazines from toppling over. Moving up next to the counter, she leaned over and beckoned Joe closer. "Charlie can mark you with a song, so if she gets out her guitar, watch where the music is going."

"You people are scary in a group," Joe snorted. "You know that, right?"

"Yes." Allie smiled. "But *this* isn't a group."

"Say the word," Charlie growled as Michael put her down, "and Brian'll have the theme music to 'Mr. Dressup' on permanent earworm."

"Let it go, Charlie."

"Right." She reached up and cupped his face in her hands. "Revenge served cold. Got it. You know where I am when the time comes."

"Thank you."

"Could be worse. If you were straight, you'd have been stuck with Allie, and it's not like *she's* all about commitment."

He grinned. "When was the last time you slept in a bed?"

"I can't remember, but I was in Halifax."

Allie caught his eye and nodded.

"Okay, then." Bending, he scooped her up and tossed her over his shoulder. "Bedtime."

"Hey! There's a whole bunch of eight track tapes up here." She grabbed one off the shelf and tossed it into Allie's hands as she passed. "Hang onto that for me."

"It's the *Saturday Night Fever* soundtrack."

"Or not." Falling forward, head pillowed on her arms, she stared down Michael's back as they exited the store. "Your ass looks amazing from this angle."

Michael's response got lost in the sound of his boots on the stairs.

"I sold a yoyo while you were gone," Joe said at last.

"Well, what do you think?" Allie asked as Michael wandered around the half-completed loft, poking at pipes and wiring. Like most of the Gale boys, he'd spent summers working construction for her Uncle Neil. Unlike most of the Gale boys, he'd actually enjoyed it and the experience had ultimately shifted his interest in art into architecture. Allie figured the renovation would keep him from dwelling on Brian's betrayal.

Brushing dirt off his hands, he returned to her side. "The plumbing and electrical's all in. If I finish the build, and you hire the retailer's people to install fixtures and counters and carpet and shit—under my supervision—this place could be livable in about a week. Maybe less."

"Carpet?"

"We run linoleum across that end, kitchen and bathroom. Put down a good, hard-wearing Berber in the remaining space." Arms folded, he looked down at her from under the edge of his hair. "It's going to take a lot of yoyos, Allie."

She smiled, reached up, and brushed his hair back. "You just make the calls and let me worry about the money."

"Allie!" Joe whirled around to face her as she came back into the store picking yet more spiderwebs off her sweater. "This person . . ." He waved at the tiny woman practically vibrating by the counter. ". . . wants to buy this painting." It was the seascape Allie'd been looking at just before Shamrocks-and-attitude had shown up.

She suppressed a grin at the way the customer just barely kept herself from snatching it out of Joe's hands. "That's great."

"Yeah, but it's . . ." Leaning closer, he dropped his voice. ". . . got a price on the back that says ten thousand dollars."

"And?"

"Ten thousand dollars? That can't be right." He waggled the painting so that Allie could see the charm sketched under the price.

The woman raised a thin hand in protest, fingers trembling slightly, the scent of linseed oil wafting up from a stain on her sleeve. "Please . . ."

"Why don't you let her hold it, Joe."

"But . . ."

"It's okay."

Still frowning, he turned back around toward the customer and barely managed to let go in time when she snatched the painting from his grip. "It's just . . ."

"A nice round number." Allie noted that half the

woman's left eyebrow appeared to be Cadmium Yellow, and asked her, "Do *you* have a problem with the price?"

The woman opened her mouth, closed it again, an internal struggle clear on her face. Finally, she shook her head, gray-streaked ponytail swaying in counterpoint behind her.

"You handle the money, Joe." Her tone suggested he table any further protests until after the deal had been completed. Allie was pleased to see he'd realized it wasn't actually a suggestion. "I'll wrap it."

"It's a bank draft." The woman's voice was also thin, the audio matching the physical, and she couldn't meet Allie's gaze.

"Bank draft's fine." Two layers of brown paper with a charm sandwiched between offered more protection than the anal retentive wrapping provided by galleries and high-end auction houses. Allie'd put her wrapping up against pretty much everything but digestion by dragons. Given dragon digestion, that was a case of *you pay your money, you take your chance*. Given the presence of dragons in Calgary—or over Calgary, at least—that was not a rhetorical observation.

"Ten thousand dollars?" The words spilled out of Joe's mouth as the door closed and the customer sprinted out of sight. "For that piece of shite? You charmed her into thinking she wanted it!"

"First, it was Gran's charm, not mine. Second, the charm's intent was to keep just anyone from recognizing the painting, merely ensuring certain specific criteria were met. Third, it's a Turner. A study for *Calais Pier*. I recognized it when I was going through the box earlier. I think he was working out the motion of the waves between the packet and the pier." She twirled a finger in the air. "The circular pattern was unique for its time."

"And that means what?"

"Back in 2006 a private telephone bidder bought Turner's *Giudecca, La Donna della Salute and San Giorgio* at a Christie's auction in New York for $35.8 million."

Joe blinked and finally managed a choked, "Dollars?"

"Dollars."

"And the yellow-eyebrow woman knew that?"

Allie nodded. "My guess is she spotted the Turner a while ago and then went looking for a buyer willing to give her part of the price up front. She's probably been panicking we were going to sell it to someone else. Or realize the actual price of what we had. Ten thousand was enough she didn't feel too guilty about not telling us how much it was worth."

"Millions. It's worth millions."

"Maybe. But, given Gran, I guarantee most of that ten thousand is profit. And . . ." Allie grinned. ". . . yellow-eyebrow woman will make enough to be able to paint for the rest of her life without worrying about starving."

"But you could have made $35.8 million!"

"No, that needs auction hysteria. But she probably was able to find a collector willing to pony up one or two million, though."

"Not the point. She'll be making it, won't she? Not you!"

"She needed it. That was one of the charm's criteria. Gran's letter said the store had become crucial to the local community." Allie watched a young couple walk by. He pushed a sleeping toddler in a stroller. She tried, mostly unsuccessfully, to get a half-grown golden retriever to heel. "When I met you, I thought she meant the *community,* but now I think she was working wider."

"So what, it's suddenly all, 'hey, let's be Robin Hood'?"

"Joe, we made a profit of ten thousand dollars. Get over it. We needed a bit of money. A bit of money appeared."

"You needed a bit of money, and a bit of money appeared?" Joe repeated, eyes wide, voice a little higher than usual. "That's how it works for you? For your family?"

"Essentially. We don't control it, though, that's darkside stuff. Sorcery," she added when he looked confused. "We don't force it; we just let things happen."

He sank down onto the stool. "Your life doesn't suck, you know that, right?"

She glanced out the back of the store toward the garage and Michael and frowned at the muting of familiar pain. Still, he was here, with her, maybe that was enough these days. "There should be new pie in the fridge," she said. "You interested?"

"Ten thousand dollars *and* pie." Joe shook his head. "Total fucking absence of suck."

"So, the Gale woman."

"Alysha," Graham muttered without looking up from his monitor. Damned spellchecker kept insisting he meant extinguished when he actually meant exsanguinated.

Dark brows drew in as Stanley Kalynchuk glared down at him. "Alysha?"

"That's her name."

"I am aware that's her name. That's all you've discovered in . . . what? Forty-eight hours? Our time is not limitless!" Kalynchuk slapped a copy of the paper onto the desk. "Or have you forgotten?"

Graham raised one hand off the keyboard to wave it at his publisher in a vaguely placating manner. "I'm working on the story about the suspicious cattle deaths—we need to put our spin on the speculation."

"Our spin?" The snort managed the complex trick of being both dismissive and accepting. "What are you blaming it on?"

"Chupacabra." And didn't the spellchecker love that.

"Goat suckers?"

"They're not necessarily goat specific," Graham muttered, backspacing. "They suck the blood from live-stock. Cattle are livestock."

"They're not being exsanguinated, they're being eaten."

"Potato, potahto."

"And we're too far north for chupacabra."

"Yeah, like our readers are going to care."

"And that right there is the problem in a nutshell. No one cares about scholarship anymore." Kalynchuk paced away from the desk, turned by the white board, and, unfortunately, paced back. Graham had been hoping he'd stomp all the way off to his office. "Imagine the hysteria if we printed the truth."

"We've printed the truth. No one ever believes us. No one is supposed to believe us; that's the point of the exercise."

"Control. Discredit. Hide behind the expectations of the masses." A beefy hand smacked down over a blurry picture of what was probably a raccoon in a dumpster. "Most people wouldn't know the truth if it bit them on the ass."

Having half expected a bad Nicholson impression, Graham reminded himself that his boss was not a fan of popular culture.

"Now . . ."

Even without looking up, Graham knew his boss was standing with his arms crossed. He was just that good he could hear crossed arms in the other man's voice.

". . . about the Gale woman."

"Alysha. I'm seeing her tonight." In three hours, twenty-two minutes, seventeen seconds. But who was counting.

"Seeing?"

He looked up at that, a little surprised by the challenge in the question. "Dinner. Unless you need me for something else."

"No, not tonight."

"You wanted me to find out what she knows. That's all this is."

"Make sure that's all it is." Challenge had become warning although he didn't think he'd let any of his conflicted feelings show in his voice. "You do your job. You find out what you need to know, and you get out."

"You make her sound like a war zone."

Kalynchuk's lip curled. "We don't know that she isn't."

"Tight jeans, low-cut white tank top, pink ballet-wrap sweater." Sprawled out on the bed, Charlie watched Allie finish dressing and frowned. "Okay, you're clearly going for mildly sexy, given the boob and ass combo, but completely harmless. How tall is he?"

"Tall enough." Allie slid her feet into a pair of pink plaid Chucks, the only flats she had with her.

"How tall?" Charlie demanded.

"Five ten. Maybe."

"Fuck a duck, I've got boots taller than that."

"Well, if I was short like you, it wouldn't be a problem, would it?"

"I gave you that extra inch, babe. Felt sorry for the chubby thing you had going in junior high." She sat up and wrapped her arms around her bare knees. "You really like him?"

Because it was Charlie asking, Allie actually gave it some thought as she twisted her hair up and clipped it. "Yeah," she said, after a minute. "I really like him."

"You going to bang him?"

"Not tonight."

"Why not? And please don't tell me it's because Michael's here, because if you do, I'll barf, I swear."

"It has nothing to do with Michael," Allie snorted, dusting bronzer over her cheeks, blending the freckles in a bit.

Charlie's turn to think for a moment. "Weirdly, I believe you."

"Tonight's still about Gran."

"Yeah, okay, allegedly dead grandmother equals death of verbal foreplay. No pre-game show, no game."

"Fortunately, tomorrow is another day." Allie leaned down and kissed the top of Charlie's head. "I think you need more sleep."

Graham drove a four-wheel drive pickup, dark blue under the grime, with a black cab over the truck bed. "It's not very glamorous," he admitted, pulling out from the store and right into an illegal U-turn across 9th, "but it's paid for."

"It's just like home," Allie told him, braced against the movement. "My family lives twenty-two kilometers outside a bustling metropolis of about four thousand people, so pickups are the default method of transportation."

"Your grandmother left, looking for something a little more exciting?"

"She may have gone a bit wild," Allie allowed, grinning at him. "Because there's nothing more exciting than spri ... cat saucers and yoyos." He was wearing jeans and a leather jacket over a white shirt with a narrow blue stripe. And on his feet ...

"What are you doing?"

"Checking for cowboy boots."

"You're mocking me."

"I am." She frowned as he turned north on 1st Street, suddenly realizing why things looked so familiar. "That's interesting. We're going back along the route the cabbie used to bring me in from the airport."

Graham turned his attention off traffic long enough to shoot an incredulous look across the cab. "He drove through downtown?"

Her grin broadened at the indignation in his voice. "It's okay. I knew I was getting hosed."

"Did you report him?"

"I didn't care that much, and I got to see something more than the expressway. That's a win." She relaxed a little when Graham turned onto 3rd. Twice over *exactly* the same route would have been more than coincidence. Turned out their destination was just west of 3rd and 6th. Allie peered north up 6th as they crossed it, her attention still drawn to something in the block north of 2nd.

"Everything okay?"

"Yeah, it's ..." Eye widening, she noticed the name of the restaurant they were parking in front of. "Buchanan's? You own a restaurant?"

He laughed. "Happy coincidence, but it is why I came

here the first time. Wanted to see what the western branch of the family was up to. Well, that and *The Western Star's* office isn't far."

It looked as though he'd have come around and opened the truck door for her, but Allie was out and on the sidewalk before he got the chance. "Seems like the western branch of the family is doing fairly well," she said as he joined her. The restaurant was a square brick building with large windows running along the two open sides. "Chop House and Whiskey Bar?"

"It's kind of a shrine to malt whiskey; they've got over two hundred brands behind the bar. But the food's amazing, too," he added as Allie's eyebrows rose. "They're known for the best bacon cheeseburger in the city, but tonight, because it's your first dinner out in Calgary, I thought we'd go straight for the cliché and a nice thick cut of Alberta beef."

Allie bit her tongue and reminded herself that Graham was actually from Quebec.

"I feel like I ate an entire cow. Just flapped down and carried it up into the mountains and gorged myself. I'll have to spend the next two days digesting."

Graham laughed as he unlocked the passenger door. "Kind of more than I needed to know, Allie."

"Just add it to all those *background* details you got for your story." He hadn't asked the kind of questions that would have required lies—and honestly, who would—so most of the details were even accurate. A few memories of Gran. Some funny similarities between the back rooms at the ROM and the Emporium. Stories about growing up surrounded by cousins she couldn't get him to share. Every time she tried to get more information about his family, the question just seemed to slide sideways and end up somewhere else. She wondered what it was sliding off of.

"Background's important," he told her, stepping back to give her room. "I believe in thorough researching."

It had definitely been more of a date than an interrogation. She hadn't had to charm him once. Her cheeks actually hurt from smiling. "Clearly."

"Are you cold?"

At nearly nine thirty the temperature had dropped, but it was the contrast between the cool night air and the warmth against the small of her back where Graham's right hand rested that had caused the shiver. "I'll be fine once I'm in the truck."

Except the cab of the truck smelled too much like Graham to allow her to dial back her reaction. Like leather and a bit like apples and a little like steak sauce and a lot like male with a hint of something she thought she should recognize. It was a scent she definitely knew. Sharp. Not clean but clearing . . .

"Allie?" He'd paused, seat belt half on and stared at her, wearing an expression that suggested a little more than she'd intended had shown on her face. "Should I take you home now?"

She considered saying, *Let's head back to your place and get naked instead.* Didn't. It wasn't so much talking about Gran that had damped her interest as knowing that however it had turned out, the evening had begun as part of Graham doing his job. Without knowing exactly why, she wanted more. So she sighed, and did up her seat belt, and said, "Please."

They were back on 9th just crossing 6th Street when Graham's phone rang. "It's my boss, I have to get it. Technically, I'm working right now."

"Since the paper paid for dinner."

"Yeah."

"Better answer, then."

He shifted the phone to his left hand and flicked it open. "What?"

Allie could hear a low rumble from the other end but no actual words.

"Fuck. You're serious? No, you're right, that's not something you'd joke about. But won't that attract . . ." Given the length of the pause after the interruption, it seemed like he was getting an earful. "Okay. Right. Actually . . ." He peered out the window. ". . . I'm almost at the parking lot. Yes, she is. Because we just finished dinner. Is there time to . . . ? No." The fingers of his right hand tightened around the wheel. "I said no."

"You have to do something for work," Allie guessed as he closed the phone and shoved it back into his pocket. "Something at Fort Calgary." She waved a hand toward the dark, empty area that delineated the parking lot on the north side of the road. "And your boss isn't happy I'm still with you."

"Good call." Deftly finding the hole between a transport and a sedan the size of a two-bedroom apartment, he crossed the westbound lane and maneuvered his truck up the dark, curved driveway leading toward the fort. "Someone reported screaming teenagers. My boss thinks that sounds like a story, and since I'm right here . . ."

"I'll go with you," Allie offered. "I could watch you work."

"I could work better if you waited here." His smile was a pale curve in the shadows. "You'd be a distraction."

With the engine off, Allie could hear the truth in his words, so she gave him some back. "I don't want to get in your way."

"Good. Thank you." He leaned back in before he shut the door. "I won't be long."

"And I won't be staying here," Allie told his shoulder through the glass as he turned toward the back of the truck. "How convenient that I didn't tell you I would." She rubbed a hand over the hair rising on the back of her neck. Graham could check out the screaming teenagers. She needed to find whatever it was that was making them scream.

Something thudded behind her.

Twisting around, she peered through the back window into the box. Although she could see a lighter rectangle where Graham had opened the tailgate, she couldn't actually see what he was doing. What would a reporter need from the back of a truck?

Then the tailgate was slammed shut and she saw the beam of a high-powered flashlight paint the trees edging the parking lot with a circle of light. It would, she allowed, be difficult to write about something he couldn't see. Leaning past the steering wheel, she watched his back in the mirror until he merged into the darkness, then traced charms onto both eyelids to boost her night sight before she opened the truck door.

Tried to open the truck door.

It wasn't locked, but when she pushed against it, something pushed back. It seemed like the *something* making teenagers scream wanted her to stay in the truck.

Yeah. Like that was going to happen. She wet her fingertip, and traced a charm onto the curve of black plastic under the window. Before it could dry, she popped the latch and kicked out with both feet. Hinges shrieked a protest as the door slammed open.

Allie waited until she was certain nothing had been attracted by the noise, then closed the door and ran toward the strongest feeling of *this is very wrong.*

Very, very wrong, she amended after a moment, star-

ing down at the gate into the fort and the creature struggling through it. It wasn't so much that it had too many
arms as that its body shape suggested it shouldn't have
arms at all. All four eyes were small and red and in the
center of what had to be a face, a large beak snapped
open and closed within a writhing mass of tentacles.

Extrapolating emotions from writhing tentacles had
to be inexact, but it looked pissed. Really pissed. And
a bit confused. A combination of arm waving and
the way the deep fuchsia skin wrinkled over the eye
ridges suggested a distinct *what the fuck* reaction to . . .
something.

It took her a moment to realize why it wasn't roaring or snarling or making any noise at all beyond a wet
squelching sound as it tried to force moist appendages
between the log posts. It was trapped and essentially
helpless. Until it had forced its way through, noise
would draw attention. Predators. Although if there was
something around bigger and badder . . .

Idiot. She snapped a picture with her phone. *The
dragons.*

About to head down to the gate and suggest moving
backward as an option if it couldn't move forward—get
the emphasis right and *Shoo! Go home!* worked on
anything from stray dogs to evangelical proselytizers—
Allie jerked back as an impact crater opened between
the two clusters of eyes and black blood sprayed out
the back of a vaguely triangular head. It swayed, began
to fall, clutched desperately at the posts, and turned to
dust.

Whoever had pulled the trigger had known where
to put the kill shot. They'd either hunted squelching,
fuchsia, tentacled visitors from the UnderRealm before
or had access to one heck of a bestiary. Not to mention
that given all the writhing around in the dark, hitting

the exact spot necessary made the gunman scarily good at what he did.

Odds that there were two gunmen in Calgary loading Blessed rounds?

Slim.

Joe was sleeping at the store from now on.

Then, from down by the river, came the scream of a teenage girl at horror movie timbre, and the feeling of *wrong* shifted toward it.

Graham was out there looking for screaming teenagers. Whoever had shot the creature jammed in the gate was, no doubt, looking for whatever was making the teenager scream. Smart money went down on a second creature. Or, technically, a first creature.

Part of her wanted to go after Graham, make sure he was all right, to not trust his safety to an unknown shooter who had already threatened one of hers. But . . .

As long as both the teenagers and the creature were covered by Graham and the shooter, Allie knew responsibility lay with the gate. Or, more specifically, closing it before anything else slithered through. Dragons were one thing—they were canny enough she could ignore them right up until they ate one of her cousins—but tentacle-mouthed, multi-armed pink things were something else again. Although she had no idea exactly *what* else again.

The creature trapped in the gate looked like a Slohath demon. It wasn't, unless they came in more variations than he cared to consider, but there were enough similarities for him to chance the head shot. Kill one of these things with a Blessed round, and they died clean.

Kill one with a regular round and there was fuck of a mess to clean up. Injure one and . . . well, there was no incentive to get a second shot off fast and aimed right like a pissed-off Hellspawn.

He went to ground in the dubious cover of a clump of dog willow and pointed his weapon toward the riverbank.

The second creature—technically the first, he amended—looked a little like a bear. Fur, claws, the whole running-on-four-legs, rising-onto-two-legs thing. But it was bigger. A lot bigger, if the pair of teenagers standing frozen in fear were any indication.

Hard to hear it growling over the sound of the river, but he could feel the rumble in blood and bone. His hindbrain suggested getting the hell out of Dodge. He told it to shut the fuck up.

No idea where the heart or brain was, but if it was bipedal, it had a spine.

His finger curled around the trigger.

Saw barbed spikes lift out of the fur along the creature's forelegs.

Felt the breeze on his cheek.

Fuck! He was upwind!

He threw himself to the right. Too late to care about the noise as the dog willow snapped and broke under his weight. Felt the impact of the first thrown spike as it buried itself in the dirt by his hip. The second missed by a slightly larger margin—he'd moved closer to the thing, not farther away. A sudden, bitter smell that caught in the back of his throat suggested poison. While the third spike was in the air, he took his shot.

The creature was still turning. The first round caught it where head met shoulders. The second, about a centimeter up. No way of telling which killed it, they hit so close together.

Silver eyes gleamed over double fangs maybe twenty centimeters long.

It held its shape for a heartbeat, then the breeze caught the dust and spread it out over the river.

The space between the posts smelled like yogurt long past its best before date seasoned heavily with cumin. The air felt damp, oily against exposed skin. Allie wondered where she'd end up if she walked through although she wasn't curious enough to actually try it. That kind of curious was just a short walk from totally bugfuck crazy.

A lack of hysteria about sudden disappearances suggested the opening to the UnderRealm only happened while the fort was closed. Something so convenient couldn't be an accidental opening but had to have been deliberately constructed.

She couldn't find any markers, so the gate had to have been opened from the other side.

By the dragons? No. Giant flying lizards were . . . well, giant flying lizards, actually, and not up to this kind of working.

Given the number of Fey in the city, it was most likely that one of their doorways had been hijacked. Someone had broken the security bindings, and the dragons had found their way through. Or been sent through. Or called through.

And now other things were following the dragons.

At best, someone in the UnderRealm had been irresponsible. At worst, the dragons were a deliberate act of aggression. Not against the family, not yet anyway, but with Gran's store so close and Gran missing . . .

Teeth clenched, Allie wrote a charm on back of a

grubby gas receipt she found half buried by the path, then tossed it through the gate. The paper disappeared. The charm, drawn not exactly neatly with the punctured tip of her finger, hung in the air for a moment.

The flash hung in the air a moment longer.

The Courts were going to be pissed.

Tough.

"It like wasn't a bear, okay! It was all furry, but it was too big!" Made shrill by terror, the girl's voice sliced an advance path through the darkness.

"It had to be a fucking bear, didn't it?" The boy was less shrill but more panicked.

"Bears' eyes don't glow!"

"Sometimes! In the right light!"

"All six of them?"

"If it wasn't a bear, then what the fuck was it? Huh? What the fuck was it?"

The quiet answering rumble had to be Graham. Allie couldn't make out the words, but the tone sounded more calming than interrogative. It also sounded as though they were about to pass right in front of her, heading for the path to the parking lot. She thought about waiting for them but decided Graham would be happier if he thought she'd stayed in the truck. When it took so little to make someone happy, why not go for it?

"A bear? That wandered down from the mountains? That got shot in the head and then disappeared?"

"Not disappeared," Graham corrected. "Turned to dust."

"A vampire bear?"

"Don't even joke about it." He waved at one of the police officers as he pulled out of the parking lot.

Allie had no idea how he'd explained away their presence, but the teens were in the back of one of the two patrol cars probably still arguing about what had happened and they'd been told they could go. "Besides," he added, changing lanes, "wouldn't a vampire bear require a stake through the heart rather than a shot to the head?"

"Depends on the mythology." She grinned as he turned to stare. "What?"

"You're just messing with me, aren't you?"

"Maybe."

"Allie."

"Yes, I'm just messing with you." She didn't know why she was laughing except that she really liked the way he said her name. "So that's what the hysterical teenagers saw; what did you see?"

"Hysterical teenagers."

"That's all?"

"Well, I didn't see a vampire bear, if that's what you're asking."

He wasn't lying. "Did you see the shooter?"

"Nope."

Also not a lie.

"Neither did the hysterical teenagers," he added. "Given there's nothing to the story but hysterical teenagers, I doubt I'll even follow up on it."

"What about tracks?"

Eyes wide, he pivoted toward her; the truck swerved to the right. "Tracks of a vampire bear?" he asked, jerking them away from impact with a parked sedan.

"Tracks of whatever the kids saw," Allie expanded, releasing her grip on the dashboard.

"If they saw anything at all."

"If they saw anything at all," she agreed as he

pulled up in front of the store. "Do you think they saw something?"

For a moment, she thought he wasn't going to answer.

"I think they saw *something*," he admittedly slowly. "But mostly, I think I want to see you again."

Allie smiled across the cab of the truck. He sounded as if he was a little surprised by the revelation. She wasn't. "That's going to be one really well researched article."

"Not for the article." When her brows rose in exaggerated surprise, he visibly relaxed. "Okay, fine. You knew that. Tomorrow . . ."

"Store's open. Monday?"

"I'll be working."

She could see schedules getting in the way until the moment was lost. This was not a moment she planned to lose. "Joe can handle the store."

His eyes narrowed as he tried to work out what she meant. "So we're on for tomorrow?"

"Yes."

"We could go to . . . uh . . ."

Allie realized she was in deep when she thought it was cute he hadn't actually thought of anything in advance.

". . . Banff!"

"Okay."

"For the day."

"Great."

"I'll pick you up at . . ."

"Ten." Allie twisted sideways on the seat, and laid one hand on his arm. "So Joe knows he's in charge. Actually, we haven't really settled Joe's hours, so Charlie may have to tell him that when he arrives."

Even through jacket and shirt, she felt muscle flex. "Charlie's here."

"Yeah. She is." Maybe he just needed reminding that Charlie wasn't a guy.

"So tomorrow . . ."

Leaning forward, Allie kissed him. He was startled at first, then he started to respond, his left hand coming across to cup the back of her neck. "Tomorrow," she murmured against his mouth as she pulled away. Before he could answer, she slid out of the truck, closed the door, and waved good-bye through the window.

Gale girls knew how to make an exit.

Now that the police were gone and the area was quiet, he retrieved his weapon from where he'd hidden it under the dog willow and placed it carefully back into the case. Having Alysha Gale actually at the site hadn't turned into the disaster it could have been, but that, he was certain, was all luck because it sure as shit hadn't been planning.

The tracks the creature had left had been mostly obliterated by traffic—cops who thought they were wasting their time weren't too careful about where they walked. He carefully erased everything that remained, keeping half an eye on the sky.

"Yes, your involvement could very well attract the kind of attention we don't want! Unfortunately, the presence of a greater danger does not change the fact that your job involves protecting me from lesser dangers as well. In this case, two lesser dangers. I have no idea what the Courts are thinking allowing these things through their gate! We'll just have to risk it."

"It turned to dust when it was shot?" Charlie frowned down at the picture on Allie's phone. "I'm thinking the guy who pointed Blessed rounds at Joe is our prime suspect, then."

"That makes sense." She paused, David's old football jersey half over her head. "We should go find Joe."

"And?"

Yanking the jersey the rest of the way down, Allie took her phone back. "Offer him a safe place to sleep."

"I thought you did that when you closed the store."

"I did." And as he had the night before, Joe'd refused the offer. Refused to *hide*. "But now we have more information."

"He knows there's a shooter out there with Blessed rounds," Michael reminded her from the edge of the bed. "You want him to hang around, you're going to have to come up with something more."

"Than potential death?"

He shrugged. "Apparently."

"You know what I think," Charlie said, frowning thoughtfully. "I think this shooter has access to artifacts, so he could have acquired something that's attracting all sorts of party people through the gate."

Allie matched her frown. "What does that have to do with Joe?"

"Nothing. He's not interested in having a sleepover, eating s'mores, and braiding your hair. We've moved on. Keep up."

She chewed her lower lip. Artifacts stored power. Power attracted more power. "It's possible," she admitted.

"You have a better idea? We need to find this shooter. Track him down."

"Not tonight." Jeans unzipped, she shimmied them off her hips.

"Tomorrow."

"Can't. Have a date with Graham."

"Allie likes Graham!"

She smacked Michael in the shoulder with her jeans. "What are you, twelve?"

"Fine," Charlie sighed, as Allie danced back out of Michael's reach, "not tonight and not tomorrow. Why should a guy with a gun come between you and your love life?"

"Exactly."

"But we have to remember, he could've gotten his artifacts from the store, and that connects him to Auntie Catherine and possibly her disappearance."

"She thinks she's Nancy Drew," Allie explained to Michael, sliding under the covers. Charlie had grabbed the middle position by the simple process of already being in it when the other two came to bed.

"You're Nancy Drew," she reminded Allie. "I'm the best friend with the gender inappropriate name."

"Who am I, then?" Michael demanded.

"A Hardy Boy."

"Which one?"

"Both of them based on how much room you're taking up in the bed!" Allie dragged Charlie's pillow out from under her head, leaned across her, and whacked him with it.

Later, after he fell asleep, Charlie sketched a new charm between his brows so he wouldn't wake and pulled Allie into her arms. "You really like this Graham guy?" she asked, fingers ghosting along the curve of Allie's shoulder.

"I really do."

"I suppose I can learn to like him for your sake, then."

Mouthing along the warm line of Charlie's collarbone, Allie murmured, "Things will work out."

Gale girls made sure of it.

Joe still hadn't arrived when Graham pulled up.

"Haven't quite got the hang of the whole having an employee thing, have you?" Charlie asked when Allie pointed out Joe didn't have regular hours. "You obviously have plans, but I could go look for him."

"It's a big city." She waved a "be there in three minutes" through the door and grinned when Graham smiled and nodded. Eyes still blue. Smile still causing her pulse to throb erratically. "How would you find him?"

"I can track your charm just as easily as you could."

That was true. Allie chewed her lip. She knew Joe wasn't dead or the charm would have died with him— and that, she'd have felt. "He knows he's supposed to come in today. If we go chasing after him because he's not here the moment the store opens, I'm afraid he'll bolt."

"Maybe he needs a little more commitment from you."

"From me?" Allie paused half into her jacket. "What are you talking about? I offered him a job."

"In a half-assed kind of way."

"So he wouldn't bolt. You didn't see him that first day, all prickly and defensive. Just watch the store until he gets here, then call me."

"Right." Charlie leaned back against the counter then jerked straight again. "Wait ... I'm watching the store? What about Michael?"

"He's working on the loft," Allie reminded her. She took her phone out of her messenger bag, stared at it for a moment, then put it back in the bag again.

"Yeah, but I fucking hate retail."

"Suck it up."

Allie paused in the doorway as Graham got out of the truck. Finally seen through the clear-sight charm, he looked no different than he did without it. Broad shoulders stretched the denim confines of a jean jacket and under faded jeans that clung to his thighs in all the best ways, he wore a pair of black cowboy boots. The halo of light and the angelic choirs were purely a product of her imagination.

On a brilliantly sunny but surprisingly cool Sunday in May, Banff was crowded, and a little tacky, and surrounded by some of the most beautiful scenery Allie'd ever seen.

"So is it in the rules that every visitor to Alberta has to be brought here?" she wondered, linking her arm with his and sidestepping a group of tourists taking pictures at the totem pole.

He tucked her in close to his side, the boots boosting his height by a good two inches. "That's what they tell me."

It was entirely possible that Gran had disappeared in Banff. And that was the story she stuck to when Auntie Meredith called.

"Where's Allie?"

Charlie turned from searching a lower shelf as Joe came into the store. "Oh, good, you're alive."

Joe's eyes narrowed. "Why wouldn't I be?"

"Shooter with Blessed rounds."

He held up the hand marked with Allie's charm.

"Right. Allie's on a date with the short newspaper dude. You know anything about a gate to the Under-Realm out by Fort Calgary?" Eyes locked on his face, Charlie stood and sighed. "FYI, your poker face is crap."

Joe sighed. "I know the gate's there."

"Your people open it?"

"They're not my fucking people. And yeah, it's one of theirs."

"Allie closed it last night."

He scratched up under his sweater and Charlie wondered just how rough he was living. She had a kickass charm to get rid of fleas. "Why?"

"A couple of creepies got through. Probably because the security had already been buggered by the . . ." Charlie cocked her head. "Do you hear music?"

"No."

Squatting, she pulled out a stack of old puzzles and peered behind it at another stack of old puzzles. "I've been hearing an autoharp off and on since Allie left."

"I don't know what an autoharp sounds like."

"Today it sounds like music no one's making."

"Oh." She heard him shuffle closer, then he said, "Your grandmother had a bunch of music boxes in here somewhere."

Charlie straightened again, wiping the dust off her fingers onto her jeans as Joe danced back again. Allie was right. Come on too strong, and he'd run. With strength she didn't know she had, she resisted the urge to say, *Calm down, I'm not after your Lucky Charms,* and said instead, "Place to start, anyway. And she's not my gran. She's my Auntie Catherine."

"Isn't that worse?"

Snapping open her phone, Charlie grinned. "Usually."

Stepping out of the truck, Allie came to a full stop as she stared at the Banff Springs Hotel. "Does everyone feel like they've been here before?"

"It has been photographed a lot," Graham allowed, closing her door and pulling her forward.

After a long lunch that Allie fully enjoyed now she knew Joe was safe, they walked around the hotel grounds then drove back to the main street and the more touristy attractions.

Sometimes they talked.

"No, no one in my family is ever called Dorothy."

"And I'm guessing there's a distinct lack of ruby slippers?"

"Good guess."

Sometimes they just walked. Hand in hand. Arm in arm. Connected somehow.

As the shadows began to lengthen, they decided to go back to Calgary for supper.

Although they never got around to it.

Graham's condo was modern; white walls, dark hardwood floors, large photographs in black frames. His furniture was minimal. And his couch, for all its modern design, was surprisingly comfortable.

Removing her mouth from his long enough to unbutton his shirt and push it back off his shoulders, Allie's eyes widened.

Intricate hex marks ran in two lines down the center of his chest.

Sorcery.

So not good.

As the calluses on his hand rubbed against the bare skin of her waist, she threw a leg over his lap and straddled him. "When this is over," she murmured, nipping along his jawline, stubble rasping against her tongue like a cat's kiss in reverse, "we're going to have to talk."

He blinked. Pulled back a little. "If you need . . . I mean, we could talk now."

"After."

When it seemed like he might be going to argue, she dropped a hand between them and began to unbutton his fly.

His hips rocked up. "After's good, too."

SIX

The clock on the bedside table read 5:14 when Allie, lying with her head on Graham's shoulder so she could watch the minutes pass, felt his breathing change. One moment he was asleep, the next, awake and, if she hadn't been waiting for it, she'd have missed the way muscles tensed as he processed the situation.

Not hard to figure out how that processing began.

Not alone.

Who?

He didn't exactly relax after memory kicked in, but given the hex marks on his chest, Allie wasn't surprised.

"So . . ." He stroked her shoulder. ". . . is this when we talk?"

He'd known she was awake even though she'd been careful to keep her body limp and her breathing deep and regular.

Good instincts. Again, not surprising.

She combed her fingernails through the patch of hair on his chest, lightly scratching at the skin. "Unless you have a better idea."

A deep breath escaped before he said, "Maybe we should wait until after we talk."

"All right." She could tell he was thinking that after they talked, it'd be too late.

Pretty much proving her theory, he released her, turned on the bedside lamp, and started to get out of bed. Allie allowed him to roll her off his shoulder but that was it. "You're working for a sorcerer," she stated calmly. He froze in place. "Given the hexes he's marked you with," she continued, "what you do is dangerous. You know who I am and as much about my family as anyone does and may have had something to do with my grandmother's disappearance although I doubt it—you knew she was gone, but you didn't know why or you wouldn't have been trying to find out what I knew about it. You'd have been angling me away from the truth. Your sorcerer didn't want her around, but he knew better than to overtly remove her. He called you last night when he realized creatures other than dragons were coming through the gate—probably because the dragons have messed up the security—and that those creatures could be a threat to him. You took a weapon out of the back of your truck. Since the west isn't wild enough for you to be waving a high-caliber sniper rifle around, there's a misdirection hex carved into it. You—and your sorcerer—assumed the hexes on the doors would keep me in the truck. You were both wrong about that. After shooting the creatures, you hid the weapon and went back for it later." The faint smell she hadn't been able to place—gunpowder. She smiled at him, rolling up onto her side. "And you snore."

His face blank, he lay back on his pillow and stared at the ceiling—further processing, deciding on a reaction.

After a long moment, he turned his head toward her, blue eyes narrowed, and said, "I snore?"

"Well, it's more of a snuffle, actually."

"How long . . ."

"As long as I was listening."

"Allie."

"Only since I saw the hex marks on your chest." She ran a finger down each line. "He should have warned you they'd give away the game."

"This . . ." He waved a hand between them, his gaze locked on hers, wanting her to believe him. "This wasn't his idea."

Allie rolled her eyes. "Duh. But he did send you to find out what I knew."

"Yes."

"You really are a reporter." If she'd only seen the issue of the newspaper he'd shown her, she might have doubted that, but she'd pulled one from a box at the airport and flipped through it waiting for Charlie. He'd had an article in it about a man from Ponoka who swore he could whistle down the Northern Lights. But seriously, who couldn't?

"I really am a reporter."

"Why?"

"Thought I'd use that journalism degree."

"Not what I meant." She flicked his shoulder with her finger. "Why work at an actual job? Your sorcerer could support you."

His left eyelid twitched. "He's not *my* sorcerer."

"Semantics." Rubbing her knee up the outside of his thigh, she murmured, "Why is he bringing the dragons through?"

"He isn't." His eyes narrowed, and he shied away from her touch. "But you knew that."

"Not until you confirmed it. The gate originated on the other side, but he could have been calling them."

After a long moment, he said, "Originated?"

"I closed it."

"You closed it?"

"Slammed it shut with extreme prejudice and hung up a sign that said, 'If you can't control the security on your gates, we'll control it for you'." When he made a noise he'd probably be embarrassed to admit to later, she laughed. "Not really. I just shut it."

"Just?"

"It's not hard." Allie lifted herself up far enough she could see Graham's face. "Openings between the MidRealm and the UnderRealm aren't natural. Because there's supposed to be a barrier, the gate would rather be closed."

"The gate has an actual opinion. Ow." He grabbed for her hand and missed. "What will they do?" A muscle jumped in his jaw. "The ones who opened the gate?"

Allie shrugged, enjoying the way her skin moved against his. "Probably open another one somewhere else."

"They won't retaliate?"

"They never have. It's not their world," she explained when he frowned. "We have the final say here. They have it there." Using the tip of a finger, she traced the white line of scar that ran along his ribs and wondered how he'd gotten it. If he'd been a Gale boy, she'd have known. Finally, she sighed. "I need to talk to your boss."

The curve of his mouth wasn't quite a smile. "He won't talk to you."

"Yes, he will."

It seemed he didn't believe her. "I can ask him, Allie, but he doesn't trust your family."

He should be heading for the hills. No sorcerer in his right mind would linger anywhere near a Gale. Allie couldn't decide if it was a good thing or a bad thing that Graham didn't know that. "Just do what you can. When do you have to be at work?"

"Nine. Why?"

Rising up a little higher, she peered past him at the clock. Five thirty-four. She smiled and slid her hand under the sheet.

"Allie!"

"Whatever's *happening* in Calgary, that doesn't change what's happening between you and me."

Blue eyes gleamed. "And what's happening between you and me?"

"Why don't you let go of my wrist and we'll find out?"

He dropped her at the store at eight forty-three, fingers drumming on the steering wheel as she unbuckled her seat belt.

"What's wrong?"

"You and I, we can't . . ."

"We already are, Graham." Leaning forward, Allie kissed him lightly. "Or are you planning on dumping me now you've had your wicked way. Multiple times."

He smiled against her mouth, one hand rising to tangle in her hair. "*My* wicked way?"

"My ways aren't wicked." She flicked her tongue against his lower lip, then backed up. "You have my cell number, call me after you've talked to him." This time the truck door opened easily. Out on the sidewalk, she turned, and leaned back into the cab. "One more thing." This needed to be said, but she carefully maintained a neutral tone; he'd recognize the warning. "If you need to talk to Joe again, come to the store."

She closed the door before he could lie to her. The thing between them was still new; no harm in granting it a little wiggle room. Unfortunately, Graham didn't seem to have gotten the memo and leaned over to roll down the window.

Lifting her arm, she showed him her watch. "You'll be late."

"Allie . . ."

He sighed as a guy leaned out of a passing truck and yelled, "Get a room!"

". . . we need to talk some more."

"Okay."

"With our clothes on."

"Sure."

"I'm serious."

"You know where I am."

He stared at her for a long moment, shook his head, and settled back behind the wheel. She waited on the sidewalk until he drove away, then went into the store and pulled out her phone.

Then put it away again.

Even without the presence of the sorcerer, there was enough going on to bring at least one or two aunties west on what they'd euphemistically call a fact-finding mission. Add the sorcerer to the mix and all euphemisms would be chucked out the window. She'd have a dozen aunties on her doorstep loaded for bear and pretty much unstoppable in a little better than a heartbeat. Might be smarter to get as much information out of the sorcerer as she could before she called in the heavy artillery and they took him apart.

They wouldn't want her to go near him.

That, she had to admit as she unlocked the door, was part of the attraction.

Funny how being so far away from home had suddenly become a good thing. It seemed the constant ache had even eased a bit.

Charlie had sprawled out on the bed leaving Michael little more room than could be filled with the width of his shoulders—which was, admittedly, a considerable width. Allie flicked on the lights, picked a pair of cushions off the floor and heaved them at the bed.

"Up and at 'em, boys and girls. There's a sorcerer in town, and I'm making French toast."

As Charlie dragged a pillow over her head, Michael blinked blearily up at her. "You're making French toast for a sorcerer?"

Allie grinned. "He's welcome to breakfast if he calls before we're done."

Graham could feel his boss' attention on him from the moment he passed under the wards guarding the entrance to the building. He couldn't see them, but he knew they were there, silent sentinels keeping the older man safe.

"You've seen what hunts me, boy. You know better than most the danger I'm in."

Except for the style of salutation, things hadn't changed much in the thirteen years Stanley Kalynchuk had been his mentor. He knew the danger because he killed those foul creatures drawn to the sorcerer's power.

Catherine Gale had not been foul, he admitted, climbing the stairs to the second-floor offices of *The Western Star*. She'd been stubborn, untruthful, terrifyingly grabby and, considering which way the wind was blowing with her granddaughter, he wasn't exactly upset when she disappeared by some other hand than his.

Alysha Gale, on the other hand . . .

"I don't believe it!"

Jerked out of his thoughts, Graham stopped just inside the door of the outer office, his way blocked by his employer who actually looked . . . disheveled. Above yesterday's shirt– still untucked—dark brows were not only drawn in but seemed thicker than usual, his cheeks were beginning to purple, and his nostrils had flared to the point where it actually looked painful.

"You slept with her!"

"Not really any of your business," Graham told him, a little surprised by how much effort it took to keep his voice level.

"Oh, you sleep with a Gale while you're working for me, the Gale I sent you out to do reconnaissance on, and it's most certainly my business. I wouldn't have cared if you'd fucked her five ways to Sunday . . ."

Graham felt his fingers curl into fists. Didn't remember consciously making the decision but couldn't deny it had happened.

". . . I have never cared about your dalliances, but you actually *fell asleep* beside her."

"I was tired." He almost smiled remembering why. "I'm fine."

"You're an idiot! Did you listen to nothing I told you about the women of this family." Kalynchuk reached out and smacked Graham on the forehead hard enough he took a step back and his fists rose. "She's marked you. Right between the eyes."

"Marked me?"

"Drawn a charm. On your forehead. The wards screamed the news when you walked through them." His lip curled. "Strip. I need to see what else she's written."

Regaining control of his hands, Graham stopped himself from touching his forehead—he'd seen nothing when he shaved and didn't expect to feel anything now—and stripped efficiently down to his boxers right where he stood. He felt stupid. And betrayed. Stupidly betrayed. She'd been playing him all along.

Except . . .

He'd have sworn it was real. Even only having known her for four days. Even not knowing what *it* was.

"She didn't mess with your protections. That's something."

Glancing up from the hex marks, Kalynchuk jabbed a thick finger toward Graham's underwear. "Those, too."

"I don't . . ."

"I do. Get them off."

Forcing himself to breathe evenly through his nose, Graham let them fall to his ankles. Detached himself from himself—the way he did when he had a target in his sights—as his boss walked slowly around him, examining his skin for more marks of betrayal. The air in the office wasn't particularly cold, but he felt himself shrinking. The metaphor made physical.

"Get dressed," the older man grunted at last. "There's just the one. Right out in the open," he added walking away as Graham began to obey. "Didn't bother to hide it. But then, no reason for her to, is there? It's not like she knows I exist, or I'd already be ass-deep in crazy old women."

Dragging his trousers up over his hips, Graham spent a moment considering a lie. "She saw the protections, Boss."

Kalynchuk froze. Slowly turned. "She what?"

"She saw the protections."

"That's impossible, they're designed not to be seen."

"Yeah, well, she saw them. She has a fairly good idea of what's going on, and she wants to talk to you."

"Talk?"

"She seemed to think you'd be willing. I expect the charm is there to get your attention," he added as he shrugged into his shirt.

"Well, it worked! And do you know why it worked?" His cheeks began to purple again. "It worked because Gale women do not talk to men of power. They swarm in like a flock of crows, pecking away a bit here and a bit there until you're blind and helpless, and then they move in for the kill."

"The kill?" Graham's fingers froze, button shoved half through a button hole. "Metaphorically?"

"Actually." His lip curled. "Gale women have a fatal hate on for sorcerers."

"But if Catherine Gale was that much of a danger to you . . ."

"Why didn't I have you take care of her? Two reasons. First of all, you take one out and a dozen more flap in to find out what happened. Second, and more importantly, by the time I knew she was here," he turned and glared at the map of the city, "she'd been here for months. We'd been here *together* for months. And that could only mean she didn't know I was here. Safest thing to do would have been to leave, slink away with my tail between my legs and start up fresh somewhere else, but why should I?" He slammed his fist against the map, the impact jumping half a dozen pushpins out to clatter against the floor. "Why the fuck should I? Goddamned Gale women! But before you could acquire any useful information from her, all of a sudden, my world went to shit. The emergence ..." He flicked up a thick finger. ". . . they started arriving . . ." Another finger. ". . . the old bitch disappeared . . ." One more finger. ". . . and the young one arrived." Fingers curled back into a fist. "Now I can't leave, and this fucking Gale girl is fucking you!"

Graham shook his head, trying to arrange this new information into some sort of order. "You should have run from Catherine Gale?"

"From what she represented, yes."

"But you're . . ."

"Yes, I am. I could turn this city into a sheet of glass and send every soul in it to perdition with a word—all right, fine," he amended, although Graham hadn't spoken, "seven words. But they . . ." He sighed and sat heavily on a corner of one of the unused desks. "They don't fight fair. There has never been a sorcerer who survived a confrontation with them. Never. Might as well try to hold a handful of water as take them on."

"Freeze water, and you can hold it," Graham pointed out as the phone on his desk began to ring.

"Trite, but true," Kalynchuk acknowledged, silencing the phone with a wave. "But while you might have been able to take out Catherine Gale, could you shoot your girlfriend's grandmother?"

"She's *not* my girlfriend." Although he could almost touch the might have beens, the way he felt before he'd been told of her betrayal.

Kalynchuk snorted. "So you say. I say they're tricky."

"The charm; what will it make me do?"

"It won't make you *do* anything."

"So it's completely benign?"

"I didn't say that."

"Then what does it say?"

"It says you should call her and set up a meeting in the probably futile hope that there's a way out of this mess before we're overrun with crazy old women."

"Boss . . ."

"You really want to know, you should ask her."

"You've never lied to me."

"Has she?" It wasn't a tone Graham recognized. Took him a moment to identify it as melancholy. "Because they don't usually. It's just one of the things that makes them so dangerous. They can eat right through your defenses with the truth, boy. Don't ever doubt it."

He touched his forehead then. Didn't know he was doing it until he felt the contact. "I need to know before I see her again."

"Forewarned is forearmed. I suppose." Kalynchuk took a deep breath and shook himself, almost as though he were surfacing from deep water. "It says, essentially and for all intents and purposes, mine."

Graham blinked, hands stilled on his final button. "Yours?"

"No, you young idiot. Hers."

"A sorcerer?" Charlie stared down at the plate of French toast and then gratefully up at Allie as her fingers closed automatically around the offered mug of coffee. "No fucking way. The family hasn't butted heads with a sorcerer in . . . well, forever."

"The seventies."

"So last millennium."

"Hex marks don't lie, Charlie."

"Yeah, but here? In Calgary?" She took a long swallow as Allie set a second full plate down in front of Michael and sat herself. "I'm sure it's a nice enough place, but there's buggerall power here for sorcerers to be drawn to."

Allie picked up her fork. "Maybe he's just ahead of the curve. Power's shifting this way. Things are happening in Calgary."

"Please stop saying that," Charlie muttered, reaching for the syrup.

"You guys don't mean . . ." Michael waggled a hand as he chewed and swallowed. ". . . *power*, do you? I mean, like the oil fields and stuff?"

"Sorcerers accumulate power." Allie mirrored Michael's wave. "Then they start using it to control things, to give themselves the other kind of power."

"You're kidding me? They want to rule the world?"

"Eventually that's what it comes to. Power corrupts. Corruption leads to abuse. Abuse has to be stopped. Or better still, prevented."

"Yeah, but what about the whole 'family doesn't interfere' thing?"

Allie shrugged. "You rule the world, you're trying to rule the family."

"So the aunties go out hunting sorcerers before it comes to that?"

"No! Well, sort of, except like Charlie said, sorcerers are rare."

"And the smart ones keep their heads down," Charlie interjected, folding the top, golden-brown slice of egg-soaked bread over a line of syrup and picking it up with her fingers.

"So it's not like something the aunties get up to every weekend," Allie finished, ignoring her. "It's just something they take care of when it comes up, when they find one. Maybe once in a lifetime. They don't talk about it though. It's an . . ." She sketched air quotes. ". . . auntie thing."

Michael frowned at the syrup bottle. "And that's what they think is going to happen to David? He's going to get corrupted by power until he wants to rule the world and they'll have to take him out?"

"It's not going to happen!" Allie hadn't realized she'd gotten to her feet until she found herself glaring down at Michael and Charlie—the former stared back at her, the latter poured herself another cup of coffee. "But, yeah, that's what they think," she sighed as she sat down.

"Why did you never tell me any of this before?" Michael wondered.

"Because even though you act like an enormous girl . . ." Charlie patted his hand. ". . . you're really a guy. Is there any way this sorcerer could be bringing the dragons through?"

Allie shook her head. "The security on the gate had to be broken from the other side."

"By who?" Charlie demanded.

"No idea."

"An accomplice. The sorcerer could be calling them."

"Graham says he isn't."

"Oh, babe, Graham's working for him. He'll say whatever the black-hearted, son-of-a-bitch wants him to say."

"I believe him."

"He must be fan-fucking-tastic in the sack," Charlie muttered, "because you've only ever been this stupidly blind about one other man."

"Who?" Michael asked. When the cousins turned to stare at him, he flushed. "Oh. Right. So, uh, when do the aunties get here?" he asked, loading up another forkful.

"I haven't told them yet."

The crack of heavy porcelain against wood punctuated the extended silence as Charlie set her mug on the table, smudged eye makeup around wide eyes making her look like a startled raccoon. "You haven't told them yet? What are you waiting for, a visit from the little people? Hang on." She threw up both hands in exaggerated surprise. "You've had that, too!"

"I'm thinking," Allie growled, "that I'd like to know what's happening, and it's a little hard to find out once the ground's been salted."

"Metaphorically?" Michael wondered.

"Sometimes. Look . . ." She pushed her plate aside and leaned forward, elbows on the table. ". . . you know what the aunties are like. Gran's gone, someone broke the security on a gate to let the dragons through, and they're going to blame the sorcerer for both those things as well as the hike in Calgary's transit fares, middle-aged women wearing jeans that barely cover their asses, and SciFi canceling *The Dresden Files*."

"Loved that show," Michael muttered around a mouthful of French toast.

"He called Graham last night," Allie continued, "so he's monitoring the gate. He knows what's going on, and he's going to tell me. I mean, bottom line, he could easily be the lesser of two evils, depending on what's letting the dragons through and why."

Charlie shook her head. "*Lesser* of two evils will mean squat to the aunties. Besides, why would he spill to you?"

"Because he won't want me to call them. He talks or I dial."

Michael saluted her with his empty fork. "You go, girl! Are you going to eat . . . Thanks." He caught Allie's abandoned breakfast as she spun it across the table and dug in.

"I don't know . . ." Charlie lifted her coffee again and peered at Allie over the rim. "I can see why he'd take any chance offered to convince you not to call, but he has to know you're going to after he . . ." She blinked, and Allie almost literally saw the lights go on. "You're not, are you? You're going to try and sort this out yourself. You're not going to call them because you know they'll take your sorcerer's apprentice down with his boss."

"He's not his apprentice." Shifting, she could feel the mark his teeth had left on her inner thigh. "He's more like his assassin."

"Yeah, that makes him working with a sorcerer so much better."

"If it comes to it, I can protect Graham from the aunties."

"You can? Really. From the aunties?"

"Shut up."

"You sure you're not doing this because of David?" Michael asked quietly. "If you talk to this guy, and it turns out he isn't corrupt, then you can convince the aunties it's not all black and white, and they'll cut David some slack."

Mouth open, Charlie swiveled around in her chair. "Fuck me blind. Every now and then I remember you're not just another pretty face."

"Thank you. Elegantly expressed as always." He reached across the table and caught Allie's hand in his. "Allie-cat?"

"I didn't . . ." She hadn't thought of David since he'd called. And he wasn't going to turn anyway, so what would be the point in convincing the aunties that maybe not all sorcerers were cut from the same cloth. She turned her hand under Michael's so she could link their fingers and said, "That might be part of the reason."

David. And Graham. And . . .

And this was hers.

"Well, okay, then." He squeezed her hand, then let her go. "Pass the syrup and answer your phone."

It came as no real surprise when the address Allie'd been given turned out to be the long stone building on 6th Street, north of 2nd Avenue. The sorcerer's power had been drawing her attention even through the extensive wards he had on the building. And *extensive* was way too mild a description. She raised an eyebrow as she put her hand on the front door and the place lit up like a carnival ride. Allie half expected to hear cheesy calliope music. According to the aunties, sorcerers were big on the whole anything worth doing was worth overdoing, and it seemed they were right about that, at least. Three charms would have been plenty; one to mask power leakages if he was so paranoid about being found, one to stop unwanted guests, and one to give warning that a guest had arrived who couldn't be stopped.

Allie paused only long enough to recheck the office number on the mailbox in the entryway, and then paused a moment longer when she saw the name on the box.

The Western Star.

She was meeting the sorcerer Graham worked for at the tabloid Graham worked for. Given that two plus two still generally equaled four, even in Calgary, it seemed safe to assume that the sorcerer had something to do with the tabloid.

She stepped over the final hex without frying, and took the stairs to the second floor.

Like the charm on Gran's door, it had been set to keep out those who intended harm. She wasn't *intending* to do anything but get some answers.

After she had those answers, her intentions might change.

The deliberate rhythm of her boots against the tiles made it sound like she knew what she was doing. Carefully not imagining the aunties' reaction to being kept in the dark, feeling reckless and wondering if it was how Charlie always felt, she took the last four steps two at a time.

All things considered, the overdone hexes on the actual office door came as no surprise.

The room beyond it was smaller than she'd imagined. The wall opposite the two huge windows—also well hexed—was one enormous bank of filing cabinets, the wall to her right was covered in maps and corkboards that were covered in turn in pushpins and clippings, and in the wall opposite was another door, painted the ugliest khaki Allie'd ever seen with *Stanley Kalynchuk, Publisher* stenciled on it in black. Given the hexes on that door, it could have said *Stanley Kalynchuk, Sorcerer* just as accurately. Allie wondered what his actual name was.

There were a lot fewer newspapers around than she'd expected. Of the three desks filling the center of the room, only one looked used. Graham was sitting on the corner of it.

"We have a person who handles all our advertising, but she works from home. Comes in Tuesday mornings to go over the layout. A lot of our content is provided by freelancers, we take some off the wires, and I fill in the rest." He stood as she crossed the office. "I thought we could get all that out of the way up front."

He wasn't smiling.

"I don't like being used, Allie."

Not a Gale boy, Allie reminded herself. Not even someone who'd grown up around the Gales. She stopped just inside his reach. Just in case he wanted to reach for her. "I didn't use you."

"You marked me."

"We do that. I'm wearing Charlie's charms and one of my mother's. When I was younger, David, my brother, used to scribble all over me." She nodded toward the inner door. "He marked you."

"With my consent." Did he even know his hand had risen to touch his chest? "Giving me his protection."

"You fell asleep beside me, Graham, knowing who I was." Hoping he'd draw the line for himself, she waited. When he nodded, reluctantly granted but still an acknowledgment of her point, she added, "And I'm offering protection as well."

"Ignoring for the moment that I don't need your protection, it says *mine*. What kind of protection is that?"

Impossible to prevent a grin at the thought of Katie's reaction. "You'll find out when you start meeting my cousins."

"When I start . . ." His mouth opened and closed a few times. Allie waited more or less patiently while he worked through his reaction. "What makes you think," he managed at last, "that I'm going to meet your cousins? What makes you think that you and I are . . ."

"Still you and I?" She finished for him when it seemed like the hand waving was going to go on for a while.

"Yes!"

"You lied about why you were in the store. You took me out to dinner under false pretenses. You threatened my friend and employee. You would have killed my grandmother had your sorcerer commanded it, and don't bother lying to me, you wouldn't have had her under surveillance if he hadn't considered her a threat and—given that he employs you, well, that kind of defines his reaction to threat, doesn't it? In spite of all that, I'm still willing to give us a chance. Then I draw a completely harmless charm on your forehead, and that's it?"

"I don't . . ."

She waited, giving him a chance to gather his thoughts because he probably didn't. Most people didn't. The family found it very frustrating.

"Given *all that,*" he said at last, one hand pushing his hair back off his face, "why the hell do you want to be with me?"

Allie shrugged, fully aware of how the motion carried on down. "You have gorgeous eyes. Your voice raises the hair on my neck, but in a good way. You make me laugh. You make me feel safe, which is edging fairly close to the border between honest emotion and bad romance novel, but considering what you do for a living . . ." Her gesture made it clear she wasn't speaking about the newspaper. ". . . I'm claiming it. And the sex is fantastic—although, to be fair, we should expand the sample. As for the rest, well, it's a mystery."

"A mystery?"

"We're attracted to power."

"We?"

"The women in my family. It's a visceral thing. I expect to have a reaction to your sorcerer when I meet him. It's one of the reasons we don't like them."

"Because you react to them?"

"And they play by different rules."

"I don't have power like that."

"I know. Like I said, a mystery. My father teaches high school."

It took him a moment to realize that statement was relevant. Most of the confrontation had left his voice when he asked, "Another mystery?"

"Sometimes the power we're attracted to is weirdly hard to define." Hooking a finger in between two buttons on his shirt, she pulled herself closer. Today the heels on *her* boots put them pretty much eye-to-eye with maybe a centimeter in her favor. He'd better be able to cope because she loved these boots. "Regardless of how we're involved independently, you and I together have nothing to do with whatever else is happening."

"So you said."

"And I'll keep saying it until you believe me."

He sighed, breath redolent with coffee fumes and warm against her face. "That's not the way the world works."

"That's not the way the rest of the world works." She wondered what he'd do if she leaned in and kissed him. Decided not to risk it when he was still so skittish although, from the way his eyes widened, she was pretty sure he knew she'd considered it. "Good thing your sorcerer already primed you for dealing with the less than usual. And, speaking of your sorcerer, didn't he want to talk to me?"

"He did."

"Well, then?"

Stepping back, pulling her finger free, he began to gesture toward the inner door, then paused. "The thing, the charm, on my head; did you put that there to get his attention?"

"No."

"But you knew that's what would happen."

Interesting that he wasn't actually asking her. "I figured your sorcerer would want to talk to me about it, yes."

"He's not *my* sorcerer."

"Then whose sorcerer is he?"

He sighed again, pushed his hair back off his face, and led the way to the inner door. "You drive me crazy."

Allie grinned, appreciating the way his pants pulled tight across a muscular ass. "Pace yourself."

The sorcerer's office was small and crowded. Allie was surprised. She'd expected a room significantly larger than the space available with dark paneling and heavy expensive furniture. While this room did hold a large desk, it was made of the same dinged gray metal as the three in the outer office. The desk held in turn a computer and a printer, at least three or four years old, a phone, and a lot of assorted papers held down by the biggest iridescent white shell she'd ever seen. Facing the desk were two uncomfortable looking wood-and-pleather chairs. The closest thing to art on the scuffed beige walls was a calendar from a local Chinese restaurant. May's picture was a not particularly good watercolor of a panda eating bamboo. A long green blind very similar to the ones that used to hang in her primary school covered the window. Hexes covered the blind. Hexes also covered the door in the wall behind the desk that logic said led to a closet.

Logic said closet. Everything else said she should leave now while she still could.

Behind that door, Allie realized, would be the sorcerer's actual room. The room where eldritch forces were confined and warped. His inner sanctum. This room was just where he played at publishing a newspaper.

Given that the hexes told her he hadn't left the building for at least a month, she'd half expected it to smell like the inside of Michael's old gym locker. It didn't actually smell that bad.

The sorcerer himself turned out to be a burly, late

middle-aged man with dark eyes behind a thick fringe of dark lashes, a lot of dark hair shot through with gleaming strands of silver, and an impressive five o'clock shadow for not quite noon. He had, Allie noted, a dimple in his chin, a cupid's bow mouth, and an old burn scar puckering the skin just under the right side of his jaw, noticeable mostly because of the stubble around it. Standing, he'd probably be no taller than Graham.

The suit didn't match the office.

In the Gale family, made-to-measure meant an auntie had bothered to check breadth of shoulder before starting to knit the sweater, but Brian had introduced Allie and Michael to the concept of tailoring, and she'd be willing to bet that the sorcerer's charcoal gray suit had cost more than anything in Brian's entire wardrobe. The maroon shirt was definitely silk, undone at the collar to show the glint of a heavy gold chain.

Artifact.

So was the enormous gold signet on his right pinkie, proving that powerfully ugly was still ugly.

Power rolled off him like smoke. Power he contained. Power he controlled.

It was a lot less enthralling than Allie'd expected although, given the gleam in the dark eyes, she had no doubt he could be dangerously charming when he wanted to.

Behind her, Graham said, "Alysha Gale, Stanley Kalynchuk."

"Shall we cut to the chase, Ms. Gale?" Light flared off the ring as he steepled his fingers. "When can I expect your relatives?"

"That's up to you." Allie thought about sitting. Decided she'd better wait for an invitation. Rumor had it sorcerers were big on the whole *quake before me, lesser mortals* thing, and the last thing she wanted to do was annoy him and prod him into reacting impetuously. Her safety depended on him considering the consequences.

His eyes narrowed. "So you haven't called them yet?" His gaze flicked past her to Graham. "Good. I am all that stands between this world and disaster. Had you reacted with your family's usual prejudice toward men of power, at the very least you'd have doomed the city and quite possibly—given how flammable the substrate is—the entire province. I alone can prevent the destruction."

Okay, that was an unexpected truth. "You're hiding in a newspaper office."

"You're aware of our visitors?" When Allie nodded, he pressed both hands down on the top of the desk and leaned forward. "They are but the precursors to an ancient enemy of mine arising from the UnderRealm."

"Arising?"

"Clawing its way through the realities to destroy me."

"Okay." She connected the dots. "So this enemy sent *our visitors* to hunt for you, and you're hiding from them?"

He scowled. "I bide my time. Should I destroy them now . . ."

"Or send Graham out to shoot them."

"Should I destroy them now," he repeated, "my enemy is forewarned that I am here."

"Right here." She couldn't stop herself. "Hiding."

His cheeks darkened. "You might want to consider that it is up to me whether or not you leave this office."

"If I don't check in with my cousin within . . ." Allie checked her watch. ". . . an hour and twelve minutes, you'll have a maximum of seven hours."

Bushy brows drew in to nearly touch over his nose. "To do what?"

"That's up to you, but we checked the airlines . . .

"This is very Jason Bourne," Michael *noted as Allie scrolled through flight schedules. "And that makes me think you're about to do something stupidly dangerous. Do you have to talk to him?"*

"It's me or the aunties."

"Can't you just ignore him?"

"Ignore a sorcerer, at least two dragons, and a compromised gate to the UnderRealm less than a kilometer from Gran's store? That would be a no."

"Ignore the short, blue-eyed dude with the big gun . . ." Charlie's gesture bordered on obscene. ". . . who just happens to work for the sorcerer? That *would be a big no."*

"I bet his gun's not that big," Michael *muttered.*

". . . and seven hours is how long it'll take a dozen aunties to get here."

"You said a maximum of seven hours."

"That's if they take a conventional airline. They'll be angry, so they'll be less likely to be conventional."

Kalynchuk leaned back, silk shirt pulling tight over his chest and considered her for a long moment. "It might be worth it," he said at last. "If only because your old women would not be able to deal with my enemy. There's a trick to it, you see, that only I know, and my life for twelve of theirs, that's tempting. Pity about Alberta, but it might be worth the sacrifice."

"I don't think so." Allie met his gaze. He was, after all, only a man. "You don't look like the sacrificial type."

"And what does the sacrificial type look like?"

"Well, for one thing, it wears a cheaper suit."

His eyes narrowed. "Aren't you clever."

"Thank you." He was sarcastic, she was sarcastic. "You can't get rid of me, not safely, so the only real question is, do I believe you when you say that the aunties couldn't deal with your enemy after they've dealt with you."

"Dealt with." He snorted. "A child's euphemism."

Allie ignored him. Stanley Kalynchuk believed the aunties couldn't deal with his enemy, but that was opinion, not necessarily an absolute truth. Except . . . Gran had left him alone. He'd been in hiding for about a month, yet according to the account books, she'd been in the city for almost a year. She had to have known he was there. And she had to have seen why it was a good idea to keep him alive—not even Gran would keep a sorcerer secret just to piss off the rest of the aunties. *Probably not,* Allie amended silently, given that it *was* Gran. But because she'd ignored him, Kalynchuk thought she didn't know because he couldn't know what she'd seen. Twisty. *Very* like Gran.

Pivoting on one bootheel, she faced Graham. "Do you believe him?"

Graham blinked.

"Answer her," Kalynchuk growled.

"I do."

"Well, okay." Allie turned back to the sorcerer. "You're going to stop your enemy because you don't want to be destroyed. I don't want the city destroyed, so I'm not going to do anything to keep you from stopping your enemy. Including calling the aunties. It seems to me that best thing for us to do is to ignore each other for a while longer."

"And then?"

"We reevaluate."

"Do we?" He shook his head. "Given your family's opinion of my profession, it strikes me that an evaluation is not likely to go in my favor."

"My family doesn't actually have strong opinions on tabloid publishers." Kalynchuk stared at her long enough that she heard the rustle of cloth as Graham shifted his weight behind her. Okay. No sense of humor. Something to remember. "I'm here and they're not."

"I see." He sighed and sat back. "The way I see it, I can't prevent you from interfering as anything I might do to stop you will bring your relatives down on me. You, in turn, don't want your relatives to destroy my associate when they destroy me." She thought she'd hidden her reaction, but from the way he snickered, maybe she hadn't. "Oh, yes, it's easy enough for me to see your actual reasoning."

Allie's chin rose. "I can protect him."

"He's not yours to protect."

"*He* is right here," Graham muttered.

"Stalemate, Ms. Gale." Looking pleased with himself, he held out his hand.

Frowning, she took it. His palm had no calluses, but his grip was strong. Her thumb itched to try a charm. Just a small one. "You know how to contact me if you need me."

"I can't imagine why I would. Remember, only I can save the city. Tread carefully."

She pulled her fingers free. "Remember, I know where you're hiding." Turning on a heel, she stepped past the chair and kissed a flummoxed looking Graham on the cheek. "I can see myself out. Call me."

He waited by the door, watching his boss carefully, assessing his mood.

"You may not be as outstanding between the sheets as I assumed."

"Boss?" A thoughtful non sequitur? Not what he'd expected.

"Your sexual prowess had been my explanation for young Ms. Gale's delay in calling in reinforcements. I'd assumed your presence by my side was my guarantee of safety; now I'm not so sure that's the only reason." Standing, he slid his jacket off his shoulders. "I'm here, they're not—that's what she said. She has reasons of her own she's not sharing. Makes sense actually, those fucking Gale women are as self-centered as they come." He hung his jacket carefully over the back of his chair and began unbuttoning his cuffs.

"That last threat," Graham began. He didn't want to bring it up, but he took care of threats.

To his surprise, his employer nearly smiled. "Posturing. She wanted me to think she'd give my position away to the hunters, but that's not the way her family works. They don't use others to do their dirty work. That would make them too much like me."

"So she's no danger to you?"

"Not on her own." The first cuff folded up, he started on the second. "And as she seems to want to be on her own . . ."

"There's a cousin with her and another one coming," Graham reminded him.

"Wrong generation. Catherine Gale may have been a danger, but we'll never know now."

"You still believe they . . ." A glance toward the ceiling since he couldn't look up at the sky. ". . . took her out?"

"Her family doesn't know what happened to her, so it's the logical explanation. And what's more, I prefer to believe she poked at them when *she* couldn't find me . . ."

The edge on the words cut deep. Graham gritted his teeth and managed not to flinch. Although Allie's grandmother would have also gotten him out of his clothes had he given her any encouragement, he didn't expect his self-control in that instance to be acknowledged.

". . . than believe there's yet another player on the field we haven't been able to identify." Sleeves rolled up, he sat back down at the desk and turned on the computer. "I want you to keep seeing her. The damage has been done. Until we know what else is fizzing in that freaky Gale head of hers, we need to maintain her interest."

Graham could almost feel the weight of the charm on his forehead. "You want this relationship to be a part of my job."

"Your job is to protect me, so . . . yes. But remember, this isn't a relationship. If it comes to a choice between what you want and what the family wants, a Gale will always choose family. You will, of course, choose me. Now . . ." Eyes on the monitor, he moved the shell to one side and pulled a stack of paper toward him. ". . . we have a newspaper to get out."

". . . so we now know what's going on, at least in the vaguest possible terms." Still buzzing with adrenaline, barely believing she'd managed to pull it off, Allie sat down with her bowl. Charlie's barely existent cooking skills extended to heating up soup although, given that the kitchen was still in one piece, she suspected Michael'd done it.

"I can't believe the mighty sorcerer is publishing a crap tabloid," Michael said around a mouthful of sandwich.

"Explains why it's still in business," Allie snorted. "And besides, newspapers are a traditional way to gain secular power." She lifted the top slice of bread, checking that the tuna hadn't been mixed with chutney or jam or something equally noxious. "Look at Conrad Black."

"Look at what happened to Conrad Black. He didn't get to rule the world."

"My point exactly."

Michael's eyes widened. "The aunties didn't . . . ?"

"They're not saying."

"But there was cackling," Charlie added.

"There's always cackling," Allie sighed. "This guy, though, he gave me the creeps, but I'd bet he's pretty much what you see is what you get. He's accumulating power, sure, but he's new at it. I doubt he's been doing it longer than the thirteen years Graham's known him. He doesn't seem corrupt; he's just arrogant."

"David's arrogant," Michael said thoughtfully.

"You're not helping."

"Sorry." His face flushed darker than Allie thought the comment called for, but Charlie didn't give her a chance to ask why.

"He's been at it long enough to acquire an enemy in the UnderRealm."

"That doesn't really have anything to do with accumulating power here, though. We've all heard how the Courts react to anything that could be used to build a power base being taken away."

Michael waved his spoon. "I haven't."

"Remember how my mother reacted when she caught us with that cigarette out behind the barn? Times a hundred," she added when his cheeks blanched. "And . . ." She turned back to Charlie. ". . . if he'd been at it longer, he'd have known better than to *make* an enemy in the UnderRealm."

"But you believe he can stop this enemy."

"I believe him when he says he knows a trick that'll

work." Allie poked at a floating noodle. "But there's definitely something he didn't tell me."

"Yeah," Charlie mocked, "like who the enemy is. Why they're enemies. What the trick is. And how come he didn't fry his minion's ass when Graham's inability to answer no when you said do you wanna give him up to someone who should've called down the wrath of . . . of . . ." She paused. Frowned. "Okay, I got nothing that doesn't sound lame, but you know what I mean. You should've called home."

"Graham's safe as long as his boss thinks *he's* safe because I don't want Graham to get caught in the cleanup."

Charlie and Michael exchanged a nearly identical look.

"Just shut up and tell me what happened here while I was gone." Looking across the table at her cousin and her best friend, Allie noticed a sudden tension. "Okay, what?"

Charlie rolled her eyes and Michael dropped his gaze, drywall dust falling off his hair to lightly season his lunch as he said, "Roland called."

Allie couldn't see why Michael would look guilty about that. She'd left her phone at the apartment rather than risk auntie-created technology that close to a sorcerer. *Tell any aunties who call that I'm still working on what happened to Gran.*

"And?" she prodded.

"And he'll be here tomorrow. I said one of us would go and get him."

"And?"

"Joe chased a guy making balloon animals away from the front of the store."

Joe had waved off her hurried explanation of what was going on with an eye roll and a terse, *"Not my business."* She owed him big time.

"And?"

"I'm nearly finished sanding. I'll get the painting started this afternoon. Flooring tomorrow. Fixtures the day after." Tradesmen made themselves available when Gales wanted them. It was just the way the world worked.

"And?"

"The stairs to the loft need replacing, but I'll wait until after we're done hauling crap up and down them. You going to furnish it?"

"Yes."

"Okay, then."

"And?"

"And David called. What?" Charlie demanded when Michael smacked her arm. "You were taking too damned long." She lifted her bowl and drank the last of the soup out of it. "Michael answered," she noted after licking the orange mustache off her upper lip.

Allie waited, suddenly not hungry.

"He asked me where you were," Michael said at last. Given the way he was working the puppy eyes, silently begging for forgiveness, that could only mean one thing.

"You told him where I was."

"It was David, Allie. I can't lie to David, you know that."

"Dude, you can't lie to anyone." Charlie reached over and ruffled his hair. "Tell her the rest."

Given the deep breath, it couldn't be good. Allie braced herself.

"He'll be here Thursday."

"Oh, great. He's going to ... wait." She frowned. If the aunties could be here in seven hours, David could be here in six. "Thursday?"

"After he stopped yelling, I convinced him you

weren't in any danger, so he shouldn't just charge out here guns blazing. You know how the aunties watch him. They see that . . ."

Allie nodded. "And they're on the next plane."

"And he's one step closer to taking over from Uncle Edward," Charlie added solemnly.

Michael sighed again. "Yeah, well, he thinks it's because the last thing *you* need right now is attention from the aunties."

"Me? Why?"

"Duh," Charlie snorted. "You're hiding a sorcerer."

"So are you."

"Your decision, sweetie."

"I didn't tell him about your plan to use this situation to make the aunties rethink the whole sorcery thing," Michael broke in, "because that would have implied or, you know, suggested that . . ." He pushed his hair back off his face. "I don't think he's going darkside any more than you do."

Picking up her spoon, Allie forced herself to eat one, two, three mouthfuls of soup.

"Allie?"

"It's okay, Michael." She put down her spoon. "But we're going to need to clean out that second bedroom and buy. . . ."

A ringing phone cut her off. Allie looked at hers, still lying by the butter dish, and then over at Charlie.

"Came in today's mail." Charlie rummaged it out of the pocket of her hoodie. "Auntie Jane's already called me twice and my mother seems to think that, now I'm not able to bounce about through the Wood, I should settle down." A glance at the call display and she left the table. "It's Dave in Winnipeg; probably about a job."

"Is Charlie leaving?" Michael asked quietly as she disappeared into the bedroom.

"You know she never stays around for long."

"But without access to the Wood . . ."

"There's these things called planes now."

They sat quietly for a moment, unable to make out what Charlie was saying, then Michael pushed his empty bowl aside. "Allie, I'm sorry for involving David."

David was not going to understand what she was trying to do. "The important thing is that you kept him from alerting the aunties." She tapped a fingernail against the tabletop as she considered things. "And you know, since we're not bringing the aunties in, it's not a bad idea to have some backup handy in case Graham's boss is wrong about being able to win this thing."

Michael frowned in turn. "Is that likely?"

"I don't know. But if I'm right, and he hasn't been at this very long . . ."

"So you want David around to back up a sorcerer?"

Allie grimaced because that was exactly what she wanted. "Think that'll be a little hard to explain?"

"I think it's going to rank right up there with the day I told the family I'm gay."

" 'Cause it's all about you." Allie poked his knee under the table with her foot, grateful for a chance to change the subject. "Brian knows you're here."

"Where else would I be?"

"No, I mean he called me. And I told him you were here. He sounded wrecked."

Michael's mouth twisted. "Good."

"Got an audition for a band." Charlie came out of the bedroom carrying her gig bag, glanced between the two of them and said, "Whoa, soap opera faces. Looks like I'm hauling ass just in time."

"Is it safe for you to travel?"

"You almost strained something turning that into a question, didn't you?" She bent and kissed the top of

Allie's head. "Relax. It's here in Calgary. Derek, the friend I was in studio with in Halifax, told his buddy Tom in Toronto that I was heading west and Tom told his ex-bandmate Dave in Winnipeg and Dave got a call from a friend whose guitarist slash backup singer just went on maternity leave and he called me."

"Great." Charlie was staying. Allie didn't bother parsing the reason. "Do you need the car?"

"Thanks." She shrugged into her jean jacket and held out a hand for the keys. "They've got rehearsal space way the hell south, on McKenzie Drive, and I'd rather not cab it."

"You just got here, so how do you even know where McKenzie Drive is?" Michael wondered.

"Well, I could point out that I have these fucking awesome powers that allow me to travel through time and space, so urban planning isn't much of a challenge, but . . ." She pulled a folded piece of paper out of one of the pockets on the bag. ". . . Allie's laptop is in the bedroom and there's a really strong unsecured wireless signal just waiting to be taken advantage of, so I looked it up. It's a bit of a drive, but I'll snag a country station and pick up an audition song on the way. Be good, kids; I won't be back for supper."

"Country?" Michael asked as the door closed.

"Not your momma's country," Allie guessed.

"Yeah, yeah, I'll dye it plaid. It'll look like I have a flannel shirt on my head. See you guys on Thursday!" Charlie waved the rest of the band off in their trio of pickups and, because the night was chilly bordering on really fucking cold, walked quickly west on McKenzie Drive to where she'd parked the car. Her hair had been deemed un-country, but she was ready to change it anyway. It wasn't like she was married to the blue, and the whole point of hair was that it was easy to change. Okay, maybe not the whole point, but she was half tempted to actually go plaid just to see what the rest of the band would say.

Dun Good was a Calgary bar band and the other four musicians were both enthusiastic about making music and realistic about making a living at it. Their day jobs would leave Charlie plenty of time to deal with the shit about to hit the fan when the aunties found out what Allie'd done.

Not to mention that David would definitely have a few words to say on the subject.

Way to go, Allie.

Charlie fully approved of kicking the coals every now and then to see what flared up. Kind of surprised her that Allie'd taken a poke at it, but maybe all she'd needed was a little distance from the family. Charlie was a big believer in distance. Not many Gales were.

Stepping over a broken slab of sidewalk, she thought about finding a park and sliding into the Wood— incognito, no music—just to see if it was safe. But then she figured Allie'd be a bit pissed about having to retrieve her car if it wasn't, and she didn't really want to have to get her ass home from Prague or Cairo anyway. Couldn't *afford* to get her ass home from much farther than where she was right at this moment given the smoking state of her credit cards.

It cost a small fortune to fly from Rio to Calgary. Who knew?

So it looked like she was stuck in Calgary for a while.

Having that choice made for her bothered her a lot less than it should. Maybe her mother was right. Maybe she was ready to settle down. Or at least stay in one place for a while, which—in no way, shape, or form—needed to mean the same thing. Give the band a couple of gigs to shake down, and she'd see about getting her other instruments from home.

"All right." At the Beetle, she shifted the gig bag to her other hand, and wrestled the key into the passenger side door. "First thing on the agenda, wheels." This thing made her want to play Simon and Garfunkel, circa "Sounds of Silence."

Bent nearly double to buckle the seat belt through the gig bag's straps, Charlie heard what sounded like wet sheets flapping in the wind. A quick check determined the Beetle's soft top had not come undone. When she straightened, squinting upward, following her ears, it looked as though a triangular section of the stars had disappeared.

"Well, hello, darkness," she muttered and had just enough time to realize the sound and the blank space in the night sky were connected when she smelled sulfur.

She dove for cover as a line of red/orange light bisected the night.

An appliance store across the street went up in flames.

SEVEN

"But the dragons are searching for the sorcerer, right? So they might have thought Charlie . . ."

"It doesn't work that way, Michael. Sorcerers have a power signature for the same reason the store does. The family uses power, we don't hold it."

"I know that."

"Then you know they couldn't have been targeting Charlie." Allie glanced toward the bedroom where Charlie was still asleep and snoring. Snoring musically, but definitely snoring. She'd called in the fire and stayed to give a statement before heading home and giving a significantly less edited statement there.

"Yeah, and I also know that your family doesn't believe in coincidence."

"I never said it was a coincidence that Charlie was there when the store burned, I just said they weren't targeting her. Not the same thing." She opened the fridge door to put the butter away, saw the blueberry pie, and wondered if Auntie Jane thought she was stupid. The thing had more charms than blueberries.

"So if it wasn't coincidence, what was it?"

"Something else, obviously." She closed the door a little harder than was necessary.

"Oh, that's mature, Allie." Michael's voice had picked up an edge. "I thought we didn't keep secrets."

Sighing, she turned to face him. "We don't."

"So tell me what's going on with the dragons."

"They're hunting the sorcerer!"

"Well, they fucking suck at it!" Michael grabbed his tool belt off the arm of the couch and stomped out of the apartment. Gran's charms kept him from slamming the door but only just. The definitive click of the latch rang in the silent apartment.

Allie frowned. Silent?

"Someone sounds less than gay this morning." Charlie, in turn, didn't sound happy about being awake. "And when I say less than gay," she added, squinting in the spill of light as Allie came into the bedroom, "I mean really fucking cranky. Call Brian. Tell him to come and pick up his boy."

"It's not about Brian." Allie sat on the side of the bed and pushed a bit of indigo hair off Charlie's face.

"Allie, sweetie, it's entirely about Brian. One, Michael's been around family all his life. He doesn't need that shit explained. Two, the only time you guys ever fight is if there's a third party involved. And, three, he hasn't been laid in days, so it's no wonder he's cranky. Call Brian."

"I'm not getting involved in this."

"As if."

"Not this time."

"Uh-huh."

"I've got errands to run before I pick up Rol. Go back to sleep." She bent and kissed Charlie's forehead to speed the healing of the scorched skin, then slid off the bed.

The mirror showed her holding a crying baby. Allie half thought she saw a lashing tail poke out of the diaper, but Auntie Vera had called to warn her about Auntie Jane's pie—not the charms, the pastry—and the vitriol distracted her. When she looked again, nothing.

Allie found Joe sitting in the food court in North Hill Center, drinking a coffee and being ignored by a belligerent-looking representative of mall security who clearly did not believe in leprechauns even if they had a *Mark's Work Wearhouse* bag and a new dark blue Henley.

"Got a minute?" she asked, sliding into the seat across from him and tracing a charm on the table that had the security guard glaring through her as well.

"Could," he said carefully. "Why?"

"Did you know there was a sorcerer in the city?"

His eyes widened. "No way, really? Those guys attract trouble like shit attracts flies. You got a sorcerer, and next thing you know you've got all kinds of nasty stuff pushing through the cracks trying to take them out." Jerking his head back, he stared up at the exposed ductwork and the ugly orange light fixtures. "Is that who they're after, then?"

They were not perched in the ductwork, and Allie only checked to be thorough. "Yes, that's who they're after." She licked dry lips. "It was his guy who threatened you."

Pale skin blanched. "With the Blessed rounds?"

"Unless there've been more threats you haven't told me about."

"No." He rubbed a thumb over the back of his hand, tracing the charm. "This is beyond not good. I mean, if a sorcerer's pissed at me, I need to be getting out of town. Now."

"It wasn't about you, it was about me. About the family. We ..." *Destroy sorcerers where we find them* was more than she wanted to admit to. And not currently accurate anyway. "... don't get along with sorcerers very well, and you'd just spent time with me. In Gran's store. But you're safe now," she added quickly as Joe jerked away from her. "I talked to him and ..."

"You talked to him? To the sorcerer?" Joe's Adam's apple bobbed in his throat. "About me?"

"No, I talked to his shooter about you, and it won't happen again." Seemed like a smart idea to keep the identity of the shooter to herself since Joe and Graham were definitely going to be interacting. "You're safe, you have my word." She frowned. "Okay, you're safe from the shooter, and I'm well aware he's not the only danger in town."

The new key on the old brass key chain she'd taken from the store had fallen to the bottom of her messenger bag and it took a moment to rummage it free. She'd barely thought of Joe all day Sunday given the whole sorcerer thing, and Charlie was right. Had been right. Was still right. Given everything that was going down, Joe needed a little more commitment from her. She laid the key chain down between them on the table. "There's no reason for you to wait outside in the mornings. Or whenever. I'd feel better if you slept in the apartment, even though I don't know that anyone's actually after you," she added hurriedly seeing his expression, "but that's your choice."

Joe stared down at the key and then up at her, pale skin paler still, although she hadn't believed that possible. "Do you know," he began. Shook his head. Pushed his hair back off his face with fingers that trembled slightly. "Stupid. Of course you know. Put a key in a cradle to keep a baby from being stolen by fairies. Give a key to a changeling, lock him in place. Give him a place. This is more than just a way to open a door. This is . . . It's . . . For me . . ."

Allie put one finger on the key and pushed it toward him, the tie that linked her to her family throbbing in time to her heartbeat. "I know."

"Really?" When he looked up, hope made his eyes as Human as she'd ever seen them.

"Yes. Really." Choosing to live unrooted was one thing; being forced to it was something else again. Allie couldn't make it right that Joe's people had used him as currency to buy the few years of amusement a mortal would provide in the UnderRealm, but she could give him a place and people to stand by him. Or occasionally in front of him. Barely breathing, he swallowed once, Adam's apple rising and falling in the thin column of his throat. Then, finally, he placed his fingertip beside hers and nodded.

"Good." She glanced at her watch and stood. "I've got to get to the airport." A step away from the table. A step back. "Joe . . ."

He paused, key halfway to his pocket.

"The sorcerer and I have come to a sort of agreement—mostly involving not doing much of anything to each other—but he did give the order to have you threatened, so if you want to . . . you know, *not,* because I didn't kick his ass, I'd understand."

Ginger brows drew in so far they almost touched over Joe's nose. "You could have kicked his ass?"

"By myself? No. But I could have called the aunties in."

"You still could?"

"Yes, but . . ."

"You're playing the long game, then."

Allie thought about that for a moment. "I guess I
am."

"Then we're good." Joe closed his fingers around the
key. "More than."

"Thank you."

On the way out, Allie took a moment to ask the security guard for directions and sketched a charm on his tie
just below the cheap brass tie clip. Moods were easy to
adjust, and she saw no reason he should make everyone
suffer for his.

Roland's plane got in on time. He pulled back from
her welcoming kiss, gently brushed an eyelash off her
cheek, and frowned slightly. "You've changed since the
last time I saw you."

Allie snorted. "Rol, last time you saw me was during
ritual and you weren't exactly at your most analytical.
And you're second circle, so it wasn't like you were paying a lot of attention to me. And it's only been a week
and a half. And you only just got here."

"All valid arguments, but . . ."

"Roland!"

They turned together as a tiny, dark-haired woman with
a brilliant smile and abundant curves crossed the terminal
toward them. She stopped in front of Roland; not so much
in front that she was obviously ignoring Allie but enough
that it was clear where her attention lay.

"I just wanted to say once again how much fun it was
to travel with you and I hope we get a chance to see

each other again while you're in Calgary. You have my number?"

"I do."

"Good."

The heat barely masked in her eyes brought Allie forward half a step. Roland started as though he'd actually forgotten she was there.

"Sandra, this is my cousin, Alysha. Allie, Sandra had the seat beside me and we ended up having to share a screen—the plane had the little ones on the seatbacks and hers refused to work."

"Pleased to met you, Sandra." Allie smiled, and the other woman blinked. "Thanks for taking care of him for us."

"My pleasure." But she sounded uncertain.

"Sorry to cut this short, but airport parking . . . you know?"

"Yes. Of course." Frowning slightly, she held out her hand. "Good-bye, Roland."

Small tanned fingers disappeared inside his. "Good-bye, Sandra."

Allie smiled again then turned to lead the way out to the car.

After a few steps, Roland fell in beside her. "It wasn't like that," he said after a few steps more.

"She wanted it to be."

"I wouldn't have called her."

"Now she won't mind as much."

"As much?"

"Hey, you're still a hunka hunka burning legal love, I couldn't change that."

He laughed as they stepped outside. "Like I said, you've changed. A week ago, you'd have ignored her."

"Maybe." Roland was David's age, so she might have

trusted him not to stray. "But I'm the only family you've got out here."

"Charlie left?"

"No, but Charlie's . . . Charlie."

As the silence extended, Allie couldn't figure out what Roland needed to think about because it was a family truism that Charlie was Charlie and the rest of them would just have to cope.

Finally, he nodded, said, "True," somewhat anticlimactically, then added, "the aunties want me to pump you for information. They think you're hiding something."

"Do they?"

"They're certain of it."

She sighed. "Wait until we get to the car and we can talk."

"I can't believe you're hiding this from the aunties!"

Pedal to the floor, Allie roared onto Deerfoot Trail. "The aunties would only make things worse."

"That's not . . ." He paused, quiet for a moment, one hand gripping the handle built into the dash, knuckles white. "Probably," he agreed at last. "But that's not your call."

"Oh, yes, it is. They sent me out here to deal with things, and I'm dealing."

"Auntie Catherine left you the store, but you *chose* to come out here and deal with things, Allie."

"And I'm dealing." When Roland opened his mouth to argue, she turned on the radio. When he sighed and reached to turn it off, she grabbed his wrist. "Wait. It's the local news. I need to hear it."

". . . third fire of the night at Web Wizards on Broadway. Although the fire marshal's office has yet to issue an official statement, an unidentified source confirms that arson is suspected."

"Web Wizards," Allie repeated, sliding the Beetle back into the righthand lane when a hole opened between a transport and an elderly Buick.

Roland turned the radio off as the weather report began. "Allie, we need to discuss you hiding a sorcerer from the aunties."

"Not now, Rol. I'm thinking. And I'm not hiding him, I'm merely letting him remain hidden."

"That's a bad defense."

"Seriously." She took her eyes off the road long enough to glare at him. "Thinking."

Charlie looked up from her guitar as the apartment door opened. "Auntie Meredith called while you were gone, Allie. If I'm still being bounced out of the Wood, they want me to grab a plane and head home so that I can take one of them traveling and they can kick shadow butt. I reminded Auntie Meredith that since the shadow was tied to your song, I was right where it didn't want me to be and planned on staying. Besides, it took them too damned long to pony up, and I just signed with a band. She told me to quit. I told her you needed me. She asked for what. I said you'd met a guy. That seemed to shut her up although there may have been cackling. Hey, Roland."

Leaving his suitcase at the end of the sofa, he bent and kissed her. "I see you're still working the punk look."

Tucking a strand of indigo hair back behind her ear, Charlie rolled her eyes. "Punk has been over for a long time. I'm thinking of dying it red, though. Red's hot for country."

"What country?"

"Not country geographically; country musically. Oh, yeah. Allie . . ." She twisted to watch Allie cross the apartment. ". . . Joe showed up. He's out back helping Michael."

"And Joe is . . . ?" Roland asked.

"Allie's leprechaun."

"He's not my leprechaun," Allie protested, heading into the bedroom for her computer.

Charlie's snort carried clearly though the open door. "You gave him a key; in what way is he not yours?"

"I didn't say he wasn't mine," she muttered as she grabbed the laptop and flipped it open. "I said he wasn't my leprechaun. I gave him a key, he's on the edge of family now."

"The edge at the foot of the rainbow."

"Let it go, Charlie." Laptop balanced on one hand as she came back into the main room, Allie frowned down at the screen. "Please tell me girlswithguitars.com isn't what I . . . Eww." It took three tries to hit delete. She didn't know a lot about guitars but that *couldn't* be good for the instrument. "Get your own computer if you're going to surf for porn!" she snapped, sitting down at one end of the big table and clearing the cache.

Roland wrapped an arm around his backpack as Charlie looked at it speculatively. "Don't even think about it."

"I can't afford a laptop. I have to buy a pickup truck."

"Because you're playing country music now?" His right eyebrow rose. His left remained neutral. "It's not like you to buy into stereotypes."

"Everyone else in the band has a pickup truck!"

"If everyone else in the band . . ." Roland frowned.

"Uh ... Wait, I've got it. If everyone else in the band dyed their hair red, would you?"

Charlie snickered. "Way to miss your save, dude. Allie! What's the anti-country music vehicle?"

"Don't know, don't care. Buy a bicycle. Look at this ..." When her cousins crowded around, she pointed at the screen. "These are the Calgary Yellow Pages online. Nothing comes up for sorcerer, but when I search for wizard, the first three—Appliance Wizard, Blizzard Wizard Heating and Air Conditioning, and Web Wizards—all caught fire last night. The dragons are trying to flush him."

"Looks like," Charlie nodded.

Roland turned to stare. "By burning down businesses with the word wizard in the name?"

"Hello! From the UnderRealm," Charlie reminded him, flicking his ear. "They know less about how the world works than you do."

"They've been sent to find the sorcerer," Allie interjected before the argument really got going. "They're supposed to clear him out of the way before his enemy comes through. This suggests they're running out of time and getting desperate."

"Desperate dragons," Roland began.

"... just what we need," Charlie finished in complete agreement.

Allie scrolled down and tapped a fingernail on the bottom entry. "This is where they'll be tonight. Wizards Of Electrostatic Painting, Beaconsfield Crescent NW. And I'll be there waiting for them."

"Why? They're not burning down family businesses," Roland continued when Allie swiveled around to face him. "This has nothing to do with us. My advice for you is to call the aunties and have them shut the whole thing down—dragons, sorcerer, gate to the UnderRealm."

"Didn't she tell you?" Charlie asked.

"Tell me what?"

"Charlie!"

"Allie's trying to work with this sorcerer, to interject a little gray into the way the aunties think about them."

"Why?"

"For David."

Roland frowned, pleating his forehead. Allie could *feel* Charlie coming up with a comment referencing hamsters and wheels, but before she could spit it out, Roland said, "You think David's going darkside and that this will help?"

"No, I don't think David's going darkside!" She turned to Charlie. "That's why I didn't tell him. I knew he'd think that! It's complicated," she added turning back to Roland again.

"You think?" Roland muttered.

"It gets better," Charlie sighed. "Not only does she think this'll help David, but she's screwing the sorcerer's apprentice."

"Assassin!" Allie snapped.

"Oh, that makes it so much better." Roland rummaged in a side pocket of his backpack and pulled out his phone.

"What are you doing?"

"This isn't dealing with things, Allie. I'm calling the aunties."

"No."

Charlie's eyes widened as Roland's thumb froze over the number pad.

"What?"

Allie took a deep breath and stood. "You haven't chosen, and I'm telling you no."

He frowned and stared at her like he'd never seen

her before. After a long moment, he closed the phone. "I'm going on record as saying I don't like this."

The situation. Not that she'd stopped him. She was within his seven-year break and, in the end, Gale boys knew where they stood. "You don't have to like it, but it's my decision. And when the dragon—or dragons—make their move tonight, I'll be there waiting for them."

"Why?"

Not Roland that time. Charlie. Who shrugged when Allie turned toward her.

"It's a valid question, sweetie. I'm beside you all the way on the new look at sorcerers thing—David deserves a better shot than he'll get from the aunties, and Graham obviously pushes your buttons. So yeah, do what you have to, to keep him from being collateral damage—but this?" She sighed and shook her head. "Neither the dragons nor the businesses they're burning have anything to do with the family. You'd be putting yourself at risk for no good reason. Besides, if they *are* getting desperate, and not just bored out of their scaly skulls, then it'll all be over soon anyway. Big bad arrives." One finger on her right hand flicked up. "The sorcerer deals with it." A second finger. "Your boy deals with the dragons." A third finger. "David's there as backup, so there's never any actual danger." A fourth finger. "And when told the story, the aunties admit sorcerers might be useful for something besides extremely high-grade fertilizer even though it was his screw up that started this in the first place." She stared at her fingers. Waggled them. And said, "I'm seeing a flaw in your plan."

"Two," Roland sighed. "The aunties assume that exposing David to a sorcerer is enough to give him ideas, and you've actually made the situation worse."

Charlie folded all but one finger down and flipped it at Roland.

Allie held up a hand and cut off his response. "I'm going out to meet the dragons because I don't want any more of this city to burn down. And when David is exposed to the sorcerer and doesn't fall, then the aunties will have to admit he isn't going to. It's as simple as that."

"Simple?" Roland asked, his tone suggesting it was anything but.

"Simple enough," Allie told him. "I'm living here, and I don't want the city burning down around my ears."

"You're living here *for now*."

"It's burning now!"

"Admit it, Allie, this is just you not coping well with living so far from home!"

"All righty, then," Charlie broke in before the argument could escalate. "They toasted the first building at midnight last night, so do we assume they're adding symbolism to their dumbass idea to flush the wizard and meet them at twelve?"

"*We're* not . . ."

"Yes, *we* are." When Allie started a second protest, Charlie smacked the back of her head. "This isn't like the sorcerer. Discretion doesn't really apply to giant, flying, fire-breathing lizards who very nearly removed my fucking eyebrows, so I'm going with you. In fact, if we're going to stop them don't you think you should be calling your boy with the big gun?"

"We're not stopping them like that." Allie offered the pronoun as surrender. In all honesty, she'd rather have Charlie with her when facing giant, flying, fire-breathing lizards.

"Okay, how are we stopping them?"

"You'll have my back; I'm going to talk to them."

"They talk?"

Allie reached out and pointed at her laptop. "They read the Yellow Pages. On-line."

The dragons' next target was as far north as the airport and tucked up close to Nose Hill Natural Environment Park.

"That's one big park," Allie murmured as they got out of the car around the corner from the targeted building. So much wilderness in the midst of so many people was an obvious oasis even in the dark—she could feel the weight of all that nothing pressing against her.

Charlie glanced across the median and then across four lanes of 14th Street at the silhouette of the hill against the night sky. "Sacred place on the top," she said as she settled her guitar strap over her shoulders and tossed the gig bag back in the car.

"Yeah, I got that." Awareness of the site lapped at the back of her neck, lifting her hair. It was old, used for centuries and abandoned for less than a hundred years; undisturbed by development, it was like a big pushpin keeping the city connected to the UnderRealm. No wonder things were happening here.

"I wonder why the Courts didn't open the gate up there."

"Easier to put a gate where there's already a gate on this side. Nothing up there but, well, a whole lot of nothing." Allie bounced the car keys on her palm for a moment as she stared into the darkness, then dropped them in her bag and headed for the curb, tossing off a casual, "You, me, and Roland should maybe pay the top of the hill a visit sometime."

"A *visit*?" Charlie's tone evoked bare skin and friction. "We going to be around that long?"

No. Maybe.

Hands shoved in her jacket pockets, Allie stepped

over a crack in the sidewalk. Roland could suck a rope. She was coping fine, but she still wasn't staying one moment longer than it took her to figure out what had happened to Gran. Or until the whole sorcerer beats the greater evil impresses aunties takes the pressure off David thing went down should the Gran question be unexpectedly answered. Well, maybe long enough to finish cataloging the contents of the store and find a cousin willing to take it over. She wasn't like Charlie, always roaming; she needed family around her, not thousands of miles back east, the distance a constant pull against her heart.

Except she'd given Joe a place.

And she heard herself say, "You just joined a band," like it was the one thing that mattered.

In step beside her, Charlie shrugged. "And Rol's just here to dot the legal *i's* and cross the legal *t's*."

"Gran used the toss it in a box filing method. He'll be here for a while."

"David'll be here day after tomorrow. I'd be more than happy to *visit* the hill with him."

The thought of David's power opened up on that hill made her snort. "That'll be the plan in case the dragons don't show tonight. Take a bottle of steak sauce with you."

"Aren't you supposed to use virgins as dragon bait?"

"That's unicorns."

"I kind of miss unicorns."

"Really?"

"No."

They followed the curve in the road around to the east as an eerie howl from the park vibrated through bone and blood and whipped neighborhood dogs into a frenzy.

"I bet the people around here . . ." Charlie's gesture

took in the houses they were passing, the blue flicker of televisions showing around the edges of curtains in the few living rooms where the residents were still awake. ". . . think that's a coyote."

Allie nodded in the direction of the nearest hysterically barking dog. "She doesn't."

Tucked back from the corner where Beaconsfield Road met Beaconsfield Crescent, Wizards of Electrostatic Painting was set up in a converted garage. It looked like the kind of business that had been built up out of hard work and a dream, and Allie wasn't going to let it burn. She'd been hoping she could use the parking lot, but as that turned out to be only a narrow strip of pavement along the east side of the building, she frowned out at the t-junction and stepped into the intersection. "You think this'll be enough room?"

Charlie glanced up at the night sky where nothing blotted out the stars. Yet. "If it isn't, this is—if possible—an even stupider idea than I thought. What are you going to do about traffic?"

"These houses all have back lanes," Allie told her returning to the sidewalk and dropping her bag on the narrow strip of dormant grass. "And given the way the roads around here twist and turn, I don't imagine there's much through traffic during business hours, let alone at nearly midnight."

"Good. Because I'm imagining you getting run over by a guy with bad skin and an ugly jacket delivering pizza."

"Well, stop."

Hidden by the angle of the roof, Graham peered through the scope and swore under his breath. After they'd cleared the air about fire-breathing not having been mentioned . . .

"I have no idea what their range is. When it comes to it, you'll just have to shoot them before they open their mouths."

. . . Kalynchuk had insisted nothing about the more mundane fires would draw Allie's attention. The destruction had occurred nowhere near the one business the Gale family owned in Calgary.

"Even if she hears about the fires," he snorted, *"she'd have no reason to think my enemies are involved and therefore no reason to work out the pattern."*

Something had clearly given her a reason.

Given that, and also given that Allie had walked blithely into the sanctuary of a man she knew would order deadly force to protect himself, he couldn't say he was surprised to see her here.

He *was* more than a little curious about what the hell she thought she was going to do.

Allie rubbed some warmth back into her fingers. In spite of sunny days, nights in early May were not exactly balmy and the radio weather forecaster had laughed, kind of high-pitched and guilty sounding, as he mentioned snow. With finger flexibility restored, she dug out the box of only slightly used sidewalk chalk she'd found that afternoon in the store, and pulled out a fat, white cylinder.

"Isn't that a little big?" Charlie asked as she bent down and started to draw the first of the three charms.

"No." With the piece of chalk laid on its side, the lines for the charm were about six centimeters wide. "I want them to see it before they burn the building down."

"Probably for the best; emergency vehicles are a big-ass distraction. You know," she continued as though imparting the wisdom of the ages, "there's no actual reason they should listen to you. Please, stop burning the city down. Bite me. Well, okay, then."

Shuffling backward, Allie dragged the chalk line out into the middle of the road.

"I'll be convincing."

"There's no actual reason why they shouldn't eat you."

"Which is why you're here."

Over supper, all three Gales and Michael had agreed that being bounced randomly around the globe by a shadowy antagonist beat being dragon chow.

"There's no proof you can even get into the Wood," Roland pointed out. *"Given the way the shadow stopped you from getting to Allie, it's entirely possible it won't let you enter in Allie's company."*

Michael wrapped his hand around Allie's wrist as though he could hold her in place. "Charlie?"

"Little Mary Sunshine there doesn't travel the Wood," Charlie told him soothingly as Roland snorted around a mouthful of pie. *"I do. And I guarantee I can get us both in. After that, who the hell knows, but since the other option is emerging digested from a dragon's ass, I'm good with a random destination. Allie?"*

Allie had admitted that wasn't really an observation she could disagree with and had spent the rest of the meal ignoring the way Roland's gaze had kept tracking back to her. At least once, she was certain he'd reached for his phone but brought his hand empty out of his pocket.

"Michael wanted to see the dragons," Allie said as she finished the last charm.

"Is that what you two were talking about? How'd you convince him not to come?"

Michael was not a Gale boy to be told no and have it stick.

"I reminded him that they flew over the store every morning and all he had to do was go outside and look."

"And?"

"And then I reminded him of the size of the car and that he'd have to sit in the backseat."

"Smart. Maybe even smart enough to . . . Allie."

"I hear it."

Wet sheets, flapping in the wind.

Allie scrambled up onto the sidewalk and stood at Charlie's right, first two fingers of her left hand tucked behind the waistband of her cousin's jeans. There had to be contact if they were going to go into the Wood together. Although, given what was dropping down into the intersection, the heavy beat of wings stirring up enough wind to snap small branches off the bracketing trees and slam against her like openhanded blows from a giant hand, comfort may have also been a factor.

Son of a fucking bitch, it was landing! They'd never landed in the city before!

Pressing his body down into the asphalt tiles, he slipped his finger through the trigger guard.

It was one thing to know that dragons were big, in the same sort of way space was big, secure in the knowledge it was unlikely the entirety of either would ever have to be faced, and it was another thing entirely to stand and watch a dragon drop out of the night sky. Around fifteen meters from branching horns to the tip of a lashing tail, this particular dragon was ebony and gold, iridescent and beautiful in the way of very, very dangerous things where admiration and terror became easy reactions to confuse.

Sitting up on its haunches, talons gouging the pavement, large enough to completely cover all three charms, it folded its wings with a sound like thunder and stared at the two Gales with enormous dark eyes.

"Holy fuck," Charlie muttered.

"Yeah." Allie pushed disheveled hair off her face as she stepped forward.

Jumped back as the dragon burst into flame.

The heat should have melted the asphalt, ignited the trees.

Ignited them.

NO!

He literally, actually, impossibly felt the world stop as Allie disappeared in the inferno.

Charlie spun away, protecting the wood of her guitar with slightly less flammable flesh.

Holding her breath, hand thrown up to protect her eyes, Allie searched the roaring flames. Trying to see through the fire to the dragon. Trying to . . .

Between one heartbeat and the next, the flames fell into their own center. Wrapped around themselves. Solidified.

Became a man.

A man?

Not a dragon! It was suddenly very hard to breathe. *Not a dragon; a Dragon Lord! The son-of-a-bitch sorcerer could have mentioned that!*

A line of white light flashed through the place where the dragon's head had been and slammed into the side of a house, the impact loud enough to rouse the inhabitants from sleep.

The Dragon Lord raised dark brows over familiar eyes.

An audience, Allie realized, was just what they didn't need.

Well, not *just*—but among the top ten.

"Charlie!"

"I know! Hang on . . ." Her left hand worked the tuning pegs. ". . . heat's pulled everything sharp."

A curtain twitched in a second-floor window.

"Now, Charlie!"

As lullabies went, it wasn't so much *close your eyes and dream sweetly* as it was *if you kids don't go to sleep immediately, I* will *come up there and you* will *be sorry.* By the time the last note faded, there wasn't so much as a squirrel awake within a five-block radius; the lullaby had bludgeoned every living creature to sleep.

Breath still fast and shallow, Allie peered at the dark starburst against the previously pristine siding, then turned her full attention back to the man in the center of the intersection. "What was that?"

"A Blessed round." The Dragon Lord's voice was unsurprisingly deep.

And suddenly it became impossible to breathe at all. She had no idea how much of what raced through her head showed on her face, but the Dragon Lord smiled.

"You're surprised," he said. "The one who fired the weapon is not here with you, then. This pleases me. Attempting to lure us into a trap would have been fatally rude."

The second dragon was green and gold. Allie thought it was smaller, but, with eyes squinted shut against the wind, she was too distracted by what it held against its chest to tell for certain. It took almost everything she had to close her teeth on a clichéd cry of denial.

Graham hadn't heard the second dragon over the roar of blood in his ears. Hadn't known it was there until claws closed around him and bones broke as it snatched him off the roof. He hung limp as it landed, weapon trapped between his body and heated emerald scales, conserving his strength, breathing shallowly to keep the shattered ends of ribs from puncturing a lung.

If they made a mistake, he'd be ready.

"He hides behind the mark of sorcery," the Dragon Lord said calmly, twitching a nonexistent wrinkle out of his suit jacket. "Ryan had to trace the bullet back to find him, and then it was scent alone that gave him away. But look there, he wears your mark as well, Gale girl, which is why he continues to live. You may correct me if I'm wrong, but that seems to indicate eviscerating him would stifle conversation. Oh, yes," he added, smiling again, "we know what you are." A nod toward Charlie. "What both of you are. And I know how a Gale girl smells. Tastes." His eyes gleamed. "Not something I could ever forget. Or ever want to."

Allie really hoped he meant *tastes* in as licentious a way as it sounded. "Let him go."

"As you wish. Ryan."

The green dragon's protest sounded distinctly sulky.

The Dragon Lord snorted, blowing lines of white smoke from each nostril. "Because I said so."

He was ready when the claws loosened. Took up the shock of landing in his knees and hips. Ignored the old pain and the new bright spike of agony in his chest. Brought up his weapon.

"Graham! Don't!"

The muscles of his hand spasmed as they tried to simultaneously obey two opposing commands.

The smell of sulfur.

Way too many teeth.

Darkness . . .

Graham collapsed as Allie reached him. She dropped to her knees on the pavement, one hand on his chest, the other reaching up, past the teeth, drawing a fast charm on the dragon's nose just where the green shaded down into gold. The scales were so hot that the skin on her fingertip blistered.

His roar suddenly more of a strangled croak, the dragon reared back, swiping at his muzzle.

She could hear the other Dragon Lord laughing, but all she could see was the blood bubbling between Graham's lips as he fought to breathe. There was a stupid vest that was obviously useless when it counted and the stupid clothing he had on under it had too many stupid fasteners or no fasteners at all, so she charmed right through and finally pressed her palm against skin.

"He needs a hospital. Charlie, go get the car!"

"Uh, Allie . . ."

"Now!" She didn't know the charms to fix this, but that didn't stop her from tracing patterns over and over and over the damage.

A scrape of claw against the road.

"I wouldn't," the Dragon Lord said.

At first, Allie thought he was talking to Charlie, but the silence stretched and lengthened to be finally broken not by claws but by the metallic jingle of keys and Charlie's boots pounding out a rhythm into the distance.

As Allie felt Graham's struggle ease under her touch, she risked a glance over her shoulder.

The green dragon, Ryan, glared down at her from under golden brow ridges, head dipped to sight along the line of his horns. She knew that look. She'd seen Dmitri wear one very like it.

The Dragon Lord stood almost directly behind her. She hadn't heard him move. He reached out, stroked the back of her cheek with two fingers and, unable to stop herself, she leaned into the touch. As the skin under his caress tightened, he murmured, "We will have the conversation we should have had tonight another time, Gale girl." A glance past her, down at Graham. "Just a suggestion, but . . . shorten his leash." Then he stepped back, and Allie found herself surrounded by fire. Impossible not to brace for pain, although the heat merely baked dry the inside of her nose and mouth, coating her tongue with the taste of sulfur.

Before she could work up enough saliva to swallow, two pairs of enormous eyes stared down at her—the emerald pair narrowed in familiar, adolescent pique, the ebony pair amused. With a backwash that nearly flattened her to the road, the dragons leaped into the air, beating their wings against the night.

"So, a Dragon Lord," Charlie said as they maneuvered Graham onto the fully reclined passenger seat.

"Dragon Lords," Allie told her, drawing another charm against Graham's right leg so she could tuck it more easily into the car. "Ryan, too."

"Did he change?"

"Did he need to?"

"No, I suppose not."

She straightened, closed the car door, and turned to her cousin, uncertain of what to say. "Charlie . . ."

"It's not a problem, Allie." Charlie held up Graham's keys. "These were in his pocket. I'll take his truck home and let the guys know what's going on." Eyes narrowed, she added, "Just a feeling, but I'm guessing his boss didn't tell you the whole story."

"Not just his boss. Graham had to have known what they were if he was supposed to be able to kill them." The keys dug into her palm as she ran around to the driver's side. "Wake the neighborhood before you go."

"Yeah, yeah, drive . . ." Charlie jumped back as the Beetle all but spun around one rear wheel and roared off. ". . . carefully."

Revelry lost a little something when played on the guitar.

"They turn into people?"

"They can take the appearance of people," Charlie amended as she came out of the bedroom in a pair of sweatpants and a faded Barstool Prophets T-shirt. "They're still dragons."

"Who look like people?"

"Yes."

Michael's eyes gleamed. "That's pretty cool."

"That's very, very dangerous." Roland looked over at his phone, lying out of reach on a pile of papers on the big table, then over at Charlie.

She shook her head, even though calling in the aunties was beginning to sound like an excellent idea. "No. This is Allie's show."

"Because Gran left her the store?" Michael asked, heaving himself up off the end of the sofa bed, crossing to the kitchen, and opening the fridge.

Charlie's turn to look over at Roland. He frowned and shrugged, unwilling to commit to the suspicions Charlie could see written out in his body language. "Yeah, that's the main reason," she said at last.

"But you guys'll stop her if she does something really stupid, right?" He turned toward them, shoving a broken piece of pie into his mouth and somehow managing to not spit blueberries and pastry as he added, "Because you're older."

"Doesn't exactly work that way," Charlie told him, sitting down in the spot Michael had vacated, wrapping a hand around Roland's bare ankle. "You know that." She stroked the soft skin of his arch with her thumb. "I wish we'd convinced Joe to stay; it's a lot more dangerous out there than we thought."

"Joe's testing that he gets to come *and* go," Michael pointed out, wiping his hands on a dish towel. "He'll stay as soon as he realizes he doesn't have to."

Roland nodded. "And he is full-blood Fey. Changeling or not, the Dragon Lords won't want to start a fight with his people, particularly not if they're already feeling annoyed about them using the gate."

"Thanks to Allie, we're his people now," Charlie snorted. Frowned. "But you have a point."

"About?"

"Joe being full-blood Fey."

At twenty after three, they finally allowed Allie back
behind the curtain into examination room one. The
emergency room in the Peter Lougheed Centre of the
Calgary General Hospital—and wasn't that a mouthful
to choke out—had been nearly empty when they'd arrived and Graham had been seen to immediately.

But only because immediately was as fast as Allie
could arrange it.

She'd used information gleaned from Graham's
wallet to fill out as much of the paperwork as possible
and lied through her teeth about the rest, tracing tiny
charms into the end of every section on the forms.
After they'd rolled him away for X-rays and MRIs and
whatever else turned out to be needed, she'd sat on
one of the ubiquitous orange plastic chairs, chewed on
a thumbnail, and concentrated on getting him fixed as
quickly as possible. Around two thirty, she'd poured a
charm into a paper cup of water and brought it to an
elderly drunk because the random shouting of obsceni-
ties had become distracting.

He'd fallen asleep, looking vaguely horrified, and
Allie'd returned to keeping the medical profession
focused.

She did not think about Dragon Lords in the city.

Much.

If the sorcerer's enemy could use *Dragon Lords* to
hunt for him, who the hell had he pissed off?

When she pushed the curtain aside, Graham was sitting on the edge of the gurney, bare feet braced against
the floor, chest wrapped in white, face nearly as pale,
uppermost hex mark just barely visible. Her charm
blazed under the fluorescent lights.

"Should you be sitting up?"

"Have to get out of here." He seemed to find the patch of floor tile framed by his knees fascinating. "Two cracked ribs—that's ..." A short struggle to breathe. "... nothing."

"Not quite nothing." Allie moved closer, resting her hand on his arm as he tried to rise, her touch enough to hold him in place. "There's impact damage to your ankles, your right knee's swollen but functional, and you've got moderate to severe bruising over seventy percent of your body—I'm assuming that's an estimate although for all I know they might have measured. They probably have charts. And that's just the new stuff— they asked me if you were into extreme sports. Given the number of old injuries they listed, they must assume you kind of suck at it if you are." She could hear herself babbling and made an effort to stop. "Still, it could have been worse."

"It was." Taking her hand in his, he tugged her around into the vee between his legs, lifted his head, and managed to lock his drifting gaze onto her face. "What did you do to me?" he demanded.

"I brought you to the hospital." She raised her other hand to push the hair back off his face, but he grabbed her wrist, the movement the careful exaggeration of someone fighting painkillers.

"No, before," he insisted. When Allie shook her head, uncertain of which *before* he referred to, his eyes narrowed. "Between the pain and breathing blood ... a punctured lung ... that's hard to miss. Heard the doctor talking ... saw recent scar tissue. No puncture."

"Oh, that."

His eyes widened. "Oh, *that*?"

"I don't know what I did." Basic first aid, the kind every Gale girl learned early to tend to fathers and uncles, brothers and cousins, didn't extend much beyond bruises and minor lacerations at third circle. Immobilizing broken bones in a pinch but better to wait for a first-or-second-circle healing rather than screw it up and have to break the bone again. "Not specifically."

"Not specifically?" His nostrils flared, once, twice, as he fought the drugs for coherency. "I'm finding your casual use ... of that much power just a little ..." He frowned as he searched through the haze of painkillers for the word. ". . . disconcerting."

"Would you have preferred robes and candles and eldritch symbols and Latin chanting and whatever it is your sorcerer does?" Allie asked. "Because given where we were and who we were with and—oh, yeah, the fact your sorcerer was nowhere around, that wasn't really an option. And ..." Using his loose grip on her wrists, she tugged herself a little closer until her hips pressed hard against the inside of his thighs and she could smell him, just a little, over the pervasive scent of antiseptic. ". . . there was nothing casual about it. I thought you were going to die."

"Me, too." The frown deepened. "I mean, not me. You."

Allie smiled for the first time since she'd realized what the second Dragon Lord carried and freed her hands so she could cup his face between them. "You thought I was going to die?"

"I did?" The frown unfolded. "I did. Why are you smiling?"

"You did something stupid for me." Bending forward, she kissed him gently. His lips were dry and sticky against hers and he still tasted just a little of blood. "And speaking of stupid," she said, backing away, "why didn't you tell me they weren't just dragons!"

"Ow!" He let go of one wrist and rubbed the shoulder she'd punched. "Injured here!"

"And way too drugged to feel that. Dragon Lords?"

"Not my information . . . to give."

"Who sent them? How many of them are there?"

Graham sighed, reached up and cupped her cheek. His fingers felt cool over the skin the Dragon Lord's touch had scorched. "Don't ask me . . . things I can't . . ."

She caught him as he began to tip left. "Come on." Dropping a kiss on the top of his head, she carefully adjusted the vertical. "Let's get you dressed enough to get you home."

"Good thing he's a bit of a shrimp."

"Michael."

"I'm just saying." Breathing a little heavily, Michael laid Graham down on Allie's bed and stepped back, rolling his shoulders. "Why bring him here instead of to his own place?"

Allie bent to untie the laces on his right boot. "He's safer here."

"From the Dragon Lords?" Roland asked, moving to Graham's other foot.

"Them, too."

Leaning against the wall by the door, Charlie shook her head. "You turned off his phone, didn't you?"

"No." Feeling the weight of regard from the other three *conscious* people in the room, Allie straightened and turned, dropping the boot to the floor. "No," she repeated. "He didn't have it turned on. I mean, he was on a stakeout; getting a phone call would be stupid."

"Stupid as shooting at a Dragon Lord?" Charlie asked.

Allie kicked the boot under the bed. "Not quite."

"He's been marked." Dropping the other boot, Roland

nodded toward the visible hex—Allie'd gotten Graham's shirt and jacket on him but hadn't bothered doing them all them way up. She'd tossed his T-shirt and vest into the backseat. Actually, she'd tossed his vest into the back before she'd gone into the hospital for help—Kevlar being harder than broken ribs to explain. "Can his sorcerer track him using those? Track him here?"

"Through Gran's protections? Not likely." Moving around to the side of the bed, Allie unbuckled his belt.

"Does he know where he is?" Roland wondered, grabbing the bottom of his black jeans and tugging as Allie lifted Graham's hips enough to clear the fabric. "Or did you put him out before mentioning the final destination?"

"Bet she didn't ask if she could charm him out," Michael muttered, yawning.

Charlie snorted. "No reason to ask when you know the answer. He'd be all macho and . . ." She dropped her voice half an octave. ". . . no puttin' me ta sleep, little lady, I don't want to be missing out on the pain."

"Little lady?"

"It's four thirty in the morning, I don't have my best stuff."

Bending to ease Graham's arm out of his shirtsleeve, Allie heard Roland sigh. "Allie, does he know you brought him here?"

"I told him." His skin was warm and a little damp and the bruises were purpling up nicely. She let her fingers rest on the curve of his shoulder. "And he heard me phone Charlie when we left the hospital."

"Did he understand?" Roland insisted.

"What difference does it make?" she sighed. "This is the only place neither the Dragon Lords nor the sorcerer could get to him." When she straightened and turned, they were staring at her again. "He took a shot at a Dragon Lord for me. Because he took a shot at a Dragon Lord, they grabbed him. They saw the hex marks. They know the sorcerer is here in Calgary."

"They knew that," Charlie reminded her. "They were hunting him."

"They were hunting *for* him. Not quite the same thing."

"Unless the sorcerer was lying about that."

"He didn't lie to me," Allie insisted. "He merely omitted details."

Roland's brows nearly disappeared under his hair. "What part of Dragon Lords are merely?"

Charlie watched her thoughtfully as she pulled the covers up from the foot of the bed. "If they'd wanted to get information out of him about the sorcerer, they had their chance tonight and blew it off."

"Because he's wearing my mark and we were right there and they didn't want to start a fight."

"Why not?" Michael asked. "I mean, I'm glad they didn't," he added when both Allie and Charlie turned to glare at him, "but you look at it from their point of view and they could have kicked your ass."

"My guess is that they don't want to risk taking damage before the big fight."

"From the aunties?"

Allie looked into memory and saw Graham hanging in Ryan's claws. Looked down at him on the bed, wearing only boxers and bandages and bruises, and said, "Them, too."

"Okay . . ." Roland sounded as though he believed her. ". . . so the Dragon Lords would like to get him alone and extract information about the sorcerer. And the sorcerer?"

Lightly smoothing the sheet over Graham's chest,

Allie considered Stanley Kalynchuk. Without meeting him, the aunties would say he was a brutal egotist, corrupted by the power he controlled, destined to abuse it. They'd feel he was significantly more dangerous than the Dragon Lords as he'd chosen his path. As much as she wanted to ease the way for David, Allie was going to go with the aunties on this one. "Like I said, Graham's safer here."

"And when he wakes up?" Charlie asked softly. "What happens then?"

Allie shrugged and brushed a strand of hair back off his face. She could hear the layers in Charlie's question, but she refused to acknowledge them. It had been a long night and all that mattered, here and now, was that Graham hadn't drowned in his own blood. "I don't know."

After a moment, Michael scratched under the waistband of his elderly pajama pants and snickered. "You're thinking about the padded handcuffs in Gran's drawer, aren't you?"

She felt the corners of her mouth twitch up in spite of herself. "Shut up."

Dragged out of sleep by the ringing of her phone, Allie glared at the clock beside the bed. Seven forty-nine. She'd been asleep for just a little over three hours. Given the aunties, that was more sleep than she'd expected to get.

When she managed to focus on the call display, her eyes widened.

"How did you get this number?"

"Don't ask stupid questions, Ms. Gale," Kalynchuk growled. "Is he with you?"

Allie's lip curled. Or would have had it not stuck to her teeth. She ran her tongue over them and said, "Don't ask stupid questions, Mr. Kalynchuk."

Behind her, Graham stirred but didn't wake. She'd removed the charm when she got into bed, but it seemed the painkillers had been enough to keep him out.

"I want to speak with him."

"I want to know why you didn't tell me about the Dragon Lords."

For a moment, she thought he wasn't going to answer. When he did, he didn't sound exactly apologetic. Or at all apologetic. "I told you as much as you needed to know."

"Yeah, well . . ." She yawned. ". . . they disagree."

"They?"

"The Dragon Lords."

"Put Graham on."

"He's asleep."

"Wake him."

If he'd asked instead of commanded, she might have considered it.

"No."

His breathing suggested it had been a while since anyone had denied him. "I am a dangerous enemy, Ms. Gale."

"Interestingly enough, you're a dangerous friend too." Yawning, she snapped the phone closed. Since it seemed highly unlikely he could get any angrier at her, she rolled over, curled up against Graham's side, and went back to sleep.

Michael and Roland both had work of their own to do, so Charlie'd gone down and opened the store.

Half expecting to see Joe already in place behind the counter—allowing her to haul ass back upstairs and grab some more shut-eye—she'd been a little annoyed to see the place empty.

Seemed no one wanted to buy crap at ten AM on a Wednesday, so she'd continued her hunt for the artifact producing the autoharp music. With no distractions, it had taken her a surprisingly short time to find it in behind a white china chamber pot. Circa 1915, according to the sticker.

Leaning against the counter, she ran her fingers over the edge of what looked to be an old presentation box for medals or jewelry. Painted gold with a red-and-black crest glued to the center of what had been the lid, the outside gave no indication of the contents. The upper edge and the long edge opposite the hinge had been beaded, allowing the box to stand on one end and be opened like a reliquary. There was no clasp to hold it closed, and when it had fallen off a pile of mildewed postcards and landed behind the chamber pot, it had opened, just a little.

Charlie opened it the rest of the way.

Inside, against plaid padding, were two drawings of young men holding instruments. Not exactly photorealism, one had long hair, one short and they were both wearing what were probably supposed to be kilts made from the same plaid fabric as the padding. Next to the drawings were rolled napkins from an American hotel.

The drawings were signed.

The napkins were sweat-stained.

Whoever had trapped their souls either really hated or really loved Celtic music.

Listening to "The Orange and the Green" being played on autoharp and pennywhistle, Charlie couldn't decide which.

"I brought . . ."

She snapped the case closed and came out of the aisle to face Joe, standing just inside the store holding a mug in each hand.

"Oh. It's you." He looked down into one of the mugs, then held it out. "Kenny gave me one with milk and no sugar. I guess he knew you'd be here. Where's Allie?"

"Sleeping. She had a late night." Charlie and the boys had been able to nap while Allie'd been with Graham at the ER. Not exactly eight hours but better than a slap in the face with a fish. "So," she asked after a moment spent worshiping the amazing aroma wafting up from the coffee. "Is there a reason why you didn't mention the dragons are actually Dragon Lords?"

Joe's eyes widened. "She met . . . ?"

"We met. Might have been nice to have had a heads up."

"I thought she knew." He jerked back a step, two spots of color burning high on each cheek. "She said she knew. I swear, she told me she knew! Fuck me, I wouldn't have not told her if I hadn't thought she knew. Even before. I wouldn't have. You have to believe me. You have to . . ."

"Joe!" As his mouth snapped shut, Charlie sighed. "At the risk of sounding last millennium, don't have a cow. I believe you."

He looked startled and she realized he hadn't expected that. "Why?"

"Why not?" To begin with, he was telling the truth. He *had* thought Allie'd known. Or he'd convinced himself she'd known, which was close enough for Charlie. She had no trouble at all seeing Allie making assumptions and Joe choosing to go along with them rather than raise the suckage in his life even a little bit more.

A flash of ebony and gold out on the street caught

her attention and, frowning, she waved Joe away from the door.

Okay.

Not so much a flash of ebony and gold as a whole freaking sidewalk full of it, framed by Auntie Catherine's clear-sight charm. In the sunlight, the highlights gleaming off the scales were very nearly aubergine.

Flipping open her phone, she called Roland.

"Hey, get Allie up. We've got company."

The sound of Joe's mug shattering against the floor almost drowned out Roland's response.

EIGHT

"He's what?"

"In the store," Roland repeated, flipping the covers back, pivoting Allie around until her legs were out of the bed, then pulling her up into a sitting position. "Right at this very moment, there's a Dragon Lord in the store. Get dressed and get downstairs."

"What about . . . ?" She twisted around until she could see Graham. With the heavy drapes still shut and the only light spilling in the open door, she couldn't tell if he looked any better.

Roland tossed a pair of clean underwear at her head. "I'll keep an eye on him."

"You're not coming down?"

He stared at her for a long moment. Opened his mouth. Closed it again. "No," he said at last as she shimmied into her jeans, "I'd just be a distraction."

Even barely awake, Allie knew *distraction* was not his first choice. She'd have called him on it, but right at the moment, Roland being a bit weird was far enough down her list of things to worry about that she could, essentially, not worry about it. She grabbed the bra she'd taken off a depressingly short time before, dug out a

T-shirt, and threw on a hoodie, turning back toward the
bed as she zipped it. Graham had his face turned away
from her, but she could see the shallow rise and fall of
his chest. "I'm worried about him, Rol. The painkillers
should have worn off by now."

"It's barely been eight hours," Roland reminded
her, handing over her shoes as she left the bedroom
and pulled the door almost all the way closed behind
her. "And you may have messed with timing when you
charmed him. But it's possible he's just catching up
on his sleep. Tabloid reporter by day, ninja by night—
working two jobs'll really take it out of you."

"If he wakes up . . ." The sudden fear of returning
to the apartment and finding him gone had her heart
pounding in her throat. "Don't let him leave."

"Fine. Now move. You don't want to leave Charlie
alone with a Dragon Lord any longer than necessary."

The mirror showed her reflection in a full suit of
armor.

Allie patted the frame as she passed. "Thanks. I'll be
fine."

As it happened, Charlie wasn't alone with the Dragon
Lord. She was standing behind the counter, one hand
clutching what looked like a gold-colored book, watching something at the opposite end of the store—*Three
guesses to what, the first two don't count,* Allie told herself silently—and Joe was by the door either wiping up a
spill or rubbing it into the floor. The dark patch of wood
offered no clues, but the mop seemed to be anchoring

him in place. Keeping him from running. She could feel the terror come off him in waves.

It had to be instinct. Joe was full-blood Fey, sure, but he was a changeling; he'd been in the MidRealm since he was a baby, so he didn't actually *know* anything more about the Dragon Lords than they did. Allie suspected that a smart person would use his fear as a cue to how they should be feeling, but it only made her sad.

"Joe?"

He jerked around to face her and gasped, "I thought you knew."

She had no idea what he was talking about and no time to figure it out. "Michael could probably use a hand in the loft. He's got tradesmen coming in to lay the floor today."

"There's, I mean . . . Coffee!"

Given the accompanying movement of the mop, she assumed that was what he'd spilled. "I think you've got it."

"I could . . ."

"You could help Michael? Yeah, that'd be great." She stepped forward, giving him a clear route to the back hall.

Knuckles white where he gripped the mop handle, he shot a panicked look at Charlie.

"We'll be fine," she said and hopefully only Allie heard she was speaking through clenched teeth.

"Customers . . ."

"Dude, there's two of us and a Lord of the Under-Realm." Without shifting her gaze, she jerked her head toward Allie. "I think we can figure out how to sell a yoyo. Go on."

He managed an eye roll and walked with exaggerated bravado to Allie's side.

She touched his shoulder as he passed. "Keep Michael from coming in here. He's . . ."

"A distraction?"

"Yeah, that, too." Second time in as many conversations she'd essentially been warned about getting distracted. Given the whole facing-a-Dragon-Lord thing, she actually planned on paying attention.

Joe squared his shoulders. "I can do that."

"Good."

She waited until she heard the back door close before she moved to stand across the counter from Charlie. From there, she could see the Dragon Lord in front of the bookshelves that covered the far wall. The shoulders of his black trench coat were spotted with rain, and Allie wasn't at all surprised when the coat made a sound like the rustle of wings as he turned to face her.

Then she stopped thinking about wings and tails and talons and conservation of mass and high school physics.

"Whoa."

"Yeah," Charlie agreed. "Kind of too distracted to appreciate it last night, but he's a hottie. Be careful. I'm staying back here so I don't embarrass myself by humping his leg."

Skin the color of burnished mahogany, the Dragon Lord had black hair cut short, a black goatee, and cheekbones that weren't so much chiseled as sculpted. He wore a pale gray suit under the trench coat with a darker open-necked shirt that framed the strong column of his throat. He was very tall, with broad shoulders and narrow hips and hands so large and powerful looking Allie had trouble focusing on what they were holding.

"This," he said, raising a tattered, leather-bound book, "should not be available to anyone able to see through the charm."

She could feel the sizzle of attraction across her skin, but she didn't seem about to succumb. Which, all things considered, was good, but the power coming off a Dragon Lord should have had her too *attracted* to concentrate on anything but him.

Where attracted pretty much meant: *Oh, baby, here and now!*

It hadn't been a problem on the street last night either.

Maybe, she thought, realizing he was waiting for her to respond, *it has something to do with the whole patronizing Prince of the UnderRealm tone.* He sounded a bit like Auntie Jane, and that was just creepy enough to put her right off.

"That's a complex charm," she pointed out. "There's not going to be a lot of people who can see through it."

"One is too many. There's enough knowledge contained in these pages to do serious harm. When we have finished our conversation, I'll take it somewhere less . . ." A glance around the store. ". . . flammable and burn it."

"The price is inside the front cover."

Charlie made a sound halfway between a gasp and snicker, but Allie refused to look away, holding the Dragon Lord's gaze determinedly if not entirely fearlessly. The whole *do me* thing aside, he could still rend, devour, and—oh, yeah—fry her where she stood. He raised a dark brow, and the temperature rose. Allie felt a drop of sweat run along her spine.

"Really?" He offered her a chance to back down. To apologize. To throw herself on his mercy.

Allie bit her lip hard enough to draw blood and squared her shoulders. "Really. We can handle whatever currency you're carrying."

To her surprise, he laughed, and it got significantly easier to breathe. "You've got fire, Gale girl. Very well." A quick glance at the flyleaf and he pulled his wallet from his pocket as he walked toward the counter.

Wallet?

"Don't worry, it's not illusionary." He pulled out a pair of fifties. "I have no interest in spending all my time on a rocky cliff eviscerating . . ."

"Virgins?" Charlie offered.

"Cattle," he said. "They're easier to find." The book disappeared inside the folds of the trench coat. "And cash is easier to obtain than a credit rating. Now then . . ."

Allie didn't remember him taking her hand. Actually, she didn't remember moving close enough to him that he *could* take her hand, but apparently she had. In direct contrast to the expensive suit, his fingers had a working man's calluses. *What did Dragon Lords work at?* she wondered.

He stroked his thumb over her palm, the rough pad leaving a path of warmth behind it. "You may call me Adam. It isn't my actual name, of course, but it has relevant symbolic value. And you are?"

"Alysha."

"I'm very pleased to meet you, Alysha Gale."

His lips burned against the back of her hand. The almost pain made her knees weak. She locked them and tried to banish the ringing in her ears.

Not her ears.

"My phone is ringing."

Adam blinked, the motion the least human seeming thing he'd done. "I beg your pardon?"

"My phone." Allie tugged her fingers free. "I have to get it." She shoved her hand into the pocket of her hoodie, closed it around the phone, and left it there for a moment while her fingers stopped trembling. When it rang again, and Adam's brows rose, she pulled it out, and flipped it open.

"Hello?"

"Why are we hearing about this man you've met from your cousin?"

This time, it *was* her ears ringing. Ear. She moved the phone out about six centimeters from her head. "I'm kind of busy right now, Auntie Ruby."

"Too busy to talk to a dying old woman?"

She sighed and gave some serious thought to beating her head against the counter as Charlie made a noise that was mostly a snicker and even Adam looked amused. "You're not dying, Auntie Ruby."

"Don't sass me, girl! What's wrong with this man that you're hiding him?"

"I'm not hiding him."

"Then bring him for dinner. And stop by your Uncle Gerald's on the way home and get milk."

Uncle Gerald had been dead for ten years. Most of the time Auntie Ruby remembered. Sometimes, she didn't bother. Allie gentled her voice as she said good-bye and hung up.

"Family," she explained, shoving the phone back into her pocket.

Adam snorted, puffing two white streams of smoke. "Tell me about it."

"Ryan?" she asked, given the interactions she'd seen.

"My youngest brother."

Which implied: "You have more than one?"

"I have eleven. And a sister."

Twelve Dragon Lords. And a . . . female Dragon Lord. A baker's dozen of Dragon Lords. She could practically hear Charlie thinking it. "They're all . . . here?"

"No, not all. Just my brothers."

Twelve Dragon Lords. Allie couldn't see how the word *just* applied any more than the word *merely* that Roland had objected to. "Why?"

Adam shrugged, the movement as elegant as every other movement he'd made. "I think you know why. The man who wears your mark also wears the mark of sorcery. You have spoken to his master."

Not a question, but she answered it anyway. "Yes."

"He has probably told you we are hunting him. But that is no concern of yours. A family matter. I'm sure you understand."

If there was one thing a Gale understood, it was how family matters were no concern of anyone outside the family. Allie didn't much like being on the other side of the fence.

Twitching a cuff into place, Adam met her gaze. "I don't suppose you'd be willing to tell me where he is?"

"No."

"I could force you."

"And bring my family into this? If you were going to do that, you'd have done it last night."

"True. You are correct in assuming we do not want your . . . aunties involved." His expression was almost fond and Allie had no intention of asking why.

"The sorcerer says you're hunting him to stop him from preventing one of his enemies from coming through. So this enemy must be some kind of 'big bad' . . ."

He narrowed his eyes at the air quotes.

". . . to be giving you orders."

"Some kind of big bad?" His chuckle lifted the hair on the back of her neck. "Oh, Gale girl, hope the *big bad* never decides to visit. It would take more than sorcery to prevent disaster. What is on its way is, in comparison, a little bad." A pause to remove nonexistent lint from his lapel, and when he looked up again, his eyes were hooded, alien, and his voice had picked up the hint of a hiss. "The sorcerer's painful death is the one thing all my brothers and I agree on. However, although each of us would happily roast his organs within his living body, if he swears to stay hidden in his coward's lair, we are willing to ignore his very existence until after the 'little bad' is dealt with."

A Dragon Lord sketching air quotes back at her was fairly close to being entirely too weird.

"And the little bad is?"

"Not commanding us, that much I will tell you. The rest, Gale girl, is as I said, a family matter."

Whatever the family matter was, it was important enough for them to agree to ignore an enemy—Stanley Kalynchuk—in order to deal with it. Allie frowned. If Kalynchuk was the one thing the Dragon Lords agreed on and their enmity was also a family matter . . .

The same family matter?

"I can almost smell you thinking." The hiss moved toward a growl. "Do not be too clever, Alysha Gale."

Auntie Elsa liked to use that warning. And that tone.

"Tell the sorcerer what I have told you. He will live a little longer if he continues to cower. Or tell the man you have borrowed from him and have him pass on the word. But for now," he added before she could take issue with the word *borrowed,* "shall we deal with the actual reason for my visit?" And once again, he became more Lord than Dragon. "I am here to discover exactly why you got my attention so charmingly last night."

"Last night?" Right. Before Graham. Chalk on pavement. Ebony and gold. Charmingly? Right. "I wanted to ask you to stop burning buildings down."

"Why?"

"Why did I want to ask you or why did I want you to stop burning buildings down?"

"Yes." His smile was wicked. Behind her, Charlie

murmured, "Holy fuck," and Allie had to agree. The longer she remained in close proximity, the stronger the attraction. Still managing not to hump his leg, though.

Drawing her tongue over dry lips, she tried not to notice that his eyes followed the movement. "I live here—that's why I wanted to ask you. Whatever you think you're doing, in the end it's nothing more than mindless destruction. Okay, maybe not mindless," she corrected when his brows lifted, "but it's petty."

"Did you just call me petty?"

"No." The air around him smelled slightly singed. "I'm calling your actions petty."

"Petty seems a bit . . ."

Stupid? Allie's brain supplied during the pause.

". . . harsh." He twitched the other cuff into place. "But you're right; we had no reason for the destruction. We were bored and spreading fire only to see if we could flush the coward from his den. My apologies if we destroyed property your family claims."

"You didn't."

"Then I take back my apology. Particularly as our efforts had such unexpectedly pleasant results. I must say, I'm well on the way to being no longer bored." He shifted his weight back on his heels. Allie braced herself, but he only folded his arms. "Now tell me, Alysha Gale, why we should we stop burning this city—which is not yet yours—just because you ask?"

"Because I ask."

"That's it?"

She thought about it for a moment. "Yes, that's it."

"Really?"

"Really."

Adam leaned closer, and his nostrils flared. Holding her ground with everything she had, Allie saw a flash of gold in his eyes. "It's like that," he said thoughtfully.

"Very well. Although not all my brothers are likely to listen to me."

She let out a long breath as he leaned away again and managed a fairly steady, "Family."

"Indeed. And speaking of family . . ." Adam's nostrils flared again as he looked past her, at Charlie. "I smell the wild lands on this one. You'll never quite tame her."

Allie turned and grinned at Charlie's affronted expression. "I'll never quite want to."

"Wise. Well, I think we have reached the end of the second measure. I thank you for the dance." He was at the door before she saw him move. A glance at Charlie's face reassured her she wasn't the only one taken by surprise. "Stay out of this, Alysha Gale. The man is not worth your family and mine coming to blows. Although . . ." This smile was almost speculative. ". . . I would like a chance to watch you burn."

He opened the door, devolved into a flash of ebony and gold and a wind that flipped a passing SUV onto its side where it lay with horn honking and wheels turning, intermittently visible through the steam rising off the wet sidewalk.

Graham woke alone in an unfamiliar bed, but the sheets beside him retained enough warmth he assumed he'd had company until recently. He felt slightly divorced from his body, like his thoughts were isolated in a bubble in his head—the lingering effects of some serious painkillers. He remembered the Dragon Lords, the hospital, and his last clear memory involved arguing with Allie's assumption that her home was safer than his.

Evidence suggested he'd lost the argument by losing

consciousness. Or, given all the red paint and draped velvet he could just barely make out in the diffuse light coming through lace-covered French doors, Allie'd split the difference and rented the bordello room at a fantasy suites hotel.

One of the doors had been left open about ten centimeters. He held his breath, and listened. Paper rustling—quietly, so as not to wake him. The faint smell of toast and coffee. Allie. Probably reading the newspaper while waiting for him to wake up and call out.

Lying back and letting a beautiful woman take care of him was a significantly more attractive proposition than admitting he'd made a stupid, rookie mistake and let his heart rule his head, but unless he wanted to hide out here for the rest of his natural life, it would be best to get it over with. The longer his boss spent waiting for the details, the worse the debrief would be.

He wasn't wearing his watch—he wasn't wearing anything but yesterday's boxers and a torso wrap. Movement reminded him of why. Cracked ribs came with distinct pain wrapped around every breath. Experience reminded him that sitting up would a bad idea, so he rolled to the edge of the mattress—not a great idea in and of itself—and let gravity take his feet to the floor. With his legs spread for stability, he used the bed to haul himself erect.

Some of his clothes had been tossed onto an ancient overstuffed red velvet chair. No sign of his weapons, but his watch and phone were on the corner of the dresser. He slid the former on and powered up the latter. Ten forty-three. No signal.

Not likely.

But it raised the odds that he was in Allie's apartment. He'd never been able to get a signal in the store although he'd seen both Allie and her grandmother use their phones.

Teeth clenched, he dragged on his jeans. His T-shirt and sweater were missing, so he shrugged his shirt on over the bandages and, after getting it more or less buttoned, settled his jacket over that. Socks might just kill him, so he shoved bare feet into his boots, then held his breath and sweated as he tied them off tightly enough to support the swelling.

"There's impact damage to your ankles, your right knee's swollen but functional . . ."

Allie's voice in memory, listing his injuries.

He wouldn't be dancing out of here, but hobbling out beat the alternative.

Ten fifty-four.

Not bad, all things considered.

Right arm tucked tight against his body, he pushed open the nearer door and stepped into what seemed to be living room, dining room, and kitchen combined. The area looked more like a loft conversion than a historic property. Rain spattered against the windows, reflected light making the day look grim and unappealing. A brown-haired man in a striped sweater vest sat with his back to him at an enormous table covered in papers.

When he stumbled over a duffel bag and clutched at the back of the nearer sofa to keep from slamming to the floor, the man turned. Looked surprised to see him.

"What are you doing out of bed?"

Ah. Not surprised to see him. Surprised to see him up.

Sweater Vest stood, frowning. "Seriously, you're lucky to be alive. Dragon Lords aren't known for their restraint. I'm amazed you came out of the experience with nothing worse than a couple of cracked ribs."

"And a punctured lung."

"You have a punctured lung?"

"Had. Allie fixed it." The expression on Sweater Vest's face spoke volumes. "Guess she didn't mention that."

"She said she took you to the hospital."

"Yeah, after." After he'd lost consciousness. "Where is she?"

"She's uh . . ." Sweater Vest glanced down at his hands and up again. ". . . busy."

She had a life. She had a business. She had her nose stuck into things that didn't concern her. But, that said, there was a whole lot of subtext Graham didn't like in that word. He doubted she was in the bathroom. "Busy?"

"I'm her cousin," Sweater Vest continued. "Roland."

"The lawyer?"

"That's right."

"Well, okay, Roland . . ." Who clearly had no intention of telling him what Allie was busy doing. ". . . tell her thanks for getting me patched up, that I'm sorry I missed her, and I'll call. Right now," he added, shuffling along the back of the sofa as he moved at his fastest pace toward the door. "I have things I have to do."

Roland cut him off. But, in all fairness, since his right knee looked like a rotting melon, his fastest pace was shit.

"Get out of my way."

"Sorry." And damn if Roland didn't fold his arms. "But Allie doesn't want you to leave."

"And I appreciate that she's probably worried, but . . ." The guy didn't look like much—like most lawyers, he probably spent most of his time at a desk—but he couldn't be moved. Graham shoved a little harder. Roland lowered his head, kind of tucked it between his shoulders, and rocked in place. "Get the fuck out of my way."

"You're already injured. I don't want to fight you." A bit of steel in his voice, and something else. Frustration, maybe.

"Good. Because I don't intend to fight you." Graham took most of his weight on his left leg, shifted, and threw himself over the back of the sofa. Rolled. Came up fast but careful, protecting his injured side, left foot back on the floor first. Took two steps toward the door and found himself facing the immovable object again.

Damn if Roland didn't have some unexpected moves under the sweater vest. But so did he. His left arm still worked. Get him in close enough. Elbow to the side of the head. Make it to the door while he was down. Except Roland *wouldn't* move in close enough. Like he knew.

"How much do you actually know about our family?"

Hello, non sequitur. "What?"

"Seriously, if you're involved with Allie, there are things you should know."

"Involved?"

He shrugged. "I'm not married to the word. What would you call it?"

Bewitched? Bothered? Bewildered? Even to his own ears his laugh sounded off, and Graham glanced up in time to see the flash of sympathy in Roland's eyes. Fuck that, he wasn't going there with her cousin. "Involved will do." He sighed. "All right, I take your quiz and I get the hell out of here. The women in your family are dangerous in groups—and they get more dangerous as they get older. The men ... Well, there aren't as many of you, and you've clearly got hidden depths."

"We choose."

"What?"

"We choose."

"Yeah, I heard you. *What* do you choose?"

This had to be the first time he'd seen a lawyer blush. "Sorry. The women. We choose the women."

"For what?"

The blush deepened.

"Oh. Well, good for you. What happens if they don't like your choice?"

"That never happens."

"Never?"

Roland shook his head—looking a little smug, the bastard. "The aunties keep the lines from getting too close and . . ."

Graham cut him off with a raised hand. "Way more about your family than I need to know. Seriously. I'll just finish up my Gale family 101 and book it, shall I? The whole family's pretty much unable to cope with anyone else having power. And when I say, unable to cope, I mean viciously unable."

"Not having. Holding."

"Yeah, whatever. Potato, potahto." Interesting he wasn't arguing about the vicious part. "Thanks for playing, I'll see myself out."

Roland sighed. "Allie doesn't want you to leave."

"Look, Allie . . ." And then the lightbulb went off. "You do what the women tell you."

"No. Yes. If we haven't chosen." He rubbed at the faint scar along the edge of his jaw. "It's complicated."

"Seems simple enough to me."

"Why did you take that shot last night?" When Graham didn't answer immediately, he spread his hands. "Complicated."

Fucking Christ, he couldn't believe this was happening. "I'm not getting past you, am I?"

"In your condition, no. If you were healthy . . ."

"I'd knock you on your ass."

"Maybe."

The bastard's smile had turned distinctly speculative.

His boss knew he was alive—the glyphs provided basic information that couldn't be shut off—and he probably had a damned good idea of where he was given that the only other place in the city able to isolate him so completely was inside Catherine Gale's wards. Not that it mattered since Stanley Kalynchuk would not ride to the rescue of the man he paid to rescue him— for a broad definition of rescue. His boss believed in a distinct adherence to job descriptions. And that was ignoring the certainty that if he left the office, he was dragon chow. If he was lucky. "How long is Allie going to be *busy*?"

"Hard to say. There's a Dragon Lord in the store."

Graham glanced down. He couldn't stop himself. The floor remained opaque. "Are you fucking kidding me?"

"It's not what you think."

"You don't know what I think."

"You're concerned about the possibility of Allie making a deal with your employer's enemy. Perhaps agreeing to turn your employer over to them. She isn't. She just wants them to stop burning the city down while they're waiting for the inevitable confrontation. That was what she intended to speak to them about last night, but you interrupted. I don't know why he's here, but I do know that's what she's telling him."

"She's dictating terms to a Dragon Lord?" Why not? She'd clearly dealt with both Dragon Lords out on the street last night, armed with a piece of sidewalk chalk, his dumbass heroics unnecessary. He rubbed his temples. "Meds?"

Roland shook his head as he walked over to the

table and picked up a prescription bottle of pills. "You shouldn't be up and walking around."

"That's not what gave me the headache," Graham muttered. He thought about making a run for the door but figured he'd had enough futility for one morning.

"You're supposed take these with food. You want some breakfast?"

"I want to get out of here."

"How about some toast?"

"I don't want any fucking t . . ."

"What?"

"Nothing." How hard had he hit his head? As Allie's cousin passed the mirror over the sink, Graham could have sworn he'd caught a glimpse of antlers branching out above his reflection.

"He'd like a chance to watch you burn?"

"I think it was a compliment. Man, those pigeons are never going to come out from under that newspaper box."

"Allie . . ."

"I mean dragons flying over are one thing—but a Dragon Lord landing, that's something else again. I wonder what the people who saw him are telling themselves? Denial, right; more than just a river in Egypt. And those marks on the outside of the door? He could have made them, couldn't he? Spacing seems right although I have to admit, I wasn't exactly measuring his claws last night. Or if not him, one of his brothers."

"Allie!"

She turned away from the window and the lights and sirens and the guy from the tipped SUV screaming at someone to see that Charlie hadn't moved from her place behind the counter. And was frowning somewhat egregiously.

"Allie, what the hell is going on?"

Allie frowned back at her. Charlie wasn't usually this dense. "Whatever's coming through, the Dragon Lords consider it a family matter and are here to attend to it."

"No shit, I got that part."

"And Kal . . . the sorcerer . . ." Sorcerers weren't named. She knew better than that. Adam must have left her more distracted than she'd thought. ". . . he's a part of it. I mean, more than just 'this is an enemy of his' part of it. He's part of the whole family matter that Adam wants us to stay out of. Graham's involved as long as he works for him, and I don't think I can get him to quit in the next couple of days unless I change his mind for him."

Charlie's eyes narrowed. "So change it."

"No." She wouldn't for Michael. She wouldn't for Graham.

"That's what I thought." Charlie sighed and rubbed at a red welt across her palm, probably made by that case she'd been holding so tightly while Adam was in the store. "You barely reacted when Adam touched you, and I bet the sorcerer barely got your panties damp. Which leads me back to my original question: what the hell is going on here?"

"With me and Graham?"

"He's got the family involved with a sorcerer and a dozen Dragon Lords, so yeah, with you and Graham."

Allie moved away from the front of the store, in behind the first set of shelves. She picked at a tangle of power cords, poked a finger into a bowl of lanyards, and finally said, "I don't know."

"Well, does anyone? Because I'm willing to ask around."

"Charlie . . ."

"Twelve Dragon Lords, Allie." She slapped her hand down on the counter. Allie jumped. "All twelve of them right here in River City with a capital D that rhymes with T that stands for fucked. Plus a sorcerer. Who you're hiding from the Dragon Lords. And something dangerous coming through from the UnderRealm."

"But just a little bad."

"To a *Dragon Lord!*"

Who'd put their egg in something that looked like an open mouth? she wondered, straightening a row of novelty egg cups. "He plans on having Graham shoot them."

Charlie took a moment to connect the dots. "The sorcerer plans on having Graham shoot the Dragon Lords?"

"Yeah."

"Ignoring the fact he's too out of it to shoot a water pistol right now, what are *your* plans?"

She shoved the offending egg cup to the back of the shelf and turned to face her cousin. Maybe it was time to actually have plans. "I plan to have Graham get through this in one piece, I plan to keep the city from burning down, I plan to do what I can to keep David from being tied down because some people are afraid of him, and I plan to keep the aunties out of things as long as possible because they've never gone along with any plan but their own."

Charlie smiled. "There we go."

"Interesting desk."

Michael had paperwork spread out over the car and was bent at an awkward angle trying to get a good look at it. He straightened, one hand against his lower back when Allie came into the garage. "Are you kidding? With seven tradesmen and a leprechaun in the loft . . ." He paused as the constant banging got temporarily louder. ". . . there's no room to spread out a paint chip let alone deal with subcontracts."

"Well, it won't free up much room, but I need Joe back. Charlie's decided to get her hair dyed red." She glanced back over her shoulder, twisting so she could see the second-floor windows. "And I have to check on Graham."

"The loft's coming along great, Allie, we'll be ready for the furniture tomorrow. Thanks for asking."

Michael wasn't smiling when she turned to face him again. He didn't look angry or hurt, but he did look uncharacteristically serious.

"I'm sorry. I'm just . . ." When she couldn't finish, he rolled his eyes, and stepped forward, wrapping his arms around her. Allie laid her head against his shirt and listened to his heart beat. If there was a place she felt safer, she hadn't found it.

Except . . .

Something was off.

She thought at first maybe he'd added a little more muscle, but that wasn't it. Her charm, her mom's charm, Charlie's charm—all there. And he smelled the same, although the drywall dust made her sneeze.

"Allie, did you just wipe your nose on my pocket?"

"Hey, you should be thrilled to get my snot on your plaid."

And then she realized: it didn't hurt anymore.

The pain of not having Michael, of knowing she would never have Michael—no happily ever after and never having enough room in the bed and ridiculously tall children with slanted fox eyes—had been with her for so long its absence should have left some kind of a void.

The total absence of void was a bit unsettling.

When she looked up, he was smiling down at her. "Does he make you happy?"

"Who?"

"The short violent dude you're having a little mental freak about."

"Can't think who you mean."

He squeezed her hard enough to make her squeak, and when he released her, she laughed—tried to laugh, it didn't actually work that well—and said, "We have a dozen Dragon Lords hanging around, something even they believe is dangerous coming through from the UnderRealm although they're just a little short of sharing details, and there's a sorcerer in town I haven't told the aunties about. And you think Graham's on the top of my list of things to freak about?"

"I know you," he said quietly against her hair, his breath warm and comforting. "I know you better than anyone knows you. Even Charlie. I watched you with him last night. You're going to present him to the aunties."

"Okay, there's something there, sure, but I haven't even known him for a week!"

"Doesn't matter."

"Michael, that's . . ." When muscles flexed in his arms, she stopped. Thought about it for a moment. Closed her eyes and took a deep breath. Realized why there was absence of void. Thought about a future without Graham in it. Sneezed again. "Oh, my God, I am going to present him to the aunties. How could you know that? You haven't even met him when he's conscious!"

"I know you," he said again. "Also my people are wise in matters of the heart." She felt him stiffen. "Okay, wise in the matters of other people's hearts. People we aren't expecting to be faithful to us."

Allie wanted to suggest that maybe he should give Brian a chance to explain except . . . "Did he know you were coming by? Because, everything else aside, if he thought he was going to get caught, he'd have never done something so stupid."

"Didn't look like he cared."

"Maybe the light reflecting off the moons of Jupiter got in his eyes, and he thought it was you." She could understand why Michael couldn't put *everything else* aside, but Brian had been either stupid or unbelievably cruel and neither quite fit.

"Allie."

"Sorry."

"Besides, we're not talking about the wreck of my love life, we're talking about the start of yours. When'll you take him home?"

Home. The thought of Graham and home, together, made it hard to think clearly. "Well, he has to choose, of course."

"Formality. He's nuts about you."

"You could tell that by the way his bruises were rising?" Allie snorted.

"I can tell because of how he got those bruises." He kissed the top of her head. "It's a guy thing."

"So he chooses, and I take him to the aunties just as soon as he's not working for a sorcerer or that sorcerer is redeemed by stopping the something dangerous in a way I can make look altruistic."

"Or the sorcerer gets killed by the Dragon Lords for trying to stop the something dangerous."

"That could happen. But it wouldn't necessarily be a good thing since Graham's likely to feel he has to avenge him."

She felt his chuckle more than she heard it. A deep rumble in his chest that made her think of tigers purring. "I'll sit on him for you. He's not so tough without that big gun and the small gun and the knife and the other knife and whatever that thing in his pocket was. Also, he's got two broken ribs and he's shrimpy. I can take him."

There was really only one thing she could say to that. "Thank you."

Graham was dressed when Allie got up to the apartment and sitting in one of the brown velvet armchairs. He brushed pale crumbs off his dark shirt when he saw her and heaved himself up onto his feet. He'd gotten most of his color back although the easy grace that used to define his movements would be a longer time coming. His eyes were half closed. His hair was a little greasy. He really wasn't very tall.

But she wanted to walk into the circle of his arms and stay there.

She wanted him to say something because she couldn't get enough of the way his voice stroked against her skin.

She wanted to fillet a Dragon Lord for having injured him.

She wanted to bake him pie.

And she was going to present him to the aunties.

They didn't always let outside lines breed in, and she wasn't sure if her father's blood made another outsider a better or worse proposition.

"The man is not worth your family and mine coming to blows."

Except he was.

"You didn't want me to leave. All right, fine, I'm here." He hobbled over to face her. "And you've proved you can keep me here. You're badass; if I didn't pick that up last night, I get it now."

It took her a moment to find her voice and she didn't manage anything close to articulate. "What?"

Graham shook his head, like he couldn't believe her response, like he couldn't believe she didn't understand exactly what his problem was. She had no idea what his problem was. "You told your cousin not to let me leave."

Why was that a problem? "You're hurt . . ."

"I'm fine!"

"No, you're not!"

"All right, I'm not." A muscle jumped in his jaw at the edge of a bruise. "But that's not your call to make. You don't get to run my life. For God's sake, Allie, I've known you for less than a week!"

"What does that have to do with anything?" Maybe his meds had him confused. Or the pain. He was probably still in a fair bit of pain. "We're good together."

"You had me held prisoner in your fucking apartment!" A half gesture with his left arm, like maybe she'd forgotten where they were standing. "That's not good. That's not even some weird ass codependent definition of good."

"But we . . ."

"There is no we!"

"But last night . . ."

"Was a mistake."

Allie stared down at her hand. She'd reached for Graham's arm, but he'd jerked back and now her hand was just there. Between them. Curling her fingers in, she pulled it back to her side, wet her lips, and looked up. "A mistake?"

"You don't need me to protect you." He threw the words at her.

This was all going wrong, but she wasn't sure how. "Well, no, but if you choose . . ."

"To leave."

"What?"

"I chose to leave, Allie. Found out I couldn't. How about now?"

"Now?"

"If I choose to leave now, do you stop me?"

"Well, he has to choose, of course."

"Formality. He's nuts about you."

Wow. When Michael was wrong, he was really, really wrong. "No." She laced her fingers together to stop them from trembling. Stupid fingers. "I don't want you to go, but if that's your choice, I won't stop you."

"That's my choice."

"Your truck is parked in the alley." Allie could barely hear Roland's voice although he was suddenly standing beside her. "Charlie drove it home. Drove it here." Because here wasn't *his* home. Allie clamped down hard on the thought. "Your weapons are in the car. In the garage. You sure you're fit to drive?"

The breath he took wasn't exactly steady, but he didn't look back as he grabbed his jacket up off the chair and headed for the door. "I've driven in worse shape."

Allie stopped herself from going after him, but only just.

As he left Michael sidled past him and came into the apartment. He looked at Graham's back, at Allie's face, and said, "That's it. He's a dead man."

Roland grabbed his sleeve. "He made his choice. You know how it works."

"Does he?" Hope made it hard for her to breathe.

"Allie?"

"Does he know how it works?" There was a chance. He'd said the words, but how could it count as ritual if he didn't understand? "Does he know?"

"We talked," Roland sighed, an apology in the exhale. "He knows the men choose."

"Oh." She could feel the ritual wrap around her like Auntie Jane's fingers wrapped around her wrist—unbreakable and uncaring. "Well, that's that, then." She waved off Michael's reaching hand and headed for the kitchen.

"Allie? You okay?"

"I'm fine."

She had a house full of family, and pies didn't make themselves.

Charlie moved closer to the wall as Graham stomped off the bottom step and hauled ass toward the back door. Still shaking off the lingering effects of the Dragon Lord's power, she took a moment to appreciate the view. He was taller when he was conscious and Allie was right, those eyes were an amazingly attractive blue even when surrounded by bruising and narrowed in a distinctly pissy scowl. "What climbed up your butt and died?"

"Ask your cousin," he growled, yanking the door open, velvet voice rough.

"You knew she was a Gale when you started seeing her," Charlie snorted at his back. "Don't blame her if you're not tall enough for the ride. Okay, fine," she added as the door slammed and the mirror showed her standing with her elbow resting on the top of Graham's head. "The height comment might have been a little tactless."

Anger kept him moving across the courtyard, out into the garage for his gear, and, with his weapons wrapped in his vest, out into the alley for his truck. If she'd started with an apology. If she'd even realized how much she'd overreacted by locking him up like a ... like a pet not trusted in traffic. Like one of those little lap dogs that needed to be protected. He didn't realize just how angry he'd been until she didn't seem to understand why he should have a problem with it.

There was another little spurt of anger when he found his keys dangling in the ignition. But hey, the Gales probably didn't have to worry about car theft. Probably had charms that sent potential car thieves straight to the police babbling confessions in the hope that a raving gang of little old ladies didn't suddenly appear and force pie on them.

Pain kept the anger hot as he drove. Too goddamned many potholes. Shifting was a bitch.

It faded a little when he took a moment to pull his thoughts together parked in his spot behind the office.

This was going to be a killer debrief.

Hard to justify what he'd done to the boss. How he'd reacted.

Roland rubbed the faint scar along the edge of his jaw. "It's complicated."

Yeah. No shit.

If the Dragon Lord had killed Allie, the old women would have flocked to the city. It had been established beyond a doubt that old women in the city before the emergence, at the same time as the Dragon Lords, would most likely be fatal. He took the shot thinking he was preventing that.

Except ...

He hadn't been thinking at all.

Not thinking of consequences. Or responsibilities. Not thinking of anything but keeping Allie safe.

And, God help him, it didn't matter that he'd known her for less than a week, he'd make the same choice again.

Complicated.

"The men choose."

"I don't want you to go, but if that's your choice, I won't stop you."

That wasn't ...

He hadn't ...

He fumbled his phone out of his pocket. "I had every goddamned right to be angry," he muttered.

"You knew she was a Gale when you started seeing her."

What if he chose to change his mind?

The number he had for her connected him with a library in Kamloops.

And a bar in Hamilton.

And a grocery store in St. Johns.

"You idiot!" The overhead lights flickered and the air in Kalynchuk's office smelled of copper and ash. "If I'd wanted them to know of your existence, I'd have had you taking potshots at them as they arrived!"

Graham kept his eyes on the desk. Experience had taught him that meeting a sorcerer's gaze when he was angry was painfully stupid. "At least we know for certain they have to trace the shot to find me. I'll have one free shot, then I'll start firing at anything that comes too close."

"You'll take as many shots as you need to destroy the creature!"

"I'll only need one."

"You missed last night."

"He changed as I pulled the trigger. I know how to compensate for that now." Which was a damned good thing since there was no way to tell what shape the boss' enemy would be wearing when he emerged. The dragon would be easier to hit but harder to kill.

Just at the edge of his vision, blunt fingers drummed on an open copy of *The Western Star*. "So you're saying last night was a trial run?"

"I'm saying we can apply what I learned last night to raise our chance of success at the emergence."

"Can we?"

There were dark stains up under the two fingernails Graham could see. It was likely another pigeon had come too close to the trap on the window while he was gone. "Yes."

"Then it's convenient you decided to betray me for that Gale girl."

"If she'd been killed, her family would have arrived to investigate."

"So you did it to protect me from old women?"

The sarcasm pulled his head up although he locked his gaze on the calendar the Oriental House Restaurant & Lounge over on 8th had sent to the paper last Christmas. "No. I did it to protect her." In all the years he'd worked for Kalynchuk, he'd never lied to him; he wasn't about to start now. "But it also protected you."

The sorcerer snorted. "Convenient. The question becomes, how do I know I can depend on you? The odds are good that the next time you do something stupid for her, it won't benefit me."

"Why are you smiling?"

"You did something stupid for me." Bending forward, she kissed him gently.

Both his ankles throbbed in time to his pulse. The support from his boots was all that kept him standing. "I ended it this morning."

"Ended it? I don't think so. If you'll recall, your relationship with her is my insurance policy."

"It wasn't a relationship, you said so yourself."

"And you're not a thirteen-year-old girl!" Kalynchuk snapped. "Keep her interested in what you can do with your dick, don't take her shopping for curtains! She's a Gale; they don't believe in hearts and flowers unless the heart's on a plate and the flowers have thorns! Go back there and apologize. I want her under surveillance."

"It's not that simple."

"It is if I tell you it is."

Graham noted the warning, but he'd already worked out how to make it simple enough for his boss to accept. "The Dragon Lords have her under surveillance. One of them was in the store this morning."

"In the store? While you were in the apartment?"

"She was asking them not to burn down the city while we're all waiting for the inevitable confrontation."

"You're certain of that?"

He only had Roland's word for it, but . . . "Yes."

"Interesting." Kalynchuk started drumming out a new rhythm, a little slower. A lot more speculative. "In the store today after she chased them off you last night. They're clearly amused by her."

The smile in his voice drew Graham's gaze off the calendar to see a matching expression.

"Dragon Lords are like cats, easily bored; amuse them and they're all over you. Catch the attention of one, and the others want to know why. The Gale girl has pulled at least some of their attention off the hunt. You . . ."

The smile disappeared as a blunt finger stabbed toward Graham. Even with nearly a meter between them, he felt it connect with one of the larger bruises on his collarbone.

". . . stay away from the store. Stay away from her. I don't want them noticing you any more than they already have. If they take you out, there's nothing between me and death." Frowning, he gestured at Graham's forehead. "You're still wearing her mark."

He clenched his hands and kept his fists by his side. "I walked out before she could remove it."

"Did you? What happens if she calls and begs you to come back?"

Not likely to happen; she'd honor his choice, but Graham didn't feel like sharing that with his boss. And if he'd known what it meant, could he have walked away from a man who'd given him the world and the skills to make his way in it? The man who'd been there for him when his family had died and . . . and he never thought about his family. What the hell was up with that?

"I'll make my own decisions," he said at last. "The way I always have."

One dark brow rose. "You've always done what you were told."

"I've always chosen to."

The silence that followed extended long enough, Graham nearly opened his mouth to explain. Nearly. He'd learned that lesson early on, too.

Finally, after what seemed like half a lifetime, Kalynchuk walked to the inner door and paused, hand holding it open about five centimeters. "Well, come on, then," he growled, "you're no good to me hobbling about like an old man. At the very least, I'll need to fix your legs. Should hardly hurt at all."

"That," Graham muttered, reluctantly following, "is what you always say."

The pie should have provided the mindless familiarity Allie needed.

It hadn't.

Given the way her thoughts had been circling, she was a little afraid to have anyone eat it.

Plus, she'd definitely overworked the pastry.

She'd punched in half her mother's number when she realized she had nothing to say.

"I met someone, but he chose to leave."

Could she be any more pathetic? It was like Michael all over again, only this time even the sex hadn't been enough to hold him.

In the end, she headed downstairs to enter the egg cups into her catalog database. Michael went back to the loft, Roland went back to Gran's paperwork, and Joe went back behind the counter in the store. She needed her head to shut up for a while, to stop nattering at her about who and why and how and what she was going to tell David when he got here tomorrow.

At least she wouldn't have to explain about Graham. A sorcerer and twelve Dragon Lords and the imminent arrival of a "little bad" involving all thirteen of them was quite enough.

And she still had no idea of what Gran was up to even though that, not sorcerers, not Dragon Lords, not . . . reporters, was what she'd come out here for.

Had Gran seen this coming and bailed because she didn't want to deal?

Or had Gran been removed before she could send up flares to the rest of the family?

The Dragon Lords were probably strong enough to hide her death from the aunties—shoving the body through to the UnderRealm would do it. Kalynchuk was strong enough to get himself involved with Dragon Lords and assume he could win—that said power even if he hadn't been in the game very long. As unlikely as it sounded, had Gran discovered and then underestimated him?

It wasn't that Allie wanted her gran to be dead, but if she wasn't, they were going to have words. And if things continued the way they were, some of those words were going to be four letters long.

"Allie?"

She set an egg cup shaped like a panda with the top of its head unevenly trepanned back on the shelf, dusted her fingers against her sleeve, and turned.

Joe rubbed at fingerprints on the glass. "Charlie told me before she left and, well, I'm sorry about you and Graham."

"It's okay." It wasn't, but it was familiar. She stared at the mail cubbies behind his head and frowned. Most of them were full to overflowing. "Why hasn't anyone else come in and picked up their mail?"

"They don't like change. You. Your cousins. You're new. It'll take a while."

"How long is a while?"

He shrugged one shoulder. "Don't know. Are you mad at me?" he asked without looking up.

"Should I be?"

"I knew they weren't dragons, that they were Dragon Lords, and I didn't tell you."

"Why not?"

"Because I thought you knew. It sounded like you knew, didn't it?"

"Then why would I be mad at you?" She sighed. "It's not your fault. We've all come into this, whatever this is, with assumptions."

He looked up then. "I heard your grandmother say once that assumptions makes an ass out of you and of me."

"But not her."

"What?"

"It may make an ass out of you and me, but not her. It's an auntie thing," she added when Joe stared at her in confusion. "Never mind. It doesn't matter what Gran would say because Gran's not here." Sighing again, she saved her file and looked around the store. "Gran's not, but I am."

Actually . . .

"Allie?"

"Gran's not here. But I am." Allie closed her laptop, set it on the shelf and walked over to the counter. "Bottom line, here and now, this place is mine."

Mine.

The word slid into empty places on the shelves, hung itself by the paintings on the walls, burrowed into boxes of odds and ends, and just generally made itself at home.

"And because this place is mine now . . ." She grinned, riding the rush as her sudden epiphany stuffed itself into the bleeding hole in her heart. It didn't fill it, it didn't even stop the bleeding, but it was a start. ". . . there's going to be some changes. Joe, pass me those salad tongs."

"These?" The ends were sticking out of a box of old silver plate. He tugged them free and passed them over.

Allie slid the back of the cabinet open, grabbed the monkey's paw with the tongs, and lifted it out, maintaining a two-handed grip, just in case. "This is not the sort of thing you just have lying around. Or, more specifically, it's not the sort of thing *I* just have lying around."

The paw squirmed and tried to twist out from between the tarnished silver paddles.

"So, what are you going to do with it, then?"

She stared down the length of her arms, down the length of the tongs at the grubby, gray paw. An excellent question. "You wouldn't know where there's a lead box, would you?"

"Uh . . ." Joe's gaze darted left and then right, as though there might be one close to hand. "No."

"That sugar bowl, then. It's silver."

"Please don't be using that thing to gesture."

"Sorry."

The sugar bowl looked big enough, but only just. The tongs and the paw wouldn't fit past the rim together, she'd have to drop it in. Joe held the lid as Allie lined things up and let go. The monkey's paw hit the edge of the sugar bowl, slid down the side, and angled off the handle as Allie grabbed for it with the tongs. It bounced once on the counter and rolled under the nearest set of shelves.

"How does something so nonsymmetrical roll like that," Allie muttered, dropping to her knees and peering under the shelves. "Joe, do we have a flashlight?"

"I think I was after seeing one in the garage."

She twisted around to look at him. Apparently he got more Irish when there was an evil, wish-granting, simian amputation rolling around loose.

It took him a moment to catch on. He flushed. "I'll go get it, then."

"Good plan."

Head resting on her outstretched arm, she fished around with the end of the tongs. The paw wasn't technically mobile, so it couldn't move anywhere under its own power. It wasn't like it was going to hide behind a box of glass doorknobs or something. Just to be on the safe side, though, she moved the box out into the aisle.

There was no mistaking the feel of it once she touched it, but there wasn't enough clearance under the shelf to open the tongs.

"Never mind the flashlight," she muttered, without looking up as footsteps stopped beside her. "Just slam that sugar bowl down over it when I knock it clear." She heard the footsteps head for the counter and when they got back she smacked the paw out toward the edge of the shelf. "Get ready!"

Once again, it moved pretty damned fast. Emphasis on damned.

"Joe!" Allie scrambled sideways as it headed straight for her . . .

. . . and was cut off and confined by a direct hit from the upturned sugar bowl. She thought she heard it scratching against the inside curve before it subsided in a sulky silence.

Releasing a breath she hadn't realized she'd been holding, Allie looked up.

Way up.

And smiled.

"David?"

NINE

Nearly two weeks after ritual made it safe enough for hugging, so Allie launched herself off the floor and into David's arms. He felt like home, and under the faint scent of what was probably very expensive cologne, he smelled like . . .

. . . the woods. Like trees and leaf mold and growing things and rotting things, and since the paper tag on his suitcase suggested he'd just gotten off a plane and then, knowing her brother's aversion to being without wheels, out of a rental car, that wasn't good. It wouldn't have been exactly wonderful if he'd walked the Wood to Calgary because the last thing David needed to do right now was start exhibiting wild talents, but it would have been better than the alternative.

She backed out to arm's length to stare up at him only to find him frowning down at her. "What?"

David shook his head, breaking the light around him into patterns that suggested more than the movement of his hair. "Something's . . ."

"Allie?"

It was almost funny to watch David's expression

change. He wasn't used to people being able to sneak up to him. Although, technically, Joe wasn't people.

"I found the flashlight." He held it up, looking from her to David, brows drawn in. He had to know David was a Gale. The Fey always knew. "Did you get the . . . you know."

"It's okay, Joe. *He* knows." Allie touched the overturned sugar bowl with the edge of her shoe. "This is my brother, David. David, this is Joe."

"The leprechaun?"

"Yes, the leprechaun," Joe sighed.

"You're tall for a leprechaun."

If Joe had been impressed by David's potential—and most people who could sense it were—that canceled it out. He set the flashlight on the counter and rolled his eyes. "No shit."

David studied him for a long moment; long enough that Joe began to fidget and Allie began to think about interrupting. Then he turned toward her, one dark brow rising. "You gave him a key?"

Joe's right hand jerked forward and down, covering the front pocket on his worn cords. Allie, used to not being able to hide things from David, sighed in turn. "Yes, I gave him a key."

"So you're staying."

Staying? That seemed a little extreme. Although, if Graham had . . . But he hadn't. "I'm not *leaving*."

Her turn to be studied. Just as Allie was about to demand an explanation, he said, "I see."

He saw more than she did, and he seldom shared.

"I hate it when you do that."

"I know." He grinned then and stepped past her, holding out his hand. "Pleased to meet you, Joe. Welcome to the family."

"Uh, thanks?" Joe glanced over at Allie, looking a little nervous as his fingers disappeared inside David's grip. She didn't blame him. Joe might be tall for a leprechaun, but David was big for a Gale and everything he could become was right there on the surface.

"David!"

He wasn't as big as Michael, though. Allie grinned as David moved Joe carefully out of the way just before Michael charged through the back door and caught him up in a hug. Michael had matched David's six one at sixteen but had still been skinny and muscled like a whippet, the fastest running back in their high school's history. By twenty, at six five, he'd begun to put on bulk and by their graduation, he had the size advantage in every way that mattered. Michael was just Michael as far as Allie was concerned, until times like this when he had his arms wrapped around David's torso and the force of his embrace lifted her big brother's feet off the floor.

"Michael. Tool belt. Ow!"

"Sorry." He backed up a step, smiling so broadly both dimples were as deep as they got. "I thought you weren't going to get here until tomorrow!"

"If I'd arrived tomorrow, you'd have been ready for me."

"Well, if you'd arrived earlier today, you'd have been able to . . ."

"Michael," Allie growled. "His choice."

"Fine. Whatever." Michael spread his hands, flashing the pale green paint smeared across one palm. "I guess we're not hiding anything. We're not hiding anything

are we, Allie?" he asked leaning out around the block-
ade of David's shoulders.

She was hiding a sorcerer from a dozen Dragon
Lords and the aunties, but since she planned on telling
David about that, it hardly counted.

"No," she said brightly, "we're not hiding anything."

"Liar," David snorted.

"You can't count things you haven't been told; you
just got here. But since you *are* here . . ." Allie put one
foot on the sugar bowl as it rocked from side to side.
". . . help."

"There's a better chance of success," David told her,
dropping to one knee, "if you have a plan going in."

"Foreshadowing," Allie muttered. When he glanced
up at her, she smiled. "What?"

His eyes narrowed.

"There's tongs," she told him. "They're silver.'"

"Technically, a monkey's paw is a neutral relic."

"I don't care. It creeps me out, and it's staying in the
basement." David stopped so suddenly on the landing
that Allie nearly ran into him. "What?" Leaning around,
she realized he was staring at the charms. She'd gotten
so used to them that she barely saw them anymore.

"Strong protections."

"You think?"

"It's unlikely Gran was this afraid of something."

About to remind David that the aunties didn't so
much not know the meaning of the word fear as rede-
fine it for their own uses, Allie traced one of the three
charms that locked into the wards and suddenly understood. "Not fear. Gran had no family here to support

her. She knew something was coming, and she knew she'd have to face it alone. This . . . All this . . ." Allie waved a hand at the door. ". . . is just a way of filling in the empty spaces. I mean, she might have gone wild, but she was still a Gale."

The force of David's regard drew her attention off the charms and up onto his face. "What?" she sighed.

"You've changed."

"Oh, for . . ." Allie decided Joe had the right idea with the eye rolling. Gales produced the most self-centered males in the universe. The moment they weren't the center of someone's attention, that someone had to have *changed*. "Roland said the same thing."

"Did he?" David was wearing his puzzle solving face. "What did he say about these charms?"

"Nothing."

"And Charlie?"

"I don't think she noticed them."

"You don't think that's strange?"

"Maybe." Allie shrugged. "It's Charlie."

David considered that for a moment, then nodded. "Fair point. But Roland is all about details. He should have had an opinion. A theory."

"He's not you."

"Clearly."

That sounded so obvious, David had to mean something else. "And?"

"What distracted him enough that he missed all this?"

"Does it matter?"

He made a face Allie didn't recognize and opened the door.

Looking past him, she saw Roland rise, turn . . .

. . . and charge forward.

The first impact rattled the windows. The second . . .

Allie threw herself between them, a palm flat on each heaving chest. "Stop it! Now!"

She shouldn't have been able to hold them, not with the amount of horn they were showing, but David backed up a step, breathing heavily through flared nostrils and Roland held his ground, one hand rising to wipe at the blood trickling down from his forehead.

Allie took a deep breath and turned to face her cousin. "What got your sweater vest in a twist?" she demanded.

To her surprise, David answered. "You. Odds are, he's been on the edge of manifesting since he got off the plane."

"That's ridiculous. He's second circle."

"And you're crossing."

Allie spun on one heel to glare at her brother. "I am *not*."

"Then explain this," he growled, his gesture took in the obvious outline of antlers rising over Roland's head and her position between them.

Her impossible position between them.

Unless she had another cousin hiding in the sofa cushions, something had sent Roland into full-on protective mode in the presence of another male. A more dominant male. Who wasn't a part of the second circle.

"Coming up the stairs, that sounded like . . ." Michael paused just inside the door, took in the tableau, and said, "Allie, do you need me to get David out of here?"

"What?" Allie glanced between her brother and her cousin, realized the implications, and stepped back, allowing the two men to put some distance between them. And her. "No. We're good."

"Who is he?" David demanded. His nostrils flared, and Allie wondered if he could smell Graham on the upholstery.

"He isn't," Allie told him, managing to include both Roland and Michael in the silent instruction to shut up. "He chose to leave."

"Did he understand . . ."

"Yes!"

David's eyes narrowed. "What happened?"

"I don't know. He got angry, and then he . . ."

"Allie."

She paced over to the window, stared down at the street, and prayed for dragons to come roaring out of the setting sun and rescue her.

No dragons appeared.

Stupid dragons.

"I'm not ready to cross."

David snorted. "Apparently, you are. And I need to know . . ."

"Wait." Hands shoved in her pockets, fingers folded around her phone, she turned to face her brother, her cousin, and Michael. The total lack of other women in the room was just . . . wrong. "If I'm crossing, then why haven't the aunties been on me about it? Auntie Ruby called this morning and she never mentioned it."

"Auntie Ruby's senile."

"True, but . . ." Her protest trailed off as she realized the aunties *hadn't* been phoning. Not for the last couple of days. No questions about Gran. No wondering when she was sending Roland home. No third degree about Graham. Allie pulled out her phone and stared at it. Flipped it open. Hit the third number in her speed dial. It rang once. Almost once.

Her mother skipped the salutations and got right to trying to run her life. "This is a special time, Allie. You're going to need family around you, so if you can't come home, I should fly out there."

"Can we talk about this later, Mom? Busy. Love you. 'Bye." She closed the phone. "They know."

"It's your journey," Roland explained. "If they're going to travel it with you, you have to invite them along."

"You got here yesterday," Allie pointed out. "You could have said something."

"In my own defense, there's a lot more happening here than my reaction to you."

Allie shuddered. Between her mother and her cousin the whole thing sounded too repulsively like those *You're a Woman Now* booklets they had to read in grade four health class. Allie had been appalled that kind of thing happened to Gales as well and had dragged Katie and Michael off after school to wait outside Charlie's grade six classroom. Charlie'd not only corroborated the information but pointed out that when it stopped happening, a Gale girl became an auntie.

"What happens to the boys?" Allie had asked *suspiciously.*

Charlie'd shrugged. "Us."

"Hang on," Michael raised a hand, claiming the pause. "Graham's not—wasn't—family. How could he tip Allie over before the aunties approved him?"

"No idea. Haven't met him." David's tone suggested that would change ASAP. Allie tried to honor Graham's choice and not dwell on how a visit from her brother would serve him right.

"Roland?"

Roland frowned, winced, and patted at the edges of the swelling as the movement pulled at the injury on his forehead. "He has power, but it barely registers. I thought it was residue from the hexes."

"That would be the hexes from the sorcerer that Allie's hiding from the aunties."

"And from the Dragon Lords as well."

"Dragon *Lords*?" David looked even less happy. "Michael told me there were dragons."

"Dragon Lords," Roland repeated, heading for the freezer. "All twelve of them. It's a Dragon Lord family reunion right here in Calgary."

"They're interested in the sorcerer's enemy," Allie said hurriedly before David's expression translated into an actual response. "The enemy that's coming through soon from the UnderRealm. Also, they *are* the sorcerer's enemy. And they don't want us involved any more than the sorcerer does. Can't think why."

"Maybe they've met Auntie Jane," Michael snickered.

"Possible," she admitted, "but too easy. I think we're missing something."

"You're missing a basic sense of self-preservation," Roland muttered, pulling out a bag of frozen peas and pressing it against his forehead. "When the aunties find out . . ."

"I'll take full responsibility."

"And at least this explains why you and Charlie went along with such a dumbass idea," David pointed out to his cousin. "Crossing to second circle moves Allie into the dominant position."

"What about me?"

"Michael, you've said no to Allie once in your entire life, and *I won't have sex with you because I'm gay* is more a biological imperative than a bid for independence."

"I also tried to stop that thing with pumpkins at the Halloween football game in senior year."

"Fine. Twice." David sat down and stretched an arm along the top of the sofa. "Now, enough stalling; let's hear it, Allie. All of it. From the top. The sorcerer. The Dragon Lords. The Fey gate. Graham."

"Actually, it starts with Graham . . ."

"How symmetrical."

She had no idea how he made that sound like a threat.

Somehow, *so one of the reasons I'm hiding a sorcerer is so we can change the aunties' opinion of sorcery just in case you go darkside even though I don't think you are but they do* sounded scarily stupid when saying it out loud to David.

By the time she finished, the lights were on, Joe had come up from the store and been told to stay, and Michael had started frying sausages for supper.

". . . and then Charlie went to get her hair colored, and Joe and I started to put the paw away, and you showed up. That's all of it."

"If the paw bothered you so much, why did you wait so long to get rid of it?"

Allie sighed and emptied her mug. David's questions had turned a relatively simple story into the extended dance version of metaphysical Calgary. "I guess because I kept thinking Gran was going to show up and demand to know what I was doing with her store."

"And now you don't believe she'll be back?"

"And now, I don't care. She had to have seen this coming. Some of it anyway." Crossing to the kitchen, Allie put her mug in the sink and got three sweet potatoes and three Yukon Golds out of the bin. "She left it to me to deal with. I'm dealing with it. Michael, pour the grease off into the other frying pan and we'll use it for the potatoes."

"Allie."

Peeler in one hand, she turned just far enough to see

David take a deep breath. "Allie, we destroy sorcerers. We leave visitors from the UnderRealm alone because most of them are either dangerous, or crazy, or both. No offense," he added to Joe.

Joe shrugged, the motion pushing him even farther down into the armchair. "None taken."

"Now, as you're no longer protecting Graham," David continued, rising to his feet, "and this sorcerer could save the world from an impending apocalypse and only convince the aunties he'd done it to gain more power for himself—which, by the way, would probably be the truth—you need to call them."

"David . . ."

"Don't worry about their reaction. I'm here to help you deal with the fallout."

"No."

"No?"

Allie picked up the cleaver and halved the first potato. "We know whatever's coming is dangerous. We know the sorcerer wants to destroy it. We know the Dragon Lords seldom agree, so we don't know they all want to destroy it. If we leave whatever's coming to the Dragon Lords by calling the aunties in and allowing them to destroy the sorcerer, then the Dragon Lords, no longer focused on a common enemy, could just as easily start fighting among themselves and not stop the sorcerer's enemy."

"The aunties will be here to stop the sorcerer's enemy."

"No." The cleaver went through the potato and into the cutting board with a crack. "We leave visitors from the UnderRealm alone, unless they threaten the family directly. The aunties will just haul us all home."

"And?"

"And I'm not leaving until I find out what happened to Gran."

"Allie . . ."

"And even if I cross fully over into second circle, which won't happen until *someone* chooses, I couldn't stop them if they tried to make me. So I'm not calling them. And neither are you. Either of you."

"Allie . . ."

"And stop saying my name like I'm five years old and I don't know what I'm talking about!" She threw a double handful of diced potatoes into the frying pan and whirled around to face her brother. "You should have chosen, David. You may have too much juice for ritual, but technically, you're still third circle. And I'm not!"

The crack of thunder was probably outside the apartment although the sudden smell of ozone suggested otherwise. The fairy lights around the pillar flared and went out, and the glasses in the cupboard chimed softly.

David snorted and tossed his head. Plaster dust drifted down from two lines gouged in the ceiling.

Allie folded her arms, glowered, and fought the urge to say, *Don't make me come over there.*

"What's going on?" Joe whispered leaning closer to Roland.

"Metaphysical head butting," Roland muttered, fingers white where he gripped the sofa cushion.

All the hair on her body had lifted—which was, Allie realized in the corner of mind still considering such things, a very creepy feeling—and every instinct urged her to give in. Gale boys got what they wanted. And maybe that was why some of them went bad. Maybe all David needed to stay on the straight and narrow was not to get his way all the damned time!

Brows drawn in, she held his gaze and gave some serious thought to smacking him on the nose with a rolled-up newspaper.

From his reaction, that may have shown on her face.

He blinked. Took a step back, shook himself, and the corners of his mouth twitched slightly. "All right, fine."

The air between them nearly twanged with the sudden release of tension. As she wondered if punching the air might be a bit over the top, David sighed. "You've made your point, Allie, but that sorcerer needs to be dealt with. Lest we forget, all power corrupts."

"Even yours?"

"If I make the same decisions, yes." This was the brother who'd explained the world to her as she grew up, carefully and objectively. "If he isn't abusing his power yet, he will be."

"So we make a preemptive strike before he's done anything?" She turned back to the stove and took the spatula from Michael's hand. "That hardly seems fair," she pointed out, stirring the potatoes.

She could hear David rolling his eyes. "Protecting innocents . . ."

"From something he might do? And what happens to those innocents when his enemy comes through and he's not there to stop it and it goes nuts on the city? Huh? What happens then?" She turned down the burner, slid a lid on the pan, and faced her brother, using the spatula for emphasis. "First we make sure it's stopped, then we reassess."

"We reassess?" Now the power struggle was over, it seemed he could poke at her again.

"Don't make fun of me," she sighed, returning part of her attention to the potatoes as Michael slid the sausages in the oven to keep warm. "I didn't exactly have a good day."

His hands closed over her shoulders and she felt the press of his mouth against the top of her head. "I'll deal with Graham Buchanan tomorrow, Allie-cat."

She could have said, no. She could have told him to let it go and he would have. But she didn't.

"It's different for everyone," Roland explained, setting down his fork. "It can happen almost instantly—one day you're third circle, the next day you've met someone and you're second—or it can take months to fully cross. Given Graham's choice, Allie's likely to take a while."

Allie sighed and chased a pea across her plate without much interest in catching it. "Can we not talk about me."

Michael squeezed her knee under the table and turned to Roland. "How did you cross?"

"It's different for men. It's always fast and it's usually tied to choosing."

"But you haven't chosen."

"He procreated," David pointed out dryly.

"So Rayne and Lucy sort of chose you?"

"Well . . ." Roland's entire face turned pink. "Rayne essentially threw me into a bedroom at her parent's anniversary party and said make baby now."

"Make baby now?" Michael snickered and snagged Allie's last sausage. "What did you say?"

"Yeah, sure."

"Yeah, sure?"

The pink darkened. "Why not? She was on my list, but I knew she'd hooked up with Lucy, and I was ready, but there wasn't anyone I wanted to choose, so we did, and I crossed, and Lyla's wonderful. And there's the added benefit," he added pointedly to David, "that it got the aunties off my back."

"Allie's got their attention currently," David pointed

out. "All they know is that she's met a man who isn't family, and that tipped her over—the missing details have to be driving them crazy."

If the day had an upside, that was it. The aunties had driven Allie crazy for as long as she could remember; she was all in favor of getting some of her own back. It didn't even begin to make up for losing Graham—she pushed her plate away—but it helped. In some ways, she'd never felt closer to her grandmother.

"Unusual for it to happen before she presented him for approval, though. Could the sorcerer have set it in motion? He has to like the idea of one of his tied to one of ours."

"It's possible," Roland admitted. "I wasn't here at their first meeting, he may have had an artifact with him."

"Hello!" Allie waved a hand between her brother and her cousin. "*I* was there, and there was no artifact. We just connected. Okay?" Apparently she'd connected a little more strongly than Graham had but Stanley Kalynchuk had nothing to do with any of it.

"I think it had more to do with the cumulative effect of the power gathering in the city," Roland continued after a moment—during which Allie just knew they'd all been waiting for her to cry. Or throw things. Well, not Joe, he was mostly trying not to attract attention to himself, and not Michael because he knew better, but David and Roland. "There is, in a relatively small area, a sorcerer, twelve Dragon Lords, and an active Fey gate until Allie closed it down. Not to mention Joe's presence in the store plus the other Fey wandering in and out to collect mail."

"Mail?"

"Gran set it up so the Fey with more complex lifestyles use the store as their mailing address," Allie explained.

David turned a raised eyebrow toward Joe. "Complex lifestyles?"

"Uh, well, there's a loireag and a pair of corbae—sisters." He started to look a little panicked as he ticked them off on his fingers, coming up short for the number of boxes. "Some brownies who work in Lower Mount Royal and, you know, Boris."

"Boris?"

Allie refused to look at Michael, refused to think about them speculating on Gran's relationship. "Minotaur."

"Minotaur?" David repeated. "There's a minotaur roaming around cattle country?"

"It sounds so dirty when you say it like that," Michael snickered. Allie punched his arm.

"Only the loireag's been in, though, and she got here before the rest of you. It's like I told Allie . . ." When Joe glanced her way, she nodded. ". . . they don't like change and three Gales—four now—that's going to make them right cautious."

"But they will be back?" Roland asked.

"Oh, sure. Eventually."

"Good. From the paperwork I've managed to sort, the mailboxes are one of the more consistent income streams." Roland stood and began gathering the plates. "I, personally, am more concerned with why a sorcerer is interfering in the family matters of Dragon Lords."

David shrugged. "Because he's a sorcerer and power blinds them to their own egos."

"I was hoping for something a little more specific."

"Maybe I should go talk to him."

"Maybe you shouldn't," Allie muttered, heading for the fridge and the rhubarb pie Katie had sent through as soon as Auntie Jane's attempt to control the situation with blueberries had been ditched.

"Does David have to do everything you say now?"

Michael wondered, proving he hadn't lost little brother timing by leaning away just as David aimed a swat at the back of his head.

"No. And why shouldn't I go talk to him?"

"Sort of," Allie amended, sticking her tongue out at her brother because sometimes five year olds have the right idea. "And since he's basically an ass, you'll lose your temper and either you'll cream him, which puts us back at we have nothing to stop the Dragon Lords' little bad . . ."

"Except me."

"You don't even know what it is, so he's still the better chance. Or you'll lose your temper and go to take him out and he'll cream you because he's been living in the office for a while now and probably has all sorts of nasty stuff stored there, or you'll go to take him out and then Graham will try and take you out and you'll flatten him and I don't want you to do that."

"I thought he chose . . ."

"He did, but . . ."

"You don't stop loving someone just because they choose differently."

They all turned to look at Michael, who was pulling ice cream out of the freezer. "What?" he asked, closing the freezer door. "I was just thinking that sometimes it sucks to be a Gale girl. You know, with the whole choice thing and all."

Allie reached over and brushed his hair back off his face, but before she could call him on it, her phone rang. Thinking it was weird his hadn't arrived yet, she pulled it out of her pocket, checked the screen, said, "Charlie." And answered it.

"Hey, babe!" Charlie wasn't quite shouting over the background noise. "I've got the perfect thing to take your mind off your woes. The band's playing tonight at The Paddock."

The band? "You've had *one* rehearsal."

"Good thing I've got more buck than a Brahma, then."

"What?"

"Never mind; the pithy country saying thing's harder than it looks. We start at eight and play a forty-five minute set."

She reached out and lifted Michael's arm to check his watch, so she didn't have to change hands on the phone. "That's in ten minutes!"

"Okay, eight-thirty, but that's my final offer because it's a work night and our keyboard player has to be on the job at six. This is kind of a shakedown flight, a favor to our drummer, Curtis, because his brother-in-law's cousin owns the bar."

"And he gets a lot of country music fans in on a Wednesday night?"

"Probably not. Which is why I'm calling you. Bring the boys." She paused while something large and metal crashed in the background. "Tell Roland to leave the sweater vest at home."

"Okay, we'll . . ." Then she remembered. "You have Gran's car."

"Use David's rental."

"How do you know David's here?"

"My mother called. Then your mother called. Then Auntie Meredith called. And then I locked my phone in the trunk for a couple of hours. So you're crossing. Thought so. Congratulations and look at the bright side. If Graham had chosen differently, you'd have probably been knocked up by morning."

"Thanks for putting crushing heartbreak in perspective."

She moved the phone away from her mouth. "Charlie's band is playing tonight. She's asking us to be warm bodies."

"Country band," Roland expanded before David could say anything. "Probably country *and* western."

David looked as close to astounded as Allie'd ever seen him. "Our Charlie? This, I have to see."

"We'll be there."

"I should," Joe began, but Allie raised a hand and cut him off.

"We'll all be there."

Charlie snickered. "Because you said so."

"Pretty much."

"Try that second circle thing on me, Ms. Bossypants, and I'll tie your hair to the bed. Later."

She hung up to find all four men watching her. "What? Joe was just unsure, and the rest of you had every intention of supporting Charlie."

Graham could drive past the store, but he couldn't park the truck. The wheel wouldn't turn, the brakes wouldn't engage, and the gears wouldn't shift. He tried both sides of the road. Same problems. He suspected that the door wouldn't open if he tried to throw himself out. Which he was not planning to do. There were limits to how far he'd let the hollow feeling in his gut take him.

He didn't know if the problem had been caused by the choice he'd so foolishly made or the direct order from his boss to stay away from both the store and Alysha Gale, but the result was the same.

The odds were better it was something to do with the freaky way the Gale family had gone all or nothing on him. His boss expected to be obeyed; he wouldn't bother wasting time and energy on a tag, not with the Dragon Lords watching for him.

He wasn't personally concerned with the Dragon Lords. They knew about him, they had his scent, but they'd also proved to be as terrified of little old ladies interfering as everyone else.

Pointless to peer at his forehead in the rearview mirror, searching for Allie's mark; he could no more see it than he could the glyphs under his shirt. Pointless, but he looked anyway.

On his third run up to the store, heading west, heading home before the evening passed from disappointing to pathetic, he saw the door open and a crowd of people come out. Allie, Joe, and Roland he recognized. The very tall young man was probably Michael, but he couldn't identify the dark-haired man in the heavy brown leather jacket. If he wanted to know what was going on, questioning the leprechaun would still be his best bet, but it looked like Allie had decided to keep the changeling close.

No way he'd been replaced already. Even Gale girls didn't work that fast.

Did they?

He moved over to the curb lane, cruising through parking spaces empty with the street's businesses closed for the evening, and slowed as far as the compulsion allowed.

The unknown man was a man of power. Business, political, metaphysical; exactly what kind of power it was impossible to tell, but Graham had spent too many years working for Stanley Kalynchuk not to recognize the attitude that came with power when he saw it. What he didn't see was any kind of loverlike interaction between this guy and Allie.

All five of them piled into a gray sedan, clearly a

rental, the unknown man driving and the probable Michael riding shotgun. An illegal U-turn pointed them back into the city.

Graham let a car and a truck get between them, then he followed.

When he saw them pull over and park in front of a good ol'boy kind of bar, he managed to make a last-minute turn down a side street before he passed them and gave himself away. An immediate left took him down the ubiquitous alley along the back of the buildings. No surprise, the bar had a small parking lot in behind. In it, the lime-green Beetle was obvious among the pickup trucks.

Charlie, the cousin, was a musician.

The Beetle out back and family and friends pulling up out front seemed to suggest she was playing tonight.

He could walk in and pretend he just happened to be out for a drink. From the outside, it certainly looked like a place a guy would go to drown his sorrow after he inadvertently set off a magic ritual that royally screwed over his love life.

Except, he'd been told explicitly not to go near Allie.

And maybe he didn't want to talk to her when she was surrounded by three other men—one a man of power, one a Gale, one fucking huge—and a full-blood Fey.

So maybe he'd just park and sit here and wait for Charlie to come out.

"You knew she was a Gale when you started seeing her."

She hadn't sounded entirely unsympathetic.

The inside of The Paddock was pretty much what the outside had promised—a not very large, not very well lit room that smelled a lot like beer with a faint overlay of damp denim. The bar, a scarred wooden slab complete with an elderly woman precariously perched on a stool and glaring into her drink, filled most of the wall by the door. There was a dartboard tucked into the front corner by the left wall, a row of booths against the right wall, a scattering of tables, a small dance floor, and a stage tucked into the far left corner just barely large enough for the four musicians setting up on it.

"When she said *red*," Roland muttered beside her.

Allie took another look at the stage. Charlie's hair blazed under the stage lights. "Wow, that's very . . ."

"Charlie," Michael finished, pushing two tables together in the middle of the room.

"I was going to say scarlet," Allie admitted, claiming a chair, "but Charlie works."

There were two other groups of people at the tables, thirteen all together and clearly there for the band, as well as four people in one booth and two in another who were just as clearly there for the beer.

Charlie looked up as they sat down, waved, set her guitar on a stand, and made her way over to them. The jeans and the cowboy boots were country, but Allie wasn't so sure about the *Joss Whedon is my master now!* T-shirt. She ruffled Michael's hair in passing, kissed Roland and David, looked speculatively enough at Joe that Allie had to grab his arm to keep him from bolting, and then cupped Allie's face between her hands.

"You okay?"

"I'm fine." It only hurt when she breathed or blinked or . . . Allie couldn't think of anything else that started with "b" except bleed and she wasn't going there.

"Really? Because I've got some great hurtin' songs lined up."

"And emo-country's supposed to help?"

"They tell me it's cathartic." Charlie shrugged, kissed her, and released her. "Although since most of the solutions seem to be drinking yourself to death, I wouldn't consider them instructive."

"Do you know enough country songs to make up a play list," David wondered.

"Darlin', I have been listening to nothing but country since I arrived."

"And how long ago was that?"

"This is me, sweet cheeks. I could boogie till the cows come home."

David glanced around. It looked like he expected those cows to appear. "And when does that happen?"

"Nine forty-five. Like I told Allie, it's a work night." She waved an answer to the call from the stage . . . "And speaking of work . . ." . . . turned on one bootheel . . . "Like them? I bought them this afternoon." . . . and headed back to the front of the bar.

The music was better than Allie'd expected.

"That's the beer," Michael explained when she leaned close and yelled her opinion into his ear.

"I've only had half of one."

Dimples flashed. "Just think how much better it'll sound when you finish!"

"I could call in a favor from the local Horsemen and get the guy investigated." David tossed back the last of his whiskey and set the glass down with a definitive thud. "He publishes a tabloid, that's suspicious activity right there."

Allie rolled her eyes, reached across the table, and smacked her brother in the arm. "Let it go, David!"

Considering that he'd spent hours in concealment at all times of the year while waiting for targets to appear, sitting in his truck out back of a bar in May wasn't particularly arduous. He'd long ago learned how to slide into a semi-meditative state that disconnected the waiting from the actual time spent.

He roused when the back door of The Paddock opened and checked the time. Twenty-three minutes made it unlikely that the skinny, pale-haired man who stepped out into the parking lot was part of the band. When he moved away from the door and fumbled out a pack of cigarettes, his reasons for leaving the bar became clear.

Graham sighed, rubbed a hand over his face pushing his hair back, and wondered what the hell he was doing. His orders had been clear. If he'd been able to park at the store, would he have rung the bell? Gone in?

Would he have been asked in?

Probably not.

Moot point on disobeying, then.

He'd never even considered disobeying a direct order until Allie.

"Less than a fucking week," he muttered as the skinny, pale-haired guy blew out a long stream of smoke while staring up at the sky.

The smoke dissipated almost instantly, caught in a gust of wind.

Wind?

Up until right this moment, the night had been uncommonly still.

Pulling his Glock from the hidden compartment in

the glove box, Graham tucked it into the back of his jeans, and got out of the truck just in time to hear the sound of heavy wings beating at the night. The sound should have faded into the distance. It didn't. It stopped suddenly.

"Did you fucking hear that, man?" The smoker gestured, the lit end of his cigarette drawing lines against the darkness. "It sounded like the world's sails were freakin' luffing."

There were a lot of guys from the east coast working in Alberta. This one sounded well lubricated.

"What the fuck was it?"

"You wouldn't believe me if I told you," Graham muttered. Just this morning—it only felt like a week ago—a Dragon Lord had dropped by the store. To talk. To be told how it was supposed to behave while in a city with Gales.

The bar was full of Gales.

Three confirmed Gales and a leprechaun and a man of power. Full enough.

It could be at the bar to talk some more over drinks and stale pretzels.

Supporting the bands Gales were in could be part of their expected behavior.

Hell, maybe Dragon Lords liked country music.

And that was the kicker: *Dragon Lords*.

The wings had almost been in sync. Almost, not quite.

He'd heard two for certain, possibly three.

Allie felt them before she saw them. Felt the sizzle along the back of her neck, felt the air currents in the room shift to accommodate them. When she turned, all three of them were staring. Eyes nearly as brilliant a blue as Graham's, golden hair brushing his shoulders and skin tanned golden brown. Eyes a glittering copper, dark hair cropped short, and skin like burnished bronze. The third gave her a moment to look, then settled dark glasses back over eyes as red as his hair. Against skin skim milk pale, the lenses looked too dark to see through.

The clichéd black jeans, biker boots, and leather jackets over T-shirts that matched their eyes detracted a bit from the effect.

"Oh, that's disturbingly gay," Michael smirked. "They look like the chorus line from *Villains on Broadway*. What?" he asked when Allie turned toward him. "I wondered what you were looking at."

David reached out and turned his head back toward the stage. "She's looking at something very dangerous," he said quietly. "When the shit hits the fan, I want you under the table."

Michael shot the area in question a dubious glance. "I don't think I'll fit under the table."

"Try. Allie . . ."

"Hey, I'm not picking a fight with three Dragon Lords. They'll have to start it."

"I don't think that'll be a problem."

If Ryan was the youngest, then these were the next three up, banding together as protection against older brothers and the indulged younger. Adjusted for swagger, they had the same elegance of movement as Adam. The same certainty of strength. The same awareness of their power.

The prickly instability that came from being near the bottom of the pecking order, that was new.

They had something to prove, and Allie would have hated to face them on her own.

Good thing she wasn't on her own.

It didn't matter that she hadn't finished crossing, it only mattered that she was the dominant female. She settled more securely into herself, feeling for the family connections. Roland would anchor, Charlie would direct, David would use. They had no one from first circle with them, but hopefully, with David in the fight, it wouldn't last long enough to matter.

And David would appreciate a chance to hit something.

She reached out just far enough to make sure Charlie was aware of what was happening, then she waited.

Bootheels rang against the scuffed hardwood floor as the Dragon Lords advanced.

Allie rolled her eyes. With the band giving all they had to a Blue Rodeo cover, they had to be amplifying the sound for effect. Trying to psych her out.

"This city is not yours, Gale girl."

The heat of his hand went through hoodie and T-shirt, intending to burn when it reached her shoulder. She didn't let it.

Turned.

Stared up at Red Eyes, flanked by his brothers, and sighed. "Nonsmoking establishment."

"What?"

Allie gestured at the two thin streams of smoke coming from his nose. "You're not allowed to smoke inside."

His lip curled. Given that his jaw was essentially human, he'd managed to fit in an impressive number of very sharp looking teeth. "And you are not funny." She could smell her hoodie scorching. "What conceit allows you to believe you can tell Princes of the UnderRealm how to behave?"

"You're not in the UnderRealm."

"That makes little difference to us."

"It should."

"Why? Because you say so? Support your claim, Gale girl."

"Or?"

Even with the glasses on, she could tell he blinked. "Or?"

"Or what? You've made an implied threat; I'd like to hear the specifics."

Blue Eyes and Copper Eyes exchanged a glance that eloquently said, *"This isn't going quite the way we'd imagined."*

Red Eyes smiled. "Or we will burn this bar down with everyone in it."

"That's pretty specific," Allie admitted.

And three things happened almost simultaneously.

Charlie began to play an entirely different song.

David stood up and said, "Get your hand off my sister."

Allie spilled the dregs of her beer, sketched a quick charm with the liquid on the table, slapped one hand down in the middle of it, and reached for Roland with the other.

Then she opened herself up to the available power.

As it surged up and through her, Red Eye swore and snatched his hand back. Charlie's song caught the power and shaped it and fed it to David, a continuous stream he didn't have to think about or conserve; all he had to do was use it.

"It's like the rest of us know where the key to the gun cabinet is kept, but David's always got a loaded gun in his hand," Allie'd explained to Michael way back when the family'd first started to worry about David. *"But he can fire all his bullets . . ."*

"Rounds."

"Shut up. . . . and then he has to reload. If he's connected to a ritual, the bullets are unlimited. If the ritual is directed toward him, suddenly he's not holding a metaphorical pistol, it's a rifle."

"But I thought your family didn't like guns?"

"Do you even know what metaphorical means?"

Blue Eyes flew backward and slammed down on the table in one of the occupied booths. The occupants, clearly veterans of many a bar fight, snatched their drinks out of the way and looked unimpressed. Copper Eyes hit the ceiling and then the floor in quick succession. Red Eyes opened his mouth and roared out a geyser of flame.

Someone screamed.

The flame folded back on him. Ignited two chairs.

Allie reached for Michael, wrapping him in protections.

David put the chairs out. Caught Copper Eyes as he scrabbled to his feet and smacked him back down again. Ducked under the swipe of Red Eyes' claws and used that momentum to spin him in place. Flicked enough power at Blue Eyes to knock his feet out from under him and slam him into the table again.

Wait a minute? Claws?

"David! They're changing!"

They'd be stronger in their true forms. Not to mention one hell of a lot bigger.

Allie wasn't sure when, but Roland had moved to stand behind her, his arms wrapped around her waist. She leaned back into his strength and opened herself further.

Charlie had the whole band playing along.

David sketched a circle in the air. It flared out and in again, enclosing all three Dragon Lords in Gale power.

Blue Eyes staggered to his feet, one of the men in

the booth helping him out with a kick in the ass. Copper Eyes stood slowly, wiping blood from the corner of his mouth. Red Eyes took off his glasses. His eyes were blazing.

Literally.

Allie could feel their combined power beating against the enclosure.

It wasn't going to hold.

This place had to have a back door. She should have just told Michael to run for it the moment the Dragon Lords strutted in through the front.

She reached farther, but even with Roland digging deep, she couldn't get more.

Red Eyes smiled as flame engulfed him.

Just a little farther . . .

Copper Eyes disappeared in fire.

She knew there was more power out there. If Charlie were closer. If Roland could hold them both.

Blue Eyes laughed and burned.

Then Allie sank into a touch that anchored her farther from her center than she'd ever been. Allowed her to reach farther than she ever had. The power surge brought her up on her toes, grinding back against Roland's body. She could feel Charlie fighting to control it, but they needed more. More family. More than one third circle, one second circle, her and David.

"What scares the old fools most about David is that they have no idea of his limits." Gran's voice in memory.

Allie threw the power to her brother, wild and unshaped and trusted him to control it.

David tossed his head, horns scoring the ceiling, the amount of power he was handling pulling them further into the physical. Into the actual. He raised his hands and closed them into fists.

The power around the Dragon Lords slammed inward.

The fires went out.

David smiled and said, "You have a count of five to get out of here."

Red Eyes stared down at his hands with their very human fingernails in disbelief. "This isn't possible!"

"One."

Blue Eyes ran.

"Two."

Copper Eyes grabbed his brother's shoulder. "Viktor, come on!"

"Two and a half."

Viktor stretched out a hand and his sunglasses slapped up into his palm. "This isn't over, Gale!"

"Three."

"Viktor!"

Viktor snarled but ran for the door.

"Four."

It hit him on the ass on the way out.

Probably Charlie.

Allie let one final pulse spread out over the bar, easing the hysterical and the only mildly impressed alike into sleep; everyone not a Gale, or Michael, or a leprechaun . . .

"Joe!"

"Full-blood Fey," Roland laughed in her ear as Joe was suddenly sitting at the table again. "No one sees him if he doesn't want them to."

Joe blushed.

"Now that's what I call power chords." Charlie unplugged her guitar and jumped off the stage trailing two broken strings. "Good thing I was using a pick, or I'd have trashed my fingers. What'd you do to my audience?"

"They'll wake up in about five minutes and have forgotten the whole thing."

"A little high-handed," Michael pointed out as he crawled out from under the table, looked down at the stains on his knees and sighed. "I don't even want to know."

"Gale girls become aunties," Roland reminded him. "And it's . . ."

Michael raised a hand and stopped him. "Told you. Don't want to know."

Allie could feel Roland's arousal; it should have been answered by her own. It wasn't . . . quite. Part of her felt almost as though it were still somewhere else. The other part—well, that part was on board with seeing things through. As soon as they got somewhere a little more private, they'd finish the ritual.

"David, Charlie can . . ."

He shook his head. "Lines are too close. Not risking it with you crossing and this much power." He fumbled the keys out of his pocket and tossed them to her. "Take the car. I'll try and be back by morning."

He was at the door, ducking to clear the spreading tines of his rack, when Michael started moving. "I'll go with him."

Allie grabbed his arm and hauled him to a halt. Here and now, the size difference was no difference at all. "We're in a bad neighborhood in a big city. He'll find someone."

"What, a hooker?"

"It has to be a woman, Michael, you know that. Charlie?"

"I'm good for now." Her fingers caressed the full curve of the dreadnought. "When she's plugged in and played that hard, she vibrates."

"Yeah, but . . ."

"Trust me, Allie-cat ..." Her kiss was sweet and wound Allie's responses up tighter. "... I got into the music. Besides, someone needs to be here when this lot wakes up."

"But the Dragon Lords ..."

"Won't be back tonight. They've scurried off with their tails between their legs."

"There's nine more," Allie reminded her.

"And you worry too much." Charlie took the keys out of Allie's hand and gave them to Michael. "You drive."

Allie nearly missed the look he shot her, a little preoccupied with Roland's teeth in the edge of her ear. Nearly. "Oh, give me a break, Michael. It's not your first ritual. Joe, we'd all feel better if you slept at the apartment tonight."

"I don't ..."

"You won't win, so don't even try," Michael sighed, heading for the door. "And you're riding shotgun. Voice of experience; don't look in the backseat."

Shoulder blades pressed hard against the wall between the men's and women's washroom, Graham opened his eyes, stared up at the grimy stucco on the hall ceiling, and tried to catch his breath. He'd been on his way into the bar when he'd felt ...

Allie.

Her touch sank past the surface and wrapped around what it meant to be Graham Buchanan. Were he a thirteen-year-old girl, he'd describe it as a perfect synergy of souls. As he wasn't, the best description he could manage involved a gasped, "Oh, my fucking God!" as his knees nearly gave out, and, about three

minutes later, after being caught up in a surge of sensa-
tion, a spreading damp spot on the front of his jeans.
Only years of experience had kept him from dropping
his weapon as his release slammed through him.

The sudden sound of a snare drum crashing to the
floor brought him out of his post what-the-hell-just-
happened fastest-response-time-of-his-life lassitude,
giving him the energy to stagger the final two meters
and shove open the door to the bar.

"About time, dude."

The blue-haired woman he'd seen out on Beaconsfield and as he'd left that morning—Cousin Charlie—
was now a red-haired woman, although the red was not
a shade usually associated with hair. She was up on the
stage bending over the drummer who seemed to have
fallen off his stool and taken the snare with him as he
headed for the floor.

Which was when Graham realized the rest of the
band was also on the floor.

And the four groups of bar patrons seemed to
be . . .

The elderly woman slumped over at the bar snarled
in a lungful of air and snorted it out, her volume
impressive.

. . . sleeping.

He could see neither Gales nor Dragon Lords, but
the air stank of sulfur and hot beer.

"Hey! Don't just stand there like a damp bump on a
log; give me a hand."

She seemed to be trying to get the drummer back on
his stool.

She had the drummer suspended in the air, unfortunately *between* her and the stool.

Graham tucked his weapon away and stepped over
the keyboard player and around behind the drum kit.

He stood the stool upright, then held it steady as she settled the drummer down on it.

"I'm Charlie, by the way." She picked up the drummer's sticks and folded his fingers around them. "We were never actually introduced." A charm on both hands held the sticks in place. "You're the moron who made the wrong choice."

"Graham."

"That's what I said." Straightening, she pushed her hair back off her face and headed toward the door he'd just come through. "All right, let's get out of sight before this lot starts waking up and wonders what the hell you're doing on the stage."

Following her seemed like the easiest option. "I'd think my presence would be the least of their concerns."

"They won't ever know they were out."

"Some of them are on the floor."

She flashed a grin over one shoulder as she stepped out into the hall, looking so much like Allie for a moment his chest ached. "Yeah, but they're in the band."

"What happened?" he asked as the door closed behind him.

"We kicked Dragon Lord ass."

"How many?"

"Three. If the eye-to-scale thing holds: blue, copper, and red."

"Trent, Delsin, and Viktor." Kalynchuk had names for them all, although Graham wasn't entirely positive that they weren't names but merely convenient labels. "And, from what I've heard, Viktor's a nasty son of a bitch." He was talking mostly to give himself time to absorb the information that, with even odds, the Gales had beaten three Dragon Lords. Wait . . . "Who was the other man with Allie?"

"Jealous?"

"No."

"Liar. But don't worry. That was David, her big brother. Oh wait, maybe you should worry, all things considered."

Four Gales. But only two women; that wasn't the way the family worked. Or it wasn't the way his boss thought the family worked.

Charlie waved a hand in front of his face. "Don't zone out on me. I need to know what the hell you were thinking."

"This morning?"

"No, when you got that haircut." Leaning back against the wall, she folded her arms and rolled her eyes. "Yes, this morning."

"I don't want you to go, but if that's your choice, I won't stop you."

"That's my choice."

"I was angry. Allie'd told Roland to keep me in the apartment. I felt . . ."

"Like you'd been de-balled? Yeah, we get that a lot. Know that we're prone to it going in and realize that's not our intent. And you're not blameless in this, boyo; when she asked, you told her you understood when clearly you didn't."

"Clearly?"

"You're here. And that mess in your pants tells me you're still connected. And that you've been keeping your fluid levels up. Good for you. Hydration's important."

He shifted uncomfortably. "What?"

"When she reached out, she found you. Now that might have had to do with this . . ." One finger flicked at the charm on his forehead. ". . . but I doubt it. In fact . . ." That same finger flicked him again. Harder. "Well, well, well. Isn't that interesting."

"Isn't what interesting?"

"Not my place to say." Her smile had edges. "But that does explain why your touch let her reach so much farther. And considering how much juice she pulled, I can't wait to see what'll happen when you two crazy kids actually get your act together. Doubt that's going to be a ritual my guitar can cover."

"What?"

She sighed. "Just tell me what you're doing lurking around here before I have to get back to three chords and the truth."

"The Dragon Lords . . ."

"You followed them?"

"No, I was here already. I came to see you."

"Me?"

"I didn't think Allie'd talk to me."

One brow went up. "Good call."

"I thought you might."

"Might talk to you?" Arms folded, she shifted her weight to the other hip. "And tell you what?"

His mouth was dry. He swallowed and wet his lips. "If there was a chance of making another choice."

Her eyes were the exact same shade as Allie's. After a long moment, she sighed again. "If you'd had a chance to talk to Allie tonight—which would probably have happened after David pounded on you for a while— what would you have said?"

"That I . . . That we could . . . It isn't as simple as . . ."

It wasn't simple, that was the problem. Not given what she was and what he did. Wanting her wasn't enough to cut through the tangle.

The other brow rose.

"I don't know," he admitted.

"An honest man." He could see the family resemblance even more strongly when Charlie smiled. "When you figure out what you want to say, I'll make sure you get a chance to say it." Grabbing his wrist, she pulled a sharpie from her pocket and scrawled a string of numbers on the back of his hand. "If you don't get through at first, keep calling. Sometimes I leave my phone in the freezer. And now . . ." She cocked her head. "Sounds like people are waking up. I need to get back in there."

"What are you going to tell them?"

"That I went to see a man about a horse." Hand on the door, she turned and grinned. "I'm getting the hang of the cowboy talk."

TEN

Reluctant to leave the warmth, Allie rolled away from Roland's side and peered at the clock. Seven twenty. The good news was, her body no longer thought it was two hours earlier. The bad news; she could tell she wasn't going to get back to sleep, and it was significantly earlier than she needed to get up.

She had two options. Get up. Or don't. Well, technically three, but she really didn't much feel like waking Roland up. If it had been Graham . . .

The floor was freezing. In cold weather she'd charm it warm before she got out of bed, but it hadn't seemed worth it in May. She really had to start remembering she was in Alberta.

A night-sight charm on one eyelid allowed her to dress quickly and find her phone. Holding her shoes, she pulled open the bedroom door and slipped out into the living room.

Michael had sprawled out over one sofa bed on his stomach, facing the bedroom with one arm tucked up under his head and the other dangling off the edge, his knuckles resting on the floor. He had the blankets pulled high around his shoulders, leaving both feet uncovered and only actually on the mattress because he was stretched diagonally across it. Leaning over, she gently kissed the top of his head without waking him and smiled when he did.

Joe hadn't bothered opening the other sofa bed and lay cocooned in blankets on the couch—although Allie had to strain to see him. Her charm seemed to have no effect on his ability to disappear. Her first inclination was to do something about that, arrange it so *she* could see him, at least, but as it seemed to be the only ability of his blood he'd kept, she decided to leave things as they were. For the immediate future anyway.

Neither Charlie nor David had come home.

Charlie did that sometimes. Better to believe she'd done it again than believe she'd been eaten by Dragon Lords. Still . . .

On her way to the door she sent a quick *Where r u?*

Out on the landing, as she bent to put her shoes on, her pocket vibrated.

Home soon!

Allie sighed and thought about calling. Wherever she was, Charlie was awake and in no danger. Or at the very least, still in possession of one thumb. And would have called her rather than texting back had she anything to say that she was willing to say over the phone.

Okay, then. Time to worry about David.

David didn't wander off.

Not ever.

She wasn't particularly worried about him being eaten by Dragon Lords—given the amount of power he'd needed to ground, the odds were better he'd have been doing the eating. She wasn't at all worried that whoever he'd found to ground off with had been more than he could handle—in any of the many ways that phrase applied. She wasn't worried about anything in particular except that he wasn't home and that was worrying. Just because.

The sun had been up for almost two hours, but the sky was so overcast that very little light made it into the back hall. If it hadn't been for the light reflected off the mirror . . .

Allie frowned at her reflection. She was holding the baby again, a scaly tail emerging from the swaddling to lash against her leg. As far as she could remember, this was the first time the mirror had repeated an image. Well, except for showing Michael naked every single time he passed but, in all honesty, given the chance who wouldn't?

"Are you warning me against the youngest Dragon Lord?" Allie asked quietly, rubbing the frame with her thumb. "Is Ryan going to try something?"

Her reflection suddenly sported a dunce cap.

"Well, excuse me for not getting it," she sighed. "I need a coffee. We'll try again later."

She glanced out the window as she passed. The courtyard was empty, the tiny shrubbery slightly disheveled. Given that at some point yesterday afternoon Michael had moved the old staircase to the loft out into the courtyard and leaned it against the wall, that was hardly surprising. Slightly more surprising that the shrubbery was intact at all given the size of Michael's boots.

The store was strangely quiet.

Given their sales, it was quiet a fair bit of the time, but this was different. This was the kind of quiet that suggested she'd just missed something. Quiet after the fact.

The glow-in-the-dark yoyos were glowing slightly.

Allie blew a charm into the air in front of her, just to make sure she was alone in the store. She was.

The cashbox was in place behind the counter.

The cash was in it.

She'd moved the monkey's paw yesterday, and none of the other artifacts were likely to be recognized by someone without power. Half of them *she* couldn't recognize until she actually came in contact with them.

Empty store. Unburgled.

The reaction of a box of phosphorescent children's toys was not enough to stop her from going next door and getting a coffee.

There was an unexpected line at the counter, which actually shouldn't have been unexpected Allie realized, given the trucks parked out front. Not that waiting was going to be a problem since David sat at one of the tiny tables, talking on the phone, two red mugs and an empty plate in front of him. She could just barely make out the reflection of horn in the window. Considering he'd probably been up all night, he looked good. Rakishly stubbled and very well grounded. Of course, given that last burst of power he'd handled, he could likely stay up for three or four nights with no ill effects.

Allie slid into the other chair and picked up the second mug.

"Yes, that's possible."

Black. When she mouthed a silent *mine* at her brother, he nodded.

"I'll deal with that if it happens."

The coffee couldn't have been sitting there for long; it was still at the perfect almost too hot too swallow but cool enough to enjoy temperature.

"Good-bye, Auntie Jane." David closed his phone and sighed. "They can't call you, so they're calling me."

"About?"

"Last night. You know they felt the working."

She knew but not on a conscious level. In all honesty, she hadn't given the aunties a thought. "Are they mad?"

"You've shut them out, Allie. What do you think?"

"They're mad."

"They're curious."

Curious aunties often ended up wondering why the object of their curiosity had stopped moving. Curious was often worse than mad.

"What did you tell them?" Because it was always *them;* that was the whole point of the aunties.

"I told them there was a bar fight. And that we won."

"But you didn't mention . . ." She flapped her hands.

David's brows went up, and he was clearly considering a facetious comment about the motion, but after a moment he decided to play along. "I didn't. You were right. You're moving into second circle . . . and I'm not. This is your play, Allie. I'll back it as long as I can."

"And when you can't?"

"Then I hope you'll take my advice." He took a long swallow of his own coffee. "Not that you have in the past."

"Hey! I got a job with that art history degree!"

"Don't have it now."

"If I was still at the ROM, I couldn't have come out here. All for the best, it's the Gale way. Now, what happened to you last night? No, wait," she added before he could answer. "Were you just in the store?"

"No. Why?"

She shrugged. "Just a feeling. And something set the yoyos off."

"The yoyos?"

"They're sensitive. Who knew." When he started to rise, she leaned forward and gripped his arm, pulling him back down. "Who or whatever it was is gone now. I checked. Back to what happened to you."

"Not really any of your business, little sister."

Allie gave him a level look over the edge of her mug. She was aiming for their mother-lite and figured she hit it when he paled slightly.

"Don't do that."

"Don't do what?"

"You know what." When she raised her brows the tiniest bit, he sighed. "I took care of it. But if you're going to make a habit of antagonizing Dragon Lords, we need more family out here."

"If they thought it would get them anywhere, the aunties would send your entire list out here in a heartbeat, hot on breeding your abilities back in before they lose them. Except they're not going to lose them." Allie reached out and wrapped a hand around his wrist. "You're not going anywhere."

He half smiled. "You won't allow it?"

Allie didn't smile back. "No. I won't."

His pulse beat hard and fast under the soft pressure of her thumb and his pupils had dilated. "You looked like Gran for a moment."

"Good." Touching him had been a necessary risk. She let him go before things escalated. "Because they're a little afraid of her."

David turned his hand over and studied the new charm. "Allie . . ."

"I mean it. They'll have to go through me."

"They're not," he began. Then he sighed again. "All right. Thank you. Now, breakfast? I'm starved."

When Allie took the empty cups back to the counter, Kenny looked past her at David, waiting by the door, and said, "Your brother." Then he returned his attention back to the customer he'd been serving. She waited until he finished, but it seemed he'd said all he had to say.

As they stepped into the store, as the front door

closed and locked, Allie heard the back door open. The muscular arm holding her in place against the glass suggested David had heard it, too. When she glanced up at his face, he mouthed: *Stay.*

So the second circle/third circle thing hadn't killed the older brother dynamic.

Allie shrugged and indicated he should get to it.

For a big man, David could move quickly and quietly when he wanted to—although since he was starting to show horn, the *quietly* probably had a bit of an assist.

"Glad to see you, too." Charlie's voice sounded a little muffled. "Now put me the fuck down!"

Allie crossed the store almost as fast and considerably less quietly than her brother had, to find David carefully setting Charlie back onto her feet. She heard a noise, suspected she'd made it, and flung her arms around her cousin hard enough to throw them both back against the inside of the back door.

"I was worried."

"Got that," Charlie gasped. "And, ow."

"Ow?" Allie pulled back. Charlie had shadows under her eyes, a shallow scratch on one cheek, and a scorch mark across the front of her *borrowed* lime-green corduroy jacket. She smelled of sulfur and the Wood.

"Just a couple of bruises. I had an interesting night."

Sulfur and the Wood and *meat lover's pizza*? "So spill."

"Upstairs." She bent and picked up her guitar case, left arm pressed against her side, sucking air through her teeth. Before she finished straightening, Allie'd taken it from her. Charlie shot her a grateful smile and added, "I only want to tell this story once so . . . Holy crap, David. Do you have Batman tucked in those tights with you or are you that happy to see me?"

Allie turned to see that the mirror had dressed David's reflection in a Superman suit.

"Man of power," she explained and gave serious thought to taking a picture. Threatening to spread the image among the younger members of the family would give her blackmail material for years. Charlie's reflection had acquired dragon wings, and Allie was holding the lizard baby again. "It keeps showing me that," she murmured, as they started up the stairs. "I wonder what it means."

"Babies . . . second circle." Charlie snorted. "Seems obvious to me."

"Allie, you didn't . . ."

She rolled her eyes and shoved David to get him moving again. "Don't worry. I like Roland and all, but we didn't make a baby. Give me credit for a little control." If it had been Graham, her answer might have been different. It seemed she'd had very little control around him right from the beginning.

The thought must've shown on her face because Charlie reached out, wrapped her right arm around Allie's shoulders, and hugged her close.

"We talked about families," she said softly, too softly for David to hear. "Back when we had that first coffee together. The whole cousins piling out of the woodwork thing came up. He'd lost a big family, six brothers and two sisters plus his parents in a fire, but he had . . . has lots of cousins, too. I told him I just had the one brother. No sisters."

She glanced up at David, already on the landing.

"Aunties would have been happier if he *was* your sister," Charlie said.

"The aunties would have been happier if he was three or four of my sisters *and* a brother," Allie told her.

"Is it weird that we talked about kids the second time we ever met?"

"Don't sweat it, sweetie, it was likely the connection manifesting early."

"Right," Allie snorted. "Some connection."

"He just chose to leave, Allie. He didn't choose to never come back."

"That's not the way it works."

Charlie shrugged as she moved past her, through the door David was holding open, and into the apartment. "Maybe it should. Work that rebel thing you've got going here. Rise and shine, gentlemen!" She'd slid into her bar voice. The windows rattled. Men woke up in Edmonton. "I have tales of daring to share!"

Charlie swallowed her last bite of scrambled eggs with fried mushrooms and garlic and sighed happily as she put down her fork. "That's better. Seems like that pizza was a long time ago."

"Tales of daring," Michael prodded, around a mouthful of toast.

She looked around at her cousins and Michael and Joe and figured she'd kept them waiting as long as she could. Which, to be honest, had been about half an hour longer than she thought she'd be able to, but ritual—and the grounding after it—worked up an appetite, and breakfast had proved to be too tempting to resist. "All right." Pushing her chair out from the table, she picked up her mug and got comfortable. "I left the bar around ten thirty . . ."

As she stepped out the back door, Charlie glanced up at the sky. Although she honestly believed the Dragon Lords had run far and fast after they'd had their scaly asses handed to them on a platter, there *were* another nine, so a little caution couldn't hurt. The rain had passed and the sky was clear, the stars as bright as they ever got over the city's lights. No triangular shape blotted out bits of the heavens and the only sound she could hear was a distant horn and what sounded like "I Don't Care" by Fall Out Boy seeping out of one of the cheap apartments bordering the far side of the parking lot. She was vaguely appalled that she recognized it.

The bartender's station wagon was all that remained to keep the Beetle company. The rest of the band had left with their friends and family pretty much the moment they'd finished the set. Two of them had babysitters to pay off.

She didn't see him until she was almost at the car and he straightened from where he'd been leaning against the hood. When he tossed his head, throwing long bangs back off his face, his eyes were a brilliant and familiar green.

Instead of his brothers' faintly ridiculous "I'm a badass" uniform, he wore baggy jeans with a T-shirt and a gray hoodie under a brown windbreaker. He didn't look much older than Dmitri, and that helped dim the *want* down to a manageable level.

As he'd obviously seen her, retreat seemed an unlikely option.

Charlie adjusted the grip on her gig bag and wished she had the guitar out in her hands. "What can I do for you, Ryan?"

He shrugged, hands shoved into his pockets. "You walk in the Wood. I could smell it on you the other night."

"Yeah, and?"

"There's something . . . around." A glance to either side, brilliant eyes searching the shadows. "Watching and stuff. I see it . . ." He waved a hand beside his head. "Here. Out of the corner of my eye. It's gone if I look at it straight. I have been hunting it because I do not trust anything that watches from the edges, but I think it hides in the Wood when I get close."

When Charlie spread her hands in the universal gesture for *Yeah? So?,* he rolled his eyes.

"You walk in the Wood. You can take me. I can hunt it down."

And bring it back and get my brothers to take me seriously, Charlie added silently. Aloud, she said, "How long has this thing been hanging around?"

"Almost two months . . . No." Ryan snorted out two streams of smoke and tossed his hair back again. "Not month, week. Thirteen days. I get days. Sun comes up, sun goes down. Weak means not strong. It's a stupid word for time."

"It's week with two ees."

"So?"

"Never mind." Brushing past him, close enough to feel the heated air, she opened the door and slid her gig bag into the backseat. It had been about two weeks ago that the shadow had first shown up in the Wood, nearly pushing her off the path when she'd gone to pick up Roland in Cincinnati and later, when she'd tried to get to Allie, flinging her out of the Wood completely. Odds were good her shadow and Ryan's watcher were one and the same. Straightening, she shoved the seat back and said, "Okay."

"Okay?"

"Okay, I'll take you into the Wood to hunt this thing."

"Oh."

"Disappointed?"

"I thought you would need to be threatened," he admitted.

"Hey, you're plenty scary just standing there." When he snorted out more smoke, she grinned. "Yeah, I didn't believe that either. Get in the car and let's go."

"Where?"

"Nose Hill. There's a lot of wild out there, and with something your size in tow, I may need to get a run at it."

"I am not that much larger than you."

"In this shape. But we'll be taking the other shape with us, right? That's plenty big," she said when he nodded.

He looked pleased as he got into the car, and Charlie grinned. Apparently size mattered even to Dragon Lords.

Traffic was light at ten forty on a Wednesday, so they made good time. Ryan tried to look like he was holding the handle on the dash because it was clearly there in front of him to be held, but his grip compacted ridges into the plastic.

"There is much of your family's magic on this vehicle," he said with forced nonchalance. "Does it make the vehicle safer for the speed it goes?"

"Not really." She turned onto 14th Street from Memorial Drive. "Most of the charms make it go faster."

"Oh."

Laughing now, *not* a good idea. "First time in a car?"

"Yes. I have never been to the MidRealm before. It is hard for us to do and all the time there are fewer places of power to ease the way."

"And that's why Adam commandeered a Fey gate?" Dragon Lord or not, UnderRealm or not, Adam was going to catch high holy hell from the Courts when he got home if he'd been responsible for the breach in security.

"I do not know *commandeered,* but when he saw what the youngest was doing, he tricked the guard, made him think the gate was closed so that he would leave." The young Dragon Lord wasn't exactly babbling, but nerves had definitely loosened his tongue and he seemed to find talking preferable to thinking about his current mode of transport. Charlie was all over that. "We were not all supposed to come, only those who agreed with Adam, but once the others knew the gate was open, there was no one to stop them. Now we are all here, and there is nothing to do but wait and avoid each other until the time for waiting is over and we know for sure who will stand with us."

"I thought you were the youngest."

"I am."

"You said Adam saw what the youngest was doing."

"No. I did not."

Charlie could smell the acrid and unforgettable scent of burning plastic. Confirmation wasn't necessary; she knew what she'd heard. "So, twelve of you, eh? That's a big family."

"Thirteen. We have a sister as well. And thirteen is not large. There were many, many more in the clutch, but . . ." Charlie caught his shrug in the corner of her eye, the move quintessentially teenage boy. "Mother sat for a long time. She got hungry."

"Your mother ate some of your brothers and sisters?"

"No, my mother ate some of her eggs. They are not brothers and sisters until they hatch. And she only ate two hatchlings. It is hard for us to ignore meat when it is helpless. Our sister . . ." He snorted. ". . . she had to be so careful and she was so angry. That was scary. We all were very careful to stay clear after she finished Mother, although Mother was large enough it took time."

"Finished ... ?"

"Eating."

"Right. And your father? No wait, let me guess. Your mother ate him before she started laying the clutch."

"Yes. You are clever because Adam says your mothers do not do that."

"So your sister ate your mother before she started laying? Why didn't she eat the father?"

Ryan shrugged again. "He wasn't around."

Smart guy, Charlie acknowledged.

"And there wasn't much meat on him," Ryan continued. "Here, cows are good and buffalo is better. Adam won't allow us to eat people."

"But not everyone agrees with Adam."

"He would make them agree with this. He knows the MidRealm best."

"He's probably right anyway." Charlie turned into the park at the first entrance past John Laurie Boulevard. "We taste like pork. Eat a pig, have the same experience, no one screams at you."

"Thank you. That is good to know."

When she turned off the engine, he released the handle, took a deep breath, and nearly filled the car with smoke when he exhaled. "I do not think any of the others have done that!"

"Good for you," Charlie coughed, all but flinging herself out into the parking lot. Ryan followed more slowly, trying to look like mild asphyxiation had been his intent all along.

"Ryan ..." Wiping her nose on her cuff, she tried again. "Ryan, does Adam know you're with me?"

"He does not keep me. And besides, he proved you were safe when he went to you this morning."

"Technically, he went to Allie, but yeah, okay, fair point." Her gig bag smelled a bit like sulfur, but the guitar inside it was fine. She settled the strap over her shoulder and closed the car door, indicating Ryan should do the same. "There's a path over there leading into the park. Let's get this show on the road."

It wasn't easy getting Ryan into the Wood. Charlie could usually slip in past a couple of bushes, but carrying the weight of a full grown Dragon Lord . . . although weight wasn't exactly right. More like essence. Presence? Charlie was pretty damned sure she felt claws on her shoulder and heard wings at one point during the walk, but she kept playing and kept walking. She'd be damned if the Wood was going to keep her out.

Eventually, she learned enough of Ryan's song that they got in.

"That," she panted, dropping down onto a log beside the path, "was not fun."

I didn't think it would be so hard. Ryan had slipped back into his true form. Charlie could still hear him although his lips didn't move. Well, his mouth didn't move. Dragons didn't actually have lips. *You can rest here while I hunt.*

"It's easy to get lost in here, I'd better go with you."

No, you would only slow me. I cannot get lost as long as I have your scent.

"You saying I smell?"

The enormous eyes blinked once.

"Never mind." She waved a hand. "Have fun, I'll be here when you need to go home."

She could feel the shadow's presence to the left, down where the trees began to grow farther apart, their heavy crowns blocking the light. Apparently, so did Ryan because he rose into the air—much more easily than he had out in the world—and sped off toward it.

Either his size was flexible here or he could adjust the landscape more precisely than she could or those trees were farther apart than she'd thought because he slipped between them with sinuous grace and disappeared.

Time passed because Charlie played her heartbeat on her base strings. Without that to ground her, she would have had no grasp of when to emerge. Time moved differently in the Wood, if and when it moved at all and, for all the time she'd spent traveling, she'd never sat still and allowed the Wood to move around her before. Usually they danced as partners. She found it interesting that no matter how much the surrounding landscape changed, the log she sat on and the gap Ryan had used to get in among the older trees stayed the same.

One heck of a lot of heartbeats later, she caught a glimpse of the shadow. It came to the edge of the trees, skidded along a gully, flowed over a dry riverbed, its movement almost familiar. It wasn't moving in the Wood, it was moving through the Wood, becoming the fixed point.

"Ryan! It's trying . . ."

It slammed into her, knocking her over. She twisted to protect her guitar and landed hard on a rock.

And it was gone.

"Trying to get out," she finished as Ryan dropped out of the sky and landed beside her, burning and changing as his feet touched down.

"I almost had it," he panted. "It is old and canny, but I have its scent now and I will find it and I will rend it!"

"Well, come on, then," she told him, rising carefully to her feet. "If we hurry, maybe we can catch it on the other side."

"You can follow it through?"

"I'm just that good. And it went through about two meters that way." The end of a song she nearly recognized still rang in her ears. They could slip out on the same notes.

Except they came out where they came in, deep in the park.

"It is the site of power, on the top of the hill," Ryan sighed. "It is too strong and it has pulled us here and I have no scent of the shadow."

Charlie's stomach growled.

"Your body is angry?"

"Hungry."

"Mine, too."

"Well, the shadow's out of the Wood and I know the song now to get you in, so I say we call the night a win. How about we go get ourselves the best pizza ever?"

"I don't . . ."

"I do. Come on, kid."

"So, we went to Chicago . . ."

"Wait." David held up a hand. "You took a Dragon Lord for pizza in Chicago."

"Yeah, there's this place I know, best pizza in the world. Ryan ate six, so he seemed to agree."

"What did you talk about?"

"He ate six pizzas," Charlie reminded them. "With essentially a human mouth. We didn't have time to talk about much."

"Who paid?" Roland wondered.

"Ryan."

"With money?"

"Adam made sure he had walking around money for when he was in skin, not scales. And speaking of Adam, he was waiting when we got back to the car. Which was an easy trip because of the draw of the hill." Charlie yawned and ran both hands back through her hair. "You know, Allie, if I'd aimed for the hill instead of for you, I don't think the shadow could have pushed me out. I could have skipped the whole ass in a plane thing."

"Builds character," Allie pointed out.

"Got lots, thanks."

"Was he mad?" Joe wondered. "Adam?"

"Not at me. Wasn't thrilled Ryan had gone offline for a while, though." Faced with a circle of blank expressions, she explained. "They have this whole telepathy thing going. Kind of Emma Frost with scales. Anyway, while Ryan was in the Wood, Adam couldn't hear him and then we left for Chicago before he arrived. He didn't have the fast pass, so he waited by the car. The scorch on the jacket—bit of Adam showing temper. They flame a bit when they yell. Sorry, Allie, I'll replace it. And this . . ." Reaching into her pocket she pulled out an emerald green scale about as big around as a loonie and slightly concave. ". . . this was on the ground when they took off. But it's all good," she added as David took the scale. "After he finished pulling the older brother shit, Adam seemed happy Ryan had found something to do now Allie won't let them burn down buildings."

"I just asked them not to," Allie protested, putting a fresh pot of coffee down on the table. "It's not like I said they weren't allowed."

"He could probably smell you were crossing and didn't want to mess with you." Charlie slid her mug over closer to the pot and looked sad. Allie sighed, poured, and slid it back. "I got the impression that motherhood is kind of fucking scary in their family."

"Kind of?" Michael snorted. "They eat their young."

"Only in the egg. Mostly only. Anyway, once Adam and Ryan left, I fell asleep in the car until Allie woke me. Then I came home." She spread her hands. "Ta-dah."

David passed the scale to Roland and scratched at his jaw, the soft *shook, shook* of his fingernails against the stubble the only sound for a moment. "The youngest is coming through," he said at last. "Some of the Dragon Lords are here to stop it. Some are here to assist it. They don't know how the numbers break down, but hopefully it'll be six of one/half a dozen of the other so they can fight themselves to a standstill."

"The youngest is another Dragon Lord, their nephew," Allie continued. "But their sister had to be careful while she was sitting, so maybe she only had one in the clutch and that distilled his Dragon Lordness, making him like you."

"Super Dragon Lord! I'm not saying David's a super Dragon Lord," Michael amended hurriedly, "just that this new guy probably is. If there was only one."

"I suspect Adam and those supporting his position want to stop the super Dragon Lord . . ."

Michael grinned.

". . . to protect their own interests and that he'll be at his most vulnerable when he first emerges," Roland said thoughtfully. "The super Dragon Lord is danger-ous enough to him, to them, that it was worth the risk of antagonizing the Courts to arrive at a place where he could be destroyed."

"Or she." They all turned to look at Joe, who blushed. "Ryan seemed scared of the females, is all."

"Smart of him," Michael muttered.

Allie smacked the back of his head. "Don't you have deliveries to supervise?"

"I do." He stood and stretched, T-shirt riding up to show a line of tanned muscle above the waistband of his jeans. "David, if you've got a minute, I could use your help finishing off those stairs before the furniture comes."

"I could . . ." Roland began, but David cut him off.

"Rol, last time you held a hammer, you nailed my boot to your mother's back porch. I've got it."

"You nailed his boot to the porch?"

Setting the scale down, Roland pushed his chair back. "I missed his foot," he muttered, heading for the bathroom and answering his phone as he moved. "Hi, baby girl! Does Mommy know you're calling?"

"I should go open the store," Joe murmured. He went to push his sleeves up his arms, realized he was in a sweater that actually fit, and all but ran for the apartment door when he saw that at some point Charlie had sketched a charm on his forearm.

When only Allie and Charlie remained at the table, Allie raised a speculative eyebrow at her cousin. "Well?"

Charlie didn't even pretend to misunderstand. "I thought about it, more than I did while lusting over Adam actually—Ryan's young enough to be a little more equal opportunity—but the package was so pretty I figured I'd be too distracted to protect myself against the inevitable third-degree burns."

"Safe sex is important."

"There's hot and then there's too hot to handle."

"No hazmat suit, no love."

"You're reaching."

"I know." Allie leaned over and kissed her gently. "Go have a shower, and I'll be in to charm those bruises for you before I head downstairs."

"Sounds good." Charlie paused just outside the bathroom door. "You should call Graham. Share information if nothing else."

"Nothing else."

"Allie . . ."

"He chose, Charlie."

She stared across the room for a long moment then shook her head. "If you say so."

"Hey! Knock first!" Roland yelled as Charlie pushed the bathroom door open.

"Dude, like I haven't seen it before."

Allie pulled out her phone. Opened it. Closed it again.

Graham might not know exactly what was coming through, but Kalynchuk certainly did. She didn't know what he'd done while in the UnderRealm to piss off the youngest of the Dragon Lords although, since the youngest in any family spent a lot of time and energy trying to prove themselves, it was possible he hadn't done much.

Either way, speculation wouldn't help Graham.

Before the imminent arrival of the Dragon Lords had driven him into hiding, Stanley Kalynchuk had lived in Upper Mount Royal. Big house, extensive grounds, a few too many rich American neighbors for Graham's liking, but he kept his opinion of that to himself. Many of the odds and ends scattered through the house were objects of power, artifacts displayed like they were nothing more than a rich man's knickknacks, and half of the enormous basement had been turned into a workshop.

Spinning the white shell around on the desk with the point of the letter opener, Graham waited to be called into the inner chamber that had become living space and workroom in one. Cramped, but he suspected Kalynchuk missed the ostentatious displays of power more than the square footage. He'd loved to show off his collection of weird.

"And this," Kalynchuk paused in front of a corner cabinet and indicated a brass hourglass about ten centimeters tall. "This contains the sand of time."

"Because it's an hourglass."

"No, the actual sand of time. Turn the glass and while the sand runs out, time stops for everyone but the one whose hand is on the glass."

There wasn't that much sand. "How long does it take."

"Two and a half seconds."

Graham'd had a little trouble seeing the point, but he'd made a polite noise and the tour had continued.

"This is a cross-section of the thighbone of the last True Hero."

That had been just a bit creepy. When Kalynchuk had moved to the more defensible position in what had been his office closet, both hourglass and thighbone had been locked into the vault by the workroom with about half of the visible artifacts. The rest, and the basics from the workshop, had been brought here.

Graham flicked the shell around again and wondered how much longer he'd be kept waiting. He'd had his ritual bath and now he could really use a ritual cup of coffee as well as a few ritual hours on his computer clearing up some ritual bills for the newspaper. *The Western Star* went to the boxes on Wednesdays, so Thursdays were light, but he still had work to do.

For his *other* job.

Maybe he'd start writing up that piece on the Emporium. He'd gone over a few of the items for sale with Catherine Gale, but he could certainly use Alysha Gale's take on them—they'd done nothing in the store itself.

His mind wandered off to the sorts of things they *could* have been doing in the store had they still been doing things.

"Thinking of that Gale girl?"

Startled, Graham jerked back and knocked the shell off the desk. Paper clips went flying. The shell bounced twice and came to rest, spinning slowly by his boss' left foot.

"Sorry, I'll just . . ."

"Get your head in the game," Kalynchuk snarled, the shell suddenly back on the desk, the paper clips back in the shell. "If these are the lingering effects, you're better off without her." He stepped back, indicating Graham should enter. "Are you able to remember the rules, or should I go over them again?"

"Don't touch anything, do exactly as I'm told; it's not rocket science, Boss."

"In your current state it could be," he muttered as Graham brushed past. "Stand there, on the right side of the table, facing the table."

The table was about a meter and a half long and no more than half a meter wide. On it was a cast iron pot with a pouring lip suspended on an iron cradle over a scorch mark on the table. In the pot, a small ingot of lead as well as shavings of a number of different metals not usually used for alloying. Next to it, a single cavity bullet mold.

"They call this Dragon's Fuel," Kalynchuk said as he set a sugar-cube-sized piece of what looked like black honeycomb down under the pot. "Ironic, isn't it. This is almost the last of the supply I brought back from the UnderRealm. When we've dealt with the threat, I may finally be able to go back and get more."

The knife he chose was the smallest on the rack, about six centimeters long and made of silver. Graham had always thought that for a man who kept a hired gun, his boss was just a little too enthusiastic about sharp objects.

"Hold your hand out over the pot. The blood must join the mixture at the moment the metals liquefy."

"And you need my blood because?" He'd given blood in these kind of rituals before, but he drew the line at bleeding without knowing why.

"To aid your aim."

"I don't miss."

"This time, you *can't* miss."

"And your blood is in there for?"

Kalynchuk paused, sleeves pushed up, old burn scars on his forearms looking shiny under the overhead fluorescent lights. Graham thought he might not answer; he didn't always, but in the end, something one of Graham's journalism profs had told him usually held true—people liked to share how clever they were.

"My blood combined with the power I'll bind to this bullet is what gives us a chance to kill the creature. You will be the system of delivery, but I will strike the final blow. From here on in, don't interrupt."

A short chant in words that sounded painful to pronounce ignited the fuel. It burned white hot, too bright to look at directly. Hand held out over the pot, Graham could feel the heat pulling the skin on the inside of his arm tight and he wondered if his boss' scars had come from learning to control the freaky stuff. But *that* he knew better than to ask.

The knife was sharp enough; he barely felt the point go in and watched in fascination as two drops of blood fell toward the metal. He'd had reason to cast silver bullets in the past, and he knew that liquid and molten metal was a bad combination.

"Step back!" Kalynchuk barked as the blood made contact.

Graham jumped back as a column of black smoke rose up and spread along the ceiling. After the first time he'd emptied the building, Kalynchuk had ordered Graham to strip the offices of all fire alarms. Graham hadn't been happy about it, not with the way his boss preferred to work, but he did as he was told.

Watching the smoke, he thought he could hear screaming. His mother's voice calling his name. His father calling for her. One of his uncles had told him the house had burned so hot and so fast that everyone had to have died instantly. That they hadn't suffered. The rubble had smoked for three days before the rains put the last of it out. They all said it was a miracle the whole town hadn't gone up. He rubbed at his forehead, trying to rub the memories away.

He never thought about the fire.

"No point in dwelling on the past." Kalynchuk's voice in his head merged with Kalynchuk's voice chanting what he assumed were words of power regardless of how made up and vaguely ridiculous they sounded.

When the smoke and the chanting died down, the sorcerer picked up a ladle.

"You need to flux the metal," Graham pointed out. Generally, he wouldn't have said anything, but generally Kalynchuk wasn't working within his area of expertise.

"The blood has purified it."

Not in the real world, but from what he'd seen, sorcery was at least one step left of reality anyway, so Graham let it go.

Kalynchuk brought the mold horizontally to the nozzle on the ladle, then rotated it to vertical, lifted it far enough to allow a small puddle to form on the sprue plate, then set the ladle back into the . . .

Empty pot.

So he'd literally only get one shot.

A carved wooden dowel to break off the excess metal, then the bullet fell out of the open mold onto a Holstein-patterned potholder. It looked like any other hand cast bullet Graham had ever seen.

"I'd like to see your Alysha Gale cook this," Kalynchuk sneered.

Last night Allie and her family had taken down three Dragon Lords, in a bar, with no chanting or fire or bloodshed. Well, none of their blood anyway. Graham just realized he hadn't told his boss about that.

Wasn't going to.

Wasn't sure why.

What would he say to her given the chance?

I've got your back.

"So, Graham Buchannan."

Charlie looked up from feeding a new A string through the tuning peg. "What about him?"

"Do I need to have a few words with him?" David spun a chair around and settled across the table, arms folded across the chair's high back, disconcertingly dark gaze locked on her face. "Or have you got it covered?"

"Don't know what you're talking about."

"He was there last night."

She should have known David had sensed Graham's presence. "I've got it covered."

"Allie didn't notice him."

"Allie had her feelings hurt," Charlie snorted, crimping the string.

"He makes her . . ."

She glanced over when David's voice trailed off.

He shrugged. "Her crazy plan with the sorcerer, whatever the hell she's up to with the Dragon Lords— since she met him, she hasn't been thinking straight."

"Hand me those wire cutters, would you? Allie used to be happy just being one of the girls," she continued as he slid them across the table into her hand. "She was a cheerleader, she was on the field hockey team, she went to a university close enough she could come home every weekend. She got a job she didn't hate and maybe she'd be chosen and maybe she'd meet someone outside the family, but either way it didn't really matter if she didn't because she had that whole Michael broke her heart thing to fall back on. And me." Charlie plucked the new string, tightened it a little further, and plucked it again. "Since she came to Calgary, Allie's started thinking for herself, she's started *doing* things. There's a fuck of a lot of Gale girls out there, David, but this, whatever the hell this turns out to be, this is Allie's chance to be something more."

"And when you say *this,* you mean Graham?"

"No, dumbass, I mean all of it. Graham, the sorcerer, the Dragon Lords, you." Charlie sighed and lifted her guitar off the table and onto her lap, running her fingers lightly over the new strings. "Gale girls get lazy, complacent, but Allie faced down a roomful of aunties when she was thirteen, so there's always been more in her. She just needed a kick in the ass to bring it out."

"And Graham?"

"Ritual needs an auntie present to be binding."

"That's not," David began. Paused. "That's exactly what an auntie would say."

Charlie grinned, picking out the first two bars of "Avalon." "And I'll say it to Allie when I think she'll listen. Like I said, I've got it covered." The sound he made next was speculative enough she rolled her eyes. "What?"

"So you and Graham?"

She didn't bother pretending to misunderstand. "He's Allie's choice. I'm willing to share."

"It looks great, Michael." Allie linked her arm through his and leaned into his shoulder. "Hard to believe that less than a week ago this was a big empty space."

The loft now had a finished kitchen along one end, complete with a breakfast bar and two stools, as well as a bathroom with a corner shower. The larger area was carpeted in a dark brown Berber and held a green-patterned sofa, two matching chairs, a coffee table, and a queen-sized Murphy bed up against the opposite wall.

Michael leaned sideways and kissed the top of her head. "Yeah, well, if I don't make it as an architect, it looks like I have a future in general contracting."

"What do you mean if you don't make it?"

"I've got time to put in with Brian's father before I can get my license and, after I walked away, well, I doubt he'll want me back."

"Do you want to go back?"

"To the job?"

"Michael . . ."

She felt him shrug. "The job, Brian, they're tangled together."

"You need to talk to him."

"Unmarried marriage counselor talking there, Allie."

And she knew that was as close as he'd come to saying, *You screwed up your love life—what makes you think you know best about mine.* "Then I need to talk to him."

"I think you've got enough going on here. And speaking of here, who are you planning to move in?"

Behind the smile and the dimples, he looked so miserable that she let the change of subject stand. He was right; she had enough going on in Calgary to keep her from hunting Brian down and demanding an explanation, but later, when it was over, Michael was top on her "to do" list. "I was thinking Joe needed a place, but, for now, I want him in the apartment. I want everyone in the apartment. With the new furniture in the second bedroom, we can sleep ten. Well, nine . . ." Her finger bounced off the muscles sheathing his torso. ". . . considering one of them's you."

"Are you saying I hog the bed?"

"I'm saying you're probably distantly related to the Jolly Green Giant. Face it, Michael, you're large."

"And proportional."

"I hate you."

He twisted out of her grip, grabbed her ears, and kissed the top of her head again. "You love me."

She did. She didn't know exactly when loving him had stopped gouging a constant and Promethean hole in her heart, but all that remained was a memory of pain and a comforting presence she knew would always be there loving her, supporting her. She dug her fingers into the ticklish spot high on his side to get him to release her ears, and when she had him on the floor, shrieking in laughter, she drew another charm just below his right ear.

Rolling off him, avoiding his flailing limbs with the ease of long practice, Allie held out her hand. "It's getting late, I should check on Joe. You coming?"

His fingers were warm when they wrapped around hers. "What's it say?"

There was no reason to either deny or lie. "It's just something visible to let the Dragon Lords know you're under our protection."

Michael snorted as he stood. "Referring to yourself in the third person now?"

"The family's protection."

"It says *mine*, doesn't it?"

"Yeah, pretty much."

The front door was swinging closed as they came into the back of the store and, just for a moment, framed in her Gran's clear-sight charm, Allie saw glossy black wings, highlights an iridescent purple under the street-lamps. Then there was a woman, tall and angular, striding away.

"Was that one of the corbae?"

"Yeah." Joe's Adam's apple bobbed as he swallowed. "She came for her mail. Allie . . ." He gestured behind him at the empty cubicles. ". . . they've all come for their mail."

"So they got used to us. Is that bad?" Some of the boxes had been pretty full. The Fey had a fondness for mail order catalogs.

"It's not good." He wet his lips. "I think it's tonight."

"Mail call?" Michael asked from behind her.

Joe shot him an exasperated look that seemed to steady his nerves. "No, *it*. It's the best reason I can think of for them to be clearing out. This lot doesn't like to be seen as picking sides."

"Picking sides? That's . . . Oh." Heart pounding, she stared at Joe, suddenly realizing what he meant. "*It's* tonight."

ELEVEN

"Tonight? Now?"

"Maybe not right now," Joe allowed. "But given the way everyone's hunkering down, real soon. Tonight some time."

Good enough for her. "Where?" Allie asked.

He shrugged, hands spread. "I don't know."

"No one said anything?"

"No." His brows drew in. "I sold a yoyo while you were gone, but that's probably nothing."

"Probably?"

He shrugged again.

"Okay, close and come upstairs. We need to have a war council."

Joe's freckles stood out in high relief. "We're going to war?"

"Well, no," Allie admitted. "But it sounds better than we need to sit around and rehash what we know and figure out what the hell we're going to do when we get out there."

"So we'll be going out there, then?"

She shot a quick glance over at Michael. "Not all of us."

"Okay, the youngest Dragon Lord is breaking out in Calgary. There's a dozen Dragon Lords already here—some of them want to stop him, some of them don't, and we have no idea of how the numbers split or what their reasons are or if we agree with any of them. We have a sorcerer who considers this Dragon Lord his enemy and is going to use a . . ." Hand waving didn't give her the word. ". . . use Graham to stop him. Those Dragon Lords who don't want him stopped are going to object. We know . . ." She pointed at Charlie. ". . . that they need a place of power to come through. That he's not coming through at a gate but trying to slip through unnoticed. We know where there's a place of power in the city."

Charlie grinned. "Nose Hill."

Allie nodded. "Nose Hill." She paced over to the window and looked up at the sky, but all she could see was the lights of the city reflecting off the low cloud cover. *Here be dragons. Or, technically, there be dragons. Dragon Lords.* She sighed. *Never mind.* "We need to be there to make sure the various factions don't burn the city down. Did I miss anything?"

"We need to be there to keep Graham from getting his ass eaten," Charlie put in.

"Graham is . . . isn't . . ." Taking a deep breath, she spun around on one heel, the rubber shrieking against the floor, and folded her arms. "Anything *else*?"

"What exactly do you plan on having us do?" David asked.

"Just what I said; we make sure the city doesn't burn down."

"And we don't interfere in the family business of the Dragon Lords."

Although David had made more of a statement than asked a question, Allie answered him. "Not unless we need to in order to keep the city from burning down."

"And if this family business includes eating the sorcerer?" Roland wondered.

"As long as they don't cook him first over the coals of the city, we don't interfere."

"And Graham?"

Allie turned to look at her cousin. "Graham . . ." When Charlie's brows rose, she sighed. "Can we just play Graham by ear?"

"Sweetie, we can play him by whatever body part you like."

"Thank you." She ignored all the eye rolling. "Michael, Joe—you'll stay here."

"We could help!" Michael protested.

Joe shot him a disbelieving look. "Speak for yourself."

"Okay, I could help."

"How?"

He frowned. "You don't even know if you're going to do anything. I can do nothing as well as any Gale. And I can duck and cover when the shit starts hitting the fan."

"No."

"Allie . . ."

She crossed the room to stand beside his chair. "Michael, if you're there, you'll split my focus."

"I was there in the bar."

And she'd never been able to forget it, but whatever they were walking into on the hill, it wasn't going to be anything as simple as a bar fight. She laid her on his shoulder and squeezed. "I can't risk it. I can't risk you. Please."

He looked down at her hand and sighed. "All right."

"I'll leave you my phone," Charlie told him, tossing it into his lap. "You'll be connected. If we need you, we'll call."

"We'll take my car," David added. "You'll have the Beetle if you need wheels."

"Strange his phone isn't here yet," Roland mused, shrugging into his jacket. "It's been over a week."

"I'm guessing Brian's keeping it close. Hoping he'll come home for it."

"Brian can kiss my ass," Michael muttered.

"See," Charlie leaned down and kissed his cheek. "You've started to forgive him."

Graham parked his truck on Beaconsfield just down from where the two Dragon Lords had landed the night he'd . . .

The night he'd complicated his life. And for fucksake, he provided protection for a sorcerer; it wasn't like his life had been uncomplicated before Allie walked into it and began tossing the metaphorical room. Okay, technically, he'd walked into hers, but that was . . .

He took a deep breath.

Head in the game.

The game came with fire and claws and certain death if he didn't get his shit together.

He doubted very much the Dragon Lords would notice another vehicle on a residential road where even they might spot a single car in the park's parking lot. The one that called itself Adam had definitely spent time here in the past.

The Dragon Lords were still circling wide, unwilling to start anything yet, but they were all up there, attention focused on the top of the hill. There was no ambient light, no moon, no stars, but by the time he jogged through the darkest of the available shadows and reached the path he'd marked earlier as maintaining cover for most of the distance he had to travel, his eyes had adjusted enough he could pick up speed. He had night vision goggles with him, but he preferred using his own senses as much as he could.

Although, thanks to Allie, they'd been less dependable of late.

Another deep breath.

Stop thinking about your fucked-up love life.

Given that nothing much overlooked that open hilltop, he was going to have to get a lot closer to the target than he'd like. At least that made the boss happy; he wanted him right on top of things.

Just before he reached the crest, he slipped off the path to the tallest of the surrounding trees, climbing it quickly and, for lack of a decent sized branch at this height, securing a sling to the trunk. Line of sight wasn't as high as he'd have liked, but it was the best the site offered given that he had no safe way to reach the small copse of trees actually on the summit. The scattering of glacial boulders offered fuck all protection from an aerial attack. That the trees were barely budding was a good news/bad news thing. It made him more dependent on the glyphs for camouflage but reduced the chance of a sudden wind screwing things up.

He raised his M24 and glanced through the scope.

Still no sign of the target. Just a brown expanse of dead grass and a few exposed rocks.

He had the special round in the chamber and a magazine of Blessed rounds as well as half a dozen more loaded up with full metal jackets ready to load as soon as he took his shot. Hopefully, once shit and fan impacted, the Dragon Lords would be too busy fighting each other to notice him.

"Are you in place?" Kalynchuk's voice rumbled out of the earpiece.

"I am."

"Remember, you're to keep me fully informed of everything that's occurring, no matter how apparently insignificant. You have no way of knowing what small piece of information may be relevant. Is there any sign of the creature emerging?"

"No." Kalynchuk had been unwilling to allow him to carry even a small camera, convinced his enemies could track him through the signal. Hell, maybe they could. How big a step was it from large, flying, fire-breathing lizards who turned into something that looked like men to large, flying, fire-breathing lizards who turned into something that looked like men and could surf video signals?

"Have you seen any sign of the Dragon Lords?"

"They're keeping their distance."

The sorcerer snorted. "So far. Remember, we don't know which of them will be acting in my best interests, so you have to get that shot off before the first of them makes their move."

"I know. You're sure Allie . . . the Gales are unaware we have a go?"

"They don't, as a family, seek knowledge. By the time they discover the emergence is occurring, it will be too late for them to interfere."

Then it would be too late for Allie to be in danger.

He took another look through the scope.

Still nothing.

"There's a man up a tree at the edge of the hill," David said quietly.

Allie glanced over at Charlie, who made several exaggerated expressions all essentially boiling down to *"Gee, I wonder who it is?"* and while it was unlikely Kalynchuk had climbed a tree . . . "Is it Graham?"

"Steel and gunpowder seems to suggest it is."

Graham.

"Can he see us?"

She could hear the smile in David's voice as she ducked under a low branch. "Not if I don't want him to. Tidier if I took him out, though."

"No. We're here as impartial observers . . ."

"Like UN peacekeepers," Roland offered.

Charlie snorted. "Who keep getting their asses shot off because they can't shoot back."

"Not like UN peacekeepers, then," Allie amended.

"So we can shoot back?"

"Back, but not first. No matter what Han Solo did," she added pointedly to Roland.

"So we just let Graham blow away Junior when he shows up?" Charlie wondered.

Allie wanted to say no if only because they'd had proof the Dragon Lords could trace the shot and, by taking it, Graham would put himself in danger, but Graham was not her concern. If Kalynchuk had been telling the truth and this emerging, youngest Dragon Lord was more than a personal danger, but also a danger to the city and beyond, then allowing Graham to try and remove that threat was the smart thing to do. If he failed, they could act as backup.

"See, Auntie Jane, we can work with sorcery. We don't need to destroy it."

"You can work with a man with a gun. The sorcerer had his ass tucked safely behind a wall of hexes."

"But David was out here, helping to save the city."

"And you think that David allowing you to stop a Dragon Lord without any of the first circle present is a good thing? Because that amount of power will corrupt!"

"Allie?"

Wonderful. Even in her head, Auntie Jane got in the last word.

"Just thinking."

"Nice change. Do we know where exactly the shit's hitting the fan?" Charlie muttered as they peered out across an empty hilltop. "Because there's a fair chunk of real estate out there."

David shifted to settle the weight of his rack, and pointed. "About six meters out."

"How the hell do . . . ?" Allie glanced up, picked a leaf off one prong, and crushed it between trembling fingers. Even though he wasn't channeling power, David was manifesting physically. She'd thought only Granddad could do that. But they were very close to the sacred site and that proximity could easily be causing strange effects. "Never mind."

She let her gaze drift out along the direction David had indicated and, suddenly, concern about her brother was no longer front and center in her thoughts. She couldn't say if it was six meters or ten, but something grabbed her attention and held it. Groping behind her for Roland's hand, she gouged a quick charm into the dirt, anchored herself, and reached out for more information.

The ambient power, this close to a sacred site, surged up through the contact and knocked her on her ass.

Strong hands pushed into her armpits and hauled her back up again.

"Allie? What was it?"

"Not what I expected." She rubbed at a stone bruise and frowned out toward the center of the hill.

"What did you expect?" David asked cutting both Roland and Charlie off one word into their own questions. Roland growled, low in his throat, but let it go.

"Something that felt like a Dragon Lord."

That wasn't the answer to the question David had asked, but he stayed with her. "And this didn't?"

Allie leaned against Roland and thought about it. "My sample for comparison is a little small; he didn't feel like Adam, that was for sure, but he felt sort of like Adam and sort of like something else. Something I know, but . . ." Lower lip between her teeth, she let her voice trail off as she tried and failed to define the second power signature.

"You said he?"

"Male, definitely." If there was one thing a Gale girl knew, it was how to identify male power. "Weirdly familiar but not."

"Patina of the UnderRealm?"

She glanced over at Charlie. "A what?"

Charlie shrugged. "You know what they say, there's nothing like the UnderRealm for leaving a waxy buildup."

"Who says that? Don't actually tell me," she added quickly. "I don't know what it is, but it's not the Under-Realm. It's something from . . ."

The middle of the hill exploded, the sound strangely muted given the violence of the emergence. A fountain of dirt rocketed into the sky surrounding a pillar of light so bright it seared afterimages on the inside of Allie's eyes. Rather than painting the bottom of the cloud cover, like a searchlight, the pillar capped out about ten meters up.

"Like a light saber," Roland murmured.

"When this is over," Allie told him, "we're expanding your knowledge of media into this millennium."

Graham had expected fire. It was how the Dragon Lords did things. It all came back to fire. A pillar of light felt wrong in subtle ways that lifted the hair on the back of his neck. Finger around the trigger, he stared through the scope and waited for the emerging form to coalesce.

Scales would be easier.

Skin wouldn't stop him.

Weird how Kalynchuk insisted on referring to it as "the creature" as if they didn't both know it was another Dragon Lord.

"What's happening?" Kalynchuk sounded as close to terrified as Graham had ever heard him. "Damn it, talk to me!"

"It's here."

David raised a hand and the falling dirt and rock dropped harmlessly around them. Allie couldn't even feel him pulling power. She'd worry about how much power he seemed to be holding another time—here and now the last thing she needed was a concussion. All right, maybe not the *last* thing, but close.

Open as she was, she could feel the power coalescing in the center of the hill.

Not quite entirely Dragon Lord. Actually, only about half Dragon Lord ...

As she realized where she'd felt the second power, she started to run. No time for explanations. No breath to spare. No option but to reach his side the moment he took physical form and pray Graham took a moment to aim.

No question her family would follow.

The light remained for a moment or two after gravity had taken care of the dirt, then it collapsed in on itself.

"The instant the light vanishes, take your shot!"

Graham's lip curled. Usually, the boss left him alone to do his job. Trusted him to do what he needed to. The backseat driving was fucking annoying.

The light had condensed to a pillar two meters high. Maybe a little less. It narrowed as he watched. Darkened.

He drew in a breath. Held it.

The light became a man. No, a boy, no more than twelve or thirteen.

Allie dove forward while the boy was still partially light, got an arm around a narrow waist, and took the slender body to the ground with her. Rolled as fire splashed against the jumbled dirt next to her legs.

He sneezed, clutched her shoulders, and squinted up at her from under messy bangs, looking a little shocky. His eyes were a swirling mix of color. "You're not my dad."

"Graham!"

"He's down!" No time to wonder why he left out the

pertinent details. Like the way Allie had appeared for an instant in his scope and nearly stopped his heart. "I have no shot."

"Then get a shot! Put the gun to his fucking head if you have to!"

Graham had dropped out of the sling before Kalynchuk finished speaking.

"Allie! What are you doing?"

She rolled again. "He's just a kid!" Standing and pulling the boy up into her arms, Allie drew charms on damp, sulfur-scented skin as she locked herself down to Roland's anchor and reached beyond. A red Dragon Lord swooped low out of the clouds, mouth open and belching flame. Viktor, if the twelve didn't double up on colors. Didn't matter who he was. Allie cut out the middleman and slapped the flame back at him.

Dragons can't fly on their backs.

Dragon Lords, however, were able to stop themselves from crashing by disappearing in flame.

"Allie!"

Right. David. She needed to let David handle the offense while she worked to protect the boy. She felt Roland's arm go around her, felt Charlie pick up the strands of power, felt David slap another Dragon Lord out of the sky.

If they had any of the first circle with them, they could have called up a wind strong enough to remove the cloud cover.

There's twelve of them! Why are we even attempting this without the aunties?

Then Graham appeared out of the night, weapon raised and Allie remembered she had more immediate concerns.

She locked his gaze with hers. Thought about saying, *I won't let you shoot him.* Decided, all things considered, that was fairly obvious. Thought about saying, *It's time to pick a side.* Remembered how badly he reacted to ultimatums. Finally let his name escape on an exhaled breath.

Saw him lower the weapon.

Over the thirteen or so years he'd protected the sorcerer, necessity had required Graham to do a number of things that might be considered cold. Even brutal. He did his job, and he walked away. But shooting a naked boy—even if it wasn't a real boy—who stood blinking and trembling, all knees and elbows, wrapped in the arms of the woman he . . .

. . . cared about, that was outside his job description.

As of right now.

"Graham! What the hell is going on? Is the boy dead?"

He reached up, eyes still locked on Allie's face, pulled the earpiece out, threw it to the ground, and crushed it under his heel.

Allie had no time to savor the victory. She felt another rush of wings and lifted her head to snarl, "He is under *my* protection!"

David pulled power through the family link; held it ready.

A pair of Dragon Lords dove in from the west, but, impossibly, before David could react, Adam dropped from the clouds and drove them off. He was larger than his brothers, his gleaming black scales an absence of color against the sky.

When he landed, the ground shook. He hadn't been that large on the street. Couldn't have been.

When he roared, Allie felt it in blood and bone.

"David! No!"

She saw David's muscles lock as he fought to ignore the challenge.

When Adam changed, the ground smoked under his feet.

"You're making a mistake, Gale girl. If he lives, his mother will follow a road of blood to the MidRealm and destroy everything in her path just because she can."

Allie turned the boy so Adam could see the charms she'd drawn. "And if you kill him . . ."

"Yes, yes." He waved a hand. "You've claimed him. Are you certain you know what that means? His life, his death, are your responsibility now." His lips pulled back, his smile all teeth. "What did I say about you . . ." A nod to David, acknowledging another power. ". . . and yours, interfering in the business of our family? It seems," he continued without waiting for a response, "that you may meet your *big bad* after all. Let us hope I can convince my brothers you've made a move so foolish we have no countermove unless we want to go to war with your aunties. I'm not ruling that out, by the way."

Above the clouds, someone shrieked a challenge.

"If you'll excuse me, Ryan requires my assistance. Some of my brothers are trying to curry favor by protecting the boy, and Ryan isn't aware we've changed sides. Should he ask . . ." This Adam directed specifically to Charlie. ". . . I had every confidence in his ability to survive. Good luck, Gale girl. Good luck, nephew." The boy stiffened, beginning to fight off the effect of emerging into another reality. "Let's hope there's enough luck to go around." Another flash of teeth. Another tower of flame. Allie braced herself against Roland as Adam took to the sky.

"Allie, I don't understand."

She looked past the boy's head at Graham, who'd lowered his weapon because she'd needed him to. "He's Kalynchuk's son."

"But he's a . . ."

"He's that, too. That lot up there . . ." She jerked her head toward the battle raging above the clouds. "They have a sister."

"What are you doing answering Charlotte's phone, Michael?"

Michael moved the phone away from his ear. Auntie Jane achieved impressive volume when annoyed. "She left it with me."

"When she went where?"

He frowned as he parsed the sentence. "I can't tell you."

"Don't be ridiculous." It sounded like a warning.

He could feel himself starting to sweat. "They went to a park."

"They?"

Oops. "Charlie and Allie."

"Charlotte and Alysha went to a park? I see." He was horribly afraid she did. Right through the phone. "And the boys? Wherever they are, they're not answering their phones. Now, you don't want their mothers to worry, do you?"

"No?"

"Are they with Alysha?"

Yes or no questions couldn't be faked. "Yeah, but . . ."

"So, the whole family is in a park. Has Alysha involved them in something dangerous or have they decided to take up midnight picnicking?"

Midnight. He glanced at his watch. "It's got to be past three AM where you are, Auntie Jane."

"I can tell the time, Michael."

"Shouldn't you be sleeping?"

"I can sleep when I'm dead." *Or when everyone else is,* was pretty strongly implied. "Answer the question."

"Uh . . . they're just observing." He motioned Joe closer. The leprechaun shook his head and backed up a couple of steps.

"The Dragon Lords?"

She knew about the Dragon Lords. That made things a little simpler. "Yeah, the Dragon Lords."

"And what are they observing the Dragon Lords doing?"

"I don't know."

She could, apparently, hear the truth in that. "I see," she sniffed after a moment. "Does this have anything to do with my sister?"

"With Gran? I don't think so. Do you think so?"

"I wouldn't put it past her," Auntie Jane muttered. "Oh, and your young man misses you a great deal."

"Brian? Why were you talking to Brian?"

"He has your phone. You should call him."

"Not going to happen, Auntie Jane."

"I've thought you were a number of things over the years, Michael, but I never thought you were a coward. Do not prove me wrong."

He listened to the dial tone for a moment, then closed the phone. "Auntie Jane," he said to Joe.

"I figured. Don't take this the wrong way, but the whole lying to relatives thing? You really suck at it."

"We have to get him to the apartment!" Allie wrapped her jacket around the boy's shoulders. "Do you have a name?"

"Yeah, I have a name!" he declared, yanking the jacket close.

"And it is?"

"Why should I tell you?" The full upper lip curled. "You are not my father!"

The special round safe in his pocket, Graham slapped in a magazine of full metal jackets and almost said, *"Your father sent me to kill you,"* but he didn't know for certain, not one hundred percent for certain, that Kalynchuk knew the creature emerging, the boy, was his son. For the sake of the years they'd spent together, he had to give him the benefit of the doubt.

"Your father couldn't make it," Allie told him. "We're here in his place."

"He sent you?"

"He sent me," Graham growled.

The boy studied Graham for a moment, eyes hazel now although other colors slipped in and out. "I can smell him on you."

"Then you know I'm telling the truth."

"Why didn't he come himself?" Graham glanced up at the sky and the boy laughed. "Oh, yeah. Them. They would devour him if they could. My name is Jack. My mother says it is a name for heroes."

Jack and the Beanstalk.

Jack the Giant Killer.

Little Jack Horner.

Jack O'Neill.

Captain Jack Sparrow.

Captain Jack Harkness.

Those were all the Jacks Allie could recall off the top of her head, but in her own defense she was a little distracted by the blue Dragon Lord falling from the sky, trailing flame from great gashes in its scales. It hit the ground with less impact than the wind accompanying it, ignited, disappeared.

Half a dozen trees turned into torches.

Allie threw power at David. The fires went out.

They almost missed the second Dragon Lord, scales a rich chocolate brown, diving toward them from the south, and the third, a much darker green than Ryan, dropping in from almost directly above.

Graham snapped his weapon up and squeezed off a shot. It hit the brown Dragon Lord in the meaty part of the muscle where the left wing joined the body. Spraying blood, he screamed and wheeled off. David filled a green wing with wind, pinwheeling the sinuous body down toward the ground. The Dragon Lord changed just before impact, ran half a dozen steps as a heavyset man with dark tattoos, changed again, and disappeared into the clouds.

"We need to talk about this somewhere else!" Graham yelled, scanning the sky.

David ground an ember out under his heel. "He's right."

"Didn't I say we had to get Jack to the apartment?" Allie rolled her eyes. "Maybe if we started *moving*!"

"I want to go to my father!"

"First, let's not get killed by your uncles."

Jack thought about that for a moment, then nodded.

Graham caught up to the rental car as they turned onto 9th Ave S.W. heading east. As they passed 6th Street, as *he* passed 6th Street, as he drove right on by without even considering turning toward the office and Stanley Kalynchuk, he realized that this finalized the choice he'd made when he let Jack live. He touched the shape of the special bullet in his vest pocket.

His blood to make it fly true and Kalynchuk's to make the kill.

Did Kalynchuk know?

He'd made enemies in the UnderRealm; Graham had already dealt with a few. He might have only sensed the power coming, known it was an enemy but not which enemy.

Until the arrival of the Dragon Lords.

Unless he'd thought it was the mother emerging and not the child.

Not hard to believe the mother'd be pissed. Given Jack's apparent age and the fact he'd fired that first shot to save Kalynchuk's life almost exactly thirteen years ago and knew the sorcerer hadn't been to the Under-Realm since, Kalynchuk had knocked up a Dragon Lord and walked away, leaving a big scaly, flying, fire-breathing single mom behind.

A trickle of sweat rolled down Graham's back at the thought. The Dragon Lords were not Human. Didn't matter what they sometimes looked like. They were . . .

Well, they *weren't*. That was the point.

For Kalynchuk to actually . . .

He might have been forced. Taken without his consent. Not ever known there'd been a child.

But blood magic wouldn't kill without a blood connection.

Would it?

Had he known?

"Put a gun to his fucking head if you have to." First

time he'd ever used a pronoun. And Graham hadn't told him what, exactly had emerged

"Is the boy dead?"

The boy. Not the enemy. Or the creature.

There didn't seem to be much doubt left to give him.

When David turned down into the alley behind the store, Graham followed. Seemed like a way to show commitment. Plenty of room in the garage for the car; room enough for him to pull up tight against the building and still leave space for the garbage truck to pass. He took his weapon with him—he didn't know if Kalynchuk could show his displeasure by de-hexing the locks from a distance, but that wasn't a risk he was willing to take.

The garage door slid closed behind him. He supposed it was a good sign it hadn't slid closed in his face.

Things had changed during the trip.

Jack now wore jeans and a black T-shirt under Allie's jacket—or a jacket that bore some resemblance to Allie's. The jeans had that baggy-ass thing going and both his boots trailed their laces. Roland was missing his shirt, Charlie was barefoot.

"Jack realized he should have more clothes, so he made some out of the available fabric," Allie told him as Jack wandered off to explore the garage.

"Made some?"

"Yeah. Dragon Lord levels of power applied to sorcery which I'm not sure he should even be able to do at his age. And I don't think the car rental place is going to be happy."

Graham glanced into the car. Most of the fabric had been removed from the back of the front seat. There were also gouges in the fabric of the roof, deep enough he could see the gleam of metal. As he straightened, he glanced over at David and saw a rack of antlers that wouldn't have looked out of place on the wall of an old Scottish castle flickering in and out of sight. "Those are . . . I mean, they're . . ."

Allie followed his gaze. "You can see them? Great." Reaching out, she swept her fingertips through the lower prongs. When she turned to him again, she was frowning. "You shouldn't be able to see them, they're insubstantial."

Behind her, David turned, and his expression shifted Graham's grip on his weapon. He knew what power barely under control looked like. "Allie."

He couldn't see her expression when she turned to face her brother, but he did see her shoulders tighten.

"David, I'm so sorry. I didn't . . ." A long step back bumped her up against Graham's chest—the car door limiting his movement. She reached behind her and wrapped her fingers around his wrist to steady herself.

To his surprise, the tension visibly eased, and David suddenly looked like less of a threat. "You're Graham."

"Yeah." They'd never actually been introduced, given the flaming flying lizards and all.

David stepped back, long legs moving him around the front of the car until the bulk of it was between them. "Later."

"He means you'll talk later," Allie murmured, releasing him.

His wrist throbbed where her fingers had been, the skin feeling hot and tight. "I got that. What's up with the . . ." A jerk of his head toward the flickering horn.

"It's a family thing. But you can thank Jack that they're not solid. I think he drew on David to fuel the transfigurations he did in the car." She wasn't exactly looking at him, but she wasn't moving away, so Graham decided to count that as a win. "I mean, it's no wonder his uncles freaked—he's an instinctive sorcerer with Dragon Lord access to power."

"Instinctive?"

"Unless your boss . . ."

"Ex-boss." *Probably.* She actually smiled at him then, and he hoped the qualifier hadn't shown on his face.

"Okay, unless your ex-boss kept trotting back to the UnderRealm to give lessons, he's untrained."

"He didn't."

"You're certain."

"As I can be. So he was right; Jack's dangerous." He wasn't exactly asking, he wasn't stupid.

Before Allie could respond, the paint can Jack had moved to the workbench to examine exploded.

Graham hit the dirt but lifted his head in time to see David clench a fist and the blast crumple in on itself. The antlers seemed to firm up for a moment.

"Jack's thirteen," Allie told him as he stood, brushing off his jeans. "That's always dangerous." They locked eyes for a moment, but before Graham could figure out what to say, Allie turned away. "Come on, Jack . . ." She tugged the boy away from the bench. ". . . let's go inside. I bet you're hungry."

"Starving!" In the low light of the garage, his eyes glowed.

"Do you like pie?"

"I don't know."

"Let's find out."

Roland followed Allie and Jack out into the yard, staying close enough that Graham had to swallow the growl rising in his throat. He looked away to find David studying him. Speculatively? Suspiciously? Hard to say.

But this was apparently not *later* as David turned his

head to maneuver his purportedly insubstantial antlers out the door. Graham fell in beside Charlie, moving a little more slowly because of her bare feet.

"So," she said as they stepped out into the courtyard, "figure out what you want to say to her yet?"

"It's not that easy."

"It's not supposed to be easy, dumbass."

He nodded at David crossing the courtyard. No way the three scrawny bushes leaned toward him as he passed. "How did he get those things into the car if it was Jack who made them insubstantial." Kalynchuk had never mentioned the abilities of the Gale men, and Roland had been able to stop him cold, sweater vest and all. David seemed like an entirely different level of problem, especially since Graham had no idea where he and Allie actually stood. Or if they stood together at all.

Charlie rolled her eyes. "Please, that was later. I had to blow him in the parking lot and bring them down a bit, or he'd have been walking back."

Graham literally felt his jaw drop. She didn't sound like she was bullshitting, and he had a reporter's built-in bullshit detector. "Seriously?"

"Why do you think Auntie Catherine drove a convertible?"

"She didn't have . . ." He waved a hand above his head.

"The aunties are first circle." Charlie's smile curved wickedly and Graham's pants felt suddenly, uncomfortably tight. "She could get as many of those as she wanted."

All of a sudden, his memories of conversations with Catherine Gale showed up in a whole new light. "So when she suggested we . . . ?"

"She meant it."

"That's . . ." Graham paused, caught by his reflection in the enormous mirror in the back hall behind the store. "Why are there fourteen of me?"

Charlie shrugged as she pushed past. "Maybe it likes you."

Jack liked pie.

Allie cut him another slice of her mother's lemon meringue—minimally and nonspecifically charmed with the Gale version of wear nice underpants in case of accidents—and slid the plate across the table.

"We don't have anything like this back home," he moaned, shoveling an enormous forkful into his mouth. "Although," he added thoughtfully, after he'd swallowed, "I did eat a nest of pixies once that tasted kind of the same, but you know . . ." Sweeping his tongue over his lower lip, he retrieved a bit of meringue. ". . . chewier."

"You ate pixies?" Joe put down his fork.

Jack shrugged as he chewed. "Not often. They're so small you have to find a nest, or they're not worth it. I like them, though."

"So are pixies . . . ?" Michael tapped his head, and Allie didn't think he meant imaginary.

"Thinking, reasoning, obnoxious little shit disturbers. Yeah." She pulled out the chair beside the young Dragon Lord and sat down. "Jack?" When he looked up from his rapidly disappearing pie, she took a deep breath. "Here, in this world, we don't eat anything we can have a conversation with."

"Not unless both parties are enjoying themselves," Charlie added.

"I don't see how that's possible," Jack admitted, frowning.

"Well . . ."

Roland kicked her under the table. "Let's not confuse him. Jack, here in this world, we have very distinct ideas of what constitutes food."

His frown deepened. "I don't know what constitutes means."

"It means we don't eat people," Allie said quickly, cutting off Roland's certain to be even more confusing explanation.

A nod down the table at Joe. "He's a leprechaun."

"Leprechauns are people."

"Those small things with wings outside?"

"Those are pigeons, you can eat those. Except not those particular pigeons," she amended, "because I know them."

"You knew this pie."

"Not the same thing."

"My mother says if you limit your food, you limit your chances. My Uncle Viktor has been trying to eat me my whole life."

"Why?"

Graham's voice lifted the hair on the back of Allie's neck. She'd been treating him exactly like the others, giving him a place at the table, feeding him, ignoring the way he made her skin feel too tight and like there wasn't enough air in the room.

Jack shrugged thin shoulders. "Because of who my father is. Mother says I frighten them because of what I can do, and that fear makes them stupid, but they really don't like that as long as I'm alive Mother won't clutch again and that makes me heir. There's never been a male heir. Mother says there's no way I'll live as long as a pureblood anyway, so they can just fuck off and she'll clutch again when she's good and ready. Also, they really, really hate my father because he showed up and messed things up. Although they don't hate him as much as Mother does, but you don't eat the only egg in the clutch. Is there more pie?"

The pan on the table was empty of everything but a few crumbs of crust.

Charlie pushed her chair back. "I'll check. You eat like Michael; he was a skinny little shit at your age, too."

"I'm bigger in my other form," Jack protested indignantly.

Flames licked at his edges, but before Allie could get out so much as a clichéd "No!" they disappeared and only his eyes showed any evidence there'd ever been a fire. She glanced over at David. He shook his head. If David hadn't stopped it, then . . .

Jack's chair tipped over as he surged up onto his feet. When the heavy wooden back slammed against the floor, everyone jumped and the lights flickered. Allie wasn't sure who was responsible. Wasn't positive it hadn't been her.

"It's gone!" His eyes gleamed gold, lid to lid. "I can't find my other self!"

"It's your father's blood." Graham glanced at Allie as everyone turned to face him. "Blood magic's the strongest there is," he continued when she nodded to let him know he had the floor. "You lot should all know that. He's in the same reality with his father for the first time in his life, and it's locked him down. You don't need scales while you're here, kid, and you'll get them back when you go home. I've picked up a bit over the years," he added in answer to David's raised brow.

"My father's blood," Jack repeated. His gaze jerked around the room like he was in a cage. "When do I get to see my father? I want to see my father."

Everyone turned to look at Graham. Who sighed.

"It's complicated, kid."

"But he sent you."

"Yeah. He sent me."

Allie wondered what Graham had in his front pocket. Every time he spoke to Jack, his hand rose to touch the small lump. She suspected he didn't even know he was doing it. It was an artifact, she could feel that much but nothing more specific, not with the amount of free-floating power in the room.

The Dragon Lord—no, Dragon Prince, she guessed if he was heir—drew himself up to his full height. "You should take me to him," he declared imperiously. "Now."

"I'm not . . ." His fingertip whitened. He was pressing against the lump so hard it had to have been digging into his chest, but he gave no indication that it hurt. "Your father might not want to see you."

"So? I want to see him."

"And they say Gale boys are spoiled," Charlie murmured, setting half a rhubarb pie on the table and dropping into her chair.

Allie bumped her with her hip as she passed. "You could call him." They were the first words she'd spoken directly to Graham since the garage, and that had been a whole pie ago.

"Call him?"

"I think we all need to know where he stands." She held out her phone. "You'd better use this. It'll make sure you get through."

"I don't . . ." His gaze slipped past her to Jack and back to her again. "All right."

When their fingers touched, Allie felt the shock race up her arm and pool warm and heavy in her belly.

David growled and pushed away from the table. "Loft."

Head cocked, eyes whirling, Jack watched David

leave, then jerked his head around toward Allie as the door slammed. "We don't have that problem," he said.

That problem. They needed more third circle here while David was or it was going to become a bigger problem. "Lucky you."

"Allie?"

Which was when she realized she hadn't let go of the phone. "Right. Sorry. You can go into . . ." She started to gesture toward the bedroom, felt power building, remembered there was now a bed in the second bedroom as well and jerked her hand more or less toward the bathroom.

"No. Better you all hear."

He wanted them to trust him. Allie could see that. Understand why. Still . . . she glanced over at Jack. "Are you sure?"

"If it goes wrong . . ." Graham's one-shoulder shrug reminded her of his injuries although there were no visible bruises, so it seemed he'd been healed. She hated that it was Kalynchuk who'd healed him. "It's better he hears it from the source than secondhand."

"The fast Band-Aid approach?"

He started to frown in confusion, then smiled up at her, eyes crinkling at the corners. "Yeah, the fast Band-Aid approach. Here, where he has people . . ." She wondered if he even knew he was reaching for her. ". . . who'll support him."

Allie wanted to take his hand. She wanted to take his hand more than she'd ever wanted anything in her life. More than Michael. But Graham had chosen, and they couldn't . . . it wasn't . . .

"Maybe you two ought to save that for later," Charlie suggested.

"They have no later," Roland reminded her.

She heard Michael sigh. "He chose to come back."

Apparently, everyone but Joe had an opinion. Allie watched Graham's hand settle on the table.

She spun around as Charlie's foot impacted with her butt, glared at her cousin, and said, "Jack, do you care if we can all hear your father talk to Graham?"

Jack's shrug was all teenage boy. "What could go wrong?"

She couldn't let him go into it blind. "Graham."

"I don't . . ."

"Tell him." It was only logical to stand by Graham's side where she could see both Jack and the phone. She was close enough to hear him sigh, see the fine muscle movement as he squared his shoulders.

"Your father sent me to kill whatever emerged from the UnderRealm."

Jack cocked his head to one side, the motion almost birdlike. If birds had evolved from dinosaurs and dragons were sort of like dinosaurs, then . . . she shook the thought away. Not the time to consider parallel evolution in metaphysical realms. "Did he know it was me?"

Graham touched the artifact in his pocket again. "He said it was an enemy."

Not the whole truth, Allie realized as Jack said, "Then he didn't know it was me."

"You're no danger to him?"

"I don't know. I haven't met him yet." He looked around the table and rolled his eyes although with the whites still barely showing Allie found it a strangely nondefinitive movement. "And *he* hasn't met me. How can you tell a person is your enemy if you haven't met them yet?"

"He has a point," Charlie admitted.

"He has a mouthful of them," Roland murmured in what Allie suspected was intended to be a warning but only came across as somewhat petulant.

"He only looks like a thirteen-year-old kid, doesn't he?" Joe said suddenly. "He's not, though, is he? He's a Dragon Prince. Heir to the sky. Stop treating him like he's fucking made of soap bubbles, remember he eats people when he's at home, and call his old man."

The silence was broken by a snicker.

From Jack.

"Is there a speaker on this thing?" Graham asked.

Allie held out her hand, and he dropped the phone in it without them touching. When she set up the speaker function, she returned it the same way.

Eyes locked on the number pad, Graham punched in ten digits and set the open phone down beside his empty plate.

It seemed Kalynchuk had been waiting for the call.

"Is it alive?"

"He's standing right here," Allie told him, watching Graham close his fingers around the artifact.

"Then you've doomed us all!"

"Overreact much?" Charlie snorted.

"It maps the way, you fools! I warned you, Alysha Gale! I warned you that disaster would follow if it was not destroyed. If you're there, Graham, kill it! Kill it now! It may not be too late!"

Graham took a deep breath and quietly asked, "Did you know?"

To give him credit, although Allie hated doing it, Kalynchuk didn't pretend to misunderstand. "Of course I knew. And that shot, that shot you didn't take, that shot was the whole reason for your existence! The stars told me my past would find me sooner or later. Those other, minor annoyances over the years—I could have lowered myself to deal with them if I'd had to. This was your task, and you failed me! Failed me after I trusted you with my life! It is most definitely safe to say I will

not look kindly upon you should we meet again, but
since the lucky ones among us will shortly be dead,
thanks to your stupidity, my displeasure seems moot.
Kill it if you want to live!"

"Father?"

The silence extended long enough Allie opened her
mouth. Closed it again when it turned out Kalynchuk
had one final point to make. "Of all the men of power,
back to the first man who claimed his birthright, only I
dared that action which brings this doom upon us. No
one else ever dared so much. I have that at least."

"Wow," Jack said over the dial tone. "He's a bit of an
ass, isn't he?"

It had rained at some point while they were all upstairs, but except for directly around the three scrawny
shrubs, the courtyard dirt had been packed too firmly
for anything less than a downpour to make much of an
impression. Graham leaned against the west wall by
a stack of lumber under a tarp and wished he hadn't
stopped smoking. Yeah, it was a filthy, expensive habit
likely to shorten his life—in point of fact, the reasons
he'd quit—but it had given him something mindless
to focus on when his thoughts slid off into unpleasant
areas.

Like how he'd spent thirteen years working for a
man willing to kill his child. Have his child killed. He
pressed two fingers against the pocket.

"You okay?"

"Just needed some time alone," he said, watching
Allie close the door and walk toward him while frowning down at the wet ground.

"Okay." She settled against the wall, close enough he

could feel the narrow strip of air between them begin to warm.

"What part of alone didn't you get?"

"You said *needed*. I figured you were done." She still hadn't looked directly at him. "Charlie said we should talk—actually, she was a little more definitive about it than *should*—but I'll go. If you want me to."

She'd started to move before he found his voice. "Stay."

They stood—leaned—silently for a moment, then Allie said, "Can I see it?"

"It?" The corners of his mouth twitched although he couldn't quite manage a smile. "You'll have to be a little more specific."

"Did I ask to see it *again*?" Her elbow impacting with his side turned out to be a lot pointier than it looked. "I meant the artifact in your pocket."

Yeah. He'd figured. It felt warm as he fished it out. Body temperature. "You're not going to see much." The fixture over the door held one of those energy-saving fluorescent bulbs, and the circle of light ended about a meter out.

Her fingers were warmer than the bullet as she plucked it off his palm. He found that vaguely comforting. "I have night-vision charms on my eyelids."

"Seriously?"

"Gale girls aren't big on eye shadow, and we like to minimize our chances of waking up the aunties."

He matched his tone to hers; all surface, no depths. "No lights on when you come home late?"

"Or go to the bathroom. Or raid the fridge. This would have killed him?" Her voice suddenly serious, she held the bullet up between thumb and forefinger. It seemed to glow with a dull, dirty light. Optical illusion. Probably. "In either form?"

"That's what he made it for."

"Your blood's in this, too."

Interesting she could sense that but not surprising, all things considered. "My blood's just there to help my aim."

Allie made a noncommittal sound, then said, "Or to give his uncles a scent when they set out to find the shooter. My charm wouldn't have lasted against blood magic."

"You think . . ."

"I think," she interrupted, "given that your target would have been standing absolutely still in the moment just after emergence . . ." The moment she'd tackled Jack to the ground. ". . . you couldn't have missed a shot at that distance."

Nice to think that. "I wasn't a lot farther away the last time I missed."

"But now you know how fast they change. You wouldn't make that mistake again. That miss, just made this shot . . ." She raised the bullet a little higher. ". . . more likely."

Graham frowned. "He'd still be in danger from the Dragon Lords. He'd need me to take out as many of them as possible."

"Unless he thought your death by Dragon Lord was the best way to get my family involved. While we're going after the Dragon Lords, he can slip away. Hide again."

"Again?"

"If the aunties haven't taken him out, it's only because they don't know where he is."

And that just begged for a sidebar. "Why do the old women in your family hate sorcerers?"

She shrugged. He didn't know if she'd moved closer without him noticing, or if he was so attuned to her, he could feel the air currents shift. "Power corrupts."

"That's a pretty nonspecific reason to kill someone."

"He ordered you to kill his son."

Yeah. Definitely a specific example of the premise.

"As much as I hate to admit it," Allie continued. "Actually managing to have a son with the Dragon Queen suggests he's a lot more powerful than I thought. Because that's, as Charlie pointed out, fucking amazing."

"He was good with fire," Graham told her dryly, remembering the blaze answering Kalynchuk's gesture in the workshop. Then, suddenly, he froze.

And that shot, that shot you didn't take, that shot was the whole reason for your existence!

"Graham?" She'd finally turned to look at him. He could feel the heat of her concern on the side of his face. And then the press of her hand against his chest. "Breathe!"

The air in the courtyard felt superheated as he drew it into his lungs and gasped it out. Then Allie started to breathe with him, her mouth near his, slowly in and out, the vise around his ribs loosening. "He was good with fire," he repeated, barely recognizing his own voice. Allie stood close enough he could see that her eyes were the cool gray of a winter sky, and he let himself fall into them. "I saved him out in the woods, made a one-in-a-million shot, and two days later my whole family was dead in a fire."

Allie made the jump with him. "You think he killed your family?"

"I think he was willing to kill his." His hands were shaking. Graham didn't remember reaching out to hold Allie's hips, but it helped. It helped to have something warm and alive in his grasp. "He showed up in the village almost before it was over and took care of everything." His family had been nearly hysterical with grief. He remembered uncles, hard men who'd fought the North Atlantic every day of their adult lives, crying like children. He remembered how Stanley Kalynchuk's hand on his shoulder had felt like the only thing he had left that was real.

This time, when the memories tried to slip away, he fought to hold them.

It was like trying to hold smoke. He had the essence but not the substance.

"Why can't I remember?"

Allie touched her forehead to his. "He doesn't want you to. He wouldn't, would he?"

"No. He wouldn't." Graham took a deep breath and loosened his hold on her just a little. Probably too late to prevent bruises. "He was there for me for all those years because he needed me today. Needed to know someone could take that shot and not miss. I'd have shot through you, wouldn't have hesitated if I hadn't gotten to know you. I'd have killed you and considered you collateral damage for the greater good."

"But you didn't."

"But I could have."

She cupped his face between her hands and repeated, "But you didn't." Then she kissed him. Softly, comfortingly.

She was all he had left. When she pulled back, he murmured, "If I could choose again . . ." and she stared at him like she was seeing him for the first time and she smiled.

"No."

"I just . . ."

"No. Not until you really understand what it means."

It took a moment to hear *not yet* instead of *no*. "But I thought I only got one chance."

"Well, you're like two people, right? The reporter

and the sorcerer's . . . person? Two people, two choices. Besides, there's a half-Human Dragon Prince upstairs eating pie. We're making this up as we go along."

"*We* are?"

"Yes. We are." And she kissed him again.

"*He needs to talk to someone,*" Charlie had said, "*and it can't be either of the boys, not with all that horn showing. He'll end up going all bantam rooster and getting damaged.*"

"*You go, then.*"

"*No.*"

"*Charlie . . .*"

"*Get your head out of your ass and get down there!*"

"*Michael . . .*"

Michael had given her the saddest smile she'd ever seen, and she knew he was thinking of Brian. "*Talk to him, Allie. It doesn't have to go further.*"

So she'd talked to him. And she'd listened to him.

She hadn't planned on kissing him, but she'd needed to do something to ease the pain. Kissing him was just the best way she could think of to say she was there if he needed her and have him believe it. Funny thing, though, she'd ended up convincing herself.

"If I could choose again," he'd said.

She'd been ready to tell him it didn't work like that when she'd realized there was no reason why it couldn't. And maybe she'd babbled a little, but he hadn't seemed to mind.

The second kiss was less about comfort and, selfishly, more about finding him again.

Turned out, he'd never been gone.

She felt as though she were sinking into him and

pulled away before she lost herself. Not the time, not
the place . . . Well, not the time and only the place when
she was sure Charlie wasn't watching from the apartment window.

"Allie . . ."

The sound of wet laundry flapping by just above the
building cut off whatever Graham had been about to
say, but when Allie leaned back against the wall beside
him, he kept his hand around hers as they watched the
sky. She half expected one of the triangular shapes to
land on the top of the building, but all three flew on by.
"What do you think they're doing up there?"

"Regrouping. Licking their wounds. Getting ready
for round two." He stroked her palm with his thumb,
and it felt so much like family that it literally made
her knees weak. "Do you think Jack's mother is on her
way?"

"It's the only thing Adam and your ex-boss seem to
agree on."

"But what do you think?"

Allie took a deep breath and tasted sulfur on the
breeze. "I don't know. It seems like the females are the
defining avatars of the Dragon Lords' power. It takes a
lot to shift that kind of thing."

"She has a way to finally get to Jack's father. That's a
lot. Do you think she *sent* Jack?"

"I don't think she'd have risked him, especially since
it seems that keeping him alive this long has been a
big 'fuck you' to pretty much everybody. But what do I
know about Dragon Lords? I'm almost positive Adam
wanted to stop Jack. To stop her. But then Jack gets
here, and he changes his mind."

"Because you claimed him?"

"It can't be me."

"Can you stop her?"

"Not alone. And I'm not exploring other options until I'm *sure* she's on her way." The aunties were still the court of last resort. "Adam's playing some weird game of his own, and I'm not taking the ravings of a man who wants to kill his own child as truth." She frowned at the sound of sirens in the distance. "Is that fire or police?"

Graham cocked his head. "Fire."

Allie sighed. That so figured. "You know what I said when we left for the hill? I said all we were going to do was stop the city from burning down." Without really thinking about what she was doing, she found herself sliding almost effortlessly through the imprint of the city until she touched the place where it went wrong, touched the fire, and put it out. Senses humming, reveling in the unexpected freedom, wondering if Charlie felt the same lack of boundaries stepping into the Wood, she reached a little farther and touched the scar on the top of the hill.

Moved down it just because she could.

Heat.

A little farther.

Rage. Surging. Consuming.

Allie didn't know where the city ended and it began. Where she ended and it began. It roared through her, scouring bleeding bits of self free as it passed. Then it came around and did it again. And again. She couldn't find herself.

Pain . . .

Hatred . . .

Burning.

Burning.

Burning.

But there, on the edge.

Something.

If she could only remember ...

Hand.

She could feel her hand.

"Allie!"

She could feel her nails digging into Graham's skin where he held her hand between their bodies. She could feel bruises rising on her shoulder blades from where she'd pressed back into the wall.

"Allie? Are you all right? You went away for a minute." He looked concerned but not terrified. That was weird because given the way her heart was slamming up against her ribs, she had to look like she'd just brushed up against the end of the world. Then she remembered he couldn't really see her.

"Sh ... sh ..." Dragging her tongue over dry lips, she tried again. "She's coming."

"Jack's mother?"

"I have to make a phone call." When he started to release her hand, she tightened her grip. "I can use the other one."

The number she needed had moved to the top of her phone book. Another time, she'd be annoyed about that. Four rings. Five. Six.

"It's the middle of the night, Alysha Catherine."

"I need a first circle, Auntie Jane."

"You need a first circle." She heard Auntie Jane yawn, teeth clacking together when she closed her mouth. "Why?"

About to say it was complicated, Allie suddenly realized it wasn't. "The Dragon Queen is on her way."

"Really?" Auntie Jane sounded more curious than angry. That was good. "How is she finding her way?"

"Her son, by a sorcerer, is here."

"Try to be more precise, girl. Her son by a sorcerer is where?"

"In the apartment. Eating pie. The sorcerer is here, too."

"In the apartment?" Allie was fairly certain she could feel frost forming on the phone. "Eating pie?"

"No. But in Calgary."

"I see."

She thought she did. "It's more complicated than that."

"No, Alysha Catherine, it is not. A full circle?"

Burning.

Burning.

Burning.

And never burning out.

"Yes. Please."

"And who will anchor a first circle, Alysha Catherine?"

Allie glanced up at the loft, knowing she'd see her brother staring down at her, knew that when he felt the burning, he'd understand. Hoped that one day, he'd forgive her. "David."

TWELVE

"They'll be here tomorrow afternoon."

No one in the room seemed surprised that the Gale family expected to be able to book twelve seats on a Calgary-bound flight with less than twelve hours' notice. Given how much of a threat both his ex-boss and the Dragon Lords had considered them, Graham knew the older Gale women were powerful, but they were clearly more powerful than he'd imagined.

"They'll be bringing Katie with them," Allie added.

Thirteen seats, Graham amended as Charlie's brows rose. She glanced over at Roland—who looked admirably neutral—before saying, "Katie's closer than I am. Way too close to do David much good."

Standing just behind her right shoulder, Graham watched the muscles tense in Allie's jaw.

"They're not bringing Katie for David." Her tone suggested that whatever was going on—and he wasn't positive he wanted it explained—was not open to discussion.

Not that Charlie didn't try.

"But . . ."

"David will be anchoring the first circle."

Roland let out a long sigh that suggested he'd expected as much.

Charlie shook her head, the mute denial as much of a denial as she could evidently make. "Oh, Allie, I'm sorry."

"It might not ... I mean, he's strong, and nothing might ..." Allie pushed a hand back through the hair that had worked its way out of her braid. "But if he does, it means at least one of the aunties will have to stay."

"Oh, sweetie, now I'm *really* sorry."

Allie cracked the first smile she'd managed since she'd hung up the phone. "So you won't be abandoning me when this is all over?"

"If the Wood stays clear ..." Her head cocked, Graham suspected she was listening to a call no one else in the room could hear. "... then I've got some traveling to do, but if you're staying, I'll base here with you." She glanced past Allie to flash an exceedingly smug smile at Graham. "With you *two*."

"So it's like that, is it?" Michael's brows rose, and his expression had enough of a warning in it that Graham had to fight to keep his hands from curling into fists.

"No," Allie told him, stepping back, bumping her shoulder into Graham's. "No one's made any choices yet. We're taking it slow this time."

"Shouldn't be a this time," Roland pointed out.

"Shouldn't be a half-Human Dragon Prince in the bathroom," Charlie reminded him. "Cope."

Roland snorted. "Then speaking to that—it's a little early to make plans for after, don't you think? If his mother is as terrifying as reports indicate, we might not survive."

"Joe."

When Joe looked over at her, Allie gestured that he should smack Roland on the back of the head.

The leprechaun sank back into the sofa cushions. "I couldn't."

"I've got it." Stretching out a long arm, Michael did the honors.

Roland dove over Joe to get to him.

Graham could just barely remember his brothers, Frank and Evan, the closest to him in age, wrestling like that, using the physical to defuse tensions rising over ... over ... He couldn't remember what, exactly, but this was the clearest memory of the time before the fire he'd had in years.

He wanted to blame it all on Kalynchuk, wanted to say it had everything to do with the way his life had been manipulated to create the man the sorcerer required, but he suspected he'd been a willing participant in dividing his life into the years before and after the fire. What thirteen year old wouldn't have wanted to stop hurting so badly?

"Hey! If the little guy is going to eat the bigger one, I should get to eat the leprechaun!"

Jack's voice drew Graham out of the smoke-filled corners in his head, and Michael's roar of laughter banished the flame.

Still laughing, he bucked up against Roland's hold. "You wish you were going to be eating me, don't you, littler guy?"

"Bite me," Roland snorted, catching Michael's flailing hand and pinning it beside the other. "Say uncle."

Dimples flashed. "Auntie!"

"Close enough."

Jack frowned as the two disengaged and dragged themselves up onto facing sofas, breathing heavily. "So no one's being eaten?"

"Not tonight. Or rather this morning," Charlie amended glancing at her watch. "I am totally bagged and I have a gig tomorrow night, so at the risk of doing Allie's job and sounding like the grown-up, it's time for bed."

"Well?"

Standing at one of the windows facing the street, Allie leaned back against Charlie's warmth as her cousin wrapped her arms around her and rested her chin on Allie's shoulder. "Well, what?" she asked just as quietly, aware of Michael and Roland and Joe asleep on the sofa beds behind them. Jack had the other bedroom—everyone seemed fine with giving a teenage Dragon Prince his space—and David had stayed in the loft.

"Well, you and Graham for starters?"

"We're . . . okay." Given all the new baggage, in some ways, it had been more like a first time than their first time had been. "No choices until all this is over."

"Sure you don't want to get him locked down before the aunties toss in their twenty-four cents' worth? They're going to want you all the way into second circle before Mommy dearest shows up."

"I want *him* to be sure this time. The aunties are going to have enough to worry about without interfering in my love life."

Charlie snorted, warm air blowing strands of hair along Allie's neck. "Yeah, like that's ever stopped them. And, also . . . well, David?"

"I can't get close to him until he gets some control back."

"You could call him."

Allie shrugged just enough for Charlie to feel the motion. "Not really the kind of thing you can do over the phone." She knew Auntie Jane wouldn't agree. Auntie Meredith, Auntie Gwen, and Auntie Carmen—Roland's grandmother—had called Roland and Charlie's mother and two of Charlie's sisters had called her. Both phones were now buried inside bags of frozen peas in the freezer. Katie had sent a brief and profane text message. *Someone* had to have called David.

A familiar shadow flickered along the street, a darker gray now the sky had begun to lighten. Charlie's arms tightened.

"There's been a flyby about every forty minutes," Allie told her. "I was lying there in the dark, and I could feel them passing—or maybe it's just one of them, I don't know. I got up to see if I was imagining things but I wasn't. Obviously. Can you . . . ?"

"Feel them? No. Probably a second circle thing."

They turned together to look at Roland, the light spilling in from the street enough to see him lying on his back, one hand tucked up under his chin, a silvered line of drool rolling toward the pillow.

"Maybe," Allie allowed. She thought of the anger and the burning and the vast weight of personality she'd touched. "Maybe not."

"So, Graham's ex-boss; you figure he's going to get involved."

"He's going to have to. He can't run because the Dragon Lords will take him out. He can't stay hidden because she'll find him no matter where he is. The way I see it, he has two choices—get to Jack before she makes it through, or take her out during that moment of disorientation right after she arrives."

"You think she'll have that moment?"

"How would I know?"

"You have to have more info than we do, sweetie. Or you'd never have called in the aunties."

"I keep forgetting you're smarter than you look."

"I'd kind of have to be."

"She's . . ." Allie took a deep breath and watched it fog the window as she exhaled. "Remember Auntie Gwen right after the change? Scarier than that."

"Wow. Okay, you think Adam and the dragon brothers up there are actually standing guard over Jack?"

"I think . . ." Allie went over everything she knew about Adam and the Dragon Lords, which was less than she knew about their sister. ". . . I think they're easily bored and angling for a front row seat."

"So, Graham's ex-boss . . ." The words were the same, but the tone had become frankly speculative. ". . . I have to say, sex with a dragon, that's impressive. Still, unless he gets his trousers made to measure, that must make him a grower not a shower."

Allie rolled her eyes. "He was in a very expensive suit; probably tailor made. Plus, he had burn scars."

"Ouch."

"No, Katie'll be staying here, but I've booked six rooms at the Fairmont Palliser for the aunties."

"The big fancy hotel by the convention center?" Joe tried not to look relieved as he wiped down the glass countertop. It wasn't a significantly successful attempt.

"That's the one. It has a spa; they'll be thrilled. The aunties are big on getting what they feel they're entitled to." Allie took a deep breath as a minibus pulled up in front of the store. "Case in point; I had to talk them down from a fleet of airport limos." She suspected they hadn't actually wanted the limos, that it was just Auntie Meredith attempting to wrest some control of the situation from Auntie Jane, but that hadn't shortened the phone call—proving that the cell service along the 401, all the way from Darsden East into Pearson International Airport in Toronto, was excellent.

Joe nodded toward the rental. "Good thing Michael had a license for driving that rig, then."

"He didn't. He had Charlie."

"And she's the driver?"

"No. She's the Gale girl." Right on cue, Charlie jumped out and beckoned from the sidewalk. "Okay, this is it. Hold the fort." Throwing her messenger bag up over her shoulder, Allie took a deep breath. "Wish me luck."

"Aren't they on your side?"

"Remember Gran?" she threw over her shoulder as she headed for the door. "Multiply her by twelve."

"Breathe," Michael suggested. "The plane's on the ground. It's too late to change your mind."

He had a point. Passing out from lack of oxygen wouldn't help.

Allie took a deep breath, let it out slowly, and tried unsuccessfully to ignore the omens that said reality was about to shift in a big way. A man in a cheap suit with a sample case at his feet moved away from the crowds before starting to talk into his cell phone, keeping his voice low and unobtrusive. Three small children sat cross-legged on the floor at their mother's feet and colored quietly. Two young men were having a quiet conversation with the young woman in the Information Booth who seemed to be actually giving them information. Outside, although construction had put a not inconsiderable ripple in the traffic flow, things seemed to be moving smoothly without horns or profanity.

It was creepy.

"Allie . . ."

"I hear them."

Twelve women all talking at once made a lot of noise. Especially since at least two of them were going deaf and refusing to admit it. Allie braced herself and then, as the aunties appeared from the baggage pickup, closed her hand around Michael's arm.

"Ow."

"Sorry."

"They know it's a real organization, right?"

"Oh, yeah. They run the local group. Actually, they pretty much *are* the local group."

"So why . . . ?"

Allie sighed. "I'm pretty sure they consider it to be gang colors."

Each of the aunties wore purple. And a red hat. Many different shades of purple. Many different kinds of hats. Four of them were wearing straw cowboy hats bought at the Darsden East dollar store, spray painted red and individually decorated. The aunties quite enjoyed being crafty

Auntie Gwen, at fifty-eight, the youngest by about six years, looked vaguely annoyed by the attention they were getting. The other eleven were reveling in it.

"It's a good thing you didn't ask them to be stealthy," Michael murmured, raising his other arm and waving it.

"This is stealthy," Allie snorted. "Nothing's blowing up."

"Alysha Catherine!" The volume of the surrounding chatter lowered considerably as Auntie Jane stopped an arm's length away. Heaven forbid the entire airport not get a chance to hear what she had to say. "Still teetering on the edge, are you?" Dark eyes narrowed. "Were you one of your cousins, I'd assume you were waiting for our approval. As you aren't and as you are, in point of fact, becoming remarkably like your grandmother, I can only assume there's something wrong with your young man."

"There's nothing wrong with him, Auntie Jane. We had a misunderstanding, we're in the middle of a situation, and we're taking it slow."

"Gale girls don't misunderstand, the situation can only be improved by you tying up loose ends, and you're taking it slow*ly*." Auntie Jane had been the terror of the Lennox and Addington County school board, teaching grade seven and eight English at every school in the district until she retired some years after the mandatory retirement age. The aunties considered government regulations to be more a set of guidelines. With Allie put in her place, she turned to Michael and sniffed, "Talked to your young man yet?"

Allie felt the muscles in his forearm tense under her hand. "No, Auntie Jane."

"And why not?"

"It's not . . . We aren't . . ."

Nudging him into silence, Allie took half a step forward. The old woman had no right to dig at Michael. "I don't think that's any of your business, Auntie Jane."

The silence in the terminal was so complete Allie felt like she'd just tried to smuggle a lip gloss through security without placing it first into a clear, one-liter plastic bag. The sound of a red Styrofoam bird falling from the brim of Auntie Christie's hat was impossibly loud.

"You don't think that's any of my business?" Auntie Jane repeated slowly.

"No, I don't," Allie told her. "For what it's worth, I don't think it's any of my business either. It's between Michael and Brian."

Auntie Jane stared at her for a long moment—didn't quite tip her head to the side so she could bring each eye to bear independently, but it was close. Then she glanced over at Michael. Then she smiled. "Well, all right, then. And you're both too old now to give me a hug?"

Michael moved first; Allie could feel the relief rolling off him like smoke. She held back just a little, just enough to come to his rescue if affection turned out to be a trap. It didn't seem to, and once Auntie Jane had gotten her hugs, the other aunties moved in, and, from the shoulders down, Michael disappeared behind a swarming mass topped off in an embarrassment of scarlet feathers.

Allie backed up to find Katie standing draped in canvas tote bags stuffed full of neck pillows filled with buckwheat and flaxseed.

"I hate you so much right now," she sighed.

"You know I wouldn't have called in a full circle if it hadn't been the end of the world."

Katie snorted. "I'd have bet serious money on you preferring the end of the world."

"So how did you get roped into this?" Allie asked, taking a couple of the bags as the aunties, singly and collectively, offered advice to every single person who'd been with them on the plane as they ran the gauntlet of red and purple in an attempt to leave the airport.

"Officially, because I'm self-employed and can take off at a moment's notice. Unofficially," she continued when Allie snorted because a first circle could have swept up as much of the family as they felt they required, "I suspect I'm competition for the young man you've found."

"Competition?"

"You're the only Gale girl he's met . . ."

"Charlie . . ."

"Please." Katie flashed a smile at the first of the
baggage handlers. He blushed and ran the loaded cart
into a pillar. "The aunties want to be sure he's serious,
they want to make sure the attraction isn't part of the
sorcerer's plot, and they figure I'm enough like you to
confuse him."

"It isn't like that."

"Good."

"It's . . ." She wanted to say terrifying but was afraid
Katie would misunderstand. ". . . real."

"Well, duh." Katie stopped, holding Allie back, keeping them from running up on the *who gets to sit next to
Michael in the bus* argument. "It's second-circle real, even
I can feel that. You're all *connected* to things." She said
connected like it was a dirty word. "I don't get why you'd
choose that, frankly."

Allie could feel herself blush and hoped none of
the aunties would turn and see her. "You'll understand
when you meet him."

"He knew we were coming." Auntie Jane patted at the
arm of her purple jacket where the fabric was still smol-
dering. "You didn't tell him you'd called us, did you,
Alysha?"

Something squished under Allie's shoe. She didn't
look down. "No, of course not!"

"No *of course not* about it," Auntie Bea growled,
picking the crimson brim of her hat up off the ruins
of the desk. They hadn't been able to keep the blast
entirely contained within the workroom. She stepped
away from the wreckage, closer to Allie. "You did keep
him hidden from us. Don't even try to deny it."

"I didn't tell you where he was," Allie admitted, standing her ground. "But I had my reasons."

"Your reasons . . ."

"Leave it, Bea," Auntie Jane cut her off. "No one thinks clearly while they're changing."

"That wasn't . . ." Auntie Jane's expression clamped Allie's teeth shut on the protest. Let the aunties believe what they wanted. They would anyway, and it wasn't like she'd done David any good.

"He's definitely made a run for it." Auntie Christie backed out of the destroyed closet, dusting ash off her hands. "But when the workshop imploded, it covered his tracks pretty thoroughly."

"It could be years before we find him again," Auntie Kay muttered. "Years."

"Don't be so defeatist," Auntie Jane told her grimly. "As long as his son's alive, anyone can find him."

"Blood magic." Auntie Meredith spat the words on the pile of dust that had been a bookcase.

"I didn't say we'd use blood magic to find him," Auntie Jane snapped. "But he won't go far as long as anyone else can. He'll remove the threat first."

"So Jack's in danger?" Allie asked.

Auntie Jane turned dark eyes on her. "How much of that blast did you absorb, Alysha? Of course the boy is in danger." Muttering under her breath, she stalked out through the newsroom.

"I was expecting someone . . . taller," the very scary old woman with the dark eyes sniffed as the dozen aunties circled Graham like cats moving in on a mourning dove, shifting him away from the counter and out into the store without touching him.

Graham sought out Allie, bringing up the rear of the pack, and didn't feel particularly reassured by her reassuring nod or her mouthed: *Auntie Jane.* It had been her idea he meet the aunties downstairs and get it over with before they were distracted by the complications of a half-Human/half-Dragon Lord sorcerer. When Auntie Jane ignored his outstretched hand, he let it fall back to his side. "I get that a lot."

"We'll have to see what we can do about having those hex marks removed while we're here."

"Thank you, ma'am. I'd appreciate that." Allie'd suspected one of the glyphs had something to do with his blocked memories.

"You and I being together, that's likely what's helping you to remember." She stroked her fingertips down the center of his chest. *"But if you want these off, we're going to need a little help."*

A slightly taller woman, steel-gray hair cropped short, eyes as dark, frowned at him over the top of her glasses. "So you used to work for a sorcerer?"

"Yes, ma'am."

"And you knew he was a sorcerer? From the beginning?"

"When I met him, I'd just saved him from being killed by a basilisk."

"How?" His confusion must've shown because she sighed and said, "How did you save him, boy?"

All things considered, he decided to let her form of address stand. "I had my hunting rifle with me, and I blew its head off."

"Quite the shot," the shortest of the aunties said thoughtfully. "Blowing the head off a moving basilisk." Shortest, Graham realized, was a relative term since at least two of the old women were Allie's height and none of them were less than five four.

"He could have taken that memory right out of your head," another auntie declared, dark eyes wide, her knitting unraveling slightly with the force of the gesture. "Left you with a big blank space you probably wouldn't have even noticed, boys being boys and all. You were what, thirteen?" She stuffed a few meters of loose yarn back into the bulging bag hanging off her shoulder. "Can't think why he didn't."

"He didn't because he saw young Graham would be useful to him," Auntie Jane snapped. "Grace is right. It was a phenomenal shot, and you know what sorts of things his kind attract. For pity's sake, Muriel, use what's left of your brains before they atrophy entirely."

One of the first lessons he'd learned was not to look the Fey in the eyes—most of them would take advantage; some of them took souls. As far as he knew, the Gales were Human. Although, as he stared as fearlessly as he was able into Jane Gale's eyes, he had to admit he wasn't one hundred percent convinced of that. Ninety percent, tops. He suspected that final ten percent would be chewing at him.

After a long moment, she snorted and allowed him to look away. "I don't actually care why you went to work for him," she said. "You were a child, so I doubt it was your idea anyway. He very likely set himself up so that he was there when you needed him, so that he was the only one there, in all likelihood. What I'm more interested in is why, after serving a power-hungry bastard with delusions of grandeur so faithfully for so long, you decided to jump ship and throw in with a family determined to destroy him and everyone like him. It can't possibly have been because of Alysha's physical attractions."

"It could have been," Allie muttered.

"Because if that's all it was," a round, apple-cheeked

auntie continued, cheerfully ignoring Allie's protest. "We wouldn't want you. First time there was a crisis, you'd be just as likely to run off with young Katie here. Her breasts are larger."

"Very subtle, Auntie Kay!"

"Well, they are, dear."

Without the extremes of Charlie's hair color, it was easier to see the family resemblance between Allie and her cousin Katie. Given that Katie was currently beating her head against Allie's shoulder, it was a little hard to pick out specific details, but she didn't seem to have Allie's golden sprinkle of freckles.

"Well, boy?"

It took Graham a moment to figure out what they were waiting for.

Right.

Why had he walked away from thirteen years with Stanley Kalynchuk? He hadn't known the emerging Dragon Lord was Kalynchuk's son when he'd refused to pull the trigger, so he hadn't exactly been struck by a sudden ethical objection. That had come later. He'd decided not to pull the trigger when Allie'd made it clear she didn't want him to. She hadn't asked him not to, hadn't said anything more than his name, but he'd chosen . . .

Son of bitch.

He'd *chosen.*

"So it's like that, is it?" Auntie Jane's voice pulled him out of his head, and he realized none of the old women—aunties, he amended silently as the youngest of them narrowed dark eyes and glared in his direction as though she was aware of his group designation—stood between him and Allie. He didn't remember any of them moving.

"As Mr. Spock said, in what was undeniably the best of the movies . . ."

"Kay has a Ricardo Montalban fixation," one of the older aunties interrupted.

"Lovely man," Auntie Kay agreed. "Amazing pecs. May his soul be at peace." She frowned. "Where was I?"

Graham wanted to kiss the corner of Allie's mouth where it curved up, fighting a smile.

"The needs of the many . . ." Auntie Muriel sighed, waving a knitting needle.

". . . outweigh the needs of the one. Of course. Had you killed the boy, we wouldn't have needed to come to Calgary to save the world."

"Knowing what you know now . . ." Auntie Jane said with a glance around the circle and in a tone that suggested interrupting would prove fatal. ". . . given the choice again, would you choose differently?"

Graham was certain she hadn't been using *choose* like that before his realization. And there was that ten percent uncertainty again. The store was so quiet he could hear the soft whisper of Allie breathing. He could see the faint dusting of freckles across her nose and cheeks, and the mole on her right earlobe. He could smell the shampoo, shower gel, *Allie* mix that made him think of her moving under him, legs wrapped around his hips . . .

And given that there were twelve older women in the store wearing at least thirty-six separate scents between them, that should have been impossible.

"If I had to do it again," he said, "I wouldn't do anything differently."

Allie raised a brow.

"She was talking specifically about last night," he reminded her.

"She is the cat's mother, Graham Buchanan," Auntie Jane snorted. "Remember it. Christie, Grace, Ellen—

go talk to David. Do not wear him out," she snapped as they surged toward the back door. "Until we know exactly when the Queen is emerging, he could have to lock us down at any moment. Just get him to the point where he can be in the same room as his sister. Vera, Meredith, and Faith, take Michael, find a grocery store, get supplies. I very much doubt we'll be able to put together decent meals from whatever Catherine has left behind. Oh, and you'd best find a hardware store as well, there's no point in leaving it to the last minute." If Michael'd had any objections, he had no chance to voice them as he was tugged back toward the bus. "Gwen get out from behind that counter. This is not the time for that sort of thing. The rest of you, upstairs, let's get that Dragon Princeling sorted before we have to start supper."

And just like that, they were gone.

Well, not exactly *gone*; he could hear them arguing on the stairs and in the courtyard and out on the sidewalk, but the store practically echoed with their absence.

Allie took a deep breath and let it out slowly as she closed the distance between them, slid her arms around Graham's waist, and rested her head on his shoulder. "That could have gone worse," she admitted as his hands spread warm and comforting across her lower back.

And all at once, the store was full of aunties again—down the stairs, in from the courtyard, spilling out of the bus and back in through the front door. Barely daring to breathe, Allie lifted her head and met Auntie Jane's gaze. She couldn't see a demarcation between pupil and iris. She could barely see any whites.

Auntie Jane's lips curled into the second scariest smile Allie had ever seen.

"Well, well, well," she said.

Then the aunties were gone again.

"Okay, that was weird." Katie's voice pulled Allie out of the circle of Graham's arms although she kept her hand in his. "Any ideas?"

Allie shook her head. "I was going to ask you."

"Not a clue. But hey, still third circle, what do I know. Hi, I'm Katie," she directed a slightly harried grin in Graham's direction. "Just so you know, if you *were* just fooling around with Allie, I'd be open to joining in because, seriously, those are a pair of fine looking shoulders and my breasts are larger, but since you clearly aren't just fooling around, it's nice to meet you. Now, please tell me Rol's upstairs running interference for that poor kid."

It took Allie a moment to realize the poor kid referenced was Jack. The Dragon Prince.

"He should be." Allie turned to Graham who nodded, looking a little stunned.

"Charlie's there, too," he told them. "I think she's teaching Jack how to download *Torchwood*."

"She's probably teaching him how to surf for porn," Allie sighed. "Just as illegal but more likely to piss off Auntie Jane."

"Either way," Katie sighed, "we need to get up there."

"Rol can hold them for a few minutes."

"Roland?" Graham asked.

"You've only seen the geeky lawyer in the sweater vest," Allie told him, searching the store for Joe. "When a Gale boy turns on the charm, even the aunties pause to appreciate . . ." She managed to keep the girly shriek down to a single syllable since she'd half expected Joe to fade in behind the counter—and there he was. "Are you okay?"

His cheeks were flushed, and his lower lip was full and red like he'd been biting it. "Your Auntie Gwen kept groping me."

"She could see you?"

He shrugged. "Didn't seem to matter, did it?"

Allie glanced over at her cousin who responded with the universal eye roll of *how the hell should I know?* "If you tell her to stop, she will. But you have to tell her flat out."

"Yeah, well . . ." Joe shrugged again.

"Are you . . . ?" Allie waved a hand, indicating the store, the counter, and the possibility of selling another yoyo.

"Oh, I'm good down here." He gripped the edge of the counter with both hands, and Allie suspected it would take all three of them working together to break his hold.

As they passed the mirror, their reflections walked by the writhing body of a white Dragon Lord being pecked to pieces by crows. Allie's reflection suddenly became a feminized version of the scarecrow from *The Wizard of Oz*. When she spread her arms, just to see what would happen, the crows flew away.

"Not exactly subtle," Katie pointed out. "And why isn't Graham naked?"

Graham's clothing began to fade. Allie touched her fingertips to the glass. "Stop it," she said quietly, and Graham's clothes returned. Plus a parka, a toque, snow-mobile boots, and a pair of enormous, gauntleted ski mitts. "Thank you. How did you know the mirror would do that?" she demanded of her cousin.

Katie sighed. "Gran's mirror." The "duh" remained unspoken but present. "And if I hadn't already known you were crossing, that would have given it away." She started up the stairs. "Second circle is so possessive it's a bit creepy."

"I'm not . . ."

"Allie, you've written *mine* on a leprechaun. And Graham. And Michael, again. And, I'm guessing, on a Dragon Prince." Leaning back, she stuck her head around the corner into the lower hall. "You've been here a week. If that's not possessive, I don't know what is."

"Preemptive."

"Potato, potahto, Allie-cat."

When Katie waved and disappeared, Allie returned her attention to the mirror. "Don't worry," she told it, lightly gripping the frame. "I won't let them destroy Jack."

"Are you sure," Graham began, touching his hair with a bare hand while watching his reflection poke at the hat with a mitten tip. ". . . that's Jack?" he finished as Allie shot him a look that said, *Don't undermine my authority with the mirror.* She knew he'd been going to say, *"Are you sure you can?"* and was impressed he'd understood her message.

"If it's possible to prevent it, I'd rather the aunties didn't eat any of the Dragon Lords alive."

"Are they likely to?"

Linking her fingers with his, she tugged him toward the stairs. "Depends." With any luck he wouldn't ask *depends on what?* "You didn't happen to count the crows did you? The ones in the mirror?"

"No, why?"

"Well, it was hard to tell since they were never still, but as they flew away, I could've sworn there were thirteen."

"Is that important? Thirteen crows?"

Allie glanced back, lower lip caught between her teeth. "It means something," she said slowly. "I'm sure of that, I'm just not sure what."

"In Mesoamerican divination, thirteen is the number of important cycles of fortune and misfortune. Loki was the thirteenth guest at a banquet where he killed Baldur beginning Ragnarok. Thirteen nodes make up the Metatron's Cube." When Allie stopped climbing and turned to face him, he grinned. "I wrote an article on Triskaidekaphobia for our second issue."

"I keep forgetting you have a secret identity."

"Had." The grin flattened. "He might have moved out of the office, but he still runs the paper."

"Remember, it isn't over until the fat lady sings." She brushed a strand of hair back off his face. "In this case, that would be Auntie Kay. If she starts in on Andrew Lloyd Webber, run."

Graham frowned. "Why?"

"She's really, really bad."

They entered the apartment just in time to see Roland step in front of Jack and say, "Auntie Bea! He's thirteen!"

Since Jack looked more intrigued than upset, Allie decided she didn't need to know the context. And anyway, Auntie Jane stepped forward before she could say anything, moving around Roland—or possibly moving Roland, Allie couldn't be positive which—and pinching Jack's chin between thumb and forefinger.

"Oh, yes," she murmured, turning his head to the right and then to the left. From where Allie was standing it looked very much like she was peering up his nose. "You're family, all right."

Allie rolled her eyes and pushed her way through the crowd of aunties—and six aunties were more than capable of seeming like a crowd. "He's family because I claimed him, Auntie Jane." All the charms but the one on his forehead were covered by clothing but should have made no difference to an auntie.

"He's family because of blood, Alysha Catherine."

"Blood?" Her cousins, standing together behind Jack in a show of generation unity, returned *I have no idea what she's talking about* expressions. "We're related to the Dragon Lords?"

"Don't be ridiculous, child. We're related to his father."

"His father?"

"My father?" Jack grabbed Auntie Jane's sleeve. "You know my father?"

"I wouldn't say that I know him, child, but I met him once. It was just before he disappeared, I was three and I remember my Auntie Anna insisting he was going to turn and his youngest sister, that would be Clara who died, oh sixteen years ago now, kept insisting he wouldn't." Patting Jack's hand, she turned her head toward Allie. "He killed Auntie Anna when she tried to stop him. Sisters are usually fairly stupid about that sort of thing."

"Clara," Auntie Bea snorted as Allie backed up until her shoulder blades were pressed against Graham's chest and his hands rested warm and grounding on her hips. "Woman was a total nut job there at the end. Eight dead, and she refused to believe her brother had done anything wrong."

"Magnificent fruitcake recipe, though," Auntie Muriel added. "Impossible to duplicate." The other five made noises of varying agreement.

"Wait, wait, wait, wait!" Roland had both hands up, his eyes so wide Allie could see the whites all the way around. "Are you saying what I think you're saying?"

"Oh, for pity's sake, Roland, law school ruined you." Still holding Jack's hand, Auntie Jane moved over to one of the sofas and sat. Jack tried to pull free, had no success, and ended up sitting beside her looking just a little freaked. "Stop it," she said as the lights began to flicker.

To no one's surprise, they stopped.

The other aunties found seats, leaving Roland, Charlie, Katie, Allie, and Graham on their feet.

"Well, Charlotte, you've always been good at jumping to conclusions, what do you . . . ?" Auntie Jane frowned up at her. Blinked. "What on earth have you done to your hair?"

Charlie tucked her hands into the front pockets of her jeans. "Red's a better color for country," she said evenly.

"And I'm sure Reba McIntyre is thrilled you approve," Auntie Jane sniffed. "That, however, is not a shade of red intended for hair. That is a shade intended for cheap lipstick and slutty lingerie."

"The blue hair made her look like a Smurf," Auntie Muriel pointed out, unrolling a long multicolored tube and starting to knit.

"I'm not saying this doesn't look better," Auntie Jane sniffed again.

Allie could tell by the curl to Charlie's lip that she was about to say something they'd probably all regret, given that the aunties believed in spreading the blame. "You're saying that Graham's boss . . . ex-boss," she corrected hurriedly as his fingers tightened, "was a Gale."

"Was a Gale?" Auntie Jane's gaze whipped around toward her so quickly Allie nearly felt a breeze. "No. *Is* a Gale."

"Is?" Allie repeated.

"They're too young," Auntie Bea snapped.

"That horse is already out of the barn, Bea. Besides, the child is sitting right here, and blood always tells. Eventually, they'd have figured it out for themselves or," Auntie Jane continued, her voice dropping into what David had always called *someone's going to get it territory,* "I'd have had something to say to the lot of them about paying attention to what's actually going on."

Katie raised a hand. "I just got here."

"And don't make me regret bringing you."

"So Alastair Bronwin," Roland said slowly, "the sorcerer the family took out in 1973 . . ."

"He had the brains to settle in Syria," Auntie Kay snorted. "Never would have found him if it hadn't been for the oil crisis."

". . . he was a Gale?"

"They're all Gales," Allie said, watching Auntie Jane's face as the last few pieces fell into place. "That's what sorcerers are. They're Gales gone bad who got away. They don't just use the power to gain more power, they use the power to extend their lives. Who was he?"

"He?"

"Jack's father."

"Before he was a sorcerer, his name was Jonathon Samuel Gale."

Allie nodded. "That's why we stop them, isn't it? Because they're Gales. They're family. They're our responsibility. And that's why we're attracted to them, it's not the power, it's because they're . . ." With an image of Stanley Kalynchuk in her head, with Roland in the room, she couldn't say *Gale boys.* "But I wasn't . . ." Graham. "I wasn't because by the time I met him, Graham and I had already connected . . ."

"Is that what the kids are calling it these days," Auntie Carol snickered.

"... and I was moving into second circle. And Graham was in the room with us. What if I hadn't ... Oh." She wouldn't have even known there was a sorcerer in Calgary if she hadn't seen the hexes on Graham's chest. Not with him locked down and hiding from the Dragon Lords. Not until it was too late. Everything came back to that first meeting between her and Graham that night in the store. Just the two of them. Because Charlie'd been delayed.

She looked up to see Charlie's gaze locked on her face and wondered how much her expression had given away. Or, with more information than the aunties had been given, whether Charlie'd arrived at the same place.

Then she took one more step.

"Jack's a sorcerer."

"Yes."

Allie realized Auntie Jane hadn't let go of Jack's hand. "And a Gale."

"Yes."

They were all looking at her now—the aunties, her cousins, Jack. Jack's eyes were gold, but Human enough for all that, and he had a curved blemish on one cheek that looked like a hockey scar. Somehow Allie doubted the Dragon Lords played hockey, but it wouldn't be the strangest thing she'd heard. His nose was a little too big for his face and he had a smudge of lemon pie filling on his hoodie. He'd just started into the all-knees-and-elbows phase and Allie hoped that his mother's heritage had gifted him with more grace than his Human side. He sat motionless beside Auntie Jane, breathing a little heavily, two thin lines of smoke trickling out of his nose—but then the one thing she knew about his upbringing was that he could recognize predators.

His uncles kept trying to eat him.

His aunties . . .

But if they truly were his aunties . . .

"Gale boys choose," Allie said, straightening and squaring her shoulders. "And he's not old enough. He's thirteen. Fifteen's the minimum for third circle, no matter how much of a pain in the ass the boys are about it."

"He's a sorcerer now," Auntie Bea reminded her. She sounded almost gleeful about it.

"That doesn't matter. He didn't choose it. His abilities are innate because sorcery was used in his conception."

"The situation is unique," Auntie Jane agreed, dark eyes narrowed. "But that in itself suggests we find a unique solution."

"If he's a Gale, then what applies to the rest of the family applies to him. Either family matters, or it doesn't. If he isn't a Gale, then he isn't your responsibility. And what's more . . ." Allie was suddenly tired of butting heads with stubborn old women. ". . . like I told his uncles, he's under my protection."

"And that's your last word on the matter, is it, Alysha Catherine?"

"Yes."

"Well, that seems like a unique solution to me." She patted Jack's hand, released it, and stood. "Muriel?"

Auntie Muriel shoved her knitting away. "With this many people, this late in the day, it had better be chili and cornbread."

"Three bean salad on the side?"

"None for me, dear. It repeats on me."

"Wait!" Allie held up a hand and the sudden, purposeful bustling paused. "What just happened?"

"You just agreed to be responsible for young Jack here until he turns fifteen."

"I what?"

"I don't need a babysitter!" Jack protested surging up onto his feet.

Auntie Jane placed her hand in the center of his chest and pushed him back down onto the sofa. "How fortunate that Alysha has always wanted a younger brother. Perfect timing," she added as the apartment door opened, "here's the girls with the groceries. Chop, chop, supper isn't going to make itself!"

"How did the women buying the groceries know what to get?" Graham asked, the question brushing warm against her ear. "They only just decided to make chili."

She turned just far enough to raise an eyebrow at him. "Do I really need to answer that?"

She could feel him thinking about it. "Actually, no."

Watching nine aunties maneuver around a kitchen was a little like watching ballet had the corps all considered themselves principal dancers. And been armed.

No. Eight aunties.

Allie frowned and moved away from Graham's touch to where Auntie Gwen was standing, staring into the middle distance. She'd only just changed over and sometimes the color of her eyes still took Allie by surprise. Tucking herself up by the older woman's shoulder, Allie followed her line of sight but as far as she could tell, there was nothing there.

"You've been awfully quiet," she said.

"I was just wondering . . ." Auntie Gwen's dark eyes gleamed. ". . . what your leprechaun's name is."

As soon as full dark fell, the Dragon Lords began flying over again, although only Allie and the aunties could feel them.

"Testing the wards," Auntie Jane sniffed. "I'll say this much for my sister, if she wanted you to stay out, you stayed out."

"Are they trying to get in at Jack, or are they making sure his father can't?" Allie twisted up a fistful of curtain and stared up at what the lights of the city allowed of the stars.

"Don't know, don't care. Who's going to Charlotte's concert and who's up for euchre?"

That was enough to turn Allie away from the window. "Charlie's playing in a bar, Auntie Jane."

"We've been in bars before, Alysha." Auntie Jane sat down at the dining room table as at least half the others started pulling on jackets and shoes. "Your Auntie Ellen used to bartend at the Royal when she was younger."

"But what if Jack's mother shows up tonight?"

"Is she going to?" Not a rhetorical or any other type of bloody-minded question, Auntie Jane looked at her like she actually wanted an answer.

"Jack . . ."

"I'm asking you, Alysha Catherine. Is she going to show up tonight?"

How was she supposed to . . . Oh. Allie slid her awareness out through the city, allowed it to be drawn to the sacred site on the top of the hill.

"Second circle makes connections, Alysha."

"I *know* that," she murmured, finding the path Jack had created between realities.

"Of course you do," Auntie Bea sniffed.

"Kids today." Auntie Christie rolled her eyes with the expressiveness of much practice. "Think they know everything."

Auntie Meredith sighed. "I don't know why we even bother to . . ."

Allie pushed the aunties' litany to the spot in her

mind where muzak lived, rested her forehead against the window, and moved carefully along the path. A little further. And back one hell of a lot faster at the first brush against the edge of the burning.

The glass had warmed under her skin, so she shifted six inches left, sucking in air through her teeth at the cool touch.

"Well?"

"Not tonight."

"Well, there you go, then. Roland, you'll stay here. Michael, you'll drive. Meredith, have you got the cards?"

"Allie, do you . . . ?"

"Guess again, future-cousin-in-law." Wearing a pair of NHL boxers and a faded Blue Rodeo T-shirt, Charlie pulled the bedroom doors closed behind her. "Allie's settling Jack. He ate a tube of toothpaste."

Graham frowned. He had a vague memory of one of his cousins doing the same. "That shouldn't hurt him."

"He ate the tube, too."

That, his cousin hadn't done. He leaned back against the dresser, unwilling to get any closer until he knew why she was in the bedroom. "Well, how was the gig?"

"Interesting. When Auntie Christie gets a couple of beers in her, she does a scary two-step."

"Any sign of trouble?"

"You mean besides there being more bowlegged cowboys in the city tonight than there were yesterday? No."

It was the expression on Charlie's face that made Graham decide he didn't want to know. "So, no Dragon Lords?"

"Auntie Ellen said a couple of them landed outside, but they didn't come in."

"Because of the aunties?"

"Or they got freaked by our kick-ass cover of 'Roughest Neck Around.' Hard to say. So, look at you two . . ." She dropped onto the end of the bed and bounced. ". . . all alone in this great big bed while I'm fighting the Jolly Green Giant for space. Plus, he's a blanket hog. He's always been a blanket hog."

"Did you want to join us?" Graham asked. He'd thought the sarcasm had been obvious, but Charlie looked like she was actually considering it.

"After things are locked down," she said at last.

"Things?"

"Between you and Allie." She tucked a bare leg under her butt, and gazed up at him. "I was hoping the aunties would bring Uncle Tom, that's Allie's dad, out west with them. He's a Gale by marriage; you've probably got some questions."

"About marriage?" He ran a hand back through his hair. "Charlie, Allie and I are . . ."

"Twinned, turbo-charged souls who have miraculously found each other and now have an eternity of bliss ahead. Also, you're really hot together. No, not about marriage, you ass, about what it means to choose a Gale—so this time, when she asks you if you understand your choice, you won't be talking through your fucking ego." She leaned back on her elbows, and Graham tried very hard not to look at the nipple poking Jim Cuddy in the eye. "Figured out what you want to say to her yet?"

"Do I need to *say* it at this point? I mean, I'm here."

"Not at *this* point." Charlie rolled her eyes. "But it's going to come up. So, since I'm here and you and Allie are still . . ." She sketched the most sarcastic set of air quotes he'd ever seen and given that she had to know about the sex, he supposed he didn't blame her. "... *treading carefully*, any immediate questions? Say, about the aunties?"

"The aunties ..." Graham remembered everything Stanley Kalynchuk had told him about the Gale women and suppressed a shudder. From what he'd seen so far, that, at least, the sorcerer hadn't lied to him about. "The aunties are self-explanatory."

"True that."

"Most of my questions ..." Most of his questions, he wanted to howl at Kalynchuk. "... you can't answer. Except ... No."

"You're thinking that if you want to know the thing you want to know, you should ask Allie, not me, aren't you?" She shifted to run a hand back through her hair, frowned at the single brilliant strand caught on a guitar callus and flicked it off onto the floor. "That means it's either about Michael or David. She loves Michael, always will."

"I'm okay with that."

"Big of you," Charlie snorted. "David ..."

"She apologized to David." It was all Allie had said to him during the whole meal. She'd said, *I'm sorry.* He'd kissed her forehead and called her an idiot.

"David's going to have to anchor the whole first circle."

"And that's dangerous."

"That wasn't a question."

"I'm not an idiot."

"About what?" Allie glanced between them as she came into the bedroom and frowned. "What have you guys been talking about?"

"You." Charlie bounced up off the bed, grabbed Allie by the shoulders of the faded Great Big Sea T-shirt *she* wore and kissed her soundly. Graham tried not to think about implications. Or east coast Canadian music meeting up with west. "I told him all about the spot under your right ear."

"He found that already," Allie snorted.

"Really? Well, did he find . . ." She shot a wicked glance in Graham's direction and bent to whisper in her cousin's ear.

Allie grinned. "No. Not yet."

"Should I . . ."

"You should leave. Joe's sharing with Michael, you and Katie are sharing with Roland."

"I could help him find . . ."

"If I need your help," Graham said, "I'll ask for it."

Charlie turned to look at him, fully at him, and just for a moment, he thought her eyes had turned a darker gray. "Deal." Then she winked, and the moment passed.

Later, with Allie's head pillowed on his shoulder, he stroked along the damp curve of her spine and thought she was beautiful and thought for the first time in a long time he was exactly where he belonged and because he couldn't entirely shut the reporter up, he thought about that niggling ten percent.

"You're thinking very loudly."

"Sorry."

"You can ask me anything, you know."

"Anything?"

He could feel her smile against his skin. "I'm fairly certain you'll keep it out of the papers at this point."

It might be the only way he'd ever find out. "Are you . . ." It sounded like such a stupid question even before he asked it. "Are you Human?"

"Was I just that amazing?"

"Allie." Graham caught her hand before it slid lower on his body.

She sighed. "Yes. No. Essentially. If the world doesn't end and you decide to stay, there will be babies."

"*He* managed that with a dragon."

"Okay, so not my best argument." Her thumb stroked the hollow of his hip and he knew she was drawing another charm. He thought about stopping her. He didn't. "Do you remember your family?" she asked softly. "From before the fire?"

Did he? He pushed through the smoke. "I remember a house too small for the number of people in it. I remember a lot of yelling and laughing and broken toys and the reek of wet hockey equipment piled in the summer kitchen. I remember knowing that wherever I went in town a spiderweb of connections defined me."

"Good." She kissed the spot under his ear. "That's what we are."

"It's not all you are."

"It's all that matters."

He wanted to believe that.

Graham lay quietly, one arm trapped under Allie's body, trying to identify the sound that had woken him. Instinct told him it hadn't come from one of the five sleeping out in the living room. Jack, maybe. But what was Jack doing up at 6:10?

Allie murmured as he slid his arm free, but he kissed her bare shoulder and she settled back to sleep. He'd left his clothing so that he could dress quickly in the dark, and it only took a moment's extra time to scoop the boxers he'd worn to bed—and not kept on long—up off the floor.

Staying low, he slipped out into the main room, silent

on sock feet, and nearly crapped himself when Auntie Kay turned from the kitchen and waved.

"I couldn't sleep any longer," she whispered as soon as he was close enough. "Time change, you know. Bea and Meredith are in the pool. Jane is on the phone with Ruby—the silly old dear was up the water tower again, wrote *Surrender Dorothy* with the paint left over from when Tom redid the trim on the farmhouse. When Christie started in on that Tai Chi nonsense, I decided to come over and get a start on the biscuits for breakfast. You wouldn't know where Allie keeps her shortening, would you?"

It seemed safest to merely answer the direct question. "Sorry, no."

"I have this terrible fear she's out and that's, well, that's just wrong."

Graham knew where this was going. "There's a twenty-four-hour convenience store just down the road. Do you want me to go out and get some shortening for you?"

"Would you, dear? How sweet to offer. Get as much as they have. If Jack's mother doesn't have us all flying about in circles today, we'll use it for pies."

She didn't offer to pay for the shortening, and Graham didn't ask. Truth be told, he was just as glad to get out on his own for a few minutes, even if it was just walking a couple of blocks to the store and back. He'd shut the newspaper down—citing a family emergency when he'd made the calls, and his whole life had devolved into waiting for Jack's mother. The Dragon Queen.

And after?

"If the world doesn't end, and you decide to stay, there will be babies."

Yeah, he could use a walk.

As he slipped into his boots, tugging them from the pile at the door, he realized his jacket was still in the bedroom. He pulled what had to be Roland's off a hook—it had to be Roland's because although the jacket he'd found was big on him, Michael's would have been like wearing a circus tent.

Leaning against the wall at the bottom of the stairs were a dozen new corn brooms.

"Do you remember your family? That's what we are."

"Oh, yeah . . ." The orange sale stickers were very bright on the blue handles. The aunties had gotten a deal. No surprise. ". . . just like my family."

When he glanced over at the mirror, fourteen reflections glanced back. Most of them were dressed. The one out front was holding a suitcase.

"I'm not leaving, I'm just going on an errand for Auntie Kay. And I'm talking to a mirror." Since he didn't have a key to the store, he went out the back door and through the garage. Since anything coming back in would have to get past David, still in the loft, it seemed safest.

He kept close to the walls of the alley and, when he reached the street, stayed close to the storefronts. The sky had lightened enough to keep the Dragon Lords flying high, but one *had* landed and walked right into the store, so daylight wasn't exactly the protection it should have been. He kept half his attention on the local pigeons. If they dove for cover, he was heading right under that newspaper box with them.

Early morning traffic had started to pick up by the time he left the store, six pounds of shortening in a bag and the storekeeper's puzzled gaze still on the back of his head. He didn't notice the big black SUV before it stopped beside him on the road.

No, he didn't *see* the big black SUV before the door opened and Stanley Kalynchuk growled, "Get in."

"No."

But he stepped up into the car.

"Hurry!"

He couldn't stop himself from dropping into the seat and closing the door behind him.

THIRTEEN

The grass across the top of the hill burned first, a circle of black spreading behind a ring of gold. Then the trees ignited with a roar, towers of flame enclosing the summit. The world burned too fast after that for Allie to see the individual pyres. Cars exploded, the slam of sound devolving to gentle popping as the fire spread.

Here and there, amidst the crackle of cooking fat, she saw faces.

Charlie. Graham. Kenny in the coffee shop. Her mother. Her father. Roland's daughter, Lyla. Dr. Yan. The aunties burned last, but even they burned, falling out of the sky trailing tails of black smoke like particularly dirty comets.

Then, when enough of the world had been remade, Jack's mother rose from the center of the circle where the flames had died to glowing embers. Thunder boomed when she spread gleaming white wings and two of her brothers, tiny against her bulk, tumbled broken from the sky. Scimitar claws extended, she gouged great gashes in the blackened, pitted rock, and roared.

And roared.

And roared.

Left hand groping for something to hold and finding only an empty bed, Allie stared up into the darkness and listened to the sound of her family moving out in the next room, to the sound of the city waking beyond the walls of the apartment, to the sound of claws on rock coming closer.

And closer.

Heat lingered in the hollows next to her so Graham couldn't have been gone long. Clock said 6:47, so she *hoped* he hadn't been gone long. If he was that much of a morning person, there were going to have to be significant adjustments made.

If they . . .

Although she was fairly certain at this point it wasn't so much *if* as when. Not that it mattered, she wasn't going to scare him away, not again. He could choose when he was good and ready to choose and not a moment before. Here and now, it was enough to know he was . . .

Wasn't.

She could feel her connection to Michael. To Charlie. But it was like Graham had suddenly ceased to exist.

"I sent him for shortening, Allie, that's all." Auntie Kay reached out a comforting hand, reconsidered, and tucked it back in her apron pocket. "He just went down to the store. He'll be back any minute."

"No." Clutching Graham's jacket closed, Allie shook her head. "I can't feel him. I can barely feel the city and I can't feel him. One minute, everything was fine, the next I'm holding the end of a broken rope!"

"He ran once before."

Pivoting on one bare heel, she whipped around

toward Roland, but Michael slid into her line of sight, hands raised, voice gentle. "Rol's right, Allie-cat. He did run once before, and you know the aunties can be a bit much for people. Even people who know them. No offense," he added hurriedly in Auntie Kay's direction.

"None taken, dear."

"You don't understand!" She cast herself out again. David. The aunties. Even the Dragon Lords circling high overhead. No Graham. "If he left the apartment around six twenty, he couldn't have gone *far* enough for me not to be able to feel him."

"Could you feel him the last time he ran?"

"Could I what?" Allie stared at Michael in astonishment. "No, of course not! I didn't try! What does that have to do with him now?"

"Maybe when he's with the sorcerer, you can't feel him. He might have run back to him this morning, Allie. I mean, he's been with this guy half his life. Hell, between the protecting and the paper, the guy is Graham's life. Maybe Graham woke up this morning, heat of the moment long past, and realized he couldn't just walk away."

"He *had* walked away." She was not going to cry.

"And you know this because?" Michael sighed and cupped one hand under her chin and lifted her head. "I hate to say this, but we both know you don't love exactly rationally."

"Who does!"

His thumb stroked her cheek. "You're a little further off the bubble than most."

"I'm a little . . ." She'd known him most of his life. He'd been the first boy she'd ever kissed. Thought he was the only boy she'd ever love. And she could see all those years together on his face. "I thought you didn't know."

"I'm not an idiot, Allie-cat."

If he'd known, and never said . . . "So you've been *laughing*?"

The fox eyes, widened. "Allie, I would never . . ."

"Patronizing me, then!" The force of the blow, although she didn't raise a hand against him—had never, would never—sent him flying over the closer of the sofa beds and slamming into the closed bathroom door.

"Yeah, so much for the not an idiot part," Charlie murmured, taking Allie's arm. "If Graham's with the ex-boss, he didn't go willingly. Come on. Into the bedroom, we'll put on some clothes, and we'll set up the search and rescue. Rol . . ."

"I'm calling."

"Michael . . ."

"Michael's fine. Joe'll pick him up, Auntie Kay'll slap a little arnica on the impact points, and he likely won't even bruise.

"I didn't mean to . . ."

"Yeah, you did." Charlie's grip moved her back into the bedroom. Twisting and trying to get to Michael only gained her a sore arm. "Oh, no. Until you've actually got your brain booted up and working, you're staying away from the noncombatants. Also, next time I tell you to handcuff your boy to the bed, you should listen to me."

"You didn't tell me to handcuff him to the bed."

"I didn't? Damn, I meant to."

"He asked if we were Human," Allie said softly as she sank down onto the end of the mattress. "He's been taught to hate everything that isn't Human. If it's not Human, it's nothing. It's . . ." She made the shape of gun with her right hand and pulled the trigger.

Charlie stopped rummaging in her drawers, turned to face her. "So you're half afraid he did fuck off?"

Allie nodded.

"Well, he didn't." A pair of clean underwear smacked Allie in the face. "And if you weren't bent on acting like a bad romance heroine, you'd know the thing between you is real and there's no fucking way he'd walk."

"Eaten!"

"By underwear?"

Which was when Allie realized she was staring at a burgundy cotton string bikini. "I forgot about the Dragon Lords! They could have eaten him."

Charlie sighed and crossed the room to crouch at Allie's feet. "Okay, one, they didn't eat him before when the aunties were just a threat, so they're sure as shit not going to eat him now when we're overrun with aunties available for immediate retribution. Two, remember how Aunt Judy reacted when Uncle Roger died?"

"I remember." The pain had drawn Allie home from Toronto and other members of the family home from farther still. The second circle had disappeared into Aunt Judy's house for five days. First and third had baked a lot of pie.

"You'd know if Graham was dead and *eaten,* well, that's pretty fucking dead. Now . . ." Charlie straightened. "Get dressed. Actually, answer your phone first." She scooped Allie's messenger bag off the chair and threw it at her.

"It's probably Auntie Jane," Allie muttered, digging through accumulated junk for her phone. Charlie had made her feel both better and worse. Better because it was hard to doubt Charlie's certainty and worse because she should have been just as certain. When she thought of tomorrow, Graham was there. When she thought of thirty years down the road, Graham was there, too. It was just today she was having a little trouble with. "I'm not sure I'm up to Auntie Jane right . . . oh, it's David."

"So, how is my nephew?" Adam wore a burgundy suit Allie was pretty sure she'd last seen Timothy Hutton wear playing Archie Goodwin for A&E. And, nothing against Timothy Hutton who she thought was getting even more attractive as he got older, but, on Adam, the suit was smoking.

Literally.

Allie stopped a careful distance away, one hand resting on Graham's truck. He wouldn't have left without his truck. Not willingly. The contact helped her ignore the remaining doubt. "Jack's fine."

The dark eyes glittered as his gaze dipped off her face for a moment. "In the bosom of his family, is he?"

She had just a little too much on her plate this morning to react to a hypersexual, shape-shifting lizard looking at her breasts. "You knew?"

The shrug was equal parts sinuous and unconcerned. "The scent of the blood is unmistakable."

"So the family business you didn't want us involved in turns out to be my family's business as well."

"I never said it wasn't." His tone dared her to challenge him on that, but she honestly didn't care enough to bother. "You must admit, it would have been much simpler for all concerned had you not become involved."

"Simpler for everyone but Jack."

"Death is not particularly complex, Alysha Gale."

Her thumbnail cutting through the dirt, she sketched a charm on the truck. "Why are you here, Adam?"

He glanced around the alley. "The store was not open; we needed to talk."

"Why?"

"I saw the man who wears your mark, taken."

Adam's smile let her know he'd heard her heart speed up. "Taken?"

"I saw him walking back to you. I saw him stop walking. I saw him disappear into a nothing in the road."

"A nothing?" The hand not on the truck held her phone, her thumb on the speed dial that would connect her with her brother. If Adam was messing with her, she was going to give David a way to work out more of the energy he still held with a little head butting. "What's a nothing?"

"A lack of something, Gale girl. There he was." Adam spread long-fingered hands. "There he wasn't."

"Did he go willingly?"

"Away from you? How could he?" His smile was heated but when Allie narrowed her eyes, it cooled. "In all honesty, I saw no coercion, but there are bonds even I cannot see."

A nothing in the road.

"The sorcerer."

"So I suspected."

"He's in his car. He's hidden it, the way he hid the office from you. It's a secondary bolt-hole—a way for him to escape, except he won't run while Jack can lead your sister to him."

"He couldn't go far enough unless he left this world entirely. For some world other than mine, of course," the Dragon Lord amended. "As that would certainly not solve his problem."

His problem. Allie appreciated the understatement. "He's grabbed Graham because Graham's still his best bet to take out Jack . . ." Lifting her hand off the truck, she closed her fingers around the bullet in the breast pocket of Graham's jacket. ". . . except we're not likely to put Jack anywhere he can get to him unless he thinks we'll just let Graham back in, which we would, because Gran's wards would strip a geis, so . . ."

"Gale girl!" His tone snapped her out of reflection. "As fascinating as time spent in your company is, if you cannot tell me how to find this nothing, I will return to the sky."

"I can't. But if the aunties can," she added hurriedly, "how do I contact you?"

"If you cannot contact me, Gale girl, I doubt you have anything to say I need to hear." He stepped back, and Allie knew the fire was a heartbeat away.

"Adam!" When he didn't begin to burn, she took a deep breath. "Just whose side are you on?"

Sulfur overwhelmed the alley's scent of old garbage, cat piss, and car exhaust as he sighed, the heat dialed back to a level she thought she could endure. "If my sister comes to this world," he said wearily, "we are bound to protect her. To serve her. I am fond of this place and there are many parts of it I do not wish to see destroyed." He twitched a nonexistent wrinkle from his suit jacket. "But mostly, I am fond of it because it has been a refuge. Here, I am not in my sister's service. I am on my side, Gale girl." His smile held multiple points. "But I suspect you knew that."

"You're probably right about the car," Auntie Jane said thoughtfully. "He'd want a way to run."

"Except if he thought he was going to be running instead of hanging about the city, he may need to keep moving to stay undetectable," Auntie Bea added.

Auntie Christie set a shallow bowl of water on one end of the dining room table. "He'll have to stop for gas, and when he does, I'll find him."

"In that?" Auntie Meredith snorted, staring into the screen of her phone.

Allie thought Auntie Christie's smile looked a bit like Adam's. "At least I don't have to scry through incoming calls."

She moved closer to Auntie Jane as the other two continued bickering. "Graham didn't go willingly."

"Of course he didn't. Stupid boy probably participated in blood magic at some point over the last thirteen years. That sort of nonsense creates ties that aren't easy to break and Jonathon Samuel is powerful enough to use them."

Allie held out the bullet. "His blood's part of this."

"So is Jonathon Samuel's." Auntie Jane snickered as she rolled it across her palm. "He's not going to be pleased he didn't get this back," she said returning it. "But it proves my point. Young men are idiots."

"He didn't know any better."

"Then you'll have a lot to teach him, won't you?"

"If . . ."

"When, Alysha Catherine." Strong fingers pinched her chin. "When."

"Allie, why do I have to be up?" Yawning and scratching, Jack slouched across the room and glared at her. "It's still stupid o'clock in the morning."

"If you can sleep through this . . ." she waved a hand at the baking and the scrying and whatever the hell Katie was doing to Charlie's hair. ". . . go back to bed."

"Thanks, Al. You totally don't suck."

"What?" she asked as Auntie Jane snorted disapprovingly. "It still *is* stupid o'clock in the morning."

Kalynchuk took a long swallow of coffee and gunned the SUV through a yellow light. "I am living in my car," he snarled, tossing the empty cup into the backseat. "Me. In my car. Like a transient. Like a mere mortal. Like I am not the only man of power to master the Dragon Queen!"

"Hiding from a group of old women who can destroy you with a word," Graham reminded him. His shoulder ached from where he'd been slamming it against the door.

"Please, they're the least of my concerns."

"You never told me you were a Gale."

"There's a great many things I never told you." He took his eyes off the road long enough to sneer in Graham's direction. "We were not friends."

"No shit." Major fail on emotional pain if that had been the intent. "Did you kill my family?"

"Did I what?" That drew his attention off the road so completely the car wandered off with it.

"Simple question." Graham reached over and jerked the wheel to the left to avoid impact with a parked car. Given the whole invisible thing, Kalynchuk had taken them onto quiet, empty, residential roads, but that didn't mean there weren't dangers. He realized too late impact could have given him a chance to get away.

From his smug expression as he regained control of the vehicle, Kalynchuk realized it, too. "Your family died years ago. Why do you care?"

"Why do I care?" Fingernails dug half moons into his palms as he stopped himself from taking another futile swing at the son-of-a-bitch. "For fucksake, they were my family!"

"It's been thirteen years, and you never asked me. You don't think that's interesting? You made a living asking questions, and you never asked me that. It's like you knew that if they'd lived you'd still be stuck in that backwoods pitiful excuse of a life. I saved you, and you know it."

"I'd always thought it." Although, here and now, he didn't know how he could have. He'd worked for Kalynchuk for half his life, had started out overwhelmed and honored to think an orphaned boy from Blanc-Sablon would be trusted to guard so important a man, had ended up thinking his life had a greater meaning than some office drone with no idea of how much larger the world actually was. Start to finish, he'd been an idiot. "The whole sex with a dragon thing? That proves your mastery of fire pretty definitively. Your enthusiasm for killing your son proves you're a heartless fuck."

"My *son*," the sorcerer snorted. "I was willing to have you kill him, which is, I admit, merely a difference of degree. You don't seem to understand that the creature is more dangerous to me than those old women are."

"And you've lost your chance."

"I didn't lose it!" The force of the words sprayed saliva over the windshield as he turned down another empty suburban street. "You took it from me."

"Damned right." Graham didn't bother hiding his triumph. "They'll never let you near him. And they won't let me near him if there's a chance I'm under your control."

"Fortunately, I don't care what they want or they intend. However, in case we can't remove him, his mother will be at least as disoriented upon arrival as he was—perhaps more, given that she has no connection to this world except through him—that's when the old women will do whatever it is they plan to do. They'll fail—they have no idea of how strong she is—but that failure should further distract her. I controlled her once, I can do it again. If I can get her into skin, you can kill her with Blessed rounds. A lot of them, admittedly, but it can be done."

"Should have thought of that before you grabbed me." He spread his hands. "No weapon."

"Not your favorite, perhaps, but I stopped by your condo and picked up your other M24."

The thought of Kalynchuk knowing how to find his very well hidden weapons cache made his skin crawl. "I won't use it."

"Stop being so stupidly squeamish. She's not Human."

"Are you Human?"

"That doesn't matter." Maybe he said it to Allie. Maybe to Kalynchuk, he wasn't sure.

"You'd like to think so, wouldn't you?"

"If she's not Human," Graham growled. "Neither are you."

"She's a Dragon Queen, you . . . Oh." The near side of Kalynchuk's mouth curved up into a derisive smile. "You're talking about Alysha. What did the little bitch tell you? That we're descended from some magical mating between a woman and the Horned God? Could be true. Could be total bullshit. What you need to remember here and now is that the creature's mother will kill you when she kills me." Years of questioning unreliable witnesses slid Graham past the sudden change of topic. "Kill you, me, half of the city, most likely. She's not exactly precise when she's in a temper. And then she'll hunt, because she'll have worked up an appetite, and more people will die. The Gale girl. The old women."

"Or they'll win."

"Unlikely."

"I'll take that chance."

"No," Kalynchuk sighed, turning on the windshield wipers as it started to rain, "you won't because in the end you will do what I tell you to do. Just like you always have."

"Fuck you."

"Touch your nose with your right thumb."

Graham fought the impulse, but his right arm rose like a puppeteer held the string. He could feel a trickle of sweat run down his side, but he could also feel his thumb against his nose. Then his body was his own again and he threw himself across the seats only to be slammed back, his head impacting with the window. The pain was strangely cleansing.

"Do your seat belt up. You may obey me now for more easy-to-understand reasons than you did," he continued as Graham did as he was told, "in that now you have no choice—but you will continue to obey. Don't worry, after it's over, I'll skip out on watching the old women swatted out of the sky by the Dragon Lords, and for all I care, you can return to your one true love. Have they told you the men choose? Also bullshit. Choose the decoration of your cage. Choose the length of your leash." His knuckles whitened as the steering wheel creaked under his grip. "Choose whose hands hold the end of that leash, but never for a moment think you can choose to be free."

"They say you chose to kill eight members of your family." Freedom being just another word for mass slaughter. "Is that true?"

"It was them, or me. All power corrupts." The laugh lifted the hair off the back of Graham's neck. "Hypocritical fucking cows."

"Jack's bored."

Glancing up at Charlie leaning against the end of the counter, Allie sighed. "I thought you were teaching him to play World of Warcraft?"

"He's a little aggressive, where *a little* means he went completely fucking nuts. Although, to be fair, the flame-thrower was a bad idea. What are you doing?"

Allie waved the dimpled metal cap covering the tip of her baby finger. "Entering this basket of thimbles into the database."

"Each individual thimble?"

"They're for sale separately, so, yeah."

Charlie slid one on, and then another, and then another until all eight fingertips were armored. "Give a thimble for luck, use a thimble to predict a death, we beg your acceptance of this elegant thimble, the dodo said solemnly." She rattled them off back into the basket. "And no, anal retentive does not have a hyphen."

"Cataloging helps me not think."

"Didn't cataloging used to be your job? I mean, I'm all in favor of a job that requires no thought but you ever think that might be why you were let go?"

"Bite me." Allie pulled a pale blue Wedgwood thimble, slightly chipped, out of the basket as Charlie sprawled over the counter. "It helps me not think of anything but cataloging, okay? When I think about her, I can feel the fire."

"That'd suck," Charlie allowed. "Let me give you something new to think about, then. Where's Joe?"

"In the bathroom." She frowned at a *Thimble Collector's International* twentieth anniversary thimble. Definitely commemorative, but was it collectible to anyone outside the club? "Does this look like actual silver to you?"

"Don't know, don't care. What do you figure Joe's doing?"

"Charlie!"

"Got you, it's a trick question. I should have asked, who do you figure Joe's doing?"

Allie turned slowly to face the back of the store. "Please tell me it's Katie."

"Nope. Now, where do you think Auntie Gwen is?"

"With the rest of the circle at the spa?"

Charlie's brows went up.

"Oh, no . . ." Allie moved out from behind the counter but before she could get any further, Charlie grabbed her arm.

"He's Fey. He'll be fine. He only looks like a kid."

That was true as far as it went. Joe'd told her the Call commanding his return to the UnderRealm had probably been a result of the Human half of the changeling bond dying of old age. That was also completely irrelevant as far as Allie was concerned. "He's my responsibility."

"Why? You're not banging him."

There was that.

"Not banging who?" Michael asked.

They turned together.

Charlie released Allie's arm and stepped away. "I'll just go over here," she said, walking to one of the center tables, "and poke through this box of . . . Okay, don't care about power cables. Have plenty." Both hands in the air, she continued backing down the aisle. "Maybe I'll look at the books."

Allie looked up at Michael, who brushed his hair back off his face, blush rising under his tan. "I could have really hurt you."

He shrugged. "You didn't."

"I could have." And then she realized he couldn't possibly hear her since he was also talking.

Apologies spilled out simultaneously, tangling in each other until he held up both hands and managed to slide "Me first" into a pause.

She owed him that much. "Okay."

Taking a deep breath, he dried his palms on the thighs of his jeans. "Allie, I'm sorry. I shouldn't have said that."

She waited but, bottom line, Michael was still a guy, and that was it. "Or maybe you should have said it years ago."

He shrugged. "How could you think I didn't know?"

"I was that obvious?"

"To the people who love you, yeah."

When he opened his arms, she hesitated a moment before moving into them. "Things are changing."

"Not us."

Maybe they wouldn't. Maybe they already had. Maybe it didn't matter because she knew Michael would stand there, with his arms open, waiting for her to find him again. Barely aware of moving, she tucked herself up against the broad shelter of his chest, resting her head against his heart. "No matter what happens between me and Graham, I will always love you."

She felt his lips against the top of her head. "I know."

"How can you *know*?"

"Because no matter what happened with me and Brian . . ."

"And Peter and Joey and Steve and . . ."

"Shut up." He tightened his grip. "Because no matter what happened with me and Brian, I always loved you."

"Medic!" The plaid of Michael's shirt might be all Allie could see, but Charlie, for all her ability to project over a crowd, was definitely a lot closer than the bookshelves at the far end of the store. "My pancreas just shut down from the sugar overload. On the bright side, I've got two verses and a chorus finished. A couple more verses, a dead dog, and a banjo, and this is going to make 'em cry."

"I thought banjos did that all on their own," Allie snorted backing out of Michael's embrace. "I should really get back to . . ."

Burning!

Raging!

She didn't remember hitting the floor, but both knees were telling her she'd dropped like a brick. The hardwood smoked slightly against her palms. It felt as though her blood was on fire.

Under Michael's panicked reaction, she could hear boots on the stairs.

"Hey, Al! My mother's . . ." The boots skidded to a stop just inside her somewhat limited field of vision. "Oh, you heard."

"At least with the rain, there won't be too many people in the park." Allie came out of the bedroom buckling her belt. Clothes suitable for thimbles didn't cut it for a potential apocalypse. Too flammable, for starters. "Auntie Gwen . . ." She slid right past the reason Auntie Gwen had a purpling bite mark just under the edge of her jaw. ". . . you're driving the bus because Michael and Joe are staying here. I don't want noncombatants anywhere near this. Pick up the others at the hotel, and we'll meet you there."

"Don't forget to remind them about the police helicopters," David growled from his place by the door. Allie was just barely coping with having him that far inside the room. With only Auntie Gwen about, and her distracted, David's presence just added to the heat in her blood. "They've got to make sure the weather's bad enough to ground them."

"Good thing it's already raining," Auntie Gwen muttered. She glanced between Allie and her brother, gestured Katie and Roland into the space between them, kissed Joe—who to his credit kissed her back in spite of the audience—grabbed the keys off Michael's palm, and ran.

Joe flushed under the scrutiny, and while his hands were shoved deep into his pockets, his shoulders were square and his chin was up.

If it worked for him, it worked for Allie.

She shrugged back into Graham's jacket, wanting as much of him near her as possible. "This also stays here," she added, fishing the bullet from the front pocket. "Just to be on the safe side." The bullet rolled along the table until Katie put out a finger just before it rolled out of reach and stopped it. "And safer yet; Charlie, can you get Jack into the Wood?"

Charlie nodded. "Don't see why not. I got Ryan in. You don't want her to be able to use him as a focus?"

Not with Graham standing beside him. "I want her confused, at least for a minute or two."

"If my mother dies here . . ."

Allie looked down at Jack's thin fingers clutching her arm, and braced herself.

". . . I get to help eat her."

Okay, that needed different bracing. She opened her mouth. Closed it again. Figured what the hell. "Sure."

"Awesome." Looking pleased, Jack gave her arm a little squeeze before he let it go. Allie could smell the fabric scorching.

"All right, the aunties may know what they're doing,

but we're going to be making this up as we go along."
She paused halfway to the door. Speaking of the aunties . . . "David?"

He nodded once, horn not quite visible but still very present. "Do what you have to, Allie, I'm stronger than you think. So are you."

Hands outstretched, their fingertips just barely touched, sending a frisson of want up her arm. She thought of Charlie wearing the thimbles, wondered if it would help. Without Graham right there to ground her, she didn't dare risk hugging him although she very much wanted to.

Eyes dark, Roland stepped between them. David would anchor the first circle, but Roland would anchor her. Today and, if they survived, every ritual where he was the only second circle male. Her father, not a Gale, had never been a part of ritual. Allie thought of explaining all that to Graham. Oh, fun.

Roland read the thought off her face. Or maybe from deeper in, all things considered. "Perhaps it's for the best Graham isn't here right now."

"Yeah." Her voice shook only a little. Little enough to ignore. "I was just thinking much the same thing."

"All right, kid . . ." Charlie led the way down the stairs. ". . . experience with your uncle suggests we're going to need to take a run at this, so we'll start at the back door. I'll begin to play, you put your hand on my shoulder, and with luck we'll be moving fast enough when we hit the shrubbery to get through."

"I don't know what you're talking about."

"Doesn't matter. Just keep up and we'll be fine." Pulling the back door open, she sighed. "Fucking rain."

Jack pushed past her, stretching out a hand so that fat drops of water sizzled against his palm. "I shouldn't be so hot. It's probably because my mother's so close."

"Your mother gets you hot? Wait." She held up a hand before he could answer. "Forget I asked. That was wrong on so many levels."

"It's too much power in one place," Jack explained, head back, catching the rain in his mouth.

"Yeah, that's where I was going," Charlie sighed. She pried a cheap plastic poncho out of its pouch and stuffed her head through an opening clearly designed for the skulls of three year olds, stretching the neck out and ripping the hood entirely off. Since the point of the exercise was to protect her guitar, her head didn't actually much matter. "You need to be behind me, kid. One hand on my shoulder," she added as he dripped his way back into the house, flipping wet bangs back out of his eyes. A Dragon Prince with emo hair and daddy issues. Her life had become Manga. "Skin contact will help, so move that one finger over until you're touching my neck and . . . God fucking damn it, that hurts!" Jerking away she rubbed at the rising blister. "You think you can keep it down to a slight scorching?"

Jack frowned at his hands as though he were still getting used to them. Probably was, when it came to it. "I can try."

"Thank you."

It wasn't hard to find his song, not with him standing right there radiating, but when she attempted to walk them over into the Wood, it was like dragging the Saddledome behind her. Ryan had been heavy, but Jack . . .

"You can't be that much bigger than Ryan," she gasped after the third unsuccessful attempt, trying to push one of the flattened bushes vertical with the side of her shoe.

"Well, yeah, I can. Size is all about power and I'm the heir. And a sorcerer." Just to prove it, it stopped raining on him. "So I'm lots bigger than Uncle Ryan."

"Yeah, well, size matters here too, kid. Don't let anyone tell you differently. Come on." Giving up on the bush, she headed back inside. "We're going to need a lot more space." The poncho came off as the door closed behind them. Leaning up the stairs, she yelled for Michael and Joe. "I need more room," she told them when they appeared. "We're heading down the road to the park."

"In what?" Michael demanded. "Both cars are gone."

"Graham's truck."

"Do you have the keys?"

Charlie snorted. "Please. How long have you known me?" Passing the mirror she flicked a finger against the frame. The reflection showed Jack, a large gold dragon and a relatively small green dragon against a shimmering white background. "Thanks. A little perspective would've been more helpful about twenty minutes ago."

"That music is really lame," Jack muttered, slouched down in the seat as far as the belt allowed, feet up on the dash.

"Hey!" Charlie smacked his shoulder. "Do not be dissing Emerson Drive."

"I want to listen to something good!" He reached for the radio, but she was faster.

"Two things," she said smacking his hand back. "One, if I'm behind the wheel we go by Winchester rules: driver picks the music, shotgun shuts his cakehole. And two . . ." The truck rocked up on two wheels as she took a sharp turn into the Fort Calgary parking lot. ". . . we're here."

Jack's nose twitched as he got out of the truck. "This is where the Fey gate was, right?"

"Yeah." Charlie nodded along the path, dragging the misshapen poncho back on over her head. "Right at the entrance to the . . . Fuck. Hang on." She pulled her phone from her belt pouch and frowned at the call display. Unknown numbers were not something that showed up on family phones. Raising a hand to hold Jack in place, she moved away from the truck. "Yeah?"

"You have Jack with you. I want to see him. I want to see my son."

Hadn't been expecting that. She smiled, and knew he could feel exactly how she meant it. "Fuck you."

"Do you think you can control him, Charlotte? Keep him from his destiny? No, you can't. He should be here, with me, embracing all that he is."

"Embracing a dirt nap if he gets close to you."

"Don't be ridiculous. We'll face his mother together, he and I."

"Yeah, like that's a convincing argument for . . ."

The roar of the truck engine cut her off. Charlie stood, free hand under the poncho resting on the upper curve of her guitar, and watched Jack peel backward out of the parking lot, wheel around through miraculously empty spots in traffic, and grind gears heading north.

On the other end of the phone, the sorcerer snickered. "I didn't have to convince you, Gale girl. His kind have remarkable hearing."

"And they learn fast," Charlie muttered snapping the phone closed. In retrospect, showing Jack how the truck worked had been a bad idea. "And more importantly," she growled, heading for the nearest trees, "how did that S.O.B. get my number?"

"I'm a little surprised that worked, actually, but I suppose it's time something went right for me." Kalynchuk unwrapped the red hair from around his phone and dropped it back into Graham's lap. "How fortunate I spotted this protruding over your waistband."

"Keep your fucking eyes on the road," Graham snarled. He stuffed Charlie's hair into his pocket. That's what he got for grabbing yesterday's boxers off the floor. When this was over, if he survived, he was definitely doing laundry.

"The freezer's ringing." Joe cocked his head and frowned. "I think it's the theme from *Boston Legal*."

Michael crossed the room in six strides, redirecting his pacing into the kitchen. "It's Roland's phone. He left it for us."

"In the freezer?"

"I guess he forgot to take it out of the peas."

Joe raised a hand. "Don't want to know."

"They haven't been gone long enough for something to go wrong." One hand digging into the frozen vegetables, he paused and shot Joe a worried glance. "Have they?"

"I have no idea."

"But you're . . ."

"Here with you, aren't I?" Joe approved of that, actually. He figured that behind Catherine Gale's wards was currently the safest place in the city. "Just answer the damned phone."

"It's me."

"What?"

"It's my phone calling. It's Brian. It has to be." Michael looked down at the phone, dwarfed by the size of his hand. "What does he want?"

"There's only one way to find that out, isn't there?"

"Yeah?"

Joe was starting to understand Allie's fondness for hitting people on the back of the head. "Answer. The. Damned. Phone."

Bottom lip between his teeth, Michael snapped it open and raised it to his ear. "Hello?"

It was Brian. From what he'd heard, Joe doubted anyone else could put that look on Michael's face.

"Where am I?"

Joe wondered if the next question was going to be *What are you wearing?* And if he should go downstairs to the store.

"Who said to meet you at the park?"

That didn't sound good. Joe watched the color drain out of Michael's face.

"What park did she tell you to meet me at?"

She?

"Brian! What park?"

Joe didn't actually need to hear the answer to that one.

"Okay, listen to me, please. Get in a cab and . . . Brian? Brian! Goddamn it!" He threw the phone across the room. Bounced it off the wall pretty damned close to where Allie'd bounced him. "Lost the signal. These phones don't lose their fucking signal!"

"Twelve Dragon Lords, two sorcerers, and an

emerging apocalypse might be messing with reception," Joe pointed out. "And he's right at ground zero."

"Thanks for that. I've got to get to him."

"Allie wants you to stay here. She'll take care of him."

"Yeah, because she'll have so much free time." He was shoving his feet into shoes as he spoke and Joe knew there wasn't a hope of keeping him in the apartment.

"How are you going to get there? It's halfway across the city."

"It's Calgary, not the middle of the tundra," Michael snapped, yanking open the door. "I'll flag a cab!"

Joe listened to him pound down the stairs, across the store, and out the front door. He sighed, followed him down, and turned the lock. Michael was nowhere in sight, so he must've grabbed a cab pretty much immediately. Seemed like he'd been around the Gales long enough for that kind of thing to rub off.

Eyes away from the shadows at the far end of the store, he rolled a yoyo along the countertop, putting out a finger to stop it just before it rolled out of reach. Allie'd told him to stay and that seemed like a good idea to him.

Besides, there was nothing he could do.

Was there?

Roland pulled the Beetle into the southeast parking lot right behind the bus, David behind them. Allie hadn't had much choice about who was driving, her blood still burned and the constant roar was nearly deafening. She had to keep reminding herself not to yell over a noise only she could hear.

None of the aunties wore rain gear, but only the aunties who didn't mind were getting wet.

"This isn't enough," she heard David say gesturing at the sky.

"We'll take care of it when we're airborne," Auntie Jane told him.

"Do we have to?" Auntie Meredith sighed. "I haven't taken down a chopper since 1968."

"Glory days," Roland muttered in her ear and Allie snickered as they ran toward the path to the summit.

"I'm not sure what I'm supposed to be doing here," Katie called out following close behind them. "This isn't a third circle thing."

"You could always cross over," Roland threw back.

"Bite me."

"You're here to pick up the pieces when it's over," Allie shouted, barely able to hear herself over the scream of rage bouncing off the inside of her skull. "Even if this works . . ."

"Oh, joy, sex in the rain. And if it doesn't work, you're talking literally pieces!"

"So call Charlie. Jack can help. And don't let him eat the aunties. I actually like the kid."

"Very funny."

Whistling in the dark, banter in the dark— It all meant the same thing, Allie knew, as they jogged out to a stop on the top of the hill and she had to clutch at Roland's arm to keep from falling. If she had this to do over, she'd . . .

Oh, who was she kidding. She'd probably do exactly the same things, and they'd still be standing in wet grass waiting for the world to end. The whole thing, from the moment she'd read Gran's will, had had a certain inevitability about it.

Up above the cloud cover, something screamed.

Well, not exactly *something,* Allie admitted silently, gouging a charm in the wet ground with the heel of her shoe. The Dragon Lords were waiting.

And they weren't going to be waiting long.

"I can't stop her from breaking free!" Stepping into the center of the charm felt like stepping into the fire. Or quicksand. Or burning quicksand. Becoming as much a part of the hill as Jack's mother. "She's too big, and she has too much momentum."

"You knew that."

"I'd hoped once we were right on top of her . . ." Allie let her voice trail off as twelve figures rose out of the woods ringing the top of the hill. They swooped once over the summit, dangling feet an advertisement for sensible shoes—although Auntie Gwen's Chucks appeared to have skulls painted on them—and then began to fly the circle widdershins. Once. Twice. Three times.

The clouds pushed back, piled higher over the city, thunder boomed and lightning cracked and the rain turned to a deluge. Over the hill, in a perfect circle, the sky all but gleamed, clear and blue.

The blue took Allie a bit by surprise; she kept forgetting it wasn't the middle of the night.

David stood across from her, grounding the lines from the twelve in the sky, the last of the rain glistening on bare skin. Roland's arms went around her, hands splayed over her belly, protecting her from the pull. Allie grabbed his wrists and reached for power as the ground erupted.

Jack's blood had pulled him into Human shape as he emerged.

Jack's mother had no such incentive.

Shimmering white, she rose and rose and rose. Ten meters. Twenty. Thirty.

As Allie fed power up to the aunties and they wrapped it around her, using the moment of *not my world* to help snap her back home, the Dragon Lords came out of the clouds.

She could hear the aunties cackling and then she had no attention to spare.

"Father?"

Tucked just inside the edge of the wood, Graham dragged his gaze off the dogfight going on overhead to see Jack pushing his way to the edge of the summit through the underbrush, looking wet, bedraggled, and more than a little pissed off. "Kid, get out of here!"

"Stop calling me kid!" Apparently, the enormous white dragon in the center of the hill held no interest for him. No reason why she should; he'd known her his whole life. He pushed past Graham, shoved his hair back out of his eyes, and stared at Kalynchuk, raking a disdainful golden gaze from head to toe and back again. "*You're* my father?"

Kalynchuk smiled. "Graham, punch him in the nose."

Trapped in his own flesh once again, Graham let the M24 drop on the strap so it rested against his back. Shifting his weight, he grabbed Jack's shoulder, spun him around, and swung. He felt the bone crack and then warmth against his knuckles just before something slammed into his chest and he flew about three meters, landing hard. He dragged the sniper rifle around and flopped over on his back, gasping for breath.

Jack peered at him over the top of the hand cupping his nose, his upper lip red. "That hurt!"

"Life is pain," Kalynchuk muttered holding a hand down to Graham.

Without thinking, a little too winded to think, Graham reached up only to have the sorcerer wipe the blood off his knuckles and onto the silver letter opener he pulled from his jacket.

"Jack, come here." He gestured with the blade. "Stand beside me."

Graham recognized the look on Jack's face as the kid began to move—he'd felt it on his own.

"It's minimal control and it won't last long," Kalynchuk admitted as Graham got to his feet, "but now, unless I'm forced to kill you myself, I may be able to bargain with your mother."

Charlie came out of the Wood at full speed, aiming for Jack, hoping that the amount of power the family had started flinging around would be enough to get his enormous teenage ass moving. She didn't catch all of what the sorcerer had to say but it didn't sound good, and there, beside him, stood Graham with a gun. With a split-second to make a decision, she shifted slightly left and wrapped an arm around Graham's waist. Momentum pushed him stumbling back—one step, two—and they were gone.

Allie had never been so far open and it wasn't enough. Any farther and Roland wouldn't be able to hold her. Any farther and they wouldn't be controlling the power; it would control them. Sweep them away. Destroy them. But if she couldn't find a way to go farther . . .

The Dragon Queen shrieked in triumph and began to twist free.

Then Allie sank into a touch she remembered from the bar. Felt Roland yanked aside and Graham's arms wrap around her.

Heard a whiskey-rough voice by her ear.

"Charlie says let go!"

But Graham wasn't family. How could he hold?

"She says I've got you!"

With no time to question whether she trusted Charlie or not, Allie let go.

If not for Graham's arms, the rush of power would have lifted her off her feet. She *was* the hill, the park, and every living thing that made it up. Grinding back against him, she poured the power up toward the aunties, felt them shape it.

The Dragon Queen shrieked again, held in place.

It was more power than Allie had ever felt, even in a full working, even with the entire family around and it still . . .

. . . wasn't . . .

. . . going . . .

. . . to be . . .

. . . enough.

She could feel the rush of air as the Dragon Queen filled her lungs.

And a familiar voice yelled, "What the hell is going on here?"

And then a still more familiar voice, twisted with fear. "Brian!"

What were they doing here? Allie fought for focus, saw Michael racing across the hill toward Brian, oblivious to the Dragon Queen pointing her muzzle toward him and opening her mouth.

Time stopped.

Or she stopped it, Allie wasn't entirely sure.

"Allie?"

Graham. Wherever she was, he was there with her. She turned in his arms.

Graham had barely registered Charlie charging out of nowhere when her arm hooked around his waist, he'd stumbled back two steps—maybe three—and suddenly found himself in an ancient wood.

"What the . . . ?"

"No time!" Charlie cut him off. She adjusted her grip but kept them moving.

None of the three Gale girls he'd met were exactly delicate, but if he'd wanted to break Charlie's hold, he should have been able to do it without even breaking a sweat. Not a chance in hell.

"This," she said, flashing him a grin that had depths so hidden they scared the piss out of him, "is where you need to know what you want to say."

And then they were on the hill again and in a complicated move he missed at least half of, Charlie spun Roland away from Allie's back and slammed Graham into his place.

"Tell her it's okay, that you've got her." A encouraging squeeze on one bare shoulder and it might as well have been just him and Allie on the hilltop.

He had no idea when he'd lost his shirt.

Okay, him, Allie, and one fuck of a big white dragon. Dragoness? Dragon Queen.

"Charlie says, let go!"

Allie didn't seem to be buying it.

"She says, I've got you!"

Then it was the feeling from outside the bar only ramped up so high it burned that memory away. If, at the bar, Allie'd wrapped herself around what it was to be Graham Buchanan, this time she didn't go around so much as through. He could feel every cell of his body attempting to spin away from the overstimulation and his spine bowed as he fought to hold them both together, his heart slamming up against his ribs so violently he could feel it bruising. His face buried in her hair, he breathed her in, every sense filled with her.

So when she stopped for a moment, he stopped with her.

"Allie?"

She turned in his arms, her eyes a dark and stormy gray.

This, he realized, with a clarity that pushed the air from his lungs, this was the choice the Gale men made. To throw themselves into the storm and trust to love to bring them safely out the other side.

"This is where you need to know what you want to say."

Turned out, it was easier than he'd thought it would be.

"Yes," he said. And let go

Allie could feel it all. Every blade of grass. Every drop of water. Every grain of sand. And everywhere she went, Graham, her anchor to the world.

Although, right now, the world was just a little more than she needed.

She pulled back until she touched the edges of the seven hundred and twenty-one square kilometers that made up the city of Calgary. Until she touched the one million, forty-two thousand, eight hundred and ninety-two souls. No, ninety-three as Jamal Badawi took her first breath. This was enough. This would be home.

She gathered it all, held it cupped in her hands, and . . .

One of the aunties fell.

The circle broke.

As fire began to blossom between the serrated rows of the Dragon Queen's teeth, Allie wrapped the power around her and whispered, "There isn't room for you here. Go home."

Then she opened a gate.

The sky over the park lit up. Even before the after-images faded, Jack's mother was gone. As one of the Dragon Lords screamed, Allie reached out again, gathered up the rest of the family, and sent them home after her. She could sort them out on the other side. Twelve smaller stars crashed to earth.

When both sky and hill were empty, the power grounded out through the only safe path.

"What scares the old fools most about David, is that they have no idea of his limits."

Allie knew. Here and now, she knew with painful clarity exactly what his limits were.

But all she could see was the blue of Graham's eyes and all she could feel was the warmth of his mouth on hers and all she could hear was an auntie shrieking, "Look out!"

They hit the ground together, rolled, and came up onto their knees like they'd rehearsed the move. All around them, she could hear the soft thuds and mild profanity of the aunties landing.

"Don't even try it!" About ninety degrees around the hill, Jonathon Samuel Gale came out of the trees holding a fistful of Jack's hair and a gleaming knife at the boy's throat. "Everyone just backs off, or he dies."

"Well, that's not much of a thre . . ." Auntie Jane began.

Allie absently reached out and shut her up.

"I could make the shot," Graham muttered.

"Would this help?" Joe asked, fading in beside them. He held out the marked bullet.

"Clever, love," Auntie Gwen murmured and the tips of Joe's ears flushed scarlet.

Graham rolled the bullet between thumb and forefinger. "I don't know where . . ."

"This went?"

Allie took the rifle from Charlie and handed it to him. Her city. Her decision. "Do it," she said.

Graham's blood to help the bullet fly true.

Jonathon Samuel Gale's blood to kill a sorcerer.

The shot wasn't as loud as Allie'd thought it would be.

They saw the sorcerer fall. Then Jack stepped back, wiping the blood from his face and roared.

"You were right." Allie laced her fingers through Graham's. "It was his father blocking the dragon shape."

"He's very . . . hungry," Charlie observed as the gold dragon ripped another bite from his lunch.

Allie shrugged, moved closer to Graham, and smoothed out the disturbance in the center of the hill before moving her attention out and around the family.

Auntie Bea had a broken leg, easy enough to heal.

Auntie Ellen and Auntie Christie had been burned. Not as easy to heal but doable.

Auntie Meredith was waving a length of . . . tail. Not her problem.

Tucked up in the completely inadequate shelter of a rock outcropping, Michael had his hands wrapped around Brian's face, their mouths locked together, their bodies so close it left no room for questions between them.

David was gone.

"What took you so long?"

Brian blushed, throwing the scattering of freckles across his nose and cheeks into sharp relief. "I was . . . I mean, because I'd . . . I don't know why I did it, Allie, you have to believe me. I didn't mean to do it. I didn't even want to, but . . ."

"You did."

"Yeah. I did. I hung onto the phone and I kept hoping Michael would call and we could talk. I couldn't go running after him. I didn't know what to say."

"I'm sorry?"

"How could that be enough?"

Allie glanced over at Michael, but he seemed willing to let Brian do the talking. The bruised look had left his eyes, and he watched Brian as though he was the most amazing, impossible thing he'd ever seen. She wondered what *had* been said. Or, if in the heat of the moment, words had been unnecessary. Didn't matter. Like she'd told the aunties, it was none of her business. It was between Brian and Michael. "If you hadn't been there, if Michael hadn't been in danger, I would never have . . ." She waved a hand because she wasn't entirely certain language was up to what she'd done. What she and Graham had done. "But the question still remains, why *were* you there?"

Fingers laced through Michael's, Brian shrugged. "I got a call from one of your aunties. She said Michael needed me. That I had to meet him at the summit of Nose Hill Park." He chewed a little on his lower lip, as though trying to decide how much to add. "She didn't mention anything about dragons," he said at last.

"Yeah, well, they tend to edit." Allie rubbed her

hand along Graham's thigh until he caught her fingers and gave them a warning squeeze. Even six hours later, the aftereffects were still wearing off, and it didn't take much for need to take over. From the way both Michael and Brian were shifting, they seem to have gotten caught up in it, too. Or maybe that was just a normal result of their reunion. She didn't want to speculate. Much. "You guys were set up."

"On the hill?"

"On the hill," Allie agreed, "because if Michael hadn't been in danger, I might not have pushed that little bit further. But before that. In Vancouver. When Brian . . ."

Michael's free hand rose and cut her off. "You're saying the aunties arranged that?" His voice had dropped about half an octave into what Charlie had once labeled the danger zone.

"One of them, yeah."

"Allie . . ."

"I'll deal with it."

"He looks like you, you know."

Allie lifted herself up on one elbow and stared down at Graham. The darkness in the room was no longer able to put a barrier between them. Walls were barely a barrier. "Who?"

"Brian. Blond hair, gray eyes, little sprinkle of freckles."

"Penis."

Graham grinned. "I'm not saying there aren't differences."

"He's a what?"

"A seventh son of a seventh son," Auntie Jane told her, watching her with the same wariness all the aunties had exhibited for the last twenty-four hours. Allie figured it'd get old eventually, but for now she was definitely enjoying it. "You didn't wonder about the strength of the attraction?"

Gale girls were attracted to power.

She squirmed around in Graham's arms until she could look up at him. "Is this true?"

Graham looked a little confused. "Well, yeah, I guess."

"You guess?"

"I spent the last thirteen years not thinking about my family, Allie. But yeah, I had six older brothers . . ." He shoved a hand into his pocket and Allie knew he was rolling the bullet. Jack had returned it, after he'd finished eating. ". . . and so did my father. But . . ."

"But nothing," Auntie Christie snorted. "The mere fact you're a seventh son of a seventh son is the only reason that stunt worked."

Auntie Muriel's knitting needles clicked an agreement. "Who ever heard of a non-Gale anchoring a ritual?"

Charlie had to have known, Allie realized. Charlie'd pushed them together on the hill. When Charlie got back from wherever Charlie had wandered off to, Charlie was going to have some explaining to do!

"Still . . ." Auntie Meredith took a thoughtful sip of coffee. "Just think what a seventh son of a seventh son of a seventh son who *is* a Gale might be capable of."

Gale girls had mostly daughters. Allie did the math. "No."

"Does the mother matter?" Auntie Grace wondered. "Charlotte could always help."

"I think it's time you all went home," Allie said more-or-less pleasantly.

Allie set the pile of folded clothes down on a rock, just inside the tree line and backed away as the stag pushed through the underbrush. He was enormous. Beautiful. Heartbreaking.

The air shimmered and David pulled on the jeans but left the rest. They looked wrong on him but Allie was grateful for the faked semblance of normalcy. He had a welt across one shoulder. Even in skin, his eyes were black rim to rim. His antlers had barely diminished with the change.

His skin was damp and hot where Allie touched it, his heartbeat slow and strong under the press of her fingers.

He closed his hand around hers, new callus already forming. "Feels strange," he said, carefully forming each word. "But more control in time."

"I know." The aunties had explained that when Granddad was young, he'd spent as much or more time at the farm as in the wood.

"Let him get used to it, Alysha. He'll come back. It's not like he ever had a steady job and he can still act as a consultant with the local police. It'll work out. It always does."

"So, Graham's going to keep the paper going." She was a little surprised at how matter-of-fact she managed to sound. "Kalynchuk—Jonathon Samuel—had everything set up legitimately, so he figures he might as well. Katie's talking about going to work for him, and Rayne and Lucy are moving west with Lyla. Roland's thrilled." Roland wasn't quite as tied as David, but he was still the only second circle male in the city and he wouldn't ever be moving far. "He'll be taking over Graham's condo and there's room there for the girls, for a while at least. Graham says Jonathon Samuel had this enormous house out in Upper Mount Royal, so Roland's going to have a look at the paperwork. I expect we'll be able to fill it easily enough. There's a number of cousins thinking of joining us."

Dark brows drew in. "Why?"

"Besides the aunties encouraging your entire list to move west?" Allie shrugged. "Things are happening here. Jack's going to stay with me and Graham in the apartment."

"Wedding?"

"It's not really necessary. But whatever we do, it won't be until you can . . ." She nodded toward David's rack and he smiled.

"Good. Want to see that."

"Auntie Gwen stayed."

"I know."

David would know where all this new branch of the family were. It was part of what he was. "She'll take care of Gran's sideline in potions and charms. She's set up housekeeping in the loft with Joe. He offered to age up a bit—first I knew he could do that—but she wouldn't let him."

"Bragging."

"Definitely." They're saying an asteroid broke up over the park. The lights were visible even through the storm. The place will probably be crawling with people looking for pieces. Be careful."

"Protected."

"Be careful anyway."

She kept her hand over his heart until he stepped beyond her reach, then she kept reaching, brushing tears off her cheeks with the other palm. "David, I'm sorry. You didn't want this. Even once you can leave the park, you can't ever leave the city!" He had become the family's tie to this new place. The living symbol of their claim.

To her surprise, he smiled again.

"Never asked what I wanted, Allie." His brows went up and just for a moment, he was her big brother, nothing more. Then he snorted, and the snort wasn't entirely Human. He only just got out of the jeans in time, one rear hoof tearing the denim.

She watched him race across the summit, heard the surprised and delighted yell of a couple of kids on BMX bikes, felt his joy in the movement, in the wind, in the sun on his back, and wished with all her heart there had been another way.

The mirror showed her reflection doing yoyo tricks. Allie didn't know what they were called, but the one that spun the hunk of enameled wood around over her head looked dangerous. As soon as things stopped whizzing about, she thrust her arm in past the surface of the glass, caught the end of the yoyo, and yanked. Hard.

Second circle made connections.

Still holding the yoyo, she stepped back as an elderly woman spilled out of the mirror into the hall, the string looped over one finger, multilayered skirt swirling, half a dozen strands of beads swinging around her neck, and a lime-green shawl slipping off one arm.

Allie released her, waited until she got her balance, then pinned her with a word.

"Gran."

Dark eyes gleamed as Catherine Gale tried to move

and found herself held. "Those old fools always worried about David," she snorted, tossing a long gray braid back behind her shoulder, setting hoop earrings swaying. "They worried he had all the power that should've gone to half a dozen Gale girls. It didn't go to David, though, did it? It all went to you just like it was supposed to. You just had to find it. And speaking of finding things, how did you . . . ?" She waved the hand with the string attached.

"There were thirteen crows in the mirror and twelve aunties upstairs."

"Clever girl."

"You saw this, didn't you?"

"Saw what, Allie-cat? That you would rise to the challenge?"

"No. Well, yes, but . . ." Her grandmother had always been able to direct the conversation. Not this time. "You saw all of this. Everything that happened. The *challenge,* if you will." Steel-gray brows rose at the emphasis. Allie ignored them. "You knew about Jonathon Samuel and the Dragon Lords and Jack—probably through Adam. He's been here before and he as much as told me he's been interacting with a Gale. You kept the museum from getting that grant so I'd be fired and have no reason not to come west. You made sure the cousins I called for help were busy to keep the number of variables down. You kept Charlie from getting here to make sure that Graham and I would connect with no distractions. The rest of them knew about the seventh son thing as soon as we touched. Charlie worked it out from what happened at the bar, so you must have spotted it the moment you met him. You knew I wouldn't call the aunties in if I thought they'd take him out with his boss, and you knew that David would come running if he thought I was in over my head. You set this whole thing up."

"Did I?"

It took Allie a minute to unclench her teeth. "Don't bullshit me, Gran."

"All right, then, I did. I saw the Dragon Queen rising, and I put the pieces in play to save the world." She rolled her eyes and adjusted her shawl. "How dreadful of me."

"You let me think you were dead."

"I'm sure that didn't last very long, Kitten."

"Not the point," Allie growled. "And not the worst of it either. Michael was one of your pieces."

Catherine Gale spread her hands, bracelets chiming. "You needed the extra push there at the end."

"I don't care about the rest."

"About saving the city, and probably half the world if Jack's mother had managed to get into the sky? Very cold, Kitten."

"I don't care that you manipulated the rest," Allie amended. "But you used Brian to break Michael's heart and then you used him to put Michael in danger, and that I cannot and will not forgive. Michael isn't family, and there are things you can do for the sake of family that you do not do to those outside the blood."

"Alysha."

She shook her head. "Take the car. Or go through the Wood if you prefer, but get out. This city is closed to you."

She'd never actually seen her grandmother look quite so astounded. Or astounded at all. "You can't . . ."

"Yes. I can. Don't make me prove it, Gran. It won't be pleasant for either of us."

They stared at each other for a long moment until Allie forced the older woman's gaze to the floor.

After a long moment, she sighed and looked up, her expression carefully neutral. "I'll take the car."

"I thought you might." Allie took a step back and released the yoyo. "I packed up your clothes and some personal things. They're in the trunk."

"Personal things?" Her grandmother frowned thoughtfully as she rolled the string onto the spool, then she snickered. "Oh, I see. And the rest?"

"You left it to me."

"So I did." Suddenly finding herself able to move, she started toward the store, then changed direction as Allie made a cautioning noise. "The garage. Of course." Back door open, she paused. "Take care of things, Allie-cat."

Allie didn't much like the smile that accompanied the words. "I will."

"Call me if you need me. And don't say you won't," her grandmother cautioned, raising her hand. Allie wondered when she'd lost the tip of her second finger. It looked like it had been bitten off just below the nail. "Charlie's not as much of a wild card as she thinks she is. Not yet."

"We'll be fine."

"Still, the offer's open." The bushes perked up as she approached, slumped a little as she passed.

They'd get over it.

Allie waited until she heard the distinctive sound of the Beetle pulling away, waited until she could feel Gran turning onto Deerwood, then she went into the store. She'd know when Gran passed the family's boundary. Or if she didn't.

"How'd you know she'd take the car?" Joe asked.

"She left the registration in her name."

"Oh." He pulled a jar of small seashells out of the latest box he'd brought up from the cellar. "If she saw everything else that happened, do you think she saw you telling her to go?"

Maybe. Probably. "It doesn't change what she did."

One of the shells gleamed unnaturally in the light. Allie sighed and made a mental note to pour them out onto the counter and check. Later. "If you're good here, I'll go next door and grab us some coffee."

"I'm good here."

Allie grinned at the way the points of his ears had turned scarlet, yet again, and noted that her charm had been definitely overwritten.

Kenny had both cups of coffee ready when she reached the counter. That sort of thing had been happening a lot lately, the city and everyone in it anticipating her needs. Rough life, she supposed, but someone had to live it.

Back in the store, Joe looked up and smiled.

"I sold a yoyo while you were gone."

Tanya Huff

The Finest in Fantasy

To Order Call: 1-800-788-6262
www.dawbooks.com

DAW 21